SHADOW CURSED

A FRACTAL FORSAKEN BOOK

J. LLOREN QUILL

Published by Jason Quill
www.jllorenquill.com

Cover design and map by Abby Haddican
Editing by Ben Barnhart
Book Layout © 2015 BookDesignTemplates.com

Shadow Cursed/ J. Lloren Quill -- 1st ed.
ISBN 978-0-9979887-2-7

For my parents, who have helped me celebrate all of my successes and supported me through all of life's misadventures.

PILLAR

THE KINGDOM OF
MALETHYA

MINOT

Ispirtu

Rue St

Regallo
Estate

Darik's Palace

THE
NOMADIC
TRIBES

Bellator

RAVINAI

Arena

Infirmary

Slate's
Apartment

Catalpa
Grove

PORTSWAIN

THE
DISENITES

CONTENTS

REFLECTIONS

Hunger. The farmer fights hunger during a long day working the fields. A traveler fights hunger with carefully packed rations. The glutton fights hunger with eager excess. Like the land of Malethya, hunger inspires people to fight. They fight for different reasons, but they all fight.

Rosana Regallo contemplated hunger while examining the plate before her. The blight had spread to the southern provinces, and it was difficult to find food untouched by the disease. Spots of wilted brown lifelessness mottled the fresh red tomatoes. The speckled rot touched everything on her plate, and she carefully carved around the sickened food with her throwing knife, conscious of the fact that this corruption was her fault. She had used blood magic to save Slate Severance and blood magic came at a cost. This time it was the blight. Even knowing the consequences of her actions, she would have made the same decision again. Her brother ruled the kingdom and enslaved the minds of all who opposed him. Rosana needed Slate's help to stop him.

If the people of Malethya needed to pick at their food and fight hunger, it was a small price to pay. Their concerns paled in comparison to Sana's hunger. Food could not quench her hunger. She set the tomato down and pushed the plate away. Her hunger ran deeper.

Some people had the slow, burning hunger for

power or wealth, insatiably striving for more and more. Theirs was the hunger of greed. Her hunger ran deeper.

Others fought the hunger of addiction. Their hunger changed to a physical need, a necessity of life that must be fulfilled. But even they could fight and overcome the hunger within.

Sana looked at her hand. Black specks periodically interrupted the smoothness of her skin. The blight slowly devoured her from within. The inevitable hunger of the blight devoured all that it came in contact with, spreading until there was nothing left. The blight's hunger could not be satisfied. The more it devoured, the hungrier it became. It would kill her, and she bore this burden by choice. It was the only way to save Malethya. If she were given the chance, the opportunity, to relive those decisions, she would make them again.

The Sicarius Headmaster did what needed to be done, because others lacked the strength to do so…

CHAPTER ONE

DECEPTION OF THE INFIRMED

"Who are you today?" the infirmary wizard in charge of her care asked. Rosana contemplated that same question with every sunrise.

Rosana sat in her padded room and obediently answered. "I am the sister of the blood mage that rules Malethya from the shadows." Rosana could convincingly masquerade as any Malethyan, but the truth was often better than a lie. "He is controlling King Darik and will bring ruin to this land."

The wizard from the mental health unit of the infirmary scribbled notes on a piece of paper. He had introduced himself as Master Meikel, and he had been in charge of Rosana's care since her recent, voluntary admittance. Meikel raised an eyebrow slightly while writing. Rosana read the mannerism as part academic intrigue mixed with pity and the slightest bit of contempt for his inferiors. After contemplating the mental state of his patient for a while, Meikel delivered the professional, slightly exaggerated smile that he reserved for masking his emotions while addressing the insane. "There hasn't been a blood mage in Malethya in centuries. They are terrors from campfire stories told to frighten children. You have nothing to worry about."

"You are right." It was impossible to argue with someone who thought you were insane. "If I'm not the sister of a blood mage, who should I be?"

"That is a question for you to answer. I am here to listen and to help. All I can tell you is that you appeared at our doorstep several days ago with symptoms of schizophrenia. So far you have claimed to be four individuals: the lost relative of a blood mage, a former member of a covert spy ring, an assassin employed by the king, and the lover of a notorious criminal. After observing you, I worry that your mind has been lost to your own fantasies." Meikel thought for a moment and then came to a decision. "Treatment will begin tomorrow. Maybe then you will regain enough of your faculties to tell me your name."

The summary of her life did reek of fantasy, but she had never anticipated that it would get her labeled insane. Rose Regallo was the compassionate sister of Lattimer, but as she grew up, she rejected becoming Rosana Regallo, splitting the older version of herself into a different part of her mind to keep the compassion of her youth alive.

Her father, Brannon, noticed her internal conflict and enlisted the aid of his Ispirtu wizards to heal her. After months of experimentation, rumors of the troubled Regallo child reached the Sicarius Guild and the Headmaster contacted her. He viewed her condition—one in which she could split her personalities but access either of them at a given time—as a rare and wonderful gift. Rosana escaped to the Sicarius Guild and became Malethya's most deadly assassin. The necessity and brutality of her craft troubled Rosana and Rose, so they created the Sicarius Headmaster, a nameless figure who did what needed to be done regardless of the means. During the travels of the Sicarius Headmaster she met

Lucus, a wizard searching for an apprentice. Seeing the opportunity for training outside of Ispirtu's walls she created the personality of Sana, whose logic and attention to detail helped her studies in pattern-based magic.

Now she was Rosana, Rose, Sana, and the Sicarius Headmaster. Her personality changed for any given situation although disagreements between herselves did arise occasionally. Right now, Sana's plan required a diagnosis that kept her in the infirmary, and jumping between herselves while talking to Meikel was a simple way to execute the Sicarius Headmaster's mission.

Rosana leaned forward in the chair that was bolted to the floor to show her eagerness for treatment. She gripped the front of her shirt in feigned trepidation and pleaded with the infirmary wizard for information, asking, "What type of treatment? Will it help me?"

"The infirmary has made dramatic strides in the areas of mental illness by applying variations of our techniques for healing other parts of the body. For typical injuries, like stabbings or blunt trauma, we use probing spells to diagnose injuries to muscle or bone and then heal the patient. We cast these spells and move very methodically through the injured tissue without lasting consequences to the patient. In our studies of the human mind, we have discovered that some patients with cases similar to yours can benefit from probing spells conducted at high frequencies. It won't hurt, so I recommend you get a good night's sleep and try to relax. We will begin the treatment in the morning."

Sana was intimately familiar with probing spells from her training under Lucus, but she wasn't familiar with this technique. It sounded like the infirmary wizards used the probing spell to jump back and forth within the brain to scramble the signals. When the spell stopped, hopefully whatever signals were crossed in the schizophrenic mind became untangled. Sana didn't want to find out what the spell would do to her brain. Rosana, Rose, and the Sicarius Headmaster agreed.

Rose looked out the locked window of her room into the courtyards surrounding the infirmary and admired the immaculate gardens with their flowers in full bloom. It reminded her that a full winter had passed since her brother, Lattimer Regallo, had seized control of Malethya. He was the first blood mage in Malethya for centuries, and he grew in power with every second that passed. *But he was the little brother who snuck into my room at night during storms because the thunder scared him. I don't want to think of him as the blood mage who has subjugated King Darik's mind and controls the kingdom's armies from his Ispirtu tower, choosing to rule through Darik and keeping the citizens unaware of the danger they face.* Sana looked at the beauty of the flowers in the gardens. *How long will it be before darkness covers the land. Time moves too quickly. The Sicarius Headmaster needs to act before all the beauty in the world disappears.*

Rose asked Master Meikel with sweetness and innocence in her voice, "Could I take a walk in the courtyards? I'm nervous about the treatments tomorrow and walking through the gardens may help me relax."

Meikel smiled at her, and this time Rosana knew it was genuine. "We believe in many forms of healing in the infirmary and encourage our patients to explore our gardens as a holistic form of therapy. I will ask an orderly to escort you." Rose smiled in gratitude as the wizard left the room.

In her few moments alone, the Sicarius Headmaster hurried to her bed. A room in the mental ward of the infirmary provided precious few opportunities to hide anything, but the frame beneath the feathered bed had a small recess where the rounded pieces of wood formed together. In that recess she had hidden a length of string painstakingly chewed from the drawstring of her hospital-issued pants after the lights went out at night. She then remade her bed and sat in her chair until the orderly knocked on her door.

The orderly entered, looking at her chart. He said, "Good evening, Miss…umm…" He scanned her infirmary records for her name and blushed after failing to find it.

"I would like to take a walk in the gardens. Would you escort me?" Rose asked politely. The orderly held the door for Rose and led the way to the courtyard entrance. Rose stepped out into the failing light of day and headed toward the gardens. The orderly followed her until they reached the garden paths and then Rose requested some privacy. Sana's plan required it. "Will you wait here for me? I start a new treatment tomorrow and would like to spend a few moments by myself. I just want to stroll through the gardens and watch the setting sun." Politeness went a long way with orderlies accustomed to behavioral issues in the mental ward.

The orderly appeared conflicted. "I'm required to accompany you, but if you stay within my sight at all times, then I think it will be ok."

Rose thanked the orderly and walked casually through the gardens, stopping to smell flowers and idly gaze at the setting sun. The centerpiece of the gardens was a hedge of rosebushes that encircled a catalpa tree. Sana scanned the branches inside the hedge and found the object of her search. Deep within the thickest part of a rosebush was a small bag. The Sicarius Headmaster plunged her arm into the thorn-covered bush to retrieve the bag while Rosana maintained a look of tranquility so as not to alert the orderly. When she pulled her arm back, the thorns had scratched and cut her forearm up to her elbow. The superficial wounds were just deep enough to draw blood, and attention.

Sana tucked the bag into her pants, securing it with the drawstring. She then tied the string she'd retrieved from her room to the rosebush. Simultaneously, she lowered her head to smell a rose blossom to maintain appearances. With this stage of her mission accomplished, she returned to the orderly at a casual pace while squeezing her arm above the elbow in an alternating pattern to increase the blood flow. Her posture was normal, if slightly hunched, as she exited the rosebushes in the gardens and came back into full view of the orderly.

He caught sight of her bleeding arm and rushed into the gardens to help. "You're bleeding! What happened?"

Rosana looked down at her arm soaked in blood and answered for Rose, who hated to lie, "I didn't notice. Isn't it pretty though? It looks like the roses in the garden." Politeness had its uses, but so did insanity. The orderly concentrated on Sana's arm so much that he never noticed the slightly hunched posture concealing the bag she'd hidden at her waist. After rushing her back to her room and dressing her arm, the orderly left her alone again while mumbling about finding a new job.

Once he left, Sana stashed the bag and pressed her ear against the wall. From the adjacent room, she heard a man singing softly. The next room belonged to Ibson, a famous wizard throughout Malethya who had suffered a tragic fall that left his brain permanently impaired. Ibson's legendary intellect was reduced to simple rhymes and a childlike demeanor. The song Sana heard through the wall had perfect pitch and a melody too complex for such a condition. Sana's resolve hardened, and she waited for her medications to arrive.

In short order, a new orderly brought in a dark liquid that Sana recognized before it was explained. "This is wormroot. We give it to all our patients who possess the ability to perform magic. The wormroot temporarily blocks your ability to access the spark and prevents you from accidently casting a spell that could harm you or those around you. Please drink it." Sana pretended to swallow and smiled with a closed mouth. The orderly left the room and Sana spit it out. By the time the infirmary wizards discovered the small pool of wormroot on her floor that signaled her disobedience, she would no longer be a patient in the infirmary.

With her last visitor gone for the night, Sana retrieved her stashed bag and laid the contents on her bed: a lock pick, a knife, and a piece of smoothed wood that fit nicely into the palm of her hand. Only the lock pick was functional. The dull knife blade collapsed when she applied pressure to it. People throughout the kingdom feared the piece of wood known as a shockstick, but it was a tool of deception. The shock that people feared came from a spell cast by Sana, a spell she couldn't cast if she had swallowed the wormroot.

Sana ran through the plan in her head and listened against the wall for the singing to stop in the adjacent room. Long after the stars were the only light in the sky, the singing turned to silence and finally the silence turned to snoring. It was time.

In the mental ward, doors locked from the outside, so the Sicarius Headmaster used the lock pick to exit. It was a standard lock, and she made quick work of it. A soft click signaled her success and she opened the door slowly, peering into the hallway. Orbs lit the hallway, but the orderlies had finished their rounds, so the corridor was empty. The Sicarius Headmaster slipped into the hallway, entered the adjacent room, and left the door slightly ajar to expedite her exit.

Inside the room, the sound of snoring and the familiar layout of the room led her silently to Ibson's bed. The Sicarius Headmaster pressed the knife against Ibson's throat, rammed the shockstick into his stomach, and whispered, "Listen to what I say or die. I know you drank wormroot and are completely defenseless. You are at my mercy." *That last part was a lie. Any mercy that Ibson receives will be from Rose.*

Ibson's eyes opened wide and his body went rigid, fighting his instinct to bolt upright because of the presence of the knife. He stammered,

Knives are mean,

> Knives are scary,
> My soul is clean,
> Don't kill—

The Sicarius Headmaster interrupted his poem, "Save the nursery rhymes, Ibson." Then she changed the inflection of her voice to alternate between high and low octaves. "Do you know who I am?"

Recognition of the distinctive style of speech invoked a fear that broke through Ibson's façade. "Yes. You are the Sicarius Headmaster and the wizard's apprentice that I once knew as Sana. What do you want from me?"

"Your life means nothing to me, since you have failed to live it. You choose to hide your recovery and ignore the world. Information, however, is valuable to me, and I believe you have been hiding information." The Sicarius Headmaster spoke. *Rose must ignore the deeds the Sicarius Headmaster carried out in the pursuit of information.*

Ibson protested, "If you need information from me, then I am in no danger until I tell you what you want to know…"

Sana appreciated his deductive reasoning, but she countered with her own. "I disagree. You locked yourself away and pretended to be mentally ill to protect yourself from the threat of a blood mage. You value your life, and this knife can take it, regardless of my motives. Stand up slowly. We are leaving." Ibson rose from bed slowly without resistance. He was an old man, and he fought with magic. Without the spark, he was simply old. "Take the knife," Sana commanded. A surprised Ibson reached for the knife at his throat. Before he reached it, Sana applied some pressure to the blade and caused it to collapse. "Don't get any ideas. This knife is harmless and you still have a shockstick to your stomach. Just play the role I tell you to play." Ibson grabbed the knife and nodded. Sana twisted so that her arm was behind her back but still pressed into Ibson's gut. "Grab my waist and hold me tight against you. Place the knife against my throat with your other hand. Now walk out the exit to the gardens. If anyone tries to stop you, threaten to kill me."

Sana, the hostage, led Ibson to the door and opened it. Ibson walked dutifully toward the exit, while Sana pretended to struggle against him. Ibson's wide-eyed, frightened stare even passed for a crazed hostile attacker. Halfway down the hallway, an orderly rounded the corner. Before Ibson could speak, Sana yelled, "Help, help me! He has a knife!"

The orderly turned and ran. Sana said to Ibson, "You are now committed to this ruse. You are a mentally ill patient holding a knife against someone's throat. No one will believe otherwise." Somewhere ahead, the orderly triggered a security orb and the alarm rang throughout the infirmary.

They rounded the final corner and saw three infirmary wizards barring the exit to the gardens. Master Meikel was in the lead and tried to reason with Ibson. "Put the knife down. You are a good person. Whatever you are dealing with right now, we can help you through it. Just let the girl go."

Ibson played his role to perfection by saying.

Step aside,
Step aside,

The girl won't die,
If my words you abide.

Sana tried to influence the critical decision in front of the wizards. "Do as he says. He's not himself. He could do anything…"

Master Meikel assessed the situation and commanded the infirmary personnel. "Allow him to leave. We can't risk harm to the girl. He has taken wormroot, so we can follow him safely. He won't get far." They stepped aside and cleared the path to the gardens. Ibson backed through the doorway, shielding himself with his hostage as the ruse demanded.

The wizards followed them into the darkened gardens with the infirmary alarms fading behind them. Ibson whispered to Sana, "Now what?"

"Walk toward the rosebushes and get behind the hedge." Ibson obliged as the infirmary wizards continued their attempts to negotiate with Ibson from a distance. Sana strained her eyes in the darkness and saw that the string she placed earlier in the day had been removed. *Help is here.*

A figure appeared on the roof of the infirmary, outlined by the ambient light from the building below but shadowed by the night sky. "Ibson belongs to me!" The pitch of the figure's voice alternated between words and pierced the night sky. A second later, a thick cloud of smoke enveloped the infirmary wizards.

The Sicarius Headmaster mimicked the alternating tones of the rooftop figure, "I am the Sicarius Headmaster!" Dense smoke reflects sound and makes it difficult to pinpoint the direction of the source. By speaking from two directions, Sana knew it would be virtually impossible to identify her or Ibson's location.

She turned to Ibson and whispered, "Our extraction point is in that direction. Move as fast as you are able. I will catch up shortly." Sana pointed toward a tall building just outside the infirmary grounds, within the capital city of Ravinai.

The figure on the rooftop said, "I defy King Darik by my continued existence. He tried to kill every member of Sicarius, his sworn servants, but I am not so easily killed. Now I serve the people of Malethya, although they are blinded to the dangers they face. I rule the world of shadows. Follow me tonight and you will never see the light of day again."

Following that bit of theater, Sana chased after Ibson, catching the old man quickly. The infirmary wizards were too disoriented and busy coughing from the smoke to give chase, but the real danger still awaited them. Up ahead, the headmaster located a tall, balconied building and quietly commanded Ibson, "Head for the alleyway just left of the building." The Sicarius Headmaster could hear the distinctive sound of soldiers marching toward the infirmary in response to the building's alarms, but they were still a few blocks away. *We made it.*

Inside the alleyway, Sana threw a canvas cover off a wooden platform. "Get on," the Sicarius Headmaster commanded Ibson. He climbed onto the platform while Sana unhooked a rope hidden amid the intricate architecture of the tall building. The rope attached to the four corners of the platform and disappeared somewhere above. The Sicarius Headmaster grasped a second rope that led to a knotted anchor against the alleyway and climbed aboard the platform. "Hold on tight. It might be a little bumpy at the top." She pulled on the rope, which released the knot and the platform started to rise immediately, gaining speed at an astounding rate. Halfway to the top, the counterweight passed them, plummeting to the ground. Their speed continued to increase and the Sicarius Headmaster jumped gracefully onto the building's balcony just before the counterweight smashed into the alleyway below. The sudden end to the platform's rise jarred Ibson, but the Sicarius Headmaster reached out to steady the suspended platform as it swung from a pulley overhead. She guided the old wizard onto solid ground.

"You played your role well, Ibson," Rosana complimented the wizard. She wanted to establish authority over Ibson, and compliments for following orders reinforced the hierarchy.

"You left me little choice. Why did you go to all the trouble of breaking me out of there? I was perfectly happy avoiding the world." Just then the Sicarius Headmaster saw motion on the rooftops, and a figure jumped gracefully from rooftop to rooftop to crouch above their balcony.

"Hello, Annarelle." The Sicarius Headmaster greeted her protégé, dressed in her likeness. The series of black wraps blended into the night, allowing for a great deal of flexibility and, most importantly, innumerable folds and pockets for darts, knives, and other tools of their craft. Annarelle also wore a Sicarius mask that made it difficult to look her in the face. The mask absorbed all light, creating a void in the visual signals the brain normally interpolates. The brain fills the void using information surrounding the mask. In practicality, this meant that the wearer of a Sicarius mask would be seen as a servant if they dressed in servant's clothes, a wizard if dressed in robes, or a soldier if dressed in armor. The Sicarius Headmaster was used to wearing and interacting with others wearing the mask, so its unsettling effect was muted. "Your timing is impeccable. I take it you found my string?"

"I left the package in the rose bush the night you were admitted and checked at sundown every evening for a signal. When I found it, I contacted Villifor, and he had his rebels occupy the army's attention tonight." Sana looked at the skyline of the city and saw smoke from several fires burning, which probably slowed the response time of the troops when the alarms at the infirmary were raised. Annarelle continued, "I'm happy it didn't take longer than a few days. How did things go inside the infirmary?"

The Sicarius Headmaster thought of the ease with which she had been diagnosed and admitted to the infirmary. It had all gone according to Sana's plan. *But I don't want to describe how easy it was to get a diagnosis and be admitted.* "I located and extracted our target before they tried to administer therapy to me."

Annarelle laughed. Most people would mistake the meaning of her laugh as jest at Sana's fear of therapy. Only a fellow Sicarius Guardsman would know the laugh's real meaning, which indicated Annarelle's relief that Sana didn't have to kill the wizard who might have attempted to treat her.

Ibson tried to take control of the situation by demanding answers. "Pleasantries aside, when do the questions start?"

Rosana waved Ibson toward the balcony railing that faced the infirmary, while Annarelle disappeared to scout for approaching trouble. Below their balcony, soldiers scoured the infirmary grounds in response to the alarm. Rosana addressed Ibson, "The Crimson Guard fights for justice throughout Malethya. The armor of the Bellator Guardsmen reflects the starlight in proud proclamation of their place in society. The robes of the Ispirtu wizards are hidden in the darkness, but you can imagine them scurrying around in a righteous display of power. I once stood in their company as a stanchion of Malethya and protector of the kingdom. Now the very people I strive to protect fear me. You let this happen."

Ibson responded, "It's true that I suspected a blood mage in Malethya, but you can't blame me for your troubles. I was put in charge of investigating how our friend, Slate Severance, the tournament champion, ended up with iron in his hand during his championship bout. During my investigation, it became apparent that he was a victim of blood magic. The blood mage attacked me in the arena and nearly killed me. I hid my recovery to protect myself, so that the blood mage couldn't come back to finish the job."

"You didn't hide from the blood mage," the Sicarius Headmaster scolded. "You hid from the world. You hid from responsibility."

Ibson shook his head in bemusement. "Responsibility is always shared, but self-preservation is the right of every man. Besides, I listened as you, Slate, Rainier, Lucus, and Lattimer worked to identify the blood mage. Slate found evidence implicating Brannon Regallo and stormed Ispirtu. I hear Brannon has been defeated, the threat of blood magic is ended, and the people of Malethya are safe. If your actions resulted in the loss of the Sicarius Guild, then the responsibility lies with the Sicarius Headmaster. Don't delude yourself."

The Sicarius Headmaster knew her own failures, and Rose mourned the loss of the guardsmen every night. "People who fail to act are adept at identifying fault in the actions of others. I will not take criticism from you." The Sicarius Headmaster's scorn permeated her words. Groups of Bellator Guardsmen and Ispirtu wizards combed the infirmary grounds below, searching for the notorious Sicarius Headmaster. Rosana explained to Ibson, "You are as blind as the rest of Malethya. We didn't defeat Brannon the blood mage. We defeated Brannon Regallo, the Ispirtu Headmaster and protector of Malethya. I stood at his side and fought with him before he was killed by his son, Lattimer. Lattimer took control of Ispirtu and the mind of King Darik through the use of blood magic. The armies loyal to Darik fight for their king, unknowingly doing the will of Lattimer. Meanwhile, Lattimer has been growing his own army of loyal subjugates. They look and act like normal soldiers until they attack. Then their eyes turn red and they attack with pure, unbridled aggression. They attack as Furies."

Ibson blanched at the mention of Furies, foot-soldiers from the days of Cantor when blood mages fought incestuously. Ibson refused to accept Rosana's story. "No, Brannon was the blood mage. Lattimer was never clever enough to accomplish what you say. It is an impossibility that he controls the kingdom and an army of Furies. Besides, Furies are mindless. Their aggression stems from a single desire to kill placed in their head by a blood mage." He pointed to toward the soldiers in the infirmary grounds. "Those soldiers aren't mindless."

"No, they are not. They attack with the aggression of Furies but the training of Bellator Guardsmen and Ispirtu wizards." Sana paused to let the reality of that threat sink in.

"I tire of your lies. Let's end these questions," confronted Ibson.

"I have told you the truth. As for questions, I have yet to ask one. However, you did ask me when the questions would start, and I have avoided answering in the hopes you would believe me. Since you refuse to see the truth, the questions will start just as soon as you wake up." The Sicarius Headmaster reached out with her shockstick and Sana cast a spell that sent a small jolt of electricity through the wizard. Ibson fell to the balcony floor.

Annarelle rejoined her and picked up Ibson's legs. "I hate this part of the operation."

Sana, Rose, and Rosana agreed with Annarelle, but the Sicarius Headmaster knew it was part of the job. "We are Sicarius Guardsmen. We need to move and hide bodies once in a while."

As they prepared to move Ibson, a large contingent of Guardsmen and wizards entered the city grounds below. At the head of the pack, a wizard carried himself with an arrogance that dwarfed the gaudiness of his robes and scepter. Even if Lattimer wasn't her brother, she would have recognized him from a mile away. It was Lattimer's first public appearance since seizing power, and he had apparently taken up their father's sense of fashion as well as his air of authority. *Despite the physical similarities to her father, his appearance only inspires hate. Lattimer killed her father. He was responsible for the deaths of Lucus and Slate's parents through the actions of Magnus. Now he has enslaved hundreds, if not thousands of soldiers to do his will. For any of these atrocities, he deserves to die.* The Sicarius Headmaster pulled out a throwing knife while Sana cast a spell to guide and speed it. The knife flew straight and actually sped up as it neared Lattimer, reaching the speed of a falcon just before its talons grasp its prey.

At the last second, the knife flew off course and embedded in the ground at Lattimer's feet, harmlessly diverted by whatever magic surrounded Lattimer. The blood mage looked down at the knife and then directly at her, locking eyes with his sister. He pointed at her as the soldiers and wizards around him turned into Furies. The soldiers sprinted toward their building and the wizards readied fireballs. Lattimer himself readied a spell and the Sicarius Headmaster didn't want to wait to find out what kind of spell it would be.

"Go! Now!" She yelled to Annarelle. They flung Ibson's body onto the next rooftop. Beneath them, the building started to shake. Lattimer planned to take down the whole building. Annarelle and the Headmaster jumped onto the adjacent rooftop just as the building was hit with a series of fireballs. It collapsed a second later in a cloud of rubble that mixed with the smoke of wizard's fire.

They gathered Ibson and used the smoke and dust as a screen to mask their escape. When they were safely away from the collapsed building, they took the time to carry Ibson more comfortably. "Well, we learned one thing tonight. My throwing knives are useless against

Lattimer."

"And if we get close enough, we run the risk of being captured and subjugated like King Darik. We need Slate. He is the only one who could ever resist Lattimer." Annarelle talked while she unwrapped a portion of her outfit around her leg. It had two long straps on either end of a fine mesh of fabric in the middle to form a makeshift stretcher.

"Slate could only resist Lattimer for a short period of time, but you are right. It would be long enough to attack him. Unfortunately, he hasn't recovered fully from his first encounter with Lattimer. We need Slate, but we need to fix him first. Maybe Ibson will hold the key." They rolled Ibson's body atop the middle portion of the stretcher, and Annarelle slung two straps over her shoulders. The Sicarius Headmaster tied the other two straps around her waist and the two set off with their cargo.

They carried him across the rooftops of Ravinai, and while the Sicarius Headmaster handled the physical exertion, Rose and her other selves were free to look at the city anew. Rose's heart warmed to the sounds of merriment that floated up from the taverns below. Rosana knew it wasn't the sounds of drunkards spending their last dime on a drink but the laughter of citizens with extra change in their pockets. Sana noted the clean streets and the quality goods displayed in the store windows. The alleyways were clear of the homeless and new construction confirmed the affluence of the citizens. Ravinai's prosperity brought conflicting emotions. When Lattimer seized power, he promised to recreate the golden age of Cantor with his unlimited power. It appeared that he was living up to his promise, but Sana knew the golden age ended in bloodshed with the blood mages subjugating citizens and using them as mindless weapons in their never-ending thirst for power. Rose hoped she could get answers before the prosperity ended and the bloodshed began.

With the fear of the future refocusing her efforts, the Sicarius Headmaster checked on Ibson. He was still unconscious as they approached an abandoned warehouse. The Sicarius Headmaster had a network of safe houses and informants in Ravinai and throughout Malethya. When King Darik destroyed the Sicarius Guild, she relocated her headquarters to this warehouse, one of her more secretive locations. The warehouse's proximity to the infirmary's morgue proved to be an advantageous location for some of Sana's needs.

The Sicarius Headmaster and Annarelle hauled Ibson's body onto the rooftop of the abandoned warehouse and toward a ventilation shaft that served as the hideout's entrance. The shaft hid a ladder and a winch, which they used for supplies or, in this case, a body. They hooked the straps of Ibson's stretcher to the winch and lowered him into the darkness until the winch stopped. The Headmaster and Annarelle descended the ladder to a small platform that hung inconspicuously from the rafters of the warehouse.

Annarelle lit a small oil lamp that cast a dim glow over the warehouse below them. The floor of the warehouse was covered with row upon row of shelving that once served as a distribution center for the king's supply of grain and stores. The offices suspended from the ceiling, so that the king's clerks and foreman could oversee the workers below and keep stock of warehouse supply. The stairwell that originally connected the offices to the warehouse floor was destroyed in a fire extensive enough to cause the building to be abandoned. The result was the perfect hideout— the warehouse offices were isolated and difficult to infiltrate. They were also heavily modified to fit her needs.

Sana reached up to a pulley system that connected the platform to the offices. She hooked Ibson's stretcher to the pulley hook before disconnecting him from the winch. "Annarelle, can you welcome our guest?" Annarelle smiled and swung freeform across the rafters, easily bridging the gap between the platform and the offices while Sana worked the pulley system. Ibson's body hung lifelessly as it traversed the span into Annarelle's waiting arms. She disconnected him and the Sicarius Headmaster swung across the rafters to join them. "His room is prepared for his arrival. Please tie him to his chair and meet me in the anatomy room."

CHAPTER TWO

TORTURED SOUL

Sana cast a spell to illuminate her headquarters and, as always, was reminded of Lucus. Lucus had been a member of the Wizard Council, a group of wizards in Malethya who acted independently from the king and weren't trained through Ispirtu. Lucus trained Sana and didn't believe in the use of magic during battle, as was true of many members of the Wizard Council. He had accompanied Slate to face Brannon anyway, and when Lattimer revealed himself as the blood mage, Lucus sacrificed himself to save his friends. What would Lucus say if he saw her now, hiding in an abandoned warehouse and kidnapping his former mentor from the infirmary?

If Lucus approved of kidnapping Ibson, he certainly wouldn't approve of her methods of questioning. The anatomy room housed a collection of texts and diagrams, but their presence was dwarfed by a large table, shelves of sample specimens, and utensils for hands-on research. She walked over to a diagram displaying the nervous system. It had been the lifelong work of a member of Sicarius. Sana concentrated on the information the diagram contained to distract Rose from the fate of the Sicarius Guardsman. That guardsman had died like the other members of Sicarius, killed by their own king.

Annarelle entered the room. "I tied Ibson to a chair in his room. He is beginning to stir and will be lucid in a few moments."

"Then our time is short. People are the most honest when disoriented." Rosana knew this from the Sicarius Headmaster's past experiences, but Annarelle's knowledge came only through the Headmaster's teaching. "I will ask the questions and you will administer any persuasion necessary to obtain answers." While the Sicarius Headmaster typically performed the physical portions of torture, Rosana handled the questions. She was the most adept at judging the responses and body language of the tortured. Her abilities to disguise herself and blend into her surroundings made it easy for her to identify when someone else was hiding something from her. Now she wanted Annarelle to try her hand at the Sicarius Headmaster's role, but not before making sure she remembered her lessons. "What are the basic tenets of torture?"

Annarelle answered quickly and without anticipation, confirming Rosana's judgment of her readiness. "One—persistent pain over a long period of time is more effective than acute pain, since pain is the only sensory stimulation that does not diminish over time. Two—extreme pain can lead to answers given solely to stop the questioning and should be avoided. Three—if time does not allow for proper technique, disregard tenets one and two."

"Excellent. Tonight we have time on our side and Ibson poses a formidable challenge. Take care that our efforts to obtain information do not provide information to Ibson in return. Any scrap of knowledge that we provide is leverage lost." Annarelle nodded her acceptance, but Rosana had also intended the reminder for Rose.

The Sicarius Headmaster and Sana could remain stoic during any set of circumstances, but Rose tended to let her emotions show from time to time. Rosana slipped on the white robe of an infirmary wizard and stopped in her storeroom for a dose of wormroot. She had stocked up for this occasion. Annarelle put on an orderly's uniform and led Rosana into Ibson's room.

The old wizard sat in a chair bolted to the floor, drooling on his chest since his neck hadn't began to regain the strength to lift his head. Annarelle had set up the room to mimic the infirmary. The walls were padded, a cheap bed was bolted to the floor, and everything was painted a sterile shade of white. The overly bright lighting orbs obscured any indication of time and disrupted Ibson's sleep cycle, providing further disorientation.

Before Ibson awoke, Rosana ran through her mental list of things that Ibson did and did not know. He knew her as Sana, but he also knew Lucus, Brannon, and Lattimer. He still believed Brannon was the blood mage and that the threat to Malethya had ended. In reality, Lattimer was the blood mage, and he had framed his father to turn Darik's armies against Brannon, using Darik and Slate to eliminate the only wizard powerful enough to oppose him. When he took control, Lattimer revealed that he had subjugated the minds of a number of Ispirtu wizards and Bellator Guardsmen who voluntarily served him. Lattimer wanted the Sicarius Headmaster and Slate to accept subjugation and to lead his army of Furies. When Slate refused, Lattimer used Slate's blood in an attempt to force Slate into servitude. They had escaped, but Sana's efforts to heal Slate before his mind could be corrupted led to the blight and left Slate only partially healed. Ibson had missed these events due to his stay in the infirmary. Rosana didn't intend to give him any of this information unless it served her to do so. Rosana needed to find out Ibson's connection to Lattimer, information about the spell being used against Slate, and most importantly, how to stop it.

"Wake up, Ibson. Tell me why you tried to escape the infirmary. We are here to help you." Rosana looked squarely into Ibson's eyes without a hint of emotion, adopting the same look Meikel had used in the infirmary while scribbling the judgments he kept hidden from the insane.

Ibson's eyes focused, and he looked around the room wildly. "What is this? I know you are the Sicarius Headmaster. Enough with the pretenses..." Disorientation. The earlier Ibson began to question fact from fiction, the quicker he would break. "Why am I so sore? Did you torture me while I was unconscious?" No, but they did throw his body across several rooftops. Rosana ignored his question and stayed in character.

Rosana raised her eyebrows and pretended to write on a notepad. "The subject denies reality even when presented the truth. This alternate reality will be enforced until the truth is accepted. Let's begin with your medication, taken for your own protection." Annarelle measured the correct dose of wormroot and administered it to Ibson, but he spit it out, spraying Rosana in the process.

Annarelle assessed the situation without reacting to Ibson's outburst. "The subject refuses his oral medication. There are only two remaining options for administration, a tube that passes the naso-gastric barrier or rectal facilitation." A look of horror passed over Ibson's face. Annarelle drew another dose that Ibson swallowed obediently and said, "The patient has become compliant."

Rosana smiled inwardly because the Sicarius Headmaster knew the first concession was the most difficult to obtain. "Ibson, you were once a prominent wizard before hiding from the world. You are responsible for teaching magic to Lucus, Brannon Regallo, and his son, Lattimer Regallo. Did you teach the practice of blood magic to all of them?"

"I didn't teach them blood magic…" Ibson began but Rosana cut him off.

"…so you did teach them all. Why did Brannon leave your tutelage?"

Ibson realized his mistake and reversed course. "What do you want? If what you say is true, Lattimer has already risen to power and has an army of Furies at his disposal. You are too late. You have failed."

Rosana addressed Annarelle. "Our patient is suffering from a delusional episode in which he thinks he is in a position to ask questions. Please begin treatment." Annarelle retrieved a series of pins from within her orderly's uniform and tied his arm to the armrest of the chair.

Rosana explained the therapy to her patient. "Pain can alert the senses. I don't know if it will help with your delusions, but it will get some answers." Annarelle placed a series of three pins in Ibson's forearm and his arm instantly flexed in agony. "The body has certain locations called plexuses that receive pain signals and transmit them to the brain. If someone knows where they are located it takes very little force to cause extreme amounts of pain." She removed two of the pins. "Do you know how many plexuses are in the body?"

Ibson went white. He'd learned his lesson and answered the question. "I do not know." Annarelle removed the last pin as a reward for her obedient patient.

"Why did Brannon Regallo leave your tutelage?" Sana repeated the question again as a test.

"Similar spells can be conjured with various combinations of spark and pattern. I taught the importance of pattern-based magic, which requires a thorough understanding of the world around you. Brannon's spark was strong, so he failed to see the usefulness of my teachings." Ibson stopped, but Sana remained quiet, so he continued on. "He left to become the headmaster of Ispirtu, where he instructed legions of wizards that the best types of spells were the ones that could be conjured the quickest in battle. Students relied upon a greater amount of spark in order to conjure more quickly." Lucus had told Sana the story of Brannon, so she could verify the accuracy of Ibson's account. Rosana had one more test before the real questions began.

"Blood magic is called spark-based magic by practitioners of the art because spells are conjured without a link or pattern." Most knowledge of blood magic had disappeared, but Lattimer had learned somewhere. "Brannon had books containing references to blood magic hidden in his personal library. Did he get them from you?"

"All references to blood magic are supposed to be destroyed, but if someone had the power and connections to track down copies of the manuscripts, it would be Brannon." Brannon was powerful, but Ibson was only offering a partial truth. The Sicarius Headmaster stood up and reached for a pin from Annarelle.

"After Lattimer killed his father, he told me that he stole the manuscripts from you and used them to implicate Brannon as a blood mage." The Sicarius Headmaster pushed the pin into the plexus of Ibson's forearm, causing him to squirm. "Each time you lie to me, another pin will be placed. Do not wait too long before giving me the answers I seek because a funny thing happens to the brain when it receives too much stimulus." The Sicarius Headmaster and Annarelle left the room but before the door closed, the Sicarius Headmaster finished her threat. "It shuts down."

Sana led Annarelle into the Headmaster's conclave, affectionately called the war room. Inside were the notes and drawings of all past Sicarius Headmasters, the most revered possessions of the Sicarius Guild. Rosana had spent countless hours poring over them to understand the personalities of the past Headmasters and any opportunities to improve her own deficiencies while Sana studiously examined the tactics and strategies of previous Sicarius missions. Rose hummed softly during the sessions to distract herself from the content.

Sana collapsed in a comfortable chair following her busy day and Annarelle produced a cup of tea without prompting. While she calmed herself from the anxiety of the day, her eyes were drawn toward the top of the wall, just below the ceiling. She had written the names of all past headmasters and the duration of their service. Josmil Santo—two years, seven months,

Hannes Windler—six months, Leotta Prinetta—two weeks. The names bordered the entire room, with Rosana Regallo finishing the circle. She had served Sicarius for over three years now, longer than any previous Sicarius Headmaster. She survived multiple attempts on her life in times of peace. Now she was labeled an enemy of the crown and would be killed on sight. If she died, Annarelle would take her place as the Sicarius Headmaster. At one time, she thought Slate would shoulder the responsibilities of the Sicarius Headmaster, but the candle of his life burned even hotter and faster than hers. How much longer would she survive? The Sicarius Headmaster's time was short and the only way to prolong it was to plan perfectly for the upcoming storm. Sana had so much to do. She put her tea down and got back to work.

"Have you checked on the locations of our friends lately?"

Annarelle pulled out a box with a series of medallions inside. "I haven't checked on them. The whole idea of tracking medallions is still confusing to me. How do they work?"

"The basic concept was developed by the researchers in Ispirtu. They tried to use magic to focus light into a beam that could be used during battle. In their experiments, they stumbled upon a phenomenon where if the beam passed through a crystal, a light particle could be split into two entangled particles. The entangled particles were forever linked, regardless of distance. They dismissed the phenomenon as irrelevant because they were only trying to develop a weapon. But I saw the pattern as perfect for tracking friends, enemies, or other people of interest. I cast a spell that used the pattern of entangled light particles and applied it to pairs of medallions. Now each of these medallions is forever linked to its entangled pair carried by our friends. With the medallions in this box, we can know precisely where they are regardless of distance."

"I have a lot to learn." The complexity of entangled particles humbled Annarelle, again proving her maturity in the months since her formal training began.

Sana set the medallions on the table, exposing a map of Malethya that lined the bottom of the box. Pins marked the last known locations of her friends, with one conspicuous absence. Rainier's medallion stopped working shortly after he left Ravinai, giving off signals so weak that Sana was unable to locate him. She placed a pin at the bottom of the map, in the general direction of the signal.

Sana reached out her hand to touch the medallion carried by Villifor while casting a probing spell to sense the pattern of the medallion. The probing spell revealed that the pattern within the medallion had been split, or entangled, and by identifying the pattern, the second half of the entangled medallion could be identified. Sana judged the strength and direction of the pattern and placed a pin on the map. As she already knew from the fires around the city, Villifor was in Ravinai. The confirmation gave her confidence in predicting the locations of the others.

Next, she searched for Jak and found Slate's Bellator friend to be in a different part of the city. "Villifor has had Jak traversing the countryside, probably with the intent to recruit aid in regions that haven't been corrupted by Lattimer yet. I guess he called him back to participate in tonight's activities."

"Is the group still together?" Annarelle was really asking about Tommy, her Ispirtu conspirator and boyfriend, but her professionalism forced her to ask indirectly.

Sana probed Tommy's medallion. "Tommy is also in the city, but they have all split up. Villifor probably put each of them in charge of separate missions."

That answer pacified Annarelle. "What about Slate?"

What about Slate? Her emotions tumbled as her hand moved toward his medallion. Rosana argued constantly with Sana over conflicting thoughts of loyalty and distrust, good intentions and poor judgment, love and logic. The Sicarius Headmaster remained uninterested in the entire argument and in the end it was Rose who had cast the deciding vote. Rose saw the same passion, strength, and integrity she had once admired in her own father, so she gave her blessing to Rosana. She probed the medallion and the entangled pattern jumped back toward her. She placed a pin on the map. "Slate is in the northern provinces, continuing his pattern of isolation."

Annarelle could sense Sana's inner turmoil. "He stays away to protect us from himself. He nearly killed us after Lattimer tried to subjugate him, and you weren't able to fully heal him. Give him time."

They didn't have time and Annarelle knew it. "While he stays away, Lattimer grows in power. I could have healed him with one more visit to a catalpa grove."

"That course of action would have required you to use blood magic, and the first time you tried it, it resulted in a blight."

"A small section of trees south of Ravinai has died by my actions. It is a small price to pay to heal Slate. You have said yourself that we need him to kill Lattimer. Slate's abilities as a Perceptor allow him to feel magic used against him and resist subjugation. He should have let me heal him in another catalpa grove. I could have finished the spell and we wouldn't be in this situation."

"The blight is spreading. Slate may be stubborn, but his heart is in the right place."

I cannot think about Slate's heart now. Sana knew that Rosana would quickly feel the need to discuss her feelings in more detail. "There is no point in arguing past actions. Slate has chosen isolation. It is our job to figure out a cure before it's too late to stop Lattimer."

That last part was only half-true. Before Slate isolated himself from the group, he'd ordered Sana to recruit new Sicarius guardsmen and track down members of the wizard council. She later reconsidered the strategy and decided someone needed to help save Slate from himself so that he could fulfill his duty to Malethya by killing Lattimer. To appease her conscience about neglecting a mission she agreed to carry out, she had sent communications to members of the wizard council warning them to stay hidden while a powerful blood mage remains in Ravinai and focused her Sicarius efforts on readying her heir apparent as the headmaster.

"And you think Ibson holds the key to curing Slate's mind from Lattimer's spell?" Annarelle asked hopefully.

"He knows more than us. If he doesn't have the answer, then he can probably lead us to it."

Sana checked Rainier's medallion out of thoroughness. The same weak signal pointed south. Had the spell on Rainier's medallion faded? Sana hoped he was safe, but she was too busy at the moment to travel to the edges of the kingdom just because of a faulty medallion. Besides, if Rainier needed her help, he would break the medallion and sever the pattern of the entangled particles would be broken. The pattern remained intact, so he must be safe. She packed the medallions into the box and Annarelle stored it on a shelf.

Her apprentice couldn't help but comment on their current state. "We are too few. Lattimer has an army and we are spread across the city with barely enough manpower to light a few fires."

The Sicarius Headmaster refused to suffer self-pity. "You are a Sicarius Guardsman. You are trained to operate alone and accomplish your missions without aid. All we need is the right information and the will to act decisively upon it." The lesson to her apprentice served as a reminder of her own previous faults. She had taught Annarelle the Sicarius way, but isolation wasn't sufficient. She learned that when she had to witness every guardsman in the Sicarius Guild butchered in front of her. If they were to win, she also had to teach Annarelle to work like a Bellator Guardsman. She needed to work as part of a team. Her decision to contact Villifor had been a good start, but that was only a start. They would need to work even closer. One thing that Villifor required from them was information, and the thought reminded her that the Guild's information networks needed tending. "While we wait for Ibson to soften up, I will check with our Sicarius contacts. My stay in the infirmary has prevented me from obtaining news from around Malethya."

Annarelle saw a chance to regain her Headmaster's approval. "I took the liberty of maintaining the drop locations in the network that I had knowledge of. Information is our lifeblood after all…"

The Sicarius Headmaster contemplated Annarelle's decision. She had acted without orders, but the headmaster had just chided her for needing to act independently. Besides, if the headmaster met her untimely end, Annarelle would need to carry on. "If you feel ready for this responsibility, then it is time I tested you to ensure it is done properly." Annarelle beamed at the headmaster, who returned her enthusiasm with measured stoicism.

Annarelle finished her immediate tasks abuzz with anticipation, cooking and serving breakfast to Ibson despite the hour. It was still the middle of the night, but the meal Annarelle served would disrupt Ibson's daily schedule and disorient him further. Sana took the time to check for signs of entry in the warehouse below and reset any traps triggered by curious rodents seeking residence in her hideaway. Happy that her residence, with Ibson inside, was safely secured, she gathered Annarelle and climbed through the roof access and out to the safety of the night.

CHAPTER THREE

THE SHADOW OF A SHADOW

"Which drop locations did you check?" the
Sicarius Headmaster had taught Annarelle a
handful of locations, but the more sensitive
contacts remained safely locked away in her
head.

"Raven's Claw, Rat Roost, and Liar's Lair."

The three locations required a variety of
skillsets to infiltrate and maintain secrecy.
They would serve nicely to evaluate Annarelle's
readiness. "Start with Rat Roost, followed by
Raven's Claw and Liar's Lair. I'll follow from
a distance."

Annarelle nodded in acknowledgment, covered
her face with the Sicarius mask that hid her
from the world, and then dashed across leapt up
to the rooftops toward the working class
neighborhoods of western Ravinai. Instead of
following, the headmaster circumnavigated
Annarelle's path and found a tall roof to
critically assess her apprentice's stealth
while traversing the city: a silhouette against
the night sky, a misstep that sent a pebble off
the rooftop to the ground, a metal roof that
thundered to the inhabitants below. These were
small errors. Small errors had killed many
Sicarius Guardsmen.

When the evaluation ended, the headmaster
moved quickly toward a raucous pub called the
Moonlight Rooster. Its patrons, like the pub's
namesake, were blue-collar workers with early

shifts and an appetite for nightlife. Clinking cups and exuberant profanities interrupted the efforts of an underappreciated singer working for tips. Money flowed freely and merriment contradicted the profanities of the patrons, again indicating that times were good in Ravinai, even in the lower patronages of the social ladder.

Sana decided to check the drop in advance of Annarelle's arrival. The headmaster circled around the back of the Rooster and opened the cellar doors. The sound of rats scurrying below greeted her. When she had first started using this drop, she had descended into the cellar, guided only by the light from the gapped floorboards above, and coined the term Rat Roost based on the cellar's inhabitants.

Since that time, Sana had devised a more eloquent method of retrieving information from the cellar. She suspended a metal box from the underside of the ceiling, spanning two gaping floorboards. Her informant simply took the corner booth in the Rooster and dropped his report through the floorboards at an opportune time. Sana came early to inspect the bracket holding the box. Angle irons held the box at each corner. If someone's curiosity got the better of them, they could slide the box out of the brackets and examine the contents, but not without alerting Sana. With the brackets in this configuration, the box could be removed, but a strategic burr in the metal bracket would scrape the box. Sana pivoted each of the corner brackets so that the box slid out in the opposite orientation. Each corner of the box had a scrape alongside it. *Annarelle probably failed to disengage the drop's trigger that marks it as safe.* But the Sicarius Headmaster couldn't count on probabilities; she hadn't survived this long by hoping for the best. *I must assume that this drop location had been compromised, and Annarelle's informant as well.*

Sana repositioned the box back into the bracket for Annarelle to find and then closed the cellar doors from within. The Sicarius Headmaster felt her way through the cellar, guided only by the light of the floorboards above, to a stack of wine casks that she hid behind. The position gave her a clear view of the suspended box and Annarelle as she entered.

The Sicarius Headmaster stood as still as a statue, even when the cellar's inhabitants became accustomed to her presence and started crawling across her feet. An especially brave rat climbed her legs to reach the shelves behind her when the cellar doors opened. The rat startled at the interruption and jumped atop the wine casks, digging into the headmaster's leg in the process. Rose, Rosana, and Sana wanted to cry out in pain, but silence was needed, and the Headmaster always did what needed to be done.

The soft moonlight of the night sky projected against Annarelle as she descended the cellar steps. She walked quietly on the balls of her feet to escape notice from the patrons above and headed for the box. Annarelle carefully switched the bracket positions and removed the box, noticing the scrape marks and confirming Sana's fears.

"The drop location is compromised." Rosana projected at just the right volume to be heard from the depths of the cellar but not be heard by the patrons above. Annarelle reached for a throwing knife in her robes, gaining the headmaster's approval by reacting to the unexpected voice with the speed and decisiveness expected of a trained Sicarius Guardsman.

"I have failed you, headmaster. I did not think I had been followed."

"Pretend it didn't happen. Gather the contents from the dropbox and finish your rounds. I will look for anyone tracking your movements at Raven's Claw and Liar's Lair. If I have need of communicating any additional orders, they will be given to you through our contact at Liar's Lair. Otherwise, finish your rounds with a scrub run and meet me at home later."

"Fractal's blessing, headmaster." Annarelle acknowledged her orders and left the cellar, leaving the Sicarius Headmaster to burn even hotter than the claw marks in her leg. Losing an informant was no small loss, but the Sicarius Headmaster had just given Annarelle orders that would compromise an additional two. Necessity forced difficult decisions, and the stakes were too high to take many losses. If her gambit succeeded, she could turn three low level informants into direct access to Lattimer. *I hate gambling, but the occasional calculated risk is necessary.*

The headmaster had to assume that the cellar doors were being watched, so she took the only other exit, the stairwell to the pub above. The Sicarius Headmaster ascended the stairs with throwing darts at the ready and threw open the door to find herself in the kitchen. Two barmaids and a cook jumped out of their skin at the sight of the notorious criminal. Before they could scream, the headmaster threw the darts and Sana added a little spark to ensure they flew straight into her targets' necks. The barmaids collapsed into the dishes they were cleaning and the chef dropped to the floor, sending a head of lettuce rolling from his outstretched hands. They would wake up in a few minutes with headaches but otherwise no worse for wear. Rose purred in approval of the headmaster's use of nonlethal force.

Rosana stole the cook's oversized cloak that hung near the door and slipped into the alleyway, walking with the slow gait of someone on her work break. She ambled across the street toward a small apartment complex with an entrance off the lighted street. Instead of entering the building, she shed the cloak and the Sicarius Headmaster scaled the building, swinging onto the overhang of the building's entrance and climbing the apartment windowsills until she reached the roof.

From there, the headmaster sped toward Rue Street, forgoing stealth in favor of speed. Annarelle would take the long, slow route to Raven's Claw so that the Headmaster could scout the area, but there wasn't any time to waste.

Rose understood the crucial need for focus, even as she wished for a moment's reprieve. *In this moment of relative safety, I wish I could enjoy the simple pleasure of a nighttime run. What I wouldn't give to feel the crisp night air on my face, and know the stars above held no Malethyan agendas.* Rose fought for these joys that every citizen of Ravinai deserved to experience. She didn't want her brother to take these joys from people by subjugating their minds. How could they enjoy the wind against their face if they were driven by a single command? Rose would not allow Lattimer to subjugate any more citizens than she could help, and she certainly wouldn't let him control her. *Under the cover of darkness, no one can catch me, and no one can control me— not even a blood mage and his army of Furies.*

The close quarters of the city gave way to the manicured lawns of the affluent, signaling that her destination neared. Many Ispirtu wizards and Ispirtu supporters chose to inhabit the estates of Rue Street, creating a neighborhood filled with egos, money, and power. Rose thought of it as home, having been raised in the largest and most condescending of estates. The last time she had come home, the Sicarius Headmaster had fought her way through a host of Bellator Guardsmen and Ispirtu wizards and left the estate a rubble-strewn monument to her troubled youth. Her mother had chosen not to rebuild the structure, making it the perfect location to observe Annarelle.

Rose picked through the charred remains of her childhood home until she reached her mother's room, giving Sana a clear view to scout Raven's Claw and strategize. Raven's Claw was the codename for the estate owned by Ms. Babblerone, a socialite of lower standing who had tired of bowing to the power of the Regallos. When approached by Rosana dressed as the Sicarius Headmaster and offered the opportunity to serve King Darik and preserve the peace in all of Malethya by providing information on the Regallos, she accepted with ambition. Rosana presumed the intrigue of the Sicarius Guild satisfied some personal craving for power. Ms. Babblerone had no idea that she spied on the Regallo family only to report their comings and goings to another Regallo. Sana had little strategic use of the information Ms. Babblerone provided, but it did serve as a connection of sorts to her previous life. Rose liked to know when her mother hosted parties or organized benefit dinners for various causes in Ravinai. She didn't necessarily approve of her copious drinking at the events, but the woman was coping with the loss of her husband and presumed loss of her daughter.

Motion near the Babblerone estate interrupted her revelry and the Sicarius Headmaster identified Annarelle as she slipped through the hedges and approached a lawn statue in the form of a raven, proudly displayed in homage to the Ispirtu Guild and the Regallo family. She ignored Annarelle, knowing she would reach the base of the statue and turn the Ispirtu insignia to reveal a hidden compartment that housed Ms. Babblerone's notes. Instead, the Sicarius Headmaster scanned the neighboring estates for movement.

All the estates were lit, even at this late hour, both to discourage intruders and as a display of grandeur. Orbs lit the mansions of the obscenely rich, while the wealthy were relegated to the candles or oil lamps of commoners. The Sicarius Headmaster didn't look directly at the lights to preserve her night vision, but then the shadows in a second story room changed. She didn't see anyone in the window, but she didn't need to. In a quiet house in the middle of the night, there would be no circulating air to disrupt the dance of a candle flame. Someone's movement in the room caused the candle to flicker. It took considerable skill for the person tracking Annarelle to break into the house that quickly.

Her paranoia validated, Sana fought the headmaster's urge to infiltrate the house and confront Annarelle's shadow. As gratifying as it would be, logic prevailed and Sana held her position. She had other plans.

Annarelle replaced the lid of the hidden compartment in the raven statue and left the dimly lit lawn for the safety of darkness, making her way toward Liar's Lair. Shortly after, the shadows in the second story room flickered again, and then a figure approached the raven statue and left something in the drop location. Annarelle's pursuer fled into the heart of Ravinai, leaving Sana with a choice. She could trail Annarelle's pursuer, but in this instance, she knew where they would end up, and she had chosen Liar's Lair for just such an occasion.

Annarelle would take a circuitous route to her final destination, giving Sana time to check out Raven's Claw again. At the drop, she found a letter sealed with the symbol of Sicarius. Sana broke the seal and read it with the ambient light of the city.

To Rosana Regallo, the former Headmaster of the Sicarius Guild,

It is a pleasure to write a note to you. In a past life, I was on the receiving end of countless notes, but I never had the pleasure of making your acquaintance. If I met you now, I would rip out your throat to put an end to the lies and manipulation that spew from your mouth. Unfortunately, my loyalty to your brother commands that I stay my hand.

Lattimer, the Great Redeemer, wishes to extend an olive branch and forgive your past transgressions in exchange for your aid. Join him and lead the new Sicarius

Guild. His intentions are true and can be witnessed in any of your rooftop runs across the city. The city is prosperous, Malethya is prosperous, and most importantly, the people are happy. He is returning Malethya to the golden age of Cantor. You can help him and join him in history as a far better person than I know you to be. You have until nightfall tomorrow to respond to this letter.

Personally, I hope you don't respond, because then the Redeemer will view you as a threat to the golden age, and he will order me to track you down and terminate the threat. I look forward to that order, for when it comes, it won't be in a letter from a coward behind a mask. It will come directly from Lattimer, giving me the single-minded focus to track you night and day, stopping at nothing until I find you. When I do, I will leave you broken and bloodied, to die a fractal-forsaken death. Only then will I be able to repay you the kindness you showed me by sending me on a doomed mission and leaving me for dead…

Phoenix

Sana slowly refolded the letter, contemplating its contents. Lattimer thought the headmaster would help him? Any prospect of that happening ended the moment Magnus killed Lucus. Sana could forgive her brother for not understanding the perils of blood magic. Sana had used it herself to save Slate, so it would be hypocritical to condemn Lattimer for the same mistake. But ordering Magnus to kill Lucus, a pacifist and friend, was unforgivable.

Lattimer's continued insistence on using blood magic to bring back the Golden Age was his final failure. Sana had used blood magic once and caused a blight. She didn't want to contemplate what repercussions were in store from Lattimer's actions. *No. I will not help Lattimer. And who was Phoenix? He writes as if he was a member of Sicarius, but what have I done to deserve such hatred?* The Sicarius Headmaster had to do difficult things in her role, but she had always tried to be fair and to protect the members of her guild. She had lost several Sicarius Guardsmen on missions, but she never would have left one of her guardsmen for dead. Whoever Phoenix was, his writing made it obvious that he was a voluntary subjugate to Lattimer. Sana had a Sicarius Fury that would be unleashed to track her down and kill her.

Sana pocketed the letter and used her rooftop run to the Lustful Lord—the highest priced brothel in Ravinai—to formulate her plans. Located in the heart of the city, this balustraded monument to infidelity was the play-place for Malethya's nobility. The numerous balconies served to propagate the prearranged nuptials through the semblance of romance. They also provided easy access to the building. The Sicarius Headmaster swung over the railing of a top floor balcony and into the only room where she didn't have to worry about interrupting a transaction in mid-thrust.

"Don't bother to scream for help. People will just assume you are getting your money's worth…" The headmaster's alternating voice inspired fear wherever she went, but here it was just part of the game.

The proprietor of the Lustful Lord faced the

Sicarius Headmaster with silky confidence. "It's been too long since you've visited me." She walked to her desk and picked gold coins from a pile, allowing them to fall through her fingers. "As for getting my money's worth, I can assure you that money is not in short supply at the Lustful Lord."

"Lady Highsmith, your services to me cannot be measured in gold… they are much more valuable."

Lady Highsmith walked over and stroked the Sicarius mask with the back of her hand. "I will provide you with the information these pompous nobles scream in excitement or cry onto the shoulders of my girls, but you will never know my true value until you take me up on the services of my trade. I may not take on customers like the other girls, but there are secrets that only a proprietor knows…"

Part of the problem with alternating your speech was that sometimes people assumed your gender incorrectly. The headmaster played along because it kept the information coming. "I am interested in taking our relationship to the next level…" Rosana was practiced at playing different roles and helped the Sicarius Headmaster's efforts by tracing the curvature of Lady Highsmith, letting her hand stop on her hip. "…but not in the manner you suggest. In a moment, my apprentice will come in here and request information. My guardsman is being followed. I need to know by whom. Can I conceal my presence in your room?"

"I've been trying to get you to stay in my room for quite some time now. What do you need from me?"

"Report your information as usual and then give my guardsman a message. Tell the guardsman to wait a few minutes in the Lustful Lord. Then pass along these exact words: 'Do not scrub too thoroughly before returning to the hideout.' If I'm correct, a dangerous visitor named Phoenix will come to your room shortly after meeting my guardsman. Do whatever you are asked and give no indication that I am here. Suggest to Phoenix that your handler usually partakes in the services of the Lustful Lord before leaving. That should be sufficient to have him pick up the trail of my guardsman, but I must confess this meeting will put you in substantial danger."

Lady Highsmith lay on the bed and purred. "I am only in danger if someone more dangerous than you walks through that door… so I am not afraid of Phoenix. I know I am perfectly safe."

"Thank you, Lady Highsmith." The headmaster opened a slatted closet door and pushed aside a collection of garments that made Rose blush and made Rosana think of Slate. Proprietor or not, Lady Highsmith had all the tools of the trade. The headmaster hid amongst the garments and peeked through the door slats. After a few minutes, a knock came at the door.

Lady Highsmith answered with the coded phrase given to her by the headmaster. "This is a place of business. State yours…"

"The business of Malethya relies upon you." Annarelle's hushed voice provided the coded response and Lady Highsmith allowed her entry. "The Sicarius Guild requests your aid in protecting the citizens of Malethya. What news do you have to report?"

Lady Highsmith reportedly professionally, "Several of the noble houses see the demise of Brannon as an opportunity for personal gain. They lack the fortitude to accomplish the task and the recent prosperity in Ravinai has tempered the need for such endeavors. A rising tide raises all ships, and the nobility are flush with coin to indulge in their personal vices." Lady Highsmith gestured toward the pile of coins on her desk.

"Thank you, Lady Highsmith. Your service is appreciated." Annarelle nodded her head in respect.

Before she left, Lady Highsmith said, "Your headmaster sends a message as well. She asked you to wait in the building a few minutes and then to return to the hideout. Do not scrub too thoroughly. I do not know what it means."

The Sicarius mask hid the frown that Annarelle surely wore upon her face. She had just been commanded to allow Phoenix to follow her back to their hideout. "I understand perfectly. Fractal's grace to you." Annarelle left the room.

The door closed, but Sana remained in hiding. She had chosen not to follow Annarelle's pursuer because of Lady Highsmith. Rat Roost and Raven's Claw were simple drops that could be turned without interaction, but Lady Highsmith preferred to give her reports in person. The pursuer would need to threaten her to turn the drop.

On cue, someone landed on the balcony and entered Lady Highsmith's room. He was of average height and immemorable build, perfectly suited for the clandestine activities of a Sicarius Guardsman. He also wore a Sicarius mask, a difficult item to obtain. "King Darik requests your services. The Sicarius Guild has been terminated and reformed with those loyal to the king." King Darik may have requested Lady Highsmith's service, but he did it as an intermediary for Lattimer. The letter she had intercepted at Raven's Claw was addressed to Rosana Regallo, not the Sicarius Headmaster. Lattimer wanted her to reform Sicarius under his control, and it appeared he would do so with or without her.

Lady Highsmith played the role of an innocent. "What? Someone just came to my room from the Sicarius Guild. Are you telling me I supplied information to a traitor? I was trying to help the kingdom!"

"You still can. I tracked the traitor to your room and realize you played no role in the Sicarius Headmaster's mutinous schemes. Your aid, however, could be the very thing I've been looking for to track down the hideout of the renegade spies and end this threat to the kingdom once and for all. Do I have your aid?" The masked man stepped forward as he spoke, clearly expecting submissive acceptance from Lady Highsmith.

"I would do anything for the people of Malethya. In fact, I can tell you that my handler typically indulges in the services of the Lustful Lord after getting my report. He doesn't know that I know this, but girls in the Lustful Lord like to talk… he might still be here."

"Now that is valuable information, and it makes me confident that you will continue to serve Malethya proudly… but you normally do it for a price." The man gestured toward the coins on the desk. "What price would ensure your loyalty?"

"The Sicarius Headmaster pays me a tenth of a week's profits every time I provide information." Sana paid Lady Highsmith nothing and knew the idea of payment offended her. "If a renegade can afford a tenth of a week's profits, then the king's coffers could surely offer a quarter of a week's profits for my loyalty..."

The masked man laughed. "It's a pleasure working with someone who knows the value of information. You will have your money." He was still smiling as he pulled a throwing knife from his sleeve and flicked it unceremoniously through the silks of Lady Highsmith's attire, pinning her to the bed. "Just don't forget what the price commands...loyalty." The man gave final instructions to Lady Highsmith before turning to leave. "Continue to give your information. Don't withhold anything, or your allegiances could be compromised. When the time is right, I will contact you again." He jumped from the balcony to the neighboring rooftop and fled into the night.

Lady Highsmith removed the knife that held her to the bed and spoke to the Sicarius Headmaster. "That man will never own my loyalty. What do you wish me to do?"

"Start by closing your balcony, drawing the shades, and turning off your lights. The assassin is probably still watching your room and I don't want him to know I overheard the conversation." Lady Highsmith carried out her instructions while looking convincingly rattled. Anyone watching would assume she was overwhelmed by the night's events and was closing up shop for the night. Sana emerged from the closet into the darkened room and removed the leather whip that had clung to her while hiding. "Your loyalty to me will be returned in kind." Sana didn't often give the backing of the Sicarius Headmaster, which increased its meaning on the occasion that she did use it. Sana walked through the darkened room and asked Lady Highsmith, "Are there any nobleman's clothes I could disguise myself with as I leave?"

Lady Highsmith went to a trunk and lifted the lid to expose a wide variety of clothing. "This is our lost and found. People come here to take off their clothes, and sometimes they are too drunk to find them later. Take what you need…"

Rosana smiled behind her Sicarius mask and pulled a nobleman's shirt over the wrappings of her Sicarius attire. The assassin may be watching the balcony window, but with the Sicarius mask and the clothes of a nobleman, she could walk out the front door. Rose walked through the dark room and grasped the hands of Lady Highsmith. "Your life is now in danger. When the danger gets too great, you will have to come with me. You will have to leave your life behind…"

Lady Highsmith looked at the dimmed opulence of her room. "I have made my living by making people's fantasies come to life. Perhaps it is time I find out what I want from life instead." Lady Highsmith managed to stare directly at the Sicarius mask. "I will go with you."

CHAPTER FOUR

THREATS UNVEILED

"You landed on rooftops with the grace of a Bellator Guardsman and your missteps sent pebbles from rooftops. Even the most dense of Ravinai's citizens know that pebbles don't fall from the sky. Assuming they didn't see you jump from building to building silhouetted in all your glory by the moonlit sky, they would have known you were on the rooftops." The Headmaster delivered her observations to Annarelle without any softening. Any guilt felt by Rose and Rosana regarding her strict tones was nullified with a quick glance at the names that bordered the room. Annarelle had only made small mistakes, but small mistakes led to death. "Tell me about the letters in the drop locations."

Annarelle used a throwing knife to slice open the sealed correspondence and read the contents from Rat Roost aloud.

Sicarius Brethren,

My eyes and ears are not my own.

Times are prosperous in the eastern provinces. King Darik's troops have redistributed a large portion of the city's tax surplus, which has sparked new businesses and new construction throughout the city. The noblemen are so flush with coin that the servant's wages have actually increased as well. These are good times.

May our enemies fear the shadows,
Careless-Thirst

Rosana digested the information from her information network. Careless-Thirst was the codename given to a barmaid with a propensity for making patrons speak carelessly. She used the proper opening line to communicate her safety. The eyes and ears of informants for Sicarius were not their own. They belonged to the people of Malethya, whom they kept safe with the information they provided to Sicarius. The letter provided little information but confirmed that the prosperity of Ravinai did not come at the expense of the outlying provinces. Lattimer intended to use blood magic to recreate the golden age, and his efforts were manifesting wealth across the kingdom. The next correspondence was from Raven's Claw.

Sicarius Brethren,

My eyes and ears are not my own.

The only thing of note is that the farmers mention a new disease affecting their crops. It kills off a portion of the plant and spreads until the whole plant dies. No amount of water or sunshine helps. The farmers believe the disease is carried by the pollen and seeds of other diseased plants along the easterly winds. These diseased particles land on the crops and the farmers have to cut off the mottled, affected areas before the disease spreads, but the particles are infrequent enough that the disease is a minor concern.

May our enemies fear the shadows,
Thistlethorn

Thistlethorn was a gardener in Mannheim's ruling estate and overheard conversations of visiting nobility as they strolled through his gardens, dutifully reporting the nature of their conversations. Sana knew he rarely was privy to sensitive information and the loss of his services was tolerable. *The disease he discusses was probably observed in his own gardens and delivered in the form of agricultural news so that his occupation could not be readily identified if his letter was compromised.* "The blight is spreading."

"We knew it was spreading, but we didn't count on the winds carrying diseased leaves or pollen when we estimated the magnitude of the effect." Annarelle spoke technically, probably in an effort to avoid mentioning that Sana's own actions were responsible for the existence of the blight. She had saved Slate's life by transferring Slate's diseased blood into a grove of catalpa trees, but the blood magic within it poisoned the trees and created the blight, a disease that wilted and killed any plant it contacted.

"Pull out the maps," Sana commanded. Annarelle pulled a map of Malethya from a desk drawer and spread it upon the table. The blight initiated in a catalpa grove south of Ravinai, and they had tracked its expansion over the previous months. The rate was slow, but if the winds created new pockets of infection, the entire eastern portion of Malethya would be infected with the blight much quicker than initially estimated. "Please overlay the wind patterns of Malethya onto these maps. When you are finished, send correspondence to all of our informants downwind of the catalpa grove. Tell them to begin storing as much food as possible."

"Yes, headmaster." Annarelle had little knowledge of the wind patterns in Malethya, but she was a Sicarius Guardsman. She dealt in information and knew how to find what she needed.

"Good, now tell me about your scrub run. Were you tracked back here as I asked?" A scrub run was a predetermined route that a Sicarius Guardsman took to shake anyone skilled enough to track them. Phoenix, having had Sicarius training, would have been suspicious if Annarelle simply returned to the hideout. Instead, Sana had asked Annarelle to perform an imperfect scrub run, with just enough mistakes for Phoenix to follow her.

Annarelle spoke with pride, "I infiltrated Ravinai's center for public works. The city needs to refill the oil in the street lamps in the less prosperous regions of town, so I strapped myself below the cart. When the driver reached a burnt-out lamp, I dropped to the ground and entered the alleyways, travelling to a drop location in which I had left clothes. After changing my attire, I entered a pub and got a well-dressed man to escort me across the city. I knocked him unconscious a few miles from here and returned to the hideout. To make sure that I could be tracked, I disabled the other carts at the public works so that only one cart left the building this evening. I also chose a location to drop from the cart with enough light to see my movements as I disappeared into the alleyway. Leaving the bar, I glanced around at the rooftops of the neighboring buildings."

Annarelle had done well. She would be difficult to track beneath the city cart and if Phoenix tracked her, he would need to maintain contact through a change of clothes and identify her as the companion of the man leaving the bar. One of the simplest and most effective ways of shedding a tail was to find a companion when they assumed you were alone. Annarelle had been just clever enough to escape suspicion from Phoenix and left just enough minor mistakes to be tracked. There was only one problem. "You chose to hide beneath an oil cart?"

Annarelle's pride slipped from her face as she realized her mistake. A single fireball from a wizard or a burning arrow would have killed her instantly. Rose decided the Sicarius Headmaster had been hard enough on Annarelle this evening. "You are progressing very nicely, Annarelle. Our work is thankless and difficult in the best of times." She embraced Annarelle to comfort her dejected apprentice. Tough love was only effective if toughness was counterbalanced with displays of affection and praise.

Annarelle pulled away after a moment, a sign of her growing independence. "Thank you, headmaster. What did you learn at Liar's Lair?"

"Lattimer has reformed the Sicarius Guild. Rat Roost and Raven's Claw are compromised as drop locations, but our efforts at Liar's Lair were not in vain."

"Did you terminate the threat?" Annarelle asked politely whether or not she had assassinated Lattimer's guardsman.

"No. I reached Lady Highsmith and asked her to play along. She responded beautifully and convinced the guardsman that she would help. They plan to pass misinformation through her and use the information to kill us."

"Why didn't you just kill him?" Politeness gave way to directness.

Sana explained her strategy, "We don't have a connection to Lattimer. You, me, Slate, Tommy, all of us would be killed on sight if we went anywhere near Ispirtu. The only way to reach Lattimer now is to make him come to us, and he would only do that for a very good reason. Before we can act against Lattimer though, we need information, and Ibson is our best source." Sana decided not to discuss Phoenix with Annarelle yet, hoping that Rosana could get Ibson to talk.

The day's first light filtered through the dilapidated roof of her hideout, reminding Rosana that it was time for breakfast. She told Annarelle, "Feed Ibson… but tell him it's lunch." She took the opportunity to break his circadian rhythms even further. "And don't forget to administer more wormroot. I don't want him recovering his strength and ruining our base." The Sicarius Headmaster was tired of waiting for answers. "While you make breakfast, I'm going to have a chat with Ibson."

The Sicarius Headmaster pushed open the door to Ibson's cell dressed in the wrapped strips of fabric that became a symbol of her notoriety. Before he could speak, the headmaster pushed two more needles into the nerves of his arm, sending pain radiating toward his neck. Ibson remained unperturbed, despite the needles in his arm. "What, no pretenses or games pretending you are an infirmary wizard?"

"I no longer have time for pretenses. By nightfall tonight, we will be attacked by Lattimer's army of Furies. These won't be peasants attacking villages but fully trained Ispirtu wizards and Bellator Guardsmen who have voluntarily subjugated their minds to Lattimer, led here by a Sicarius Fury. I am not leaving this hideout without answers. You can talk to me and live or keep your silence and die."

Ibson shook his head. "You act as a child holding her father's sword. Your ignorance makes you a danger to yourself and to those around you."

The headmaster's threats didn't make any headway, so Rosana tried a more tactful approach. "Perhaps you would enlighten me with your wisdom."

"I know you are lying because you speak of the impossible. The mind of a Fury is burnt out and replaced with a single command. They are mindless killing machines, not the trained wizards and soldiers you speak of. Since you are lying about this portion of your story, I still contend that you lied about anyone showing up here tonight. I don't believe Lattimer has an army of Furies. I believe Brannon was the blood mage. I believe he was defeated. What I don't understand is what you are trying to accomplish with this charade."

Ibson was talking. Rosana considered this progress. "I have told you my goal. It is to save the people of Malethya from Lattimer's control, even though they don't realize the threat he represents. Lattimer is the blood mage and he is powerful. He has discovered a way to control willing minds without burning them out. He has an army that he can turn on like a switch. Normal people turn into Furies at his command and attack with relentless aggression. They feel no pain or remorse for the destruction they cause. Do you doubt me?"

Ibson looked into the cold, hard eyes of the Sicarius Headmaster. "I do not doubt you believe what you say, but I side with reason. I do not believe you."

The Sicarius Headmaster shared her own form of reason. "By tonight, you will believe me. Your belief in the truth is the only thing that will save your life. I don't need to know your motivations for living, but someone who spent the past year of his life locked in the infirmary has a very strong sense of self-preservation." The headmaster picked up a few more needles and began placing them in the various nerves of Ibson's extremities. With each one she placed, Ibson writhed in agony. His eyes glazed over from the pain and the Sicarius Headmaster grabbed his chin to turn his eyes to her gaze. "The brain shuts down when it gets overwhelmed." She held up a final needle. "When you wake up, consider how much you value your life. It will be your last chance to contemplate the question." The Sicarius Headmaster plunged the needle into the nerves of Ibson's neck and he lost consciousness.

Annarelle entered the room with a plate of food and some wormroot. "I guess Ibson won't be eating for a few minutes."

Sana replied, "He'll wake up soon enough, but I don't believe he will be cooperative. I have more to tell you about this evening's activities. We are in danger and our timetable has moved up. We may have need for the third tenet of torture."

CHAPTER FIVE

THE HIDDEN ROSE

"Annarelle, you deserve to know the truth. The man tracking you is a former Sicarius Guardsman now serving as a Fury under the control of Lattimer. He goes by the name of Phoenix, an identity he must have assumed after a near-death experience for which he blames me. He calls Lattimer the Great Redeemer and promises to hunt me down with relentless hatred starting at nightfall tonight." Sana handed Annarelle the letter left at Raven's Claw.

"I will not let him—" Annarelle began before Sana interrupted.

"And neither will I, apprentice, but he is a formidable enemy and I am now playing a very dangerous game. We must make preparations for my demise."

"Death awaits us all, headmaster." The fatalism of the Sicarius Guardsman was delivered with a smile. "You had me lead this monster to our hideout… why?"

Sana explained, "I had two reasons. The first is that there is no place to face Phoenix in which we would have a better advantage than here. We have set traps and know when to expect an assassin's arrival. How are your studies of exploding orbs progressing?" Annarelle began her training as an Ispirtu wizard, but her weak spark prohibited her from casting strong spells using Ispirtu techniques. Even the creation of a simple blue orb to light their hideout was beyond her capabilities. However, Annarelle became intrigued by the spell that protected Ispirtu's walls and had set to studying the pattern of exploding orbs in great detail. During their attack, exploding orbs could not trigger within a certain distance of its walls, but Lattimer had created a pocket just large enough to place an exploding orb. Lucus found the weak spot in the defense, and they infiltrated the Ispirtu compound following the explosion. Sana had encouraged Annarelle to continue her studies in magic, but suggested she focus on a single pattern and learn it well. Her interest in exploding orbs was a logical, and potentially useful, pattern to learn.

Sicarius professionalism couldn't mask Annarelle's pride in her progress. "When orbs explode, they cause damage through the rapid expansion of the air around them. I've gotten quite good at encouraging or suppressing the rate of expansion." The practical advantages of Annarelle's studies meant that she could amplify the power of an exploding orb or prevent it from exploding at all. Her painstaking progress was evident to Sana by the deconstructed orbs riddling the desk of her room and the sounds of various small explosions in the middle of the night.

Sana needed the hard work to be put into practice tonight. "How large of an area can you suppress?" Annarelle smiled and Sana filled her in on her plan. "The second reason for leading Furies here tonight is Ibson. He has closed his eyes to the truth of the world. Phoenix will help me open them."

"You always think five steps ahead of everyone else, headmaster." Annarelle commented with admiration. Sana considered the events that would unfold soon. *I wish I had the same confidence in my own cleverness. Intricate plans are clever when they work, but more often than not, the added complexity simply brings new things that can go wrong.* She had learned the value of a simple plan by working with Slate. He didn't always form the cleverest of plans, but he was the first to react when plans changed. The thought of Slate made Rosana's thoughts wander, so Sana refocused. *I have work to do.*

"What will you do to prepare for Phoenix?" Annarelle asked before leaving.

"I'm going to try to think six or seven steps ahead so that we have more than six or seven hours to live." With less than a day's time to prepare for an attack by Furies, Sicarius Guardsmen humor felt appropriate. "Do you know the safe house down by the docks?"

"It smells of rotten fish, and it floods when the river rises in the spring." It was also unknown to everyone but Annarelle and would serve as their next hideout.

"That's the place. I periodically stock it with dead fish to preserve the strong smell and discourage the curious. Beneath the leaky home is a watertight series of rooms that can be accessed via a stairwell behind a false wall. Start transferring our stores. Empty everything but the anatomy room. We'll have need of that before leaving. I'll meet you back here at dinner and expect the preparations to be made."

"You can count on me, headmaster."

"I know I can, Annarelle." Before facing the activities of the evening, she needed to prepare herselves. That meant more than just laying out some throwing knives. She needed a break from being the Sicarius Headmaster. Rose gave Annarelle a hug. "Thank you for being more than my apprentice. It has been a long time since I truly had a friend."

Annarelle spoke with wisdom beyond her years. "This is Malethya. We do what must be done when times require it. When times don't require it"— Annarelle pulled away from Rose—"we take comfort wherever it can be found." Annarelle left Rose to begin packing their things, starting with the histories of the Sicarius Headmasters.

Rose went to her bedroom, a former warehouse office. The room had a small closet with a cot inside for sleeping. The odd arrangement was explained by the remainder of the furnishings in the room. Racks of clothing dominated the space, bearing the colors of every noble family and every profession imaginable. Off to one side of the room, a small desk overflowed with makeup. With these tools, Rosana could become anyone she needed to become.

Rose sat in the desk but the reflection of the Sicarius Headmaster stared back at her. The Headmaster had to keep her hair tied up. Long, flowing hair would identify her as a woman if anyone saw her jumping across the rooftops at night. The Sicarius Headmaster cannot be a man or a woman. The Sicarius Headmaster needs to be an enigma, a symbol to the people of Malethya. She slowly removed the pins holding her hair, removing the mystery of the headmaster with each fallen lock. Her hair framed the hard lines of her cheeks and jaw, softening her appearance and soothing her soul. Next, she brushed her hair, and the simple act conjured up memories of her youth. *I would sit quietly while my mother brushed my hair and hummed peacefully to me, her only daughter.* Rose's face reflected in the mirror, but she couldn't be Rose right now. She needed to be Rosana, someone with her own unique style and self-confidence that was born of maturity. The long, straight hair wouldn't do. She styled it according to Ravinai's current fashion. Then Sana, the wizard's apprentice, recalled her training under Lucus. *He showed me how some animals changed colors with the changing season. I must concentrate on the pattern of a fox, whose white winter fur brightens to red in the summer while I apply just a trickle of spark.* Her raven hair changed to a dark claret and then auburn as she adjusted the amount of spark. She would need to hold the spell to maintain the effect, but it required little spark. Finally, she applied a generous amount of makeup, darkening her skin tone and softening her most defining features. Rose no longer looked back at her in the mirror. She was Rosana.

Rosana stood up and perused her wardrobe for the appropriate attire, eventually finding a server's uniform from the Refined Palate, one of Ravinai's finer dining establishments. She dressed in the attire she had worn many times before and left the Sicarius hideout, allowing herself a temporary reprieve from the demands of her chosen way of life.

Rosana walked through the streets of Ravinai toward King Darik's palace. Nestled close by for the convenience of its upscale patrons, the Refined Palate served as a testament to the obscenely rich, with the golden décor recently updated to reflect the prosperity of King Darik's rule. Rosana allowed herself to admire the grandiosity; Sana would despair that the growing riches reflected the use of blood magic, but Rosana wasn't concerned with such matters. Rosana was a server and knew nothing of magic. Instead, she entered the office of the restaurant manager.

"I'm ready to begin my shift." Rosana announced amicably, although she knew her shift would last only as long as she wanted it to last.

The manager shifted uncomfortably in his chair. "Of course, of course. Your employer negotiated your schedule in advance, and you have been assigned to the section of his choosing." The Sicarius Headmaster had previously visited the restaurant manager in his home and convinced the man to allow Rosana, a Sicarius informant, to work a section of his restaurant. The frightened man agreed to the arrangement even faster than he soiled his pants. "I will rearrange the servers' assignments. You can begin your shift immediately."

"Thank you for your service to Malethya. I will tell my employer of your devotion to the cause." Rosana left the office and started wiping tables in her section. She knew the routine the servers followed after working here on a recurring, if infrequent, basis.

While she awaited the arrival of a patron that warranted the Sicarius Headmaster's need for an informant, Rosana took an order from her first table. Seated around the table were a group of prominent merchants in Ravinai that the Sicarius Headmaster identified immediately, surmising that their conversation would likely involve the price fixing of Ravinai's textiles, for which they would all mutually benefit. Rosana asked, "May I take your order, gentlemen?"

The headmaster identified Mr. Radcliff, an importer of dyes and other less mundane items into Ravinai, who asked, "What would you recommend? These menus do nothing for me. All the descriptions mix together and create indecision."

"I recommend the soup à la Darik. It is served with a light bread for dipping and the freshest fruit in Ravinai." Rosana knew the menu by heart.

"Beautiful and decisive. If you ever tire of serving food and offer more profitable services, I would be your first client." Hearty laughter filled the table at the forwardness of Mr. Radcliff's proposition. Rose was disgusted and mortified. Sana wanted to slip a hidden knife into his throat. The Sicarius Headmaster knew the location of Mr. Radcliff's estate and the easiest way to break into his house at night. None of them responded though. This was Rosana's mission, and Rosana smiled coyly and blushed before taking the remaining orders. Any decent server knew that a little flirtation always led to more coin at the end of the meal.

Rosana dropped off the order with the kitchen and picked up the food for another one of her tables. As she was delivering the order, she heard a woman's voice and smiled in recognition. Her mother, Caitlyn Regallo, had entered the Refined Palate for her afternoon social hour. Due to the size of her group, she always reserved the largest table in the restaurant. Prior to Brannon's death and subsequent allegations of blood magic, Caitlyn Regallo had enjoyed life as Ravinai's most influential socialite. Invitations to join the group were fought over by every manicured fingernail in the city. Now the Regallo name had been smeared with the worst of labels, but the family's money and Lattimer's continued influence in Ispirtu ensured that the table remained full.

Rosana chose to serve the tables in the section next to her mother, banking on her altered appearance and the social etiquette of the elite to prevent her mother from looking too closely at the restaurant's help. Caitlyn was dressed immaculately in a form-fitting outfit, diverging from Ravinai's current fashion just enough to draw notice but not so much as to stand out. Within weeks, tailors would copy the style and mass-produce it for the citizens. While the rest of the patrons studied Caitlyn Regallo's style and noted who her dining companions were, Rosana studied her mother's face with concern. She bore Sana's calculating eyes with the hard-lined borders of the Sicarius Headmaster. The hard lines around her eyes had started to appear after Brannon's death. Rosana couldn't blame her mother for having difficulty coping with the loss of her husband, but it pained Rose that Caitlyn's face was devoid of the love and comfort she knew as a child.

Rosana delivered the food to Mr. Radcliff's table, encouraging the pig's advances due to the proximity to her mother's table. From this distance, she could overhear the conversation but escape direct interaction.

"Caitlyn, how do you live in that tiny apartment?" Ms. Babblerone asked her former neighbor. Caitlyn had chosen not to rebuild the Regallo estate on Rue Street, instead taking up residence in an opulent loft in the heart of Ravinai. It was anything but tiny.

"I find it invigorating to be a part of the

city, instead of being locked away in the solitude of a mansion." Caitlyn answered the question in a manner that avoided mentioning Brannon. The less attention she drew to his transgressions, the higher her stock remained.

"Yes, but the inconvenience of it all… I much prefer to have invitations sent to my door where I can read them and take the time to invent convenient excuses for not attending the less prestigious functions." Everyone knew that several key members of Ravinai's social circle had been conspicuously absent from some of Caitlyn's most recent gatherings.

Despite the statement's accuracy, such subterfuge could not be tolerated. Comments like that festered and proliferated if left alone. Caitlyn was too seasoned at this game to allow it. "If you have so many invitations to turn away, Ms. Babblerone, you must have trouble deciding who should attend the small gatherings in your home. You may take me off your invitation list if this is the case. Please do not feel any obligation to me." Ms. Babblerone was of the lesser nobility and having Caitlyn Regallo attend her gatherings was still a huge boost in her social status.

"Caitlyn, my friendship comes without obligations. You know that." Ms. Babblerone backpedaled quickly and turned the subject toward a source of Regallo pride. "Tell me about Lattimer. I hear he has risen to favor quite quickly in the eyes of King Darik."

Cailtyn flashed a broad smile, but Rose noticed the hard lines didn't completely disappear. "He is the only wizard in the Malethya who can claim to have killed a blood mage. That triumph alone would garner the attention of the king." The Sicarius

Headmaster's blood boiled at the memory. She had stood by Brannon's side until a fireball from Lattimer engulfed him in flames. After killing his father—the only wizard powerful enough to oppose him—Lattimer claimed his father's scepter and revealed himself to be a blood mage. Sana escaped Lattimer by sending a shock through his body when he removed the mask of the Sicarius Headmaster and saw his lost sister, Rose. Rosana cleared the plates from another table.

"Lattimer's research since then has only increased the honor of the Regallo name. He has discovered several treatments for previously incurable diseases. The infirmary has plans to send wizards to Ispirtu for training to learn his new techniques." Thoughts of Master Meikel and his plans for unscrambling her head came back to Rose. Apparently she had her brother to thank for teaching Master Meikel such methods. What other techniques did they experiment with? Caitlyn continued, "The Bellator Guild is also excited about Lattimer's efforts to enchant their armor and weaponry. The rumors of what the guardsmen may soon be capable of are astounding. I only hope half of them are true."

The Sicarius Headmaster cringed at the news, even though the valuable information justified her time in the Refined Palate. Infirmary wizards sent to training in Ispirtu would soon become subjugates of Lattimer. *If Lattimer succeeds in enchanting armor and weaponry, then his Bellator Furies will become even more dangerous.* With Lattimer growing in strength this quickly, the need for expediency increased. The Sicarius Headmaster anxiously awaited the end of Rosana's shift.

"Lattimer's accomplishments are remarkable.

You should be so proud of him." Ms. Babblerone spoke before thinking, as she was prone to doing. "However, given the family history, aren't you concerned at his broad range of interests? What if he follows in his father's footsteps and…" Ms. Babblerone trailed off as her brain caught up to her mouth. In asking if blood magic ran in the Regallo family, she'd harkened the permanent stain on the Regallo name caused by Brannon's presumed transgressions. Such a direct insult put Caitlyn in a difficult situation. It warranted a harsh response, but in doing so, she would create a scene that would undoubtedly reflect poorly as well.

Rose felt sorry for her dear mother and Sana hated to see Rose's innocence dampened. Before Caitlyn could respond, Sana concentrated on the pattern of the wind catching the sail of a ship. The sail caught the force of the ship and propelled it forward, harnessing its power. Sana released her spell and directed a concussive wave of air toward a server who was serving Ms. Babblerone water. He held a tray full of water glasses in one arm. Sana sent the spell at his elbow. The tray crashed downward, soaking Ms. Babblerone along with half the attendees. The socialites stood in horror and defended against the wet attack with general shrieking and commotion, saving Caitlyn the indignity of a response. A joyous smirk danced across her face at the plight of Ms. Babblerone.

Rosana joined the other servers in rushing over to the table to clean up the mess. Sana laughed silently at the chaos her prank had predictably caused. Even chaos could be controlled with logic. Rosana knelt at the table nearest Caitlyn and dabbed a towel onto the wet floor. *Being so close to Mother makes me tremble inside.* Rose longed to reach out and give her mother a hug and tell her, "I'm your little girl. I'm still alive and I have missed you since the day I disappeared." The Sicarius Headmaster and her other selves fought the childhood yearnings of Rose, knowing that Caitlyn would be in danger if she knew her daughter was alive. If Lattimer discovered that Rose conversed with Caitlyn, it would make her mother a target. She would be another way to get to the headmaster and the headmaster didn't tolerate such ties.

Rosana stood from beneath the table and ever so subtly grazed her hand against the leg of Caitlyn Regallo, delighting Rose. She sighed contentedly and averted her face from her mother's gaze, walking to the manager's office to end her shift. Satisfied, Rose would wait. The world needed her to be the Sicarius Headmaster a little while longer.

CHAPTER SIX

THE THIRD TENET

"Have you prepped the anatomy room?" The Sicarius Headmaster took a chisel to the names of the previous Sicarius Headmasters inscribed in the wall of her partially disassembled hideout. Sicarius Headmasters had to keep their identities secret, and she felt obligated to maintain secrecy even in their death. The names served as a physical reminder of her mortality, but she didn't need to be reminded of the list. The names were burned into her memory. She couldn't have forgotten them if she'd tried.

"Your tools are laid out and the room is prepped. Do you need any additional help from me?" Annarelle asked whether she would be involved in the questioning.

"I will talk with Ibson in the anatomy room. If things progress beyond the first two tenets, I will need your help. I expect our visitors promptly at nightfall, and we will need to work quickly when they arrive." While the Sicarius Headmaster issued orders to her apprentice, Sana fretted over the uncontrolled variables in her plan. Ibson was at the heart of her troubles. All she could do was evaluate possible outcomes and give the Sicarius Headmaster time to get the answers they needed to help Slate.

"I will be sure to finish stocking our new hideout and return before nightfall. I will set the traps on my way out." Annarelle turned to leave, but hesitantly consoled, "I know you don't want to use the third tenet. I hope it doesn't come to that."

"I hope it doesn't come to that either," Rose replied and Annarelle left.

The Sicarius Headmaster finished chiseling the names and, with her vow of secrecy preserved, went to check on Annarelle's work. She trusted her apprentice, but a person's survival was no one's responsibility but their own. First up were the security orbs. The Sicarius Headmaster had accumulated many orbs from Sicarius missions, and they were currently set to announce any unexpected visitors. The ground floor of the warehouse was littered with security orbs and explosive orbs. If someone made the mistake of triggering a security orb, it would be the last mistake they ever made. The only safe way into the hideout was the rooftop entrance, but she couldn't trap that yet. Annarelle was still using it to relocate the hideout.

The real cleverness took place inside the anatomy room, which was centrally located within the former warehouse offices and heavily modified by Sana. Around the middle of the walls was a metal hinge. Sana released the top portion of a wall in sections that folded downward, revealing a cage of sorts. The metal cage surrounded the top half of the room, but left a small gap about the span of a hand at chest level. Below the hinge, the folded upper portions of wall tucked neatly against the permanent lower wall. Rose examined the structure. *It looks like a large, caged version of the ticket counter from the traveling shows I saw as a child.* At the top of the cage, where it attached to the rafters of the warehouse, a nondescript metal rail circumnavigated the room. Sana checked to make sure the rail was well-greased and that the rail's release mechanism was fully engaged. All the rooms adjacent to the anatomy room had a similar, stationary metal rail. These rails served didn't have release mechanisms like the anatomy room, because they served a different purpose. The all touched snugly, forming a network of metal rails that spread throughout the far reaches of the hideout.

Contact was important.

Next, Sana arranged a series of smoke orbs that were set to simultaneously trigger around the center of the room. She placed the triggering orb near the metal table in the middle of the room. Finally, she checked a carefully concealed rope that traversed the rafters of the warehouse. Sana was satisfied with her preparations and turned her attention to Ibson. She would ask the questions since Ibson seemed to respond well to logic. The Sicarius Headmaster would handle the rest. She did what needed to be done without the burden of morality.

The Sicarius Headmaster grabbed some wormroot from storage and walked into Ibson's room. "Drink this."

Ibson drank the concoction without complaint. That was some small measure of compliance. The Sicarius Headmaster removed needles from his arm and Ibson's face relaxed as he sighed in relief. Rose delighted at the removal of the needles.

"If you think the removal of those needles will change my mind, you are mistaken." Ibson started the conversation.

Sana responded logically. "I have removed the needles because I no longer have any need for them." The Sicarius Headmaster untied the straps that bound Ibson to the chair. "Please follow me into the next room."

They walked through the disassembled hideout and into the partially furnished anatomy room. At the sight of the instruments laid out around the steel table, Ibson whitened. The Sicarius Headmaster flashed a throwing knife before Ibson got any ideas about trying to obtain her instruments as potential weapons. The old man realized the futility of the attempt and instead asked, "Is this how you intend to make me talk?"

The Sicarius Headmaster simply said, "Please lie on the table." The Sicarius Headmaster restrained Ibson on the table and wandered over to the table of instruments. She chose one with a flat, sharp edge and turned it over in her hands. "This tool was discovered in travels across the northern mountains before the Twice-Broken Wars. It fits perfectly, and painfully, beneath the fingernail. I've never had to use it on more than two fingers before getting answers to my questions." She set the instrument down and picked up another that looked like it would be excellent at cracking walnuts. "This tool was invented within the Sicarius Guild. If you withstand the pain of the first round of questions, this tool can remove the tip of a finger at the top knuckle." The Sicarius Headmaster reset the tool in its position and motioned to the remaining devices. "Sicarius has built a reputation for practicality. You have information that I need. I will be as practical as I need to be to obtain that information." Rosana and her other selves ignored the Sicarius Headmaster's comments and tried to focus on different things. They didn't have the stomachs for the third tenet.

Ibson interrupted her, "You haven't even asked me a question yet."

The Sicarius Headmaster answered, "And that is because I want you to truly understand the situation you are in. All of these tools are at the disposal of Sicarius Guardsmen, but who do people tell stories about to scare their children? It is me, the Sicarius Headmaster. Do you know why I am so feared?" Sana didn't wait for an answer to the rhetorical question. Instead she formed a spark in her hand and answered as a wizard's apprentice. "I have studied under Lucus. Whenever you start to lose blood, I can close your wounds and resume questioning. If you start to black out from the pain, I can bring you back, but that's not all…" Rosana thought back to her time with Slate, listening to his tales from Primean's Pain Tolerance Laboratory. She remembered the scars laced across Slate's body. She remembered the ghostly complexion of his skin. Sana said, "I also know every means of inflicting pain researched within the depths of Ispirtu. I can inflict so much pain upon you that you won't remember what words come out of your mouth." Rose quivered at the pain and sorrow she had witnessed in her life. On Rose's behalf, Sana said, "I tell you all of this in the hope that it is unnecessary."

Ibson did not shake in fear at the threat though he undoubtedly knew the threats were real. "I have experienced much in my life, but there is so much beyond your comprehension. You have my attention though. Ask your questions..."

Sana handled the questioning. "I'm a quick

study and may comprehend more than you think. Let's start with the easy questions. Did Lucus, Brannon, and Lattimer apprentice for you and receive training in magic?"

"Yes. Brannon and Lucus studied together. Lattimer was a more recent student of mine."

"Did you ever teach them blood magic?" The Sicarius Headmaster approved of Sana's direct line of questioning.

Ibson waited a second before answering. The Sicarius Headmaster almost reached for an instrument on the table, but Ibson was only considering his response. "I taught them magic, and not the watered-down crap that Brannon taught his Ispirtu wizards. I taught them real magic. I believe Lucus taught you the basics. What do you know?"

Sana didn't expect that response, but it got Ibson talking. She decided to answer his question and see where it led. "Lucus taught me that magic consists of two parts, the spark and the pattern. A spell could be cast with infinite combinations of spark or pattern to produce the same result. A pattern must be held in your mind and then linked to the correct amount of spark to achieve a spell with the desired results. He often said that the ability to control how much spark is linked to a particular spell is the difference between a wizard and a simple conjurer of tricks."

Ibson slipped comfortably into the role of lecturer, despite being restrained to a table in a room built for torture. "Lucus was a wise man, which is a higher compliment than being a powerful wizard. Brannon was a powerful wizard, but his strength in the spark led to shortcuts. He taught Ispirtu wizards that the best spells were those most useful on the battlefield. He'd say, 'Hold a loose pattern and throw some spark into the spell to create the biggest fireball you can muster.' His strategy worked in the Twice-Broken Wars, but it has done a disservice to wizardry since then. Sometimes I think the only thing those Ispirtu wizards are capable of anymore are throwing fireballs, shaking the ground, and creating concussion waves. If Lucus wasn't a pacifist and decided to play a larger role in the Twice-Broken Wars, things might have been different. He could have led the Ispirtu Guild, and he wouldn't have died at Brannon's hands." He continued on before Sana could correct the old man. Magnus had killed Lucus, but it was at Lattimer's command. "Lucus taught you correctly, but he only taught you the beliefs of Malethya. What did he teach you about the Twice-Broken Wars?"

"The Disenite ships came under the guise of peace, but then mounted an invasion. Slate's father, Villifor, slowed the invasion long enough for King Darik to gather the nobility under one army. Darik turned back the Disenites, but he had to resort to using magic in battle. Brannon and his wizards decimated the invading Disenite army, and the destruction they wrought on the land of Malethya sparked a second war centered on the ethos of magic in battle. The Wizard Council formed as a group of pacifist wizards who opposed Brannon and his Ispirtu wizards, while Villifor formed a band of rebels to stand against Darik." Sana's curiosity began to give way to the Sicarius Headmaster's anxiety. "What does this have to do with your teachings to Lucus, Brannon, and Lattimer?"

"Everything. This land has forgotten the lessons of its past. It doesn't even know the reason the Disenites attacked in the first place." Annarelle stepped into the room, and her presence interrupted Ibson's lecture. He seemed to catch himself from saying something he hadn't intended.

Sana paused her line of questioning to address Annarelle. "How are the preparations coming?"

Annarelle looked tired from the day's activities. Rose hoped that Annarelle would get a few minutes to rest before Phoenix arrived. "The preparations have been made and everything of value is secured, save the items in this room."

"Thank you. You have arrived just in time for Ibson's lecture on magic. He was about to tell us why the Disenites attacked during the Twice-Broken Wars. He was also going to tell us how it relates to our more immediate concerns….namely, Lattimer." The Sicarius Headmaster turned an instrument idly in her hands.

"None of this matters. Brannon was the blood mage, and he was defeated. You are both wasting your time." Rose sighed in frustration. *I hate to think of the pain Ibson will have to receive.* The Sicarius Headmaster examined the instrument in her hands, and then looked to Ibson.

Annarelle reminded her headmaster of the time of day and its implications. "The sun is nearly set, headmaster. I even saw a squadron of Bellator Guardsmen attempting to hide in a building down the street. Their armor glinted off the setting sun and made noise at every movement. I would have to be blind to miss that many guardsmen in one place. They are preparing to attack. I believe we are running out of time for the first two tenets."

The Sicarius Headmaster gripped the instrument tightly in her hand. *Even the third tenet of torture takes time and with each passing moment, my opportunity slips away.* Sana had witnessed many of these events before and she knew that Ibson's initial response would be silence. He would subconsciously withhold any information that Sana requested because of the pain being inflicted. Rosana took Ibson to be the type that liked to talk. He was holding back information, but she was very good at putting people at ease. If she could do that, he would talk on his own accord. Rose knew Ibson was misguided, but not an evil man. *I don't want to see him suffer.* The Sicarius Headmaster loosened her grip on the instrument and Sana responded to Annarelle. "The first two tenets will be sufficient."

Annarelle protested, "But the third tenet is required when time is short. We should proceed with those activities immediately before it is too late."

The Sicarius Headmaster stared back at her guardsman with unquestionable authority. "Who taught you the three tenets of torture? I wrote the guidelines. I know when to deviate from them. The first two tenets will suffice."

Admonished, Annarelle nodded. "Yes, headmaster. You have my apologies." The apprentice instead began to lay out an arsenal of throwing knives, kunai, and poisoned darts. Even if she didn't agree with her master's decision, she would prepare for the coming fight and fend off the Furies as long as possible.

Rose chose to address Ibson. "You are very fortunate. The Sicarius instrumentation will

not be used against you." She then handed off
the questioning to Rosana, who wanted to put
Ibson at ease. She sallied over to Ibson and
ran her finger along the length of the table
restraining him. "Why do you think I decided to
spare you from a more direct means of obtaining
information?"

Ibson responded, "There are several
possibilities. One possibility is that you
never intended to question me in that manner,
but your reputation and my own judgment rule
out that possibility. You seem utterly
confident in your ability to get the answers
you seek, so I will also eliminate the
possibility that you don't believe I will talk
when tortured. Presumptively, you have
something in store for me that you think will
convince me to talk with even more
effectiveness."

Sana appreciated Ibson's deductive reasoning,
but Rosana was doing the questioning now. "I
refrained from torture because I believe you
are a good man, albeit a man with secrets. I
also believe that you question my motives. I
have told you nothing but the truth, and I
don't believe further explanation will sway
you. I believe that if you see the truth with
your own eyes, then you will agree to help me
out of your own volition." An explosion on the
warehouse floor momentarily deafened the
anatomy room. "Ah, it appears that night has
fallen and our guests have arrived. It will
take them a few moments to realize that there
is no entry from within the warehouse. I
suggest we use those minutes for less
contentious points of discussion until you can
be convinced of my motives. I believe you were
about to tell me about why the Disenites

attacked during the Twice-Broken Wars?"

Ibson looked perplexed as he weighed his belief that the headmaster spoke lies against the explosion he heard on the warehouse floor. "This is an elaborate ruse if you are lying to me. If you are not, then I question the sense of a history lesson." Ibson sighed before saying, "Nonetheless, you are correct in that this is not a contentious point with me. People believe the Disenites came here under the guise of peace and then attacked. That is not true. They came with the intention of peace. They only attacked once they realized how dramatically their beliefs differed from our own."

Footsteps echoed down from the warehouse roof, indicating that the soldiers were searching for a new point of entry. "What beliefs? Malethya has schemes aplenty but few beliefs."

Up above, the footsteps stopped and muffled orders were heard. Ibson's eyes darted to the rooftop before answering with less certainty than before, "It's a belief you have already confirmed for me. Like most conflicts in Malethya's history, it has to do with magic. You stated that magic consists of two parts, a pattern and the spark. We are taught to hold a pattern and to throw spark into it until the spell is cast. The disenites also use magic, but they learned that the source of magic is the pattern and not the spark. They hold the spark and cast a spell with their understanding of the pattern." The decidedly unmagical pattern of feet upon the rooftop stopped near the ventilation shaft. Sana calculated they would bypass her locks in less than a minute. Ibson concluded, "This difference might seem minor to you, but the Disenite rules regarding magic run much deeper than ours. They are no longer rules. They are religion. Wizards are their priests and the pattern is their god. When they discovered our beliefs, they began a holy war against us. We are heathen, and they will cleanse the land of Malethya from our toxic existence. We defeated them once, but they will come back. Their pattern demands it."

Rosana held the old man's hand as if he were an old friend despite the fact that she had restrained him to the table and he had no choice in the manner. "That was an excellent history lesson, but what does it have to do with Lattimer and blood magic?"

Crack! The ventilation shaft popped open and a Bellator Guardsman dropped to the platform beneath. He stood in shining armor that bore the golden lions of King Darik. Sana determined he would have difficulty crossing from the platform in his heavy armor. The Sicarius Headmaster eyed the vulnerabilities in the glistening armor that a throwing knife could fit between. Rosana only noticed the soldier's golden eyes that could have been torn from a Bellator recruiting poster. Ibson noticed the eyes too and said, "It seems my story has nothing to do with Lattimer. Didn't you say we would be attacked by Furies?"

Before Rosana could respond, the monument to Malethyan honor standing on the platform across from her spoke, "I am looking for Rosana Regallo. Her brother has extended her a generous offer of peace, and I intend to return her answer."

"Acceptance of my brother's offer signals my acquiescence to his plan that enslaves and subjugates the minds of all that oppose him. I refuse his offer." The Sicarius Headmaster, Rosana, Rose, and Sana unanimously and emphatically agreed.

The soldier shook his head. "Your response is noted. I will tell my commander." He began to climb the ventilation shaft ladder but was halted by the Sicarius Headmaster.

"Tell Phoenix that I was mistaken to leave him for dead. If I could do it all over again, I would make sure to finish the job." Rose cringed at the Sicarius Headmaster's harsh words. Sana knew why the Sicarius Headmaster antagonized Phoenix and considered it a necessary step in her plan. The soldier finished climbing the ladder to relay the message to Phoenix.

Rosana challenged Ibson. "You still don't believe that Lattimer is a blood mage and that Furies are about to attack us?"

Ibson balked at the idea. "The man's eyes were golden, not the red eyes of a Fury. What you claim is an impossibility. The knowledge from the days of Cantor is lost to Malethya... it would take a blood mage of the highest order to accomplish the feats you suggest. Bah! You suggest feats that weren't even accomplished in the days of Cantor. Lattimer can turn soldiers into Furies without losing their minds? It's ridiculous."

Whoosh! A fireball burned through the warehouse roof and Bellator Guardsmen jumped through, bypassing the platform entry point and giving the soldiers direct access to her hideout. The soldiers advanced in groups through the empty rooms, their well-trained teams searching for traps while maintaining defensive formations. Rose spoke to Annarelle, "Don't kill the Bellator Guardsmen." Sana's plan was complex but it was coming together. She commanded Annarelle, "I need them as close as possible." Plan or not, the Sicarius Headmaster's instincts for self-preservation issued the final command, "Kill any archers or wizards on sight." None of the guardsmen attacking her had the red eyes of a Fury, and she didn't want to kill her fellow countrymen if she could help it.

Rosana tried questioning Ibson again. "You have admitted to training Lattimer Regallo. Lattimer placed manuscripts on blood magic within the personal library of Brannon Regallo as evidence of his transgressions. If you trained them both, then I must assume Lattimer got the manuscripts from you."

Ibson, fully restrained and defenseless on the table, knew he was in a vulnerable position, but he also knew the guardsmen were after Sana, not him. He didn't take the bait. "Manuscripts from the days of Cantor have been destroyed."

Rosana responded persuasively, "Yet I saw them with my own eyes, right before the Regallo mansion burned to the ground. Malethya is full of tales and legends. Perhaps Cantor didn't destroy all knowledge of blood magic? Perhaps some wizards couldn't see knowledge destroyed, even knowing the damage blood magic had caused Malethya?" Rosana ran her finger up Ibson's arm and pointed at his chest. "I think you, the wizard who was so willing to give a lecture on the history of Malethya, would be unable to destroy manuscripts of such historical importance if you had them in your possession." Sana detected the slightest dilation of Ibson's pupils. Rosana had been correct. The Sicarius Headmaster itched to get the information out of him quickly, with the surrounding guardsmen advancing, but it was too late for torture.

The Bellator Guardsmen cleared Ibson's cell and advanced through the emptied headmaster's conclave toward the anatomy room. A group of archers dropped down to cover the advancement of the Bellator Guardsmen. Annarelle threw kunai at a rapid pace, but the archers had their arrows notched and ready to go. She wouldn't stop them in time. The Sicarius Headmaster reached for her throwing knives before the archers could set their stance and find their targets. Sana concentrated on the pattern of candlelight spreading across a room, slowly dividing as it traveled. Then she attached the spell to the knives with some spark as the Sicarius Headmaster released all five knives at one time. They flew through the waist-high opening in the wall and spread out as they flew. Each knife cleanly found the exposed necks of the archers. They fell to the ground. Rose blessed their fractal-forsaken souls.

The Bellator Guardsmen reached the anatomy room's walls. The teams of soldiers tried to use exploding orbs to break through the walls, but Annarelle had prepared for that possibility. She held a spell that took the pattern of expanding gases during an orb explosion and created an opposing pressure from the air that surrounded the orbs. The soldiers triggered the exploding orbs, but they remained inert and would fail to explode as long as Annarelle held her spell. Rose hoped that the Guardsmen vacated the area before Annarelle released her spell.

Ibson's discomfort in his situation only increased with the headmaster's display of lethal proficiency. He asked, "Isn't it about time you got us out of here?"

Rosana patted his chest. "Now what good would that do? You don't believe me yet. Why don't you tell me how Lattimer obtained the forbidden manuscripts on blood magic?"

The Bellator Guardsmen regrouped after finding their exploding orbs to be useless. Behind them, the masked man known as Phoenix descended the ladder to the platform beneath the ventilation shaft. There were too many Bellator Guardsmen between them to get a clean shot with a throwing knife. Ibson began his denials. "I don't know what you are talking about. I don't know anything about any forbidden—"

"Hold your tongue Ibson. You are about to believe."

"Rosana Regallo, sister of the Great Redeemer and Master of Lies—to my delight, you have rejected your brother's gracious offer of peace. With this response, you have labeled yourself a threat to the Redeemer's plans for peace and prosperity throughout Malethya. It falls to me to end this threat to the kingdom. I will take the utmost pleasure in killing you."

Rosana used her charm to further agitate Phoenix. "I'm sorry, Phoenix, but I already have a bunch of suitors who came calling tonight." She gestured toward Bellator Guardsmen, "and if I'm not mistaken, some Ispirtu boys are waiting in the wings. They are the shy types who like to keep their distance." Then she lowered her voice and winked at a female guardsman. "I even have a few ladies showing interest. I'm afraid you will have to wait your turn… besides, I'm not interested in you. I don't go for the I-should-have-just-laid-there-and-died type. This whole reincarnation angle you are playing just isn't for me."

"You fractal-forsaken bitch!" Phoenix ripped off his mask to reveal a hideously deformed face. "You sent me on a lone mission to investigate a fallen Sicarius Guardsman in some tiny forgotten northern village. I arrived there to find the town deserted. Then animals started rustling in the woods, birds began circling overhead, and rats emerged from the cellars. The birds came at me first, swooping down around me. The ravens pecked away at my arms and face, forcing me to run for the cover of one of the town buildings. Then the rats greeted me and I kicked them back. When they kept coming at me, I started using my knives, but there were too many. They climbed up on me and chewed any bit of exposed flesh." He pointed toward his face, where half his cheek was eaten away. "I fled the town and ran for the woods, but a stag lowered his rack into my abdomen, gutting me. I lay on my back as rats feasted, and the birds treated me like carrion. A mountain cat came from the woods to finish me off, but just before he went for my neck, a fireball blew him off my half-dead body. Moments later, the Great Redeemer appeared above me. I begged for him to finish me off, but he said he had bigger plans for me. He offered to heal the parts of me that he could and to give me the power to never feel defenseless again. I took his offer. Lattimer healed parts of me and then burned out the portion of my brain that registers pain. Now I stand before the person responsible for sending me to that town. I have power that you ignorantly turned down. I will take a pound of your flesh to replace what was eaten off me. I will have my revenge."

Sana recalled sending Phoenix on that mission. *This was when Lattimer was still learning his powers and the attacks in the northern villages weren't as widespread as they became later.* The Sicarius Headmaster had traveled to the town personally to investigate Phoenix's disappearance and reported to the Guild that he had died. Sana should have sent more guardsmen, but Sicarius Guardsmen were used to working alone, and she didn't think the danger in such a small town could be that great. It was a calculated risk and Phoenix had paid the price. Rose felt compassion for the man and a failure as the Sicarius Headmaster to protect the guardsman in her care, but Sana's plan didn't allow for compassion. "You fool. You are working for the very man who created the animals that attacked you. He burned out their minds just as he burned out your sense of pain. He didn't offer you power. He offered servitude. You willingly gave up your freedom for the worst form of slavery… slavery of the mind. You know nothing of power. I don't know what power a man such as you could possess. You, someone who nearly died at the hands of a few songbirds, come here and expect to kill me? ME?!? I hope you brought more than the guardsmen before you. They are nothing more than target practice for my knives."

Phoenix heard enough. "Your knives mean nothing when compared to the power of the Great Redeemer. You say he enslaved me, but you are wrong. He entrusted me to command his troops. He entrusted me to kill you." Phoenix raised his hand in a fist, and the eyes of the

Bellator Guardsmen turned red. Phoenix smiled and it turned Rose's stomach. It was a smile of pure joy, but it was a joy driven by the madness of his red eyes. He commanded his Furies, "Kill the Shadow Bitch."

The Bellator Furies rushed the anatomy room, their charge fueled by the command burned into their mind. Annarelle threw some kunai, but they were useless. Nothing short of decapitation would slow these Furies. The Furies crashed into the metal wall of the anatomy room, using their armored bodies as a siege weapon. The wall buckled toward Sana, but it didn't break. She didn't think it could withstand another such blow. Phoenix yelled to his troops, "Bellator Furies, attack again! Ispirtu Furies, join me on this platform."

The guardsmen retreated from the wall, leaving the bodies of several guardsmen crumpled against the wall. They had the unfortunate luck of being the battering portion of the Bellator ram. Ibson yelled from his table. "What are you waiting for? Get us out of here! We will be killed!" Belief. That was what Sana waited for. She stood casually from the metal table restraining Ibson and walked to the metal wall that had buckled, examining it. While she talked to Ibson she faced away from him, hiding her concentration.

"This wall won't survive another assault." Rosana asked the next questions with the patience of Lucus. "Do you believe me, Ibson? Do you believe that Malethya is under the control of Lattimer? Do you believe he has figured out a way to activate his army of Furies? Do you believe they will kill us?" One look at the unbridled hatred on the faces of the Bellator Furies rendered the last question pointless. Sana waited for a response as she concentrated on a pattern she knew well. It was the pattern of energy and desire. The energy needed to be released.

The Bellator Furies rushed the anatomy wall and Ibson cried out, "I believe you! I believe it all!"

Sana raised her hand to touch the metal wall and cast her spell with all the spark she could deliver. She didn't know why, but she knew the energy liked metal. It jumped from her and the bright spark ran through the metals walls, radiating outward from the anatomy room, trying to reach the ground. The energy always tried to reach the ground, looking, searching, for the quickest means to reach it, even if it meant arcing across the air and through the armor of the approaching Bellator Furies. It burned through them and jumped to the network or metal rails surrounding her hideout, blissfully traveling down them to ground below. In its wake was a pile of armor and smoldering flesh.

Phoenix, still standing on the platform across from the destruction, yelled for his Ispirtu Furies to hasten their descent. "Get down here! Turn that room into kindling." Ispirtu Furies climbed down the ventilation shaft and others jumped from the hole in the rooftop. With the encouragement of Phoenix's command, they didn't lack the bravery to jump, but they did lack the training of the Bellator Guardsmen and sustained serious leg injuries from the feat. The stationary targets were easy to dispatch with throwing knives. Annarelle made short work of them while the Sicarius Headmaster targeted the Ispirtu Furies climbing down the ladder. Sana had used all the spark she could handle on the Bellator Guardsmen, so she wasn't able to guide the flight of the knives. The Sicarius Headmaster was a good shot, but a lethal throw from this distance was too much to ask. Sana briefly considered taking aim at Phoenix, but he was her only connection to Lattimer. She still needed the bastard.

Rosana questioned Ibson. "Lattimer obtained manuscripts from somewhere. Was it you? We have very little time before those wizards start casting fireballs at us."

This time Ibson did not hesitate. "I didn't give Lattimer any manuscripts, but I can help you. I think I know where to find the answers you seek. Just get me off this table and out of here!"

Rosana knew she could get Ibson to come around and carry out Sana's plan. "I strapped you to this table on purpose. It is about to save your life." She ran from the anatomy room wall to the trigger orb and plunged her knife into it. The anatomy room filled with smoke so thick that she could hardly see the red eyes of the Ispirtu Furies who stood next to Phoenix. She counted as Slate had taught her. "Annarelle, get on top of Ibson. Now!" Sana raced to the hidden rope and unhooked it from the wall. ...1 She jumped onto the table and fastened the rope to it before stomping on a switch at the base of the metal table that released it from the floor and released the anatomy room from the rails supporting it. ...2

The room plummeted downward, pulling the rope with it. The rope looped over a pulley hidden in the rafters and propelled the metal table upwards, with Ibson, Annarelle, and Sana with it. Sana had created the anatomy room to be one large counterweight, a larger scale version of the lift she had used to extricate Ibson from the infirmary. The smoke from the orbs hid their ascent into the rafters where the metal table snapped into a fixture. The weight of the room easily snapped the rope, hiding all evidence of their escape. The walls and floor of the anatomy room crashed into the rotted wooden floor of the warehouse just as a series of fireballs destroyed the remainder of her hideout.

Phoenix yelled, "Down there! This is just like the trick she used to escape Darik's cleansing of the Sicarius Guild. Turn that floor into kindling!" Sana breathed a sigh of relief as she silently unstrapped Ibson from the table and motioned Annarelle down the hidden crawlspace. Eventually Phoenix would discover that the rotten wood floor of the warehouse didn't hide an escape route and figure out what happened. She wanted to put some distance between them before he did.

Annarelle unlatched the roof access and checked for any additional guardsmen, but Phoenix hadn't kept any soldiers in reserve after getting his target in sight. They ran to the edge of the rooftop, confident that their steps were covered by the sound of fireballs and crackling wood. At the edge, a rope and hidden pulley connected to a distant building. Annarelle took out the sling they had used to carry Ibson's unconscious body and placed her legs through two of the loops. The Sicarius Headmaster copied the motions of her apprentice, carrying out Sana's escape plan that they had practiced many times. After they both fit within the harness, they attached the free end to the pulley, grabbed Ibson, and jumped before he could offer a complaint.

The trio slid down the rope and halfway down,

a look of concentration appeared on Annarelle's face. She struggled for a few moments and then gave in, relaxing as she released her spell that prevented the Bellator Guardsmen's orbs from exploding outside of the anatomy room. Without Annarelle's spell to suppress them, they all exploded, sending an immense ball of flames through the warehouse roof.

They crashed through the thin wall of the building and the Sicarius Headmaster quickly flicked a throwing knife at the suspended rope, severing it from their destination. The group untangled themselves from each other and looked back at the burning remains of the warehouse. After a moment, Phoenix climbed through the ventilation shaft. His clothes burned and his body crisped from the heat, but he moved with the grace expected of a Sicarius Guardsman. He didn't feel the pain of his burning flesh. He only focused on one thing—finding and killing Sana.

At the sight of Phoenix climbing from the smoldering building, Ibson spoke. "As you mentioned earlier, Malethya is full of legends and stories. Most of the true ones have been forgotten, but I know of one that might explain the abomination I see before me."

That was all the Sicarius Headmaster needed to hear. "Tell me where we are going."

"Have you heard of Minot?"

REFLECTIONS

Rosana looked up from the mottled signs of death on her hand to the warm smile of Slate Severance. His ghostly complexion masked his compassion. The scars that riddled his body hid the strength of his determination beneath them. The red eyes of a Fury concealed Malethya's best hope for salvation. She loved the complexity of the man.

Slate saw her examining him. "The Sicarius Headmaster would never get caught staring at someone so blatantly, so I'm guessing Rosana wanted to have breakfast with me today?"

"You are correct, although I think even the Sicarius Headmaster is learning to enjoy your company. Very few people have survived long enough in her presence to establish a relationship."

Slate slipped a box onto the table. Rosana opened her gift hurriedly, finding four objects inside. Slate explained, "I heard that an antiques dealer had a rudimentary tool rumored for use in torture, and I couldn't help but buy it for the headmaster. The second item is a book with detailed observations of lightning that I thought Sana would appreciate. The hairbrush is for Rose." Then Slate's skin hid the color that would have risen to his cheeks at the mention of the last present. "And for Rosana, Lady Highsmith suggested this…"

Now Rose blushed, but Rosana beamed in excitement. She had lived her life in solitude, hiding herselves from the world. Then she had confided in Slate, and he had accepted herselves into his life, embracing her hidden complexities.

She looked back at her hand, embracing the mottled death. She chose this disease for herself. She chose it to save Slate. She chose it to save Malethya. She couldn't save them without sacrificing herself. At one time, she had thought she could.

CHAPTER SEVEN

MINOT MYSTERY

"Where am I?" This common question was as foreign as it was rare for Rosana, whose livelihood depended on a keen awareness of her surroundings. She lay in a stationary cart and stared up at the few stars that filtered through the canopy of tree branches above her. Recollection came quickly.

After escaping Phoenix, they retrieved supplies from one of her stashes in Ravinai and freed a horse and cart from a stable as they exited town. Rose hated stealing, but even she saw the necessity. Annarelle drove the cart under the direction of Ibson, while Rosana lay in the back and succumbed to exhaustion. She hadn't slept since breaking Ibson out of the infirmary, and the events of the past two days had emptied her stamina.

Sitting up, she found Ibson wide-awake despite the hour. He sat idly against a nearby tree, crunching on an apple. "What's going on? Where are we and where is Annarelle?" Rosana hated her compromised position. Without information, she felt as vulnerable as the citizens she protected.

"Your apprentice has disappeared into the forest and is presumably protecting our position from owls and nightcrawlers. She picked this position to set up camp but prohibited me from starting a fire to warm my old bones. We have been here for hours and I'm stuck sitting here watching the bark grow on that oak tree. Did you know that the bark of oak trees is..."

"And where is here exactly?" When did old men develop the ability to ramble on and forget the simple question that was asked of them? Ibson seemed particularly likely to carry the conversation on a tangent if she didn't focus him back. Was that part of his nature or a disguise he wore to hide his thoughts?

"We are east of Minot. Dense forest covers the area for miles, but Annarelle chose this spot for camp. We rode around half the night before she found it. It was slow going. With the horse and cart, she needed to stop her travels to set aside fallen branches and trees every time she encountered an obstacle she couldn't navigate around." He bit into the apple with a shake of his head.

"Why did she choose this spot? And why are you awake? Are you too nervous about our situation to sleep?"

"I'm old, the need for sleep and ability to rest peacefully die away with youth. Plus, you knocked me unconscious and drugged me so many times in the past two days that I've had a week's worth of rest during my captivity."

"I thought you planned to help us now. Captivity is a strong word." Strong, but technically correct.

"I will stop using the word captivity when you stop administering wormroot. Until then, you might as well keep me in shackles."

Annarelle emerged from the woods. "Headmaster, I thought I heard your voice. The perimeter is secure, and I have no disturbances to report. I didn't wake you for fear of startling you." Smart girl. Many headmasters had died in their sleep, and Rosana didn't intend to be one of them. Out of self-preservation, when startled from sleep, the Sicarius Headmaster acted first and counted the bodies later.

"Thank you, Annarelle." Sana replied. Until she no longer felt compromised, she needed to focus on their plan. "Tell me our situation and your strategy."

Annarelle reported, "We approached Minot from Ravinai along the road. Before getting close to the village, I left the trail and circled around Minot while you slept, searching for soft mud and low foliage to easily mark the trail. After meeting up with my original tracks, I searched for hard ground to break away, eventually locating this spot. I have spent the last hour covering our tracks from the rutted trail through the woods that I created."

Sana commended the foresight and deductive reasoning of her apprentice. "You have done well. Phoenix will eventually discover that we left Ravinai, and he will try to track us. We can expect him to follow the rutted track around Minot before he discovers this area, alerting us to his presence. By circumnavigating the town, he will have no indication where we are truly hiding."

Ibson agreed. "Your apprentice is not as crazy as I first believed. Fractal's blessing that some of Malethya still has common sense. If what you say is correct, however, Phoenix will know our target once he traverses the rutted path once. You might as well have pointed to Minot and proclaimed your intentions to the masses."

Before Annarelle could let her disappointment in her actions show, Rosana challenged Ibson.

"Intentions? How can I proclaim our intentions to the masses when I don't even know why we are here? Tell me, Ibson, why did you point us to this tiny town in the middle of nowhere?"

"Not in the middle of nowhere, Ms. Regallo. We are at the exact location in which Slate encountered Furies for the first time. There is no place more relevant than Minot."

Rosana encouraged the old man to talk while holding back the headmaster's first reaction to strangle the answers from him. "Would you enlighten me as to why Minot is relevant to Lattimer and Phoenix, the man you described as an abomination?" Rosana also wanted to know the relevance of Minot to Slate, but she had made it through her questioning of Ibson thus far without revealing any new information about his condition, namely that Lattimer held some of Slate's blood and could reduce him to a quivering pile of uselessness just by being in his proximity.

"I do not know if Minot bears relevance for Phoenix, but I am fairly certain Lattimer knew of its secrets before the initial attack on Minot ever occurred. In fact, I believe the Fury attack on Minot had an entirely different purpose than Villifor or King Darik ventured to surmise." Rosana waited patiently for the explanation while Sana searched for potential implications but found none. Minot was an isolated and tiny village without any real significance. How could an attack on Minot be important? Ibson continued, "Lattimer rose to power extremely quickly, even considering his family tree. How could an aspiring blood mage progress so rapidly in skill in such a short period of time? In one moment, he pushed a little iron around in Slate's blood. Now, if you are correct, he has gained control of Malethya, created an army of Furies, and discovered a manner to maintain the minds of those voluntarily subjugated to him. He has accomplished feats of magic unseen since the days of Cantor, all in a time when knowledge of such spells has been completely and utterly suppressed."

Sana remembered the books on blood magic from her father's personal library that Lattimer had planted. What if he'd possessed more of them? "Lattimer isn't making discoveries into blood magic. He is simply casting long-forgotten spells from the days of Cantor."

Ibson concluded, "Lattimer stayed in hiding, slowly growing in power, until Minot. Then he risked an attack on Bellator troops with subjugated peasants, clearly exposing his presence. What would be worth that risk? There must be something here he desired greatly. Cantor was an extremely gifted wizard who devoted a large portion of his life to spark-based magic. Do you really think he could destroy all knowledge of his life's work?"

Sana quickly scrolled through the timeline of events and everything checked out. After the initial attack on Slate's home, the northern villages were attacked randomly but regularly. Lattimer had been searching for something, and he had found it in Minot. Ibson's story was sound, but the Sicarius Headmaster questioned whether he was telling the complete truth. Ibson had been under duress during questioning and few people made such complex connections under duress. Rosana reasoned that Ibson had plenty of time to contrive the story to mask his real reasoning while traveling from Ravinai. In the end Rose trusted his intent, even if Rosana questioned his motives.

Annarelle summed up Rosana's mixed feelings succinctly. "You brought us all the way out here on a hunch that Lattimer may have found some books related to blood magic? The attack on Minot occurred months ago. You'd better hope there is something worthwhile still here." She drew her knife. "If you are wrong, I'll kill you myself."

Ibson remained unperturbed, strengthening the headmaster's concern that he was holding back information. She chose to play along with Ibson for the time being. "The Furies attacked Slate in the village of Minot, but they were defeated by Magnus and his troops. If you are correct, Lattimer succeeded in whatever objectives he had in the Minot encounter. That means he intended for the Furies to be seen, and he intended for them to be defeated."

"What would he have to gain from such an encounter?" Annarelle asked.

"He pointed the attention of Villifor and King Darik away from Minot, which means…"

Ibson smiled as Sana caught up, "Whatever Lattimer was doing in Minot required more of his time to complete. Getting the King to attack Ispirtu accomplished two goals—displacing his father and securing the mystery of Minot. Shall we discover what the mystery holds?"

Nighttime belonged to the Sicarius Headmaster. *There is no better time than now for a reconnaissance mission. Having to focus on a mission will also help mask Sana's disappointment in her failure to link Lattimer's rise to power with the attack on Minot.* "Annarelle, Minot is nestled beneath a northerly rock face. Can you lead us from camp and approach from the north? From the rock face, we will have a clear vantage point of the town and the surrounding area."

"Of course, headmaster." Annarelle took off at once, leaving Rosana to accompany Ibson while she searched the surrounding woods for any threats.

Ibson started the discourse, "You still don't trust me."

"You only helped us when your life was in imminent danger, and that isn't counting the fact that you abandoned Slate and me by hiding in the infirmary. If you want trust, you will have to earn it."

The old man ambled slowly through the woods, with Rosana helping him up and over any fallen trees that crossed their path. "I saw Phoenix and the Furies. I know the truth and I am on your side. What would earn your trust?"

"You can start with the truth."

"You don't believe me that Minot is important?"

"I believe Minot is very important. I don't believe you deduced the importance of the town during Phoenix's attack. You knew about it beforehand and didn't tell us about it. You knew of Minot's importance when Slate first told you about it in the infirmary, and you kept your silence. Until I understand why, I have no reason to trust you."

Ibson sighed. "You are very astute. The reasons for my silence are the same as the reasons for my seclusion in the infirmary." After his admission, he continued apologetically. "The reasons for my silence are my own, however, and I will not share them." The methods of the Sicarius Headmaster were still available for future use, but Ibson preempted that thought process. "Even your unique talents would have failed to make me talk. I am bound to my word." *Bound?* Rosana thought the use of the word was more than happenstance.

Annarelle appeared ahead and signaled the Sicarius Headmaster that they were approaching their destination. Before she took the point, Ibson gave one final promise. "There are things I can't tell you, Sana, but you of all people should understand that secrecy is a burden that must be borne. I can assure you that I believe Lattimer is a blood mage and that our causes are aligned. I will help stop Lattimer, but my secrets are my own."

The Sicarius Headmaster commanded Ibson to stay hidden and then concluded the conversation, "I have enough secrets of my own, and I will not help you bear yours. If your secrets stand in my way, you will pay the price."

She moved ahead to get Annarelle's report. "We are approaching the rock face on the north side of town. I have checked the surrounding area for guardsmen and believe the area is clear."

"Thank you, Annarelle." *Maybe Ibson is wrong about Minot?* The headmaster moved silkily through the night. Years of honing her talents meant that only highly trained scouts could have seen her, but the magic of the Sicarius mask made her into the lethal legend that she was, capable of killing her foes before they even knew she was there. The headmaster smiled in satisfaction. Talking was done, and they had a mission to complete. This was her time.

At the top of the hill, she crawled on her belly, inching over the rock face to view Minot without forming a silhouette for anyone watching below. She expected to see the burnt shells of the village houses and abandoned roadways. She expected to see the dense forest growing in to retake the land stolen from it by the villagers. What she saw shattered her expectations.

The blackened ground had been cleared and in its place stood the stone barracks of a Bellator squadron. A sprawling bunkhouse of poor construction sat off to one side of the barracks, while an estate comparable to the ones found on Rue Street rose on the far side of the barracks, with orbs lighting the rooms and hallways inside. Ispirtu wizards roamed the hallways, fulfilling whatever whims the favored disciples of Lattimer had in the middle of the evening. Ibson was right. Lattimer's intentions for Minot were much grander than a simple attack by village Furies.

We have waited too long. I should have acted sooner. The Sicarius Headmaster condemned the patience of her other selves. Sana ignored the headmaster, but the comment from her other self hurt deeply. She had planned according to the information she had, but she had failed to make the connections that Ibson made. Rose provided some comfort, but the bitter taste of failure coated her throat.

With the intent of making up for her lapse in logic, Sana tried to piece together the everyday actions of the army camp below. Based on the layout, the Bellator barracks were placed to protect the Ispirtu wizards from interacting with the occupants of the bunkhouse. That meant that whatever work was actually being done in this camp required Ispirtu magic, manual labor, and some soldiers to keep things in order. She instantly made the bunkhouse her primary target. These occupants were of little significance to the Bellator and Ispirtu Guardsmen, so her presence among them would likely go unnoticed. For gathering her first bits of information, this was the safest plan of action.

With her mind made up, the headmaster returned to Annarelle and Ibson to inform them of her plan. "Minot is filled with Lattimer's people and I need to find out more information. There is a poorly constructed bunkhouse down there that I will infiltrate. I will go alone."

Annarelle knew better than to object to her headmaster's plan, but Ibson did not. "Why go in there alone? Surely you could use our—"

Before the wizard continued with his foolishness, the Sicarius Headmaster cut him off. "Meet me back at the wagon. You would get yourself killed in that camp and increase the chances of my capture or death in the process." Sana thought her odds of survival were slightly better with Annarelle on the mission, but she needed Annarelle to watch Ibson. *I need to do this alone.* "Your death is your own choice, but if your presence might get me killed, then I take issue. Get him out of here."

"Yes, headmaster," Annarelle said immediately.

Ibson foolishly continued his objections. "If you'd just quit administering the wormroot…" The headmaster simply nodded to Annarelle, who delivered a blow to the base of Ibson's neck. He crumpled to the ground and Annarelle unfurled the sling from her garment and carried the old man away.

Alone, the Sicarius Headmaster carried out the plans formulated by Sana. She circled around Minot to the easterly side and observed the barracks from the dense woods. Up close, the structure wasn't just poorly constructed, it was dilapidated. The residents within were not held in high regard by the wizards and the soldiers next door. More importantly, dilapidated structures provided ample opportunities for entry by rodents or wooded creatures seeking warmth… or a Sicarius Guardsman. The windowless structure had a single door at either end of its length and a multitude of loose boards that held the structure together.

Before going in for a closer look, the headmaster checked the premises for Bellator Guardsmen. After watching for nearly an hour without seeing movement, she threw a rock into the middle of camp. The noise didn't set off any alarms or spark the interest of any guards. If this place was so important, why didn't they post any guards?

Cautiously, she approached the barracks within the shadow cast by the lit hallways of the Ispirtu estate. The headmaster flattened against the wall and listened through a loose wallboard. Inside, she heard the deep breathing of the tired and the groans of the physically exhausted. Following closely after, the stench of the occupants' exertion confirmed her initial assessment of the situation. *What are they working on? What makes them so tired that they cannot bathe?*

Before she could reason through the answers to her questions, the door opened and someone sprinted for the woods. Sana wanted to stay but was overruled by the Sicarius Headmaster, Rosana, and Rose, who were all too curious about the escaped man. The Sicarius Headmaster took off into the woods to track the escapee, following his smell as much as his clumsy trail through the woods. Since he was heading away from the camp, the headmaster took her time trailing him. The farther into the woods he got, the safer her interrogation would be. The promise of additional information appeased Sana's desire to investigate the bunkhouse.

About a half mile into the forest, she found the object of her pursuit. The escaped man looked wildly around the trees, trying to capture his bearings. Rose took pity on the man and took control of the conversation, although she spoke in the alternating speech of the headmaster. "You are a half mile east of a village normally known as Minot. Please don't run, or I will be forced to incapacitate you."

Of course, the frightened man took off at the sound of her voice. The Sicarius Headmaster smoothly flicked one of her easily accessible darts at the man. Sana concentrated and cast a spell to make it fly straight. The dart embedded in the man's hamstring, and he immediately dropped to the ground. The fast-acting poison on the tip of the dart prevented his nerves from contracting his muscles.

Rose continued to comfort the man as he writhed on the ground and attempted to figure out why his leg had suddenly stopped working, "The effects of the dart are temporary and will wear off in a few minutes." Rose continued to ask questions before the headmaster got any ideas. "Who are you and what are you doing in Minot?"

"Minot?" Confusion spread across the man's face. "I don't know what you are talking about. I'm in prison."

Prison? Now it was Sana's turn to be

confused. Rose dropped the alternating speech and responded comfortingly, "Why don't you tell me how you got here."

Instead the man saw an opportunity to ask the question that had burning in his mind ever since he heard the telltale voice from the shadows. "You are the Sicarius Headmaster. Are you going to kill me?"

Rose replied, "I don't want to kill you. I do, however, need to know what is going on in your prison camp. If you help me, I will have no reason to kill you. In fact, I might even help you… now why don't you tell me about yourself."

"My name is Josef and there isn't much to tell. I am a single man who spent his life living day to day. I picked up odd jobs when I could find them and drank away any profits I made. One day, I took a delivery job from Mr. Radcliff that ended up being less than legal. The delivery went sour, and I fled for my life, leaving the imported merchandise behind. The next thing I knew, King Darik's men pounded down my door and threw me in jail. It wasn't until the hearing that I discovered I was being tried for robbery and murder. There had been a great deal of bloodshed at the exchange, and King Darik was looking for answers. The empty crates bore the symbol of Mr. Radcliff's trading company, and he claimed they were stolen from his warehouse and implicated me. Several of his company men testified to having witnessed the robbery, and I was sentenced to death." Rosana remembered Mr. Radcliff as the suggestive patron of the the Refined Palate. The Sicarius Headmaster simply added another name to her mental list of miscreants.

Josef continued his tale, "The night before

my execution, King Darik visited with me. He offered to spare my life if I pledged servitude to Malethya in a work camp. It was an easy choice at the time…"

Rose interrupted to question an untold part of his story. "Did an Ispirtu wizard accompany King Darik when he made the offer?"

"Yes, Darik said that I would work under the direction of the wizard. He didn't give his name. All he required was that I speak some words of loyalty, but I haven't seen him since."

"Do you remember the exact words?" Sana asked.

"Yes, having one's life spared on the eve of execution makes for a keen memory of the occasion. It was a simple sentence. I said, 'I open my pattern to do your bidding.' King Darik thanked me for my service to Malethya, and they left me alone in my open, unguarded cell."

"Didn't you run? How did you end up here?"

"Of course I ran. I ran straight to the tavern and toasted my good fortune. I awoke in the morning with an intense headache and decided to go for a walk. Walking seemed to help with the headache, but for some reason I wandered directly into the Bellator complex. They expected my arrival and directed me toward a holding area with the other prisoners."

"You have called Minot a prison, but there are no stationed guardsmen and you easily escaped camp."

Josef's wild eyes turned adamant. "I escape every night! I run as far and as fast as I can, but every morning I return."

That explained the lack of guards. Josef had voluntarily subjugated himself to Lattimer in exchange for his life, and now he was tied to

Lattimer's command. Josef was tied to the work camp more tightly than any group of guardsmen could have maintained. Rose's pity for the man increased tenfold. "What do you do during the day?"

"When we wake up, we are given time to dress, eat our rations, and use the communal latrine. We put on work clothes, grab mining tools and those of us that choose to eat do so. Others simply waste away and are replaced by new arrivals. It is one of the few choices we still have."

"What do you work on?"

"I have no idea. My memory stops after our allotted time in the morning and doesn't return until I come back to camp at nightfall. I arrive exhausted and starving and consume my rations. When night comes, I try to escape, but I always end up back at camp. Can you help me?" His wild eyes momentarily cleared at the prospect of the headmaster's aid. She had no hope to give him, but she needed Josef.

"I will do what I can." Rosana spoke the half-lie to protect Rose's innocence. She would do what she could for Josef, but there was nothing she could do.

"Thank you!" Misguided hope flooded through the wildness of Josef's thoughts. "What do you need from me?"

Rosana said, "I need to follow you tomorrow morning and find out what you are working on. I can't help you until I find out more." Even then, Josef had little hope of breaking Lattimer's bonds, but the headmaster needed to conceal that truth.

Rose rubbed Josef's leg to disperse the poison, and he soon stood under his own volition, eager to aid the headmaster in any way possible. They returned to Minot as dawn approached, just in time for Sana's plan. "Josef, are there extra work clothes and mining tools available?"

"We go through a lot of workers… they leave their clothes and tools behind."

"Can you get me some tools and clothes from the bunk house and bring them back to the woods?"

"Easily. The other prisoners have their own issues to deal with. They don't question my comings or goings."

"Perfect. Please get them and leave them at the edge of the forest. Then return to the bunkhouse and go about your daily routine."

Josef turned and ran back to camp with renewed purpose. His devotion to her would switch the moment Lattimer commanded. Rose felt compassion for the tortured soul of the subjugated. *Is it better to be a Fury and have your mind wiped out completely? At least then you wouldn't wake up to know what was taken from you.* Josef's tale only served to steel Rosana, the Sicarius Headmaster and Sana in their mission. The rest of Ravinai and Malethya may be blinded by prosperity, but Josef was proof of things to come. *I need to stop Lattimer before more Malethyan's lives are sacrificed in the name of the new golden age.*

The sun ascended above the treetops, directing its morning light farther down the Bellator barracks. A group of Bellator troops already stood at attention in a dueling courtyard. When the first ray of light touched the sand, a man stepped forward and barked orders at the troops.

"I'm surprised the lot of you could find the dueling courtyard and avoid the pointy ends of your swords. Lucky for you, you have the best trainer in the fractal-forsaken kingdom. I will make soldiers out of you yet." He limped to the center of the dueling courtyard, and the distinctive gait of the battle veteran identified him as Hedok, Slate's trainer from his days in Bellator. During the battle with Brannon, he had sided with Lattimer, along with a small contingent of Bellator Guardsmen including Magnus Pudriuz and Cirata LaRossa. Several of Jak Warder's men had died by Hedok's blade and the Sicarius Headmaster longed to return the favor. "Today's topic will be the same topic you fail to learn every day—aggression wins. You three… the ones with faces so ugly you couldn't bed a whore." Hedok pointed to three decidedly normal-looking soldiers. "You will attack the other three at my command. Pretend you've held a weapon before and make a decent show of it."

"Are the blades dulled?" One of the chosen soldiers asked. Blades could be dulled for training purposes with the aid of Ispirtu wizards.

"Blades aren't dull in battle, and you've failed to learn your lessons. I think live blades would be the motivation you need. Then you would learn your techniques or die trying!" Hedok threw his head back and roared at his own teaching prowess. "Unfortunately, Magnus thinks my techniques have thinned our ranks unnecessarily. The blades are dull. Attack!"

Two soldiers attacked with extremely offensive techniques while a third hesitated. "Stop!" Hedok limped over to the hesitant soldier and threw him to the ground in disgust. Before his tirade could begin, Magnus stepped into the courtyard.

"Let me handle this, Hedok." Magnus was the most physically imposing man the headmaster had ever seen. He towered over most of his opponents, and anyone who rose above his stature would still be overpowered by the massive man.

Sana eyed the soft spot on his neck while the Sicarius Headmaster playfully fingered her throwing knife. *The blade could sever his artery and kill him before an Ispirtu wizard could be summoned for healing, but I need him alive.* Her goal was to stop Lattimer. Killing Magnus would deprive Lattimer of a faithful servant, but it wouldn't get her any closer to saving Malethya, or Slate, from Lattimer's reign of blood magic. *I need to find out what Lattimer is searching for in Minot.* Magnus' presence solidified the town's importance in Lattimer's schemes.

Magnus picked up the fallen soldier from the ground and roughly set him on his feet. He stumbled backward and needed to be caught by two fellow Guardsmen. "The lesson of aggression must be learned. It has numerous advantages in battle. Learn them now." Magnus raised his closed fist, mimicking the motion of Phoenix, and three guardsmen turned to Furies. "Attack!"

The three Furies attacked with primal rage. They delivered powerful offensive swings of their weapons that the remaining guardsmen deflected with ease. Instead of returning to their forms, though, the Furies continued their attack without regard for their own well-being. One dropped his sword, grabbed the sword arm of a Guardsman and bit into his wrist. Another Fury tried to strangle the guardsman, letting his armor absorb the soft blows of his opponent who couldn't muster a strong blow from such close proximity. Before this soldier passed out, Magnus commanded the Furies, "Stop!"

Magnus lowered his fist, returning his hand to a pocket. Sana assumed he held some enchanted artifact created by Lattimer to control the Furies. Rosana thought through the easiest way to lift the artifact from Magnus' possession for a later date. Rose pitied the soldiers as they regained their senses from their time as Furies. The soldier that bit into his opponent was particularly mortified to find his teeth in the act of gnawing through his fellow guardsman's arm.

Magnus bellowed at his guardsmen, "Why do we train you?" He walked over to the soldier who was now spitting blood from his mouth in disgust. "We train you so that you don't end up like this, with blood dripping from your mouth like a ravenous dog. Aggression is powerful. It gives you an advantage in combat if you can harness it. You are not mindless peasants who only know how to attack with their teeth. Your mind has been spared by the Great Redeemer. Use his gift to channel your rage, overcome your fear, and become a Bellator Fury." He turned back to the barracks. "Cirata, would you care to grace these soldiers with a demonstration? Maybe if they see the beauty that aggression can become, they will embrace it as they must."

Cirata Larassa stepped into the dueling courtyard and Rosana could barely hold her emotions in check. Cirata had attacked her while she retreated to save Slate's life. Because she had to engage and fend off Cirata, Lucus was forced to sacrifice his life. The Sicarius Headmaster helped to temper Rosana's hatred. The mission was important and emotions threatened its success. Rosana's hatred of

Larassa and Rose's mourning for the death of Lucus could wait.

"You better give me some dulled blades, love. Otherwise, your lesson will be rather short-lived." Cirata placed her short swords on a table while Hedok ran to accommodate her request. He delivered two practice swords that Cirata quickly twirled around to get a feel for their weight. "I am ready."

Magnus reached to his pocket and then raised his fist. "Show these guardsmen what it means to be a Bellator Fury. Attack!" Ciratta ran straight toward the guardsmen and didn't slow as she approached. She knifed between two soldiers and delivered blows to the back of their legs as their defensive blows met air. They crumpled to the ground at the force of her blow, but their hamstrings were saved by the dulled blades. Magnus reinforced his lesson by shouting, "Aggression negates fear. The time it takes you to decide your next action is all the time you need to die." Without slowing, she twirled to touch the neck of another guardsman. "You are thinking while she is killing." One guardsman took the offensive, stepping from his fellow guardsmen toward Cirata, but she reacted immediately, continuing her onslaught with a dive. In one fluid motion, she took out the ankles of the two guardsmen in the rear with quick strikes from her swords while locking her legs around the advancing soldier and whipping him to the ground. His head bounced in a manner unexpected from sand and his eyes rolled to the back of his head. "You are all dead. Cirata, you can stop now."

The Sicarius Headmaster marveled at the beauty of what she just witnessed. *Larassa's attack was fluid, relentless, and executed at full speed.* Sana contemplated the consequences of such a technique in battle and Rosana's concern for Slate was immediate. Slate could move at high speeds and deliver blows with incredible force thanks to an experiment performed by Lattimer before they knew he was the blood mage, but even he would be in danger when fighting Larassa because she attacked at full speed anyway.

Magnus was equally impressed with Cirata, giving her a kiss before her eyes even returned to normal. "It is a privilege to watch you flow through battle." He then turned toward the soldiers who were still conscious. "This is what you must aspire to become. Use aggression but do not get lost in it. Only when you learn this lesson will you be worthy of joining me." He turned and nodded toward Hedok before leaving the soldier on the bloodied sand.

Hedok wrapped up the morning's lesson. "I planned to give the losers of the match kennel duty. Since you all lost, go feed the dogs and take them for a walk. Only after you return can you visit the Ispirtu estate for healing. Let your injuries reinforce your lessons! Now get out of my sight!"

The Sicarius Headmaster returned to the woods to find that Josef had acquired the clothing she requested. She slipped them on over top of her Sicarius garments and kept the Sicarius mask on. With it, she would appear as Josef did to the other workers.

Meanwhile, Rosana copied the dejected gait and hunched shoulders of the workers, making her all but invisible. Right now the mission required her to blend in, and Rosana was the master of her environment. She transformed her herself into a prisoner in both disguise and mannerisms.

One of the guardsmen rang a bell and the workers started to file out of their prison. She slipped into their haphazard ranks as they formed a line outside the Bellator barracks to receive their morning rations. Rosana kept an eye of Josef, taking her cues from his actions. He didn't look up at the Bellator Guardsmen that plated his food, so she averted her eyes as well. A beaten dog didn't look at his master. There weren't tables for the prisoners to eat at, so they stood around in a general collection of apathy, well-versed at the practice of eating with one hand while holding their trays with the other. She stood next to Josef, within the relative safety of his fellow prisoners. He looked around for Sana. With her Sicarius mask on, his eyes slid past her. The longer he looked around, the dimmer the spark of hope in his eyes became. Rose wanted to reach out and just let him know she was here. She wanted to maintain his hope, stoke it like the first spark of a campfire, but this wasn't the time.

A Bellator Guardsman banged his hand against a metal plate, signaling the end of breakfast. The prisoners dropped their plates in a pile and grabbed an assortment of pickaxes and shovels on their way to the edge of camp, where Magnus awaited them.

"You all deserve to die, but the Great Redeemer has spared your lives in exchange for servitude. Fulfill your service to Malethya." He raised his fist and the prisoners around Rosana turned to Furies with red eyes starving for direction. "Follow the Bellator Guardsmen to the pit and obey their commands."

The Bellator Guardsmen, all of whom were

partially wounded from their encounter with Cirata, started jogging into the forest. The prisoners immediately followed suit, sprinting to catch up with the guardsmen in their eagerness to obey Magnus. Rosana ran in the middle of the pack of Furies, realizing that she was probably the first person in the history of Malethya to do so and live to tell about it. At least Sana hoped she would survive this mission. *The presence of Magnus and Cirata have turned this mission from simple recon into a high-risk job.*

The Bellator Guardsmen delivered a welcome distraction from the danger of the Furies that surrounded her by discussing their training in Minot. The guardsman who had bitten his fellow soldier started the conversation. "How does Cirata control herself like that? I can't even remember what I do when I turn into a Fury."

"I'm not sure, but that's what they are trying to teach us. Just think of the power we'll have when we figure it out." Sana wanted to hit the girl in the back of the head for her stupidity. Power that someone else controls isn't power. She was a mindless weapon of Lattimer, even if she learned to keep her wits in battle.

"We'd better learn quickly. I don't know if I can take too many more lessons from Cirata." One of the guardsmen referenced the swollen ankle he was running on after having it taken out by Cirata. "I don't want to find out what a lesson from Magnus would be like either…"

The soldier who'd been hauled to his feet by Magnus concurred with a grunt. "At least we have plenty of time to learn the lesson. The dogs can't find a bone no matter how often we bring them to the graveyard."

The others laughed at the inside joke. Rosana hated inside jokes when she wasn't an insider. Nonetheless, it gave her some information, which appeased the headmaster and Sana. The Furies were being used to search for something that they weren't finding. Now she just had to learn what they were searching for, why Lattimer wanted it, and if she could use it to save Slate.

Before Sana could weave the new bits of knowledge into the other sparse information at her disposal, the guardsmen stopped their run. Rosana slowed her feet in unison with the Furies but took in her surroundings from behind the safety of the Sicarius mask. A small hunter's cottage sat undisturbed in the middle of the forest, less than a five minute run from Minot. The grass leading to the cottage's door was trampled and muddied, and the only detail that disrupted the tranquil scene. It was obvious that many people had been in and out of this cottage on a regular basis, but that didn't make any sense. The cottage was too small to fit more than a person or two inside at a time, much less an entire group of prisoners. *What's going on here?*

CHAPTER 8

A SIMPLE HUNTER'S COTTAGE

"Dogs, enter the cottage. Inside, run towards the sun and start digging. Now go!"

How will we all fit? Run towards the sun? What is he talking about? Rosana ran forward, matching the eagerness of the other Furies while contemplating what their instructions would be. She stepped through the threshold of the cottage and her eyes took a moment to focus. Rather than a small dim room, she found herself in a great open expanse.

Rosana had traveled all of Malethya and scoured the kingdom's libraries in search of information. If she had combined the libraries of Malethya, they would barely equal the expanse of the collection of blood magic transcripts that filled the room she beheld.

Shelf upon shelf reached skyward to an elegant cupola recessed into the ceiling to provide natural light that bathed the entire room. Ladders wheeled along the floor and enabled young Ispirtu scholars to search the ranks of books above. At eye level, tables were filled with scholars actively scribbling notes or transcribing the collection of works contained in the cottage.

A sudden realization almost stopped Rosana in her tracks, but the headmaster kept her feet moving to maintain the disguise of a prisoner.

When Lattimer had gained power, he'd spoken of his short-lived tutelage under Ibson, when he was blindfolded and shipped to a shanty in

the woods in which he wasn't permitted to
enter. It was during this time that Lattimer
got his first taste of blood magic in the form
of illegal texts. Ibson dismissed him from his
teaching and cast a spell to put Lattimer to
sleep during his return trip to Ravinai.
Lattimer had been looking for something during
the attacks on the northern villages. He was
looking for Ibson's shack in the woods, where
he first encountered blood magic. *Did Ibson
know more about this shack then he let on? Was
this shack actually Ibson's home?*

The Furies continued at a run through the
library, so Rosana was forced to pull her eyes
away from the treasure in front of her and
follow their lead. Looking ahead, she saw an
even more incredible sight. A door labeled
storage led to a vast expanse of sand and
stone. She crossed the threshold and
immediately felt the hot sun burning down on
her. The Furies spread out and chose locations
at random to dig. Some chose to dig in holes
begun from previous days' work while others
started anew. Shovels of sand flew overhead in
an attempt to satisfy their masters. They
performed this back-breaking work with the same
determination and vigor the soldiers had
exhibited in battle.

Rosana picked a location very near the
entrance. Sana theorized that she needed to
fulfill the duty of a Fury, but there was no
harm in digging close to the library. If
anything of interest was going to happen today,
it was probably going to happen in the library,
where the Ispirtu wizards and Bellator
Guardsmen congregated. She set to work digging,
though without knowledge of what she was
seeking.

Just as she got into a steady rhythm, a Bellator Guardsman passed through the doorway and stood right next to Rosana. She once again found herself thankful for the Sicarius mask that hid her identity. The guardsman commanded the Furies, who listened attentively. "You will dig all day long. If you begin to sweat, keep digging. If you stop sweating, walk to the threshold and wait for a guardsman to provide you with water, and then get back to work. If you need to relieve yourself, you are surrounded by wasteland… use it. Search for any tool, weapon, or artifact that you can find within these sands. If you find anything you think matches this description, bring it to me."

With these directions, the group of Furies restarted their exercise in tedium. Rosana dug for the better part of the day and when she tired, the Sicarius Headmaster took a shift. It was critical to her mission that she maintained the appearance of a Fury, and if that meant a day of strenuous labor, then she would do it. While Rosana and the Sicarius Headmaster dug in shifts, Rose and Sana discussed the purpose of the wasteland labeled storage and the actions of the wizards and Guardsmen visible within the library.

How is it possible that a library so large can be hidden within a tiny cottage? Rose wondered. *And this wasteland… there's no telling the size of it. There is a sky and sun, and it continues as far as the eye can see.*

Ibson suggested that this place housed the secrets of the blood mages. The spells used to create this place probably stretched even the limits of the blood mage's abilities. Sana pieced together the information logically, but the idea that this place existed stretched the bounds of her imagination. That's where the childlike wonder of Rose flourished.

If a world as expansive as this wasteland fits inside a library, which itself fits inside a hut, how do we know another world isn't fit inside this wasteland…

…or that Malethya isn't itself fit inside some long dead library of a blood mage? Sana finished Rose's question. *We don't know that, but let's work with the tools at our disposal. If we presume a blood mage created this wasteland, then the creator likely lived in Malethya. As impressive as this magical display is, I imagine it would be more difficult to take the world you live in and hide it inside a library then it would be to create a barren wasteland devoid of life. Let's not slip into the existential until reason fails us.*

Rose could not be discouraged. *Think of the possibilities, though. Someone created this, but why? What is its purpose? If it was intended to remain hidden, how did Lattimer find it? What has he learned since discovering it?*

Now you are asking the right questions. Are you sure you don't want to be a wizard's apprentice? Sana used her favorite inside joke, and it stretched the limits of her repertoire. Rose had turned into Sana, so of course she had the skills to become an apprentice, or an assassin like the headmaster or a chameleon of her surroundings like Rosana. Sana moved on from her rhetorical question. She would leave the jokes to Rosana. *The first question you asked has already been answered for us. This is a storage facility. It says so on the door.*

But what does it store? Why bury them in the

hot desert sand?

Lattimer seems to think there are magical artifacts buried here. Why else would he give these instructions to his Furies? Whether he is right or not, I have no idea. I haven't seen a single Fury turn up an artifact since we got here this morning. And the guardsmen say the prisoners have found nothing during their time here. Rose said a fractal's blessing toward the continued failure of the Furies' efforts and Sana rationalized that a desert was the perfect place to store items, with its lack of humidity and protection from the sun beneath the sands. She continued on, *Whatever information or artifacts Lattimer obtains from this storage room will be transcribed and stored somewhere more accessible to him. We need to find out where those Ispirtu wizards are taking their transcriptions.*

Rose remembered, *Lattimer used to have a rock collection when we were growing up. He would meticulously catalog them and group them into similar categories.* Rose's memories of childhood were always given with a state of melancholy. The brother she loved, the one that collected shiny rocks, turned into the ruthless man she now fought to remove from power. *He will do the same thing now. All of this information will be summarized, categorized, and lumped into a single location. If we find that location, we won't have to read through all of these books.*

The Sicarius Headmaster took a break from shoveling to grunt in agreement. She knew a suicide mission when she saw one, and spending an inordinate amount of time in a room full of Ispirtu wizards and Bellator Guardsmen who wanted to see you dead qualified as a suicide

mission. Even if she did dress in an Ispirtu
robe and don the Sicarius mask, she could only
read so fast. Lattimer would be getting
information from his army of Ispirtu scholars
faster than she could catch up. Putting aside
the notion, Rosana decided it was time for some
water. The heat of the overhead sun eliminated
her need to relieve herself, but that also
warned her about sun sickness. If she was
drying out, she needed to replenish her fluids.
She walked back to the library door and stood
patiently at the threshold, waiting for a
guardsman to address her as she had seen the
other Furies do.

A Bellator Guardsman approached with a glass
of water, saying roughly, "Drink, dog, and get
back to work." While she drank her water,
Magnus and Ciratta entered the library via the
cottage door. He located an Ispirtu wizard who
seemed to be in charge.

"Have you entered the vault?" *The vault?*
Rosana hadn't seen anything that would be
described as a vault when she entered the
library.

"No sir, Magnus." It was fun to see an
Ispirtu wizard, trained to treat anyone without
the spark with thinly veiled condescension,
speak in submissive fear, even if it was toward
Magnus. "Our wizards are probing the safeguards
on it and searching through texts for any hints
on how to circumvent the spells that bar us
entry." Rosana drank her water more slowly to
catch more of the conversation.

"That sounds very similar to what you
reported yesterday. In fact, it sounds similar
to what you reported last month. Let's try
something new." Magnus turned his attention to
one of his Bellator Guardsmen.

"Have   the   prisoner's   uncovered   any artifacts?"

"No, sir!" The Bellator Guardsman that issued their orders in the morning reported to Magnus.

"Then let's give them a different purpose, shall we?" He raised his fist and yelled into the wasteland, "Come here, dogs!"

Rosana dropped her water and ran to Magnus with an overzealousness that interrupted the transcribing of the library's wizards. The prisoners assembled into a mass of sweat and dirt masked by the stench of bodies forced to work tirelessly day in and day out. Magnus barked, "Follow me to the vault."

The Furies obeyed in comical fashion, clamoring for position behind the large man, with Rosana in their midst. Rosana thought that when they weren't attacking, lemmings would be a more apt name for the Furies. Their simple obedience masked the ferocity that was only a command away. In their current state, however, the lemmings followed Magnus obediently through the library. They walked past the storage room, the cause of their sore backs, without so much as a glance. With new orders to follow, they completely forgot how they had spent their day.

Magnus descended an elaborately designed staircase with the sound of eager footsteps in his wake. They circled down the winding staircase as it magically cut through the stone that surrounded them. The weight of the walls around them began to take on · a tomb-like quality as they descended. Rose wondered if they were deep in the heart of Malethya or simply in the cottage's cellar. Before Rose put any more thought into the geometric conundrum, the staircase opened onto a room that dwarfed the library above.

The vault, as Magnus had described it, was more city than vault. Stone structures as large as King Darik's palace and as sprawling as the infirmary were encompassed within a shimmering dome in which Ispirtu wizards actively probed and tried to penetrate. Rosana had expected a dark, hidden structure with thick metal walls and not this beautiful, translucent work of magic. But given the other magical feats exhibited within the cottage, she should have been prepared. At the very least, the Sicarius mask hid her surprise.

Magnus interrupted the Ispirtu wizards. "Have you made any progress breaking into the vault?" He already knew the answer from his conversation in the library, but Magnus took the opportunity to see an Ispirtu wizard admit their failures whenever possible. Rosana grudgingly agreed with the strategy.

"We are probing every inch of this wall, General Pudriuz, but so far we haven't found a weak spot. Its construction is flawless. We can't identify the pattern used to construct it, so we can't deconstruct it." The wizard's awe at the construction of the vault was tempered by the reaction he anticipated from Magnus.

"Besides gaping at the magnificence of each square inch of the wall for hours on end, have you tried anything else?" Magnus gestured past the wall. "The real treasure is inside. Lattimer says the people inside have stored the knowledge of the spark-based magic since the days of Cantor."

The beauty of the translucent wall and the magnitude of the buildings inside had distracted Rosana from making a very important observation. Inside the city, people walked around the buildings, peacefully ignoring the wizards on the other side of their wall. They carried out menial tasks, walked from building to building, sold wares from shop windows, and generally looked like the citizens of Ravinai with the exception that they all wore robes and walked with the self-assurance and wisdom of experienced scholars. Rosana, the master of her surroundings, was ashamed at her glaring mistake. She wouldn't tell that portion of the story to Annarelle when she briefed her, assuming she survived this mission.

"No, General Pudriuz, we did not want to risk damaging the city within through direct assault."

"That proves once again why you are not in command. We'll try a physical attack first." He raised his fist and pointed toward the Furies closest to him, thankfully omitting Rosana from the group. "You three Furies… breach the wall."

The already red eyes of the Furies trained on the wall, and they sprinted toward it with raised shovels and mining equipment. Their attack was short-lived. The second their weapons touched the shimmering wall, a shockwave traveled through weapons and bodies leaving behind Fury husks. The smell of burnt flesh from the charred corpses permeated the air. Weapons clattered to the ground and the areas of the shimmering wall in which they struck grew in thickness.

Magnus contemplated sending in the remainder of his Furies, in which case Rosana would need to break cover and was unlikely to escape with her life, but the charcoal husks of the first wave of Furies restrained his hand. Instead he asked the wizard, "Can you probe that section of the wall? What do you see?"

The wizard concentrated and then spent several uncomfortable moments staring at a shimmering wall while everyone watched him. When he finished, he said, "The pattern of the wall is identical to the sections around it, but it has gotten thicker."

"Did the wall get thicker or did it reinforce itself in this area by stealing from the areas around it?"

"It's difficult to say, General. The wall is so large that it could shift material to this section with very little consequence to the other areas. I can't detect the difference."

"Worthless wizards… they have magic at their disposal and can't find a decent use for it." Magnus grumbled under his breath in a rough approximation of Hedok's derision. Their time together in Minot must have been lengthy if their personalities were beginning to rub off on each other. "We need to find out, which means we need to attack it with more strength. If the wall is just reinforcing itself using other parts of the wall, we can attack one area continuously to intentionally thin out the sections around it. Then we can divert our attack at the thin section of wall. Will you and all your wizards send fireballs at the section my Furies just attacked?"

"We don't know what effect a large attack will have on the wall. Maybe we should start small with a trial run of a smaller spell?" The wizard tried to reason with Magnus.

"You just admitted you can't tell what effect a small spell will have on the wall. Let's learn something about this thing instead of staring at it all day long." He reached in his pocket but the wizard conceded before Magnus had to issue any orders.

"You are right, General. Wizards, fireballs on five." Wizards conjured spells at different speeds, so it was necessary to set the end goal when they coordinated attacks to occur simultaneously. 1…the weakest wizards began concentrating. 2…a few middling wizards joined the mix. 3…the strongest wizards began to apply their craft. 4…Rosana took a subtle step toward the staircase. 5…fireballs formed in the hands of the Ispirtu wizards and shot toward the wall, crackling the air as they flew by. The fireballs slammed into the wall in a fireworks display of magical power.

The wall flexed inward under the force of the erupting fireballs, but it didn't break. A few of the vault's citizens casually looked up at the wall before going back to their business. The flexed wall absorbed the energy of the fireballs and the heat turned the wall white-hot. The energy quickly dispersed from the area of attack, turning from white to red to a soft yellow. As soon as the wall recovered its original shape, a blue pattern of light grew inward toward the point of the attack. The pattern reminded Sana of when she cast one of her stunning spells. She could never predict the path of the spell—it expanded outward and took on a life of its own—but she could often tell the direction. The wall acted in the same way, but on a much larger scale.

"Do it again!" Magnus ordered upon seeing the flexed wall. Rosana didn't expect an improved result based upon the citizens' lack of concern.

The wizards went through the same five-second process before sending a second wave of fireballs crashing into the wall. This time the wall didn't bend. It didn't change color. It absorbed the energy of the spells within the intricate pattern that spider-webbed across the wall. The pattern within the wall glowed with its natural blue energy before sending it back at the Ispirtu wizards. It arced from the wall into the wizards, just as Sana's stunning spell did, and killed them where they stood. It all happened so fast that no one had time to react.

Magnus looked around the corpses at his feet in disbelief. He absently kicked the crisped body of the wizard who'd questioned his order to attack the wall. "Congratulations. You've proven me wrong." He then raised his fist and commanded his Furies, "Carry these corpses up the stairs and into the woods. I don't want them stinking up the place."

Rosana joined the remaining Furies in picking up the bodies and traversing the long stairwell to the library. After a long day of shoveling in the badlands her muscles screamed, but the will of the Sicarius Headmaster kept her going. She was going to survive this mission, and all she had to do was carry a body. That was something at which she had a lot of practice.

The long march up the stairs gave Sana time to contemplate the day's events. Lattimer had been searching for Ibson's cottage near Minot, inside of which was a library from the days of Cantor and spark-based magic. Lattimer employed countless Ispirtu wizards to filter through the information and bring the most important to his attention. He would be gaining power at an incredible rate, which didn't even take into account any artifacts of power that were discovered in the wastelands. Based on today's efforts, he hadn't discovered many artifacts, but he had the advantage of time and tireless Furies. Eventually, Lattimer would obtain the right artifacts and figure out the key to unlocking the vault and whatever knowledge the citizens held within its shimmering walls.

Rosana reached the top of the stairs and followed the other Furies toward the main entrance. Magnus followed after them, · but a voice called for his attention. "General Pudriuz, may I have a word with you?" Rosana looked from behind the safety of her Sicarius mask to see Phoenix standing on the second floor of the library. She almost dropped the corpse on her tired shoulders from shock, but the Sicarius Headmaster held her nerves in check. "I have been tracking the former Sicarius Headmaster and believe that she is somewhere in the vicinity." *I'm right below you, asshole.*

"We were just finishing up here. Let's head back to Minot and make some plans. I'm ready for some real work anyway. I've spent too much time watching people dig in the sand." He raised his fist. "After dropping off the bodies, return to your bunks. You will not remember anything from the time you left Minot to the time you returned." Lowering his fist, he addressed his Bellator Guardsmen with a smile. "You can walk back to camp with me and get filled in by our Sicarius brethren about his current plans. Tonight, we go Shadow hunting."

Rosana happily followed orders and hauled her corpse through the library, out of the cottage, and into the late afternoon sun. It felt good to feel the warm Malethyan sun and the cool northern breeze on her face after spending the day in the dry heat of the wastelands. She deposited her corpse in a pile in the woods and ran back toward Minot in formation with the

Furies, trying to use the run to coax the soreness from her back and shoulders after shoveling all day.

When she approached camp, she dipped out of formation and disappeared into the woods, silently thanking Magnus for holding back his Guardsmen. Rosana could have slipped away once they reached Minot, but this just made it easier. She circled around the village and made her way toward the location that Annarelle chose for camp.

As she approached, she made the sound of a chickadee. Annarelle responded with the sparrow's song and hopped down from a tree where she was watching for anyone wandering from Minot.

"Annarelle! I'm so happy to see you!" Rose greeted her friend after a long day's mission. Rosana and the Sicarius Headmaster were exhausted from the day and happy to let Rose do the talking.

Annarelle gave Rose a hug. She had worked with Rose, Rosana, Sana, and the Sicarius Headmaster long enough to be accustomed to a wide range of greetings, even if she didn't know the reason. "I'm happy to see you too, headmaster… I just wish I didn't smell you quite so strongly."

Rose became aware of the smell of exuded sweat and charred corpse. "I'll wash up quick at camp while we make plans. Phoenix is here and he's coming for us tonight."

"How do you know that?"

"Because he told Magnus."

"Magnus is here too?" Annarelle's surprise was tempered by her Sicarius training and quickly transitioned into more practical questions. "What is going on in Minot? What did you find out?"

"More than I expected but not what I was looking for… let's get back to camp and I'll tell you what I saw."

Annarelle navigated through the traps she had set around camp, and they found Ibson making a cold dinner in the clearing. "Would you like some flatbread, fruit, and cheese? It's the best I could contrive without a fire. Your apprentice wouldn't allow it."

Annarelle explained, obviously for the umpteenth time. "Fires send up smoke, which any woodsman can locate from a long way off."

"If you quit feeding me that wormroot, I would gladly create a smokeless fire. It is simply a matter of coaxing the particulate in the smoke out of the air." *I know that spell from Lucus' teachings, but I haven't had the need to teach Annarelle yet. We spent our time training in Ravinai, where campfires weren't particularly useful. If we make it out of Minot, it will be a good lesson for my student.* Ibson continued, "As it stands now, we all get cold food and mine will taste like wormroot. I might as well eat a strap of leather off the horse's dressings. Wormroot spoils the taste of everything." He spat in disgust, trying to get the taste out of his mouth.

"You asked me earlier what you needed to do to earn my trust. I am a trusting person, and you can start right now." *Rose was trusting. Ibson was just lucky to be dealing with her at the moment.* "Annarelle, please stop administering wormroot to Ibson. With any luck, the effects will wear off before we are attacked."

"Are you sure that is wise, headmaster…?" Annarelle questioned with kindness in her voice. The Sicarius Headmaster would have told her to obey her orders but Rose wanted to know her friend's opinion on matters.

"I don't trust him yet, but I do not believe he would side with Magnus or Phoenix. He has his own motivations, and they are still secret to me."

"What attack?" Ibson's previous encounter with Phoenix made him appropriately serious.

"I'll tell you about it as I get cleaned up." Rose went to the far side of the cart and began to take off her clothes. "Please keep your eyes on your plate."

Ibson looked up at her and said, "I'm too old to notice such things. Don't worry about me."

"Those sound like the words of a dirty old man hoping to get a glimpse of a young naked woman. Keep your eyes on your food." Ibson looked down and Rose finished disrobing, briefing Annarelle and Ibson while she rubbed the exhaustion from her muscles and the sweat from her skin. "Lattimer has discovered a hidden tribute to the days of the blood mages. It is a colossal library, barren wasteland, and protected city all magically shoved into a hunter's cottage in the woods. Ispirtu wizards comb through the books every minute of every day, filtering the vast supply of books into useful knowledge for Lattimer. His power is growing faster than we once believed. Bellator Guardsmen oversee criminals-turned-Furies as they search an endless desert for magical artifacts from the days of Cantor. These are just the consolation prizes though. Within that hut lies an entire city protected by a magical wall that Magnus and his Ispirtu wizards cannot breach. Magnus called it the Vault, a name that shows the perceived value of the city to

Lattimer even if it fails to convey what he expects to find within those magical walls."

Before Rose could continue, Ibson jumped up excitedly and started talking. "The library is a compilation of all blood magic, which they would have called spark-based magic." His youth-like excitement made him start pacing back and forth. It even momentarily held off the Sicarius Headmaster's condemnation of the old man for failing to inform them that the shanty in the woods was also his inhabitance. "Its discovery led to the golden age, and it was considered the greatest advancement in Malethya's magical history. Unfortunately, some wizards used the principles of spark-based magic to gain personal power. Their greed brought about the destruction of Malethya and a period of darkness to the land. The library was set up as a scientific record of those advances in magic."

"You knew this existed. And this is where you trained Lattimer in the arts of blood magic! Why didn't you tell us?" The Sicarius Headmaster would wait no longer.

"But this isn't my home, although I am tied to it. I didn't teach Lattimer blood magic either. I dismissed him when I discovered his interest in those sections of the texts I used for training. I would have spoken of Lattimer's time with me at the cottage once you convinced me of his transgressions, but I could not without mentioning the library. Some bonds are too deep to break. But now I can discuss the library with you because you've seen it!" The excited old man ran over to Rose while she was still washing, grabbed her soapy shoulders, and kissed her on the forehead. Even with the Sicarius Headmaster resting, Rose contemplated finding a knife but his actions were too innocent to act upon. Ibson was like a child showing a new toy to the other kids in the neighborhood. Rose worked too hard to maintain her own innocence to condemn him for his. Rose wanted to ask more questions regarding Lattimer, but it was apparent that Ibson was freely speaking now that the ties holding his tongue were broken.

Annarelle asked, "How can such an expansive library be shoved inside of a hunter's cabin?"

"Oh! That is a clever piece of magic and since you have seen the hut, I can describe it to you!" Ibson danced a jig—an actual jig—in the middle of camp. "Our world is constructed in three dimensions: height, width, and depth." Ibson searched the ground for a suitable teaching aid before settling on a rock. "Take this rock for example. It doesn't change size and it doesn't change shape. It is boring in every sense of the word." Ibson smoothed a patch of dirt so he could sketch on it. "Now imagine what I can do with this rock in two dimensions. If I depict just the width and height of this rock right at its tallest point, I get a point." He drew a point on the ground with a stick. "If I take a different plane that cuts through the rock, I get an ellipse. I can make the ellipse grow bigger or smaller just by choosing a different plane." *Where is he going with this?* "My point is that if we want to alter the world around us, we shouldn't use a three-dimensional object. We should use a four-dimensional object."

"…but you just said everything in our world was three-dimensional. There are no four-dimensional objects."

"Of course there are four-dimensional objects

in our world! I just showed you this with the rock. A three-dimensional object can have two-dimensional representations like the rock appearing as an ellipse. A four-dimensional object can exist in our world, but it appears as a three-dimensional object to our limited view. Try to keep up."

Sana was used to this form of lecturing from her time with Lucus. "That doesn't explain how an entire city got shoved inside a hut."

Ibson was unperturbed. Indeed, he nearly bubbled over with excitement. "Yes, you are correct. A four-dimensional object is only part of the solution. It allows us to change the shape of an object in our world but it lacks the flexibility to create." Ibson wrapped his hand around the rock. "It is surface area that allows us to fold or unfold an object into a new volume. My hand has enough surface area to wrap around the rock and form a similar shape. To create more complex items, like a city, one needs much more surface area and volume. Are you familiar with a fractal?"

Annarelle covered this one. "Fractal's blessing, fractal-forsaken—I've been called them all at one point or another."

"Yes, but the true meaning of a fractal has been lost. Specifically, it has a very unique property in that the two-dimensional geometric representation of a fractal has an infinitely long border. A three-dimensional fractal has infinite surface area, and a four-dimensional fractal has infinite volume…"

Finally Sana understood, "…and that means it can be molded, folded, and unfolded into infinite possibilities."

Ibson smiled at his students. "Yes! And a four-dimensional fractal could be folded or unfolded to create anything we wished in the three-dimensional world. This is how the hut was created, although the knowledge of its existence has been lost for a very long time."

"Can you make such a four-dimensional fractal?" Rose asked somewhat fearfully. The implications of such power inspired trepidation.

"There are ties deeper than you know." Ibson's animation was instantly sapped, and his mouth closed even though the twinkle in his eye longed to continue. Whatever ties held Ibson's allegiance, they weren't totally broken. It was just as well. As interesting as Ibson's discourse on four-dimensional objects was, it didn't change the fact that Phoenix and Magnus had plans for their impending doom. It also didn't help her save Slate.

"You've said that phrase a few times now. I don't know what bonds prevent you from speaking, but for now I'm satisfied." Rose finished dressing and as she adorned the suit of the Sicarius Headmaster, that part of her began to reawaken as well. A new mission was about to begin. "You can join us as we infiltrate Minot this evening. My brother will have summarized the findings from the library somehow, and we must find where that is."

Ibson interjected, "…but you just found out about Cantor's library. Surely that is sufficient intelligence for one day! Phoenix is too close. We need to leave!"

Rose was satisfied with the day's activities. She had cracked Ibson's shell. Sana was intrigued by the revelations of the magical spells used to create the hut and the Sicarius Headmaster walked into the heart of the enemy's base and left unscathed. The experience only reinforced her confidence. "You are too passive." She again condemned her other selves. "No one can stop me. The time to act is now." Rosana agreed they should continue the mission, but for entirely different reasons. Rosana came here to find out how to break the spell that Lattimer had on Slate. She would succeed. Her will convinced Rose and Sana to extend the mission in Minot. Sana created a plan and issued orders. "Although I have learned a lot today, I have not found what I came to Minot for… and I'm not leaving until I do. As for Phoenix, let's give him a surprise. Annarelle, what traps have you set?"

"There are exploding orbs set around the perimeter of the camp. I also set a couple of security orbs for early warning." This was standard practice. Sana wasn't going for standard. Phoenix would search for exploding orbs following the events of Ravinai, so she needed a different sort of trap.

"Retrieve them and set a single security orb in the middle of camp." Sana walked into the woods and cast a spell to coil vines around her arm. During her tutelage under Lucus, she had studied the pattern of snakes. Snakes coiled up when they slept and straightened to move around. The pattern she used in her spell to coil the vines actually encouraged the vines to fall asleep, to relax their grip on the trees they clung to and to coil upon her arm for a restful slumber. Sana then suspended the vines at ankle height at strategic locations around the camp by casting a spell that awakened them and encouraged them to move to the location she specified. With that part of her trap set, she checked on Annarelle.

"You know the pattern of a trigger orb,

correct?"

"Yes, trigger orbs—" Annarelle's explanation of the pattern was cut short by Sana.

"Good. Cast the spell on the vines I just suspended. If they stretch or break, make them trigger the security orb." Sana knew the translation of the trigger orb spell to work with the vines wasn't a simple task, but her plans weren't done yet. She left her apprentice with a contemplative look on her face. By the time she left camp for the woods, she was in deep conversation with Ibson, trying to figure out how to accomplish such a spell. Maybe the old wizard's lectures would finally come in handy.

Sana set to work on her second trap, one of the secrets Phoenix hadn't learned about yet. She traveled half the distance to Minot and sat on the forest floor. If she collapsed afterward, it helped to already be on the ground. The spell she was about to cast was powerful and required a large amount of spark because she needed to utilize multiple patterns to cast it. Sana started with a probing spell that she coupled with the first pattern of her spell—a hunting snake constricting its prey. Some snakes used venom to subdue their prey while others twisted around, constricting so tightly that they either crushed or suffocated their victims from the pressure. It was this constricting pattern that married nicely with vines. They wound around trees and eventually constricted the life from the much larger trees they preyed upon. Sana's probing spell searched for this constriction in the woods around her. The snake pattern identified all the tree-choking vines that the probing spell contacted and Sana held them in her mind. Sana then expanded the probing spell outward, straining until she had identified every vine between Minot and her camp. She then modified the snake pattern, amplifying the natural pattern of the vines. They wanted to cling to anything they touched, climbing upward while they wrapped tighter and tighter. Sana then used the second pattern—that of a hunting snake waiting in the weeds. This part of the spell gave the vines hunger but also patience to wait for an opportune time to strike. Sana poured her spark into the spell and completed all of it, with one exception. She held onto the pattern of the snake waiting in the grass. They wouldn't strike until she released the spell. Sana might not know the pattern of a trigger orb like Annarelle did from her studies in exploding orbs, but she could hold this small portion of the spell as long as she needed in order to ensure Phoenix had a very unpleasant surprise in store for him.

CHAPTER 9

A MINOT-SCULE PORTION OF THE PUZZLE

Rosana, Annarelle, and Ibson watched Minot's Bellator and Ispirtu complexes from the safety of the prisoner's barracks. Josef had directed the Sicarius Headmaster and her guests to a few cots made empty after the day's losses. The amnesiac, hopeless prisoners didn't question their presence. No one even attempted to talk with them.

Through a crack in the hastily constructed barracks, Rosana watched as Magnus assembled his search party in the Bellator courtyards. The still night air easily carried Magnus' speech to the assembled troops and Ispirtu wizards.

"You joined Bellator to make a difference. You joined for the glory of battle and to claim your stake as a protector of Malethya." Several swords banged against shields in anticipation. "Tonight, we are afforded the opportunity to chase down and kill one of the greatest threats to peace and prosperity within our lands. We will be hunting Rosana Regallo, Brannon's daughter and the former Sicarius Headmaster. She exposed herself as a traitor to King Darik and sided with her father on the day of his death. You offered your allegiance to Lattimer, the great Redeemer, in exchange for the power you now hold. Use it to capture or kill his sister and ensure his benevolent rule for years to come."

"For the Redeemer!" shouts filled the air and adrenaline pumped through the veins of the soldiers.

"The man Lattimer hand-picked to reform the communication networks within Ravinai and throughout Malethya has tracked Rosana to a location near Minot. Phoenix, please share your findings with the troops."

Phoenix, wearing his Sicarius mask, stepped forward and stood beside Magnus. It served to solidify his position as a Sicarius Guardsman and to hide his deformities from the troops, which were grotesque even by Bellator standards. "I have been tracking Rosana Regallo, but you are more likely to know her as the Sicarius Headmaster, the Shadow of the Night, or a host of other names from your childhood. I can assure you that she has earned these names and more. Her Sicarius endeavors earned the names heard throughout Malethya, but I hold a few names in private. I reserve them for when I get to look into her eyes right before I kill her. She has earned these private names as well. She is responsible for this…" Phoenix tore off his mask in theatrical fashion, and the Guardsmen and wizards flinched at the sight. In addition to his previous injuries, burns from the explosion in the warehouse added to the effect.

"Several days ago, Rosana kidnapped the famed wizard Ibson from the infirmary. After tracking her accomplice to a hideout within Ravinai, we now believe Ibson is aiding their criminal activities. Upon attempted apprehension by a squadron of Bellator Guardsmen and Ispirtu wizards, Rosana blew up the warehouse, killing everyone inside. I alone escaped their treachery and have followed them to Minot." Phoenix paused to let his words of heroism sink in.

Rosana could almost hear the soldiers' thoughts—if the Sicarius Headmaster killed an entire squadron of Guardsmen and wizards already, then what makes me think I'll survive the night? Every highly skilled soldier knew to play the odds when your life was at stake, and the odds were never good against the Sicarius Headmaster. Phoenix had to be more careful with his pep talks. This one wasn't getting the intended effect.

"Magnus has assured me that the camps have been secured all day, so I have reached you in time. She is likely camped in the outlying wilderness plotting to secure knowledge of the activities at Minot. We will enter the woods tonight and prevent Rosana from accomplishing her mission. I must warn you that Ibson, if he is helping Rosana, is a master of defensive magic and will be a difficult target to hit. Additionally, Rosana's apprentice has shown an affinity for explosives, so leave them at camp. They will only be used against you if she is present. Finally, Rosana is a wizard with a proclivity for shock spells. I recommend that you leave your metal armor, or it could be your demise."

I hate that Phoenix knows my secrets. The more secrets an adversary keeps, the harder they are to defeat. Now I will need to add tricks to my arsenal to stay a step in front of the abomination.

The soldiers looked to Magnus for confirmation of Phoenix's orders. "A Bellator Guardsman is not a Bellator Guardsman without his armor. Phoenix might as well order you to leave an arm at home for all the sense he makes. We will not be following that order."

Phoenix interrupted Magnus by saying, "Then you will all die unnecessarily." But Magnus had already continued his speech.

"Thanks to the Great Redeemer, we are prepared for the tricks of the Sicarius Headmaster. Lattimer witnessed the Headmaster's shock spell first-hand and has been working to discover a means of enchanting our armor. I am pleased to announce that on Lattimer's last visit, he extended this blessing to all of his favored soldiers in Minot. You need not fear the Headmaster's shock spell." A roar went up from among the soldiers.

Sana wondered about the enchantment. Her shock spell traveled poorly through some materials, but the armor still looked like metal. *Has Lattimer found a pattern to give the metal the correct properties to inhibit the flow of spark or is he just using blood magic?* The Sicarius Headmaster quieted Sana's musings, since they weren't relevant. Lattimer had created the armor; that was the important thing.

When the soldiers quieted, Magnus continued, "Even with the gift of the Redeemer, the headmaster is dangerous. Her throwing knives can be just as dangerous as her shock spell." Magnus looked down at his foot and Rosana smiled. She had left a throwing knife buried to the hilt, pinning his foot to the ground on the night Magnus destroyed Pillar, Slate's hometown. Magnus then tried to restore the confidence of his troops. "As for the ability of Rosana to kill a squadron of Bellator Guardsmen, I believe your claims. But I don't believe that this group of soldiers is as mindless as the Guardsmen you describe." Magnus walked up and down the ranks of troops. He stopped in front of one of the guardsman that Rosana recognized from the morning lessons. "My troops are taught to control their anger and channel their rage." He stared down the soldier in front of him, reinforcing the morning's lessons and setting his expectation that the lesson had been learned. "They are better than Bellator Guardsman. They are Bellator Furies."

The soldiers loosed an impressive battle cry into the night air. Sana sighed at the idiocy of such an adrenaline-induced display. *They abandon the element of surprise so willingly.*

Phoenix had the same thought. "Let us leave before all of Malethya knows we are coming. I left the trail when it became clear that they were circling the outskirts of Minot in search of a campsite. We will return and pick up the trail."

Magnus gave the order to the contingent of Bellator Furies and Ispirtu wizards with a raised fist. "Follow Phoenix and corner Rosana in her camp. Attack with aggression. Feel no pain. Attack with absolute impunity. Feel no fear. Attack with control. Leave no one standing."

The testosterone-driven group left Minot for battlefield glory, and the Sicarius Headmaster pondered her own mortality as the mission entered its most dangerous stage. The names of the previous Sicarius Headmasters floated through her head, as they always did before embarking on a dangerous mission. *I will pay that sacrifice eventually, and if it happens to be tonight, then this was a mission worthy of death.* Committed to the mission, she addressed Josef, who was integral to her success. "We will enter the Bellator complex. If you hear an alarm or the group returns from the woods, you must carry out your part. Can you do this?"

"I will, headmaster, if it means I have a chance to escape from here."

"You will not escape tonight." The brutal truth from the headmaster was softened by Rose. "…but I hope what I find within the Bellator complex will free you soon." She did hope to free these prisoners and she ignored Sana's calculated odds of her statement coming true.

"That's all I can ask. I'll do my part."

"Good, now let's make sure you have the authority you need to implement my plans." The headmaster called on Rosana to persuade the group of prisoners. She stood on top of a cot so that she was visible to everyone in the room and projected the alternating voice of the Sicarius Headmaster to the far corners of the room, trying to convince the prisoners to participate in Sana's plan.

"I am the Sicarius Headmaster. You have grown up fearing me, but tonight I am your friend." The dull eyes around the room looked up at her with only a small spark of interest. "I know you are ordered around by Bellator Guardsmen and forced to sleep in this filthy hole. You work all day only to return having forgotten the reason your muscles are sore in the first place. Well, I can tell you why your muscles are sore." The dull eyes brightened momentarily. Sana had guessed that the greatest motivating force to these prisoners was to fill in the blank holes in their memories. She'd seen more eager audiences, but at least the headmaster had their attention.

"When you pledged obedience to King Darik in exchange for your lives, you pledged obedience to Lattimer Regallo. He forces you to work all day and then forget what you were working on, but I traveled with you today. You dig. You dig relentlessly for every hour of the day. You dig to find magical artifacts that will increase Lattimer's power and further strengthen his hold over all of you. The longer you work here, the more difficult it will be to free you from the oaths you swore." Before the direness of their situation slipped into their minds and the hunger for freedom disappeared from their faces, Rosana brought home her plea. "Help me tonight and I will try to break the bonds that tie you here. Will you help me?"

"I will help you." Josef stated. It was always good to have a plant in the audience.

At Josef's participation, the crowd's silence broke, turning to nods and then verbal confirmations. "Fractal's fortune to you, headmaster!" "May your shadow be silent!" Words of encouragement were offered in hushed tones. Rosana told them to follow Josef's lead and to be ready.

She left the complex with Ibson and Annarelle in tow.

"That was impressive. I thought that hopeless group was beyond motivation." Ibson congratulated the Sicarius Headmaster.

"Not every mission can be completed with a spell. It takes more than just magic." Sometimes it took different selves.

"Why aren't we going to the Ispirtu complex?" Ibson asked. "You said the scholars in the library were wizards. Surely the information they collect will be compiled within their own walls."

Annarelle answered his naïve question. "The wizards answer to Magnus, and he will demand a

filtered down report of the most important
information to present to Lattimer. That is the
list we want."

Sana added some thought to the strategy. "It
will also be less guarded. Magnus called his
best troops to duty tonight, leaving behind a
skeleton crew in the Bellator complex. The
Ispirtu complex, by comparison, houses all of
the scholars that we saw in the library. Their
number is far greater than the few wizards that
joined Magnus and his troops."

They raced toward the darkest corner of the
Bellator complex, cognizant of Ibson's lack of
training in Sicarius ways. A straight sprint
was the best bet, even with the slow speed of
the elderly wizard. As they neared the complex,
the Sicarius Headmaster tempered the
conversation. "No more talking unless it is
required. Do your jobs and complete the
mission." Rosana couldn't agree more. She had
her own mission and she didn't care to share it
with Ibson. She needed to end Lattimer's hold
on Slate and she would find out how tonight.

In the darkened corner, Ibson caught his
breath while Annarelle went ahead to scout for
Guards. The two-story complex was a mixture of
utility and grandeur, indicating that it had
been built quickly to serve a temporary purpose
before it was remodeled. A square hallway lined
with doors along the outer wall framed the
layout of the first floor. It looked like every
building constructed to provide sleeping
quarters for as many people as possible. The
inner hallway had an open doorway into a
darkened kitchen and dining area. The lights
were poor and the construction cheap. Fine
artwork adorned plain walls, reminding Sana of
makeup on a pig. Lattimer hadn't intended for

Minot to be a permanent outpost for his army, and Magnus' presence here meant his frustration was rising. He wouldn't send his most trusted servant to Minot unless he was unhappy with the progress they were making. Sana took Lattimer's frustration as a positive sign for the rest of Malethya.

Annarelle made it halfway down the hallway when the latch of a door sprung her into action. Before the door fully opened, Annarelle slit the throat of the room's occupant, opening her airway to prevent her attempted screams from alerting the other guards. The Sicarius Headmaster had taught her student to only kill when necessary, but this mission warranted the crude technique. Annarelle wiped her blade on the guard's clothes and quietly shut her door, effectively hiding her body from sight. She then advanced to the end of the hallway, looked around the corner, and signaled Ibson and the headmaster to follow now that the hallway was cleared.

Sana made a quick stop into the dead soldier's room. She found the soldier to be unarmored, but a Bellator soldier never left their armor too far away. Sana wanted to check this enchantment. Rosana moved quickly to the soldier's armor stand and Sana released a shock spell into it. The spark dissipated. Magnus had not lied; her shock spell would not work against Magnus and his troops.

The headmaster joined Annarelle and Ibson a moment later, and Annarelle gave her scouting report. "There is a stairwell halfway down the next hallway. I looked inside the guardsman's room when she opened the door and it is a simple room. Assuming the rest of the rooms on this level are similarly constructed, then we shouldn't waste our time down here. I'll head upstairs and signal you to follow."

"Agreed." Rose hated to put her friend in danger by giving her the lead, but she deferred to the Sicarius Headmaster's judgment because she was living on borrowed time. She knew the headmaster felt obligated to train the next headmaster for when she died. No amount of training could substitute for experience. She helped Annarelle the most by slowly giving her more autonomy and preparing her for life without guidance from Rose, Rosana, Sana or the headmaster.

Annarelle cleared the stairs, and Ibson and the headmaster advanced to the stair's landing. Sana considered it the most defensible position with its views of both floors. The first floor remained quiet, so she looked up to the second floor.

Heavy doors barred the way, but Annarelle came prepared. She set up two tiny orbs near each of the door hinges and concentrated. A second later, a directional blast pulverized the hinges and a small area surrounding the wood door. Such a technique would normally cause an alarm to be raised, but Annarelle also suppressed the air surrounding the blast, muffling the noise. Sana and the Sicarius Headmaster nodded in approval at the improving techniques of their star pupil. Annarelle caught the falling door and moved it to the side.

Unlike the utilitarian bottom floor, the second floor bordered on opulence. It had been added on top of the original structure and the builders had spared no expense. The center of the room was dominated by a larger-than-life reenactment of Lattimer's victory over his father. Lattimer stood at the head of a group including King Darik, Magnus, Cirata, and Hedok, with his arms extended forward in the exaggerated motion of a fireball spell. Brannon stood in front of them, looking treacherously defiant, right before he was consumed by a bronzed fireball. Sana couldn't help but notice that she was conspicuously absent from the scene, along with Slate and the others that managed to escape Lattimer's coup, but she understood the long practiced tradition of victors writing history in their favor. Beneath the sculpture was an inscription: "Power returns to Malethya." Several comfortable chairs surrounded the gaudy centerpiece so that the Bellator soldiers could be inspired by the acts of the Great Redeemer. Rose thought, *I know that my brother is vain, but this is a bit much even by his standards.*

Around the outside of the room were doors of varying size, with the largest being a double door carved from catalpa trees. Sana reasoned that the biggest doors belonged to the biggest man or the biggest ego. In the case of Magnus, they were one and the same. Several other posh rooms surrounded Magnus' rooms, with slightly smaller doors that likely belonged to Cirata and Hedok. *Their acts of treason against Malethya have benefitted them well.* The Sicarius Headmaster wanted to end their good fortune but tonight was not the night for revenge. It was a night for information, and that's why the far wall from their stairwell held her attention. A large room screamed command center with a map table at its center and papers strewn throughout.

The Sicarius Headmaster motioned to Annarelle, who used hand signals to acknowledge her orders. The map room was the target and she quickly traversed the room scanning for guardsmen. Time didn't allow her to clear all the individual rooms, so she just positioned herself to view the doors if they opened. Ibson and the Sicarius Headmaster joined her a minute later.

In the command center, Sana quickly processed the information, starting with the map table. Tokens with wizards and soldiers inscribed upon them were positioned around the map. Blue tokens were distributed around the far reaches of Malethya while black tokens were concentrated near Ravinai. A small number of red tokens were set in Minot. They didn't exist anywhere else on the map. Sana interpreted the blue tokens as ordinary soldiers in King Darik's army or wizards unassociated with Lattimer, the black tokens as soldiers and wizards under the direct control of Lattimer, and the red tokens as the elite soldiers that Magnus described as Bellator Furies. If her assumption was correct, Lattimer hadn't focused his efforts on expanding his power yet, choosing instead to keep it concentrated near Ravinai. What reason did he have for doing this? There was no one left in Malethya powerful enough to oppose him.

Sana shifted her attention to the stacks of papers and read the top report entitled, "Status Report for the 39th Squadron." Rose immediately smiled. Her brother had always been fastidious in his attention to details and filed everything with systematic order. She remembered Lattimer as a young boy with an affinity for collecting rocks. He would scour the ground for anything of interest and then toil over whether they should be organized according color, type of striations, or the location of origin. One look at the orderly piles and Rose knew that Lattimer demanded documentation from his troops with the same level of detail. Rose said to Annarelle and Ibson, "These piles will be organized according to some pattern. Determine the pattern and gather the most important documents."

Rrrreeeeeeaaaaaahhhhh! The screech of a distant security orb reverberated through the walls of the Bellator complex. There was little doubt about the origin. Annarelle commented while sifting through reports. "Phoenix has located our camp."

Fractal's luck. They had even less time than Sana hoped, but that was why Sana had laid her second trap. Upon discovering an empty camp, Phoenix and Magnus would quickly realize that Minot had been infiltrated and come rushing back. It wouldn't be an easy journey.

Sana completed the spell she had been holding at the ready, no longer requiring the vines to wait with predatory patience. The vines in the forest would now attack anything they touched with the hunger and force of a constricting snake. There would be a lot of dead squirrels in the morning, but more importantly, a lot of distracted Bellator Furies and wizards. Her spell wouldn't be strong enough to kill her highly trained adversaries, but it would require them to slash and burn their way back to Minot.

Even with the aid of the spell, Sana's time was short. Any remaining Bellator Furies would take up defensive positions around the camp, and the Ispirtu wizards sleeping next door would awaken, searching the grounds for target practice with their fireballs. She issued orders as the Sicarius Headmaster. "You have five minutes to gather documents. Then you will signal Josef and the criminals to proceed with the plan. I will meet you at our extraction point." Rosana wanted to check Magnus' room. She needed information that could help Slate, and that type of information wouldn't be in status reports.

"Yes, headmaster." Annarelle responded without looking up from the reports.

Ibson, who had been thoughtfully deciphering the reports as well, told Annarelle, "These two stacks of reports are laid out according to the regions of Malethya. What have you found?"

Rosana left the two to their work and headed for Magnus' room. The two large doors made of catalpa wood were locked, but this wasn't the first locked door she had encountered in her life. Rosana took out a simple lock pick like the one she had used in the infirmary and popped the lock within seconds. Before opening the door, Sana did a quick probe of the door handle and didn't find any variances in its pattern, suggesting that it was free of magical traps.

The simplicity of the lock angered the Sicarius Headmaster. If you had something worth protecting, why trust a simple lock? She thought back to the door that hid the entrance to the Sicarius Guild. It appeared to be a normal door, but if someone used the doorknob, they were in for a nasty surprise. The true door opened from the hinged side. When the hinge was pulled up, it slid into the doorframe and opened. Now that was a locked door… this thing was… an insult. Didn't they know who she was? Rosana opened the door with disgust.

A large bed dominated Magnus' room, which was

a necessity for a man his size. Expensive furnishings speckled every corner of the room, but Rose knew her mother wouldn't approve of the decorations. She had been told on numerous occasions that "Money can't buy taste," when visiting influential members of Ravinai in her childhood. Off to one side of the room was a private office area. Rosana headed there while Sana kept track of the time. *I have four minutes.*

The first things she noticed were various awards bestowed upon General Pudriuz by King Darik through official channels. Unofficially, Lattimer had bestowed the awards upon Magnus, but few in Malethya would know the distinction. The one that caught Rosana's eye was a plaque that hung on the most prominent section of the wall. It was simple compared to the rest of the awards, so why would it have such prominence? The plaque stated:

I, King Darik, honor Magnus Pudriuz and elevate him to the position of general. In this capacity, it shall fall to Magnus and the other generals to protect the blood of Malethya. Your selfless offering makes you stand alone among the armies of redemption. Let the selfless command the selfish. Use your power for the good of Malethya. Protect the blood. Protect the kingdom.

While interesting in its choice of words, the award wasn't what Rosana wanted. The description used the words redemption, blood, and selfless offering. They were obvious ties to Lattimer's self-proclaimed title of the Great Redeemer, his use of blood magic, and Magnus' voluntary subjugation to Lattimer's rule. It also explained Magnus' ability to control Furies. Lattimer had created a magical artifact that granted Magnus the ability to command his subjugated troops. Sana rationalized that Phoenix was also one of Lattimer's generals, given his ability to command Furies. The information was helpful, just not to Rosana. How would she find out more information about Slate? Outside, the distant fireballs erupted in the forest, slowly approaching Minot. *Three minutes left.*

The Sicarius Headmaster tossed the room, searching for anything on how Lattimer actually subjugated his Furies. Frustrated, she threw open the doors to find Cirata's room. *Two minutes left.*

Cirata apparently considered herself something of an artist, but her taste in subjects was egregious. Cirata had taken to painting the object of her affection, Magnus, in all of his historical victories. In one painting, he stood victorious following a tournament match. In another, he stood with dead Sicarius Guardsmen at his feet. Some images were less historical and presumably inaccurate. One depicted a naked Magnus in various acts of Cirata's fantasies. This one was definitely embellished. Of more interest were the ones depicting battles yet to come, the most important one showing Magnus decapitating Slate while Cirata plunged her short sword into the body of the Sicarius Headmaster. The thing that interested Rosana most, however, was the setting of this painting. It was painted in great detail, but of a room Rosana had never seen before. It contained row after row of blood, neatly contained within sealed vials or jars.

She recalled the words she saw on the plaque in Magnus' quarters. *Protect the blood.* She had assumed the words referenced Lattimer, the blood mage. Maybe they were more literal? Lattimer used blood to subjugate the minds of the unwilling. What did he do with it after taking over his subjugate's minds? Did he need to keep the blood to maintain control of their minds? If he did, he would need somewhere to store it and he would use his most trusted allies to protect it. Sana ventured a guess that if the room Cirata painted was real, then destroying it would significantly reduce Lattimer's power. The Sicarius Headmaster just wished they had started the mission sooner. *In one night, I have uncovered more information about Lattimer and Slate than in the previous months of passivity combined.* Rose defended the perceived inactivity of Rosana and Sana to the headmaster, but it was hard to argue with the effectiveness the headmaster displayed today. Rosana rolled up the painting and took it with her.

Outside, Rosana heard the banging of metal on metal between the roar of fireballs coming closer to camp. Any guards remaining in camp would be alerted by the fireballs approaching anyway, so Annarelle had signaled Josef to begin his portion of the mission. Sana could envision the prisoners running around in groups of three, banging their shovels and pickaxes together while yelling loudly.

In her last minute, Rosana left a present in the form of a Sicarius Headmaster letter to Cirata with the intention of spreading misinformation and doubt amongst her enemies. She used the naked Magnus painting as a canvas for her correspondence. She scrawled hastily:

Dear Cirata,

I see you are off fighting vines in the woods. I'm glad you were able to find someone of your own skill level to fight against. I would offer myself up for training, but if we ever meet, you will be dead before you draw your swords.

Thank you for the pleasant stay within Minot. I had the joy of watching Magnus nearly kill himself trying to break into the vault. Do you know its purpose? I'm sure Lattimer hasn't revealed the true nature of what is inside to his lowly minions. Be careful with your progress in breaching the wall. If what is inside is more valuable than you, you will have rendered yourself useless to your master.

Tell your lover and the disfigured disgrace called Phoenix that their ineptitude is only surpassed by their predictability. My purpose for coming to Minot has been accomplished, and I will leave as easily as I arrived. You can't catch a Shadow, and you can't protect the blood.

The unmistakable sound of fireballs neared, so Rosana threw the painting on Cirata's bed where she would be sure to find it and headed for the exit. At the bottom of the stairs, a few of the guardsmen still in the Bellator complex gathered in the hallway to form a plan of defense. The Sicarius Headmaster produced a smoke orb and rolled it toward the group before they even saw her coming. They started coughing and a few brave souls rushed toward the stairwell to attack her, but the headmaster had already escaped into the central kitchen and bypassed the group during their momentary blindness. She left the building without any further excitement.

Outside, the chaos of Sana's plan was in full effect. Josef and his fellow criminals ran around in groups of two or three in seemingly mindless directions. A large group of Ispirtu wizards had climbed to the roof of the Ispirtu complex to give themselves a clear line of fire to anyone approaching, but they didn't fire on Josef and his fellow criminals. Sana had gambled that the "dogs" of camp were considered useful if not respected by the wizards and guardsmen. A master took care of his hunting dog because it helped put food on his family's table. No one in Minot wanted to take the place of the criminals in the barren wasteland, digging for artifacts they may never find, so they didn't kill them when they began running around aimlessly. They knew that one command from Magnus would make them the useful, obedient diggers that they relied upon.

Whoosh! A large fireball cleared away a section of trees heading into the Minot camp, exposing their pursuers. The armor of the Bellator Furies glistened from the blue hot heat of wizard's fire, distracting Sana from the red eyes that normally drew her attention. Magnus stood at the front of the group, with his battle-axe searching for a target. Cirata cut through a vine that had tangled around the arm of a Bellator Fury and found its way down the dying man's throat. Sana hadn't anticipated that consequence of her spell.

Hedok cursed at the sight of Josef and his friends. "Who let the dogs out of their cage?"

"I believe Rosana Regallo has paid a visit to your camp," Phoenix snarled. "She has probably been here for some time without your knowing it. Lattimer will hear a full report of this incident, beginning with your failure, Magnus." Magnus raised his battle-axe in response, but something kept the man from decapitating him. Phoenix laughed. "You've already spoken your bonds to Lattimer. Only a stronger bond can supersede your oath to protect the blood. Only a direct command from the Redeemer would let you hurt another general in his army. Your axe does not threaten me."

Magnus roared in frustration but lowered his axe. "This isn't over yet. Surround the town. We can kennel the dogs later. If Rosana is here, we will find her." The Ispirtu wizards and Bellator Furies sprinted around the tree line, but the Sicarius Headmaster had already been moving during their discourse, shifting between groups of criminals and making her way to the woods. She slipped into the relative safety of the trees and made her way to the extraction point, looking for Annarelle and Ibson.

Instead, the headmaster found only their supplies hidden in a hollowed stump at the extraction point. Where were Annarelle and Ibson? They had obviously left the Bellator complex if Josef and his men were signaled. Rose panicked. *Have I placed Annarelle in danger? Have I compromised the safety of my friend?* Had the Sicarius Headmaster rushed her training?

The Sicarius Headmaster sprinted toward Minot, stopping just short of exposure in the clearing to scan the town. The Bellator Furies slowly formed a perimeter around the town and were about halfway finished with sealing entry or exit from the town. Cirata, Magnus, Hedok, and Phoenix searched the town's buildings under the protection of Ispirtu wizards, starting with the prisoner's barracks. Wherever Annarelle and Ibson were, they would be found soon enough. Sana tried to decide what she would do in Annarelle's situation. The chaos created by the prisoners made sprinting a viable option, but Ibson's age ruled out the likelihood of that choice. No, if they hadn't made it to the forest by now, they were likely pinned down for some reason. Had Josef's men started their portion of the plan too early? If they had, Ibson would have difficulty blending into the crowd due to his age and lack of Sicarius training. They would be easy targets for the alerted Ispirtu wizards and would need to find a different escape route. If they were pinned down at the Bellator complex, they would take the most readily available disguise and wait until the timing was right…

There! Two figures dressed in armor ran from the Bellator complex. At first glance, they appeared to be fulfilling Magnus' orders to secure the town, but a closer examination revealed the imposters. They had only fitted the most visible portions of Bellator armor and taken whatever size was available at the training grounds. Most guardsmen were considerably larger than Annarelle or Ibson and no respectable guardsman would wear such poorly sized armor into battle.

The Sicarius Headmaster readied a throwing knife as she searched for any guardsmen alerted to Annarelle and Ibson's flight to safety. Sana prepared a spell with the pattern of a diving falcon to make the knife fly straight, holding the spell at the ready. The Bellator Furies had nearly closed off the perimeter, but Annarelle and Ibson were close to the tree line now… just a few more seconds.

A glow from the top of the Ispirtu complex caught the attention of the Sicarius Headmaster. A wizard with a look of concentration on her face stared intently at the two figures escaping town dressed in oversized armor. She formed a blue fireball in her hands.

No! Terror filled Rose.

The Sicarius Headmaster threw the knife and Sana released her spell, sending it straight toward the Ispirtu wizard.

Please, fly faster! Rose silently urged the knife toward its victim, but watched in horror as the wizard atop the Ispirtu complex unleashed a massive blue fireball a moment before the knife embedded in her chest. She crumpled to the ground, but the fireball flew forward, straight for Ibson and Annarelle.

The Sicarius Headmaster ran through the list of names she held in her head. Usually she reminded herself of her own mortality by recalling the fallen Sicarius Headmasters, but on this occasion she used a different list. This list had all the names of the Sicarius Guild, the people under her supervision who had died while she watched King Darik order their execution. Annarelle would be one more name on the list, one more person she had failed to protect.

Rose was paralyzed with the fear of seeing someone else close to her die. She relived in excruciating detail the moment when Slate knocked the scepter from Brannon's hand and she'd been forced to watch Lattimer engulf her father in flames. Now Annarelle, her closest friend, would meet the same fate. Regret and failure flickered between Rose and the Sicarius Headmaster in increasing doses as the fireball raced toward Annarelle and Ibson. They would be burned to the ground where they stood…

…except they weren't.

The fireball dispersed a few feet from Ibson and Annarelle, and they escaped into the woods. Rose ran through the woods to meet them at full speed. Her relief overcame all of her Sicarius training, and she almost tackled Annarelle in an outpouring of relief. What had happened?

"The wormroot wore off and Ibson shielded all of us with a counterspell to wizard's fire," Annarelle answered Rose's unspoken question.

Rose grabbed both sides of Ibson's face and kissed him with the gratitude and innocence of a young girl. "Thank you, Ibson. You asked what you could do to earn my trust. Well, you have earned it!" Although Rose was speaking, her gratitude was complete. Ibson hadn't just saved Annarelle. He had saved the Sicarius Headmaster's successor, Rosana's friend, and Sana's apprentice.

The old wizard beamed and his cheeks flushed. Rosana wasn't sure if he sought the headmaster's praise or was simply bashful about the kiss. His cheeks quickly recovered and he said, "That fireball will have created quite the stir. We should keep moving." Shortly after, a series of fireballs razed the tree line where Annarelle and Ibson had escaped, but they were safely in the deeper sections of forest. Heavy footsteps of Bellator Guardsmen followed. Sana imagined unbridled anger on the face of Magnus as his foe escaped his grasp and the slow burning, thoughtful evil of Phoenix analyzing the scene and plotting his next move.

Annarelle provided the strategy, "The thickest woods are to the east. We should head in that direction and force them to follow us on foot. We no longer have a horse to speed our travels, so we'll have to make it difficult on our pursuers." Sana nodded in approval.

"Let's discuss as we travel. Distance is the most important factor right now. Phoenix tracked us from Ravinai. We have to assume he will be capable of following us from Minot. Josef's men ran in every direction, so tracking us will be difficult and I can compound the difficulty by attaching moss to our feet to hide our trail. We need to capitalize on that advantage."

"But where are we going? Minot was our only lead." Annarelle asked as they retrieved their supplies for the journey ahead.

The Sicarius Headmaster smiled. This wasn't the friendly smile of Rosana, Sana, or the innocent smile of Rose, and it had an unsettling effect on anyone that saw it. This was the smile of a trained assassin who finally knew where to aim her knives.

"There is a room full of blood that we need to destroy. Nothing will stop me from finding it and completing this mission, even if that room is protected by Magnus and Phoenix. This mission requires a particular skill set, and there is only one person with the skills we'll need. We are going to find Slate Severance."

REFLECTIONS

The black, mottled spots on her skin were the price Rosana paid to learn the secrets of that bloodied room and get one step closer to killing Lattimer. She was succeeding, but the cursed blight within her veins reminded her always of the cost, and sometimes she questioned her own actions. In this moment, when she shared a meal with Slate, and he surprised herselves with thoughtful gifts, she longed for more time. She longed for a cure. She longed for a life like the lives of the Malethyans she tried to protect.

Sana looked up from her forsaken hand to see that Slate had moved from the table to an open window. The salty sea air wafted the curtains back and forth in the same pattern that billowed his shirt and messed his hair. It was a simple, powerful pattern that mimicked the motion of the waves, and the waves owned the coast. Slate stared out the window in contemplation, but he must have felt her eyes on his back.

"Did we do the right thing?"

Rose answered gently. "We've been over this many times. I did what I had to do and I would do it again. It was the right thing to do."

"I wasn't referring to your actions, my love." Slate still looked out the window. "I have come to grips with your decision and who you are. You gave Malethyans their minds—and their lives—back. There aren't many people that could have done it, especially knowing the cost. If anyone ever finds out the sacrifice you have made for Malethya, they will sing your name in songs for generations."

Silence passed for a few seconds because they both knew what he feared. Rosana had the same fear, and it corrupted her soul as quickly as the blight did her hand.

Slate finally voiced his concern. "Have we doomed all of Malethya?" Rosana stood and joined Slate at the window.

Disenite ships, with their towering sails, sat in the harbor of Portswain just beyond the city's defenses. They had come back, and their presence in the harbor grew more ominous the longer they sat idle. Without firing a single shot, the proud sails of the Disenite ships weighed upon all of Malethya like a black cloud. Rosana could see the black cloud settle upon Slate.

"There is still reason to hope."

Sana had seen Slate slide into darkness before, and she had succeeded in pulling him out of it. She'd tracked him through towns littered with dead guardsmen and Ispirtu Furies. He had been hunched over the bar in a tavern, staring into his cup the way he currently stared at the sails of the Disenite ships…

CHAPTER TEN

On The Trail

The stench of death littered the town. The townspeople removed the guardsmen's armor and piled the bodies, but decay set in faster than they could work. Trails of blood stained the streets as a fatal reminder of the power of Slate Severance.

"Can you tell me what happened?" Rose asked the innkeeper gently. Rose sat at a table in the back corner of the man's establishment. They had been tracking Slate using the stratego medallions when they came across the massacre in this town. As urgently as Sana wanted to continue to keep their distance from Phoenix, the Sicarius Headmaster couldn't resist the opportunity to gather more information.

The innkeeper started his story warily. Rosana could see that he was confused about the events he'd witnessed and uncertain of whom he was talking to. Rose wore simple traveling robes, but she spoke with command as well as innocence to coax the man into discussion. "The women of town quietly whispered that Slate Severance was in the area. I took my son out into the street to practice some forms in case the rumors were true. I don't know very many, but my father was in the King's Army during the Twice-Broken Wars, and he taught me the basics." A serving girl came to their table to pour glasses of water.

"How did the women of town know that Slate was in the area?" The serving girl giggled and almost spilled the pitcher. "Perhaps you could answer for him?" Rose asked the girl.

The girl's cheeks flushed, and she looked to the innkeeper, who seemed relieved to have avoided the question. Stuck, she said, "From what I hear, Slate Severance isn't just the most wanted criminal in the kingdom, he's also the most wanted man. Women in Malethya like a man who can take care of himself. A man that can defy a king and live… that is straight out of a fairy tale."

"I see." Rose flushed. Rosana seethed. Sana and the headmaster turned the topic of conversation away from Slate's bedroom exploits and back to the innkeeper's tale. "What happened while you trained your son?"

Back on comfortable ground, the innkeeper continued. "I heard a rumble in the distance and looked up to see approaching horses bearing the Lion of Darik. The King's army doesn't have reason to visit villages like ours, so I was confused by the sight. I was still trying to make sense of it all when someone jumped from the second-story window of my inn. There he was, the most notorious man in Malethya—Slate Severance. He looked as pale as a ghost and as deadly as the stories. I could barely believe he was hiding in the tiny town of Landon and staying in my inn. I'm already contemplating changing the name. What do you think of the Clean Slate? It would speak to our most famous patron and the fresh linen." The man laughed at his own cleverness.

"I think it is a fine name. Did he say anything to you?" Rose asked.

"He told me to leave, and that it would all be over soon. My son and I ran to our home and watched from the windows, ready to run for the hills if he came for us. Then do you know what he did?" The innkeeper spoke incredulously as the serving girl stood nearby with doe-like eyes. Rosana wanted to slap her. "He stood alone in the middle of the street without armor and only a staff for a weapon, and called out to the approaching troops. He mocked them. He stood alone against the largest group of soldiers I have ever seen, and he laughed in their face." The innkeeper looked like he wanted to smile at the memory, but his fear from the encounter was still too fresh. "The soldiers rode straight for him as wizards shot fire and turned up the earth and Slate just darted through them all in a dance of death. He moved faster than any human, and I could barely keep my eyes on him as he carved his way through those soldiers. He disposed of the first few wizards so quickly that the remaining ones blew themselves up before he could reach them. Then he turned on the remaining soldiers, and I saw him crush the armor of a man's helm with his fist. One soldier got a lucky blow into Slate's shoulder, and by fractal's fortune, he didn't even bleed. All the stories are true. He must be a demon or something. He killed them all and left us to pile the bodies in the blood-stained streets."

"Didn't he talk with you afterward?" Rose asked. The serving girl returned to the bar now that the exciting portion had been told.

"No. What could he say? He is a monster. He just killed King Darik's men. Many of our sons and daughters left Landon to join the army and protect the citizens of Malethya. It could have been our son's or daughter's bodies out there."

Rosana sighed and took over the conversation from Rose. She understood how difficult it would be for Slate to change his reputation, but he hadn't even tried to tell these villagers the truth. Rosana would try to convince them of the truth even if they didn't believe it. "Slate saved all of your lives." The innkeeper laughed, but Rosana pressed on. "The soldiers that came here were sent to kill Slate by King Darik, but they would have killed everyone here and burned the buildings to the ground if they'd succeeded. They no longer serve Malethya. The soldiers—and Darik as well—are under the control of a blood mage named Lattimer Regallo. Slate has unique abilities, as you witnessed, and he is the only person to ever resist Lattimer's power."

"What are these stories? I have offered you and your friends the warmth of my inn and you repay me with fantastical tales. Quiet your fractal-forsaken tongue." The normally jovial innkeeper turned serious.

"Did Slate hurt any of the villagers while he stayed in Landon? No. He only killed those that intended to kill him. I can tell you how Slate got the scars across his torso. I can tell you that Lattimer watched as Slate was whipped within an inch of his life, but I know these things won't convince you." Rosana saw the man's resistance to the truth in his eyes, but if she couldn't convince a single man of the truth, then she would never convince all of Malethya.

"Have you noticed any black specks on the plants in this area? Those specks are called the blight. They were unleashed by blood magic and they will slowly get worse and choke the life from the world around us." Though Sana had accidently caused the phenomenon, Rosana wasn't above using it as an agent of persuasion to

help the man see the greater truth. The
resistance in the man's eyes softened just a
bit. As an innkeeper, he would have heard the
stories of farmers for miles around. Someone
was sure to have mentioned the blight to him.
"I can see you have an open mind, even if my
words are difficult to believe. I will only
attempt to gain your trust with one more
argument. My friends are outside by the pile of
rotting bodies and their actions may sway your
belief." The innkeeper held her gaze and then
slowly nodded, giving her the benefit of the
doubt. He got up from the table to go outside
while Rosana collected her things.

On the way out of the tavern, the serving
girl said, "Did you enjoy the innkeeper's tale?
If you want to hear my version, I can confirm
some of those other rumors we talked about."
She winked at Rosana, whose anger was mollified
by the actions of her other selves. The
Sicarius Headmaster jumped the bar, grabbed two
knives, and stabbed them through the sleeves of
the woman's dress, pinning her arms to the wood
counter. The serving girl squealed in terror.

Rose, in defense of Rosana, spoke in the
alternating voice of the Sicarius Headmaster.
"You like spreading rumors and tales of
dangerous people? I will give you one more
tale. I am the Sicarius Headmaster and Slate
Severance is mine." Sana said, "When you wake
up, you will let every woman in this fractal-
forsaken kingdom know that if Slate comes to
town, there will be no late night visits to his
room." The Sicarius Headmaster grabbed the
trembling chin of the serving girl and
whispered in her ear. "There is only one
difficulty when dealing with dangerous people
like Slate. They have dangerous friends. If I

hear of you or anyone else so much as flirting with him again, I will come back here and kill you myself." She pulled out her shockstick and touched it to the neck of the serving girl. Sana sent some spark through her body, and the girl crumpled against the bar. Rose knew that Sana wouldn't cause any lasting damage with her spell, but she didn't necessarily agree with the tactic. The whole series of events with the serving girl troubled her innocent mind.

Rosana wrote a note to the serving girl to appease Rose and let out her bitterness.

Dear Wench,

I do not know your name and I doubt that Slate did either. If you ever hope to be remembered in this world, do something worth remembering.

I apologize for any physical or lasting pain you endure from our encounter. It was not my intent to hurt you. I simply wanted you to know the seriousness of my request and the resolve of my threats. I expect you to carry out my wishes and spread the word to women considering Slate. I also urge you to examine yourself and the choices you have made. Those are the choices that have resulted in your being pinned and unconscious, hanging from the bar. Make smart choices. Don't be a wench.

Rosana folded the note and shoved it in the girl's mouth with a distinct lack of tact. She left the bar with her mind racing. *What am I going to do about Slate? I haven't even tracked the guy down yet, and my thoughts of him already tie my insides in knots and I've pinned a wench against a bar.* Rose had become fairly practiced at managing her various personalities, and it was rare to have such an emotional and conflicting reaction from herselves. Slate's actions contributed to her father's death, but he hadn't known Brannon was her father at the time. Slate had hurt her deeply with his mistrust, but she hadn't trusted him with her identity in turn. Most disturbingly, Slate had left her, but he had done it to protect her from himself. The whole thing unsettled her deeply.

While trying to pull her mind from the abyss that was Slate Severance, Rosana looked around the town. The once-flat streets of Landon had been turned into a series of hills and holes by the wizard's blasts in their battle with Slate, but the tallest hill in Landon wasn't made from dirt. Flies buzzed over the pile of bodies and carrion circled above, drawn by the stench that repulsed the senses of every other living thing. At the base of the pile she saw Annarelle and Ibson speaking with the innkeeper. She walked over and heard Ibson talking with the man as if they were old friends.

"Silar once told me that unless I could fix the axle of his broken cart, then having a wizard around was about as useful as a wife who refused to cook." Ibson chuckled, "His wife boxed him upside the head faster than he could turn to judge her reaction to his joke."

"That sounds like my father. He was a good man with a sense of humor that could get him killed. He always spoke highly of you…"

"That's because I fixed his axle." This time the innkeeper chuckled.

"You knew this man's father?" Sana asked. She knew Ibson was old, but the innkeeper wasn't a young pup either. How old was the wizard?

"In my younger days, I traveled more frequently. My previous deeds still hold weight in many towns in Malethya. Shall we get back to the problem at hand? I won't get this smell out of my clothes for a week."

In all the recent events, Sana reminded herself of Ibson's celebrity status among wizards. It was easy to forget when your thoughts were occupied with Lattimer, blood magic, and rooms full of blood that held hostage the minds of countless people. "Yes, can you teach Annarelle the pattern for smokeless fire?"

Ibson quickly slid into the comfortable role of teacher. "I will let her discover it on her own with a question. When fire burns, energy is transferred from the material of the object to the fire in the form of heat and light. Smoke is created when some of the heat carries particulate matter into the air with it. How would you create smokeless fire?"

Annarelle contemplated the question for a minute, and then answered the impromptu quiz. "You would need to burn the object completely so that no particulate was left to form smoke. Or we could suppress the particulate from rising in the heat of the flames."

"Excellent! You have a student with a sharp mind," he said to Sana. "In practicality, we can do both. Wizard fire burns hotter than a campfire, so we can use it to our advantage here. We also use the pattern of a fishing net wrapped around the fire, catching the particulate as a net catches fish. Try it."

Annarelle tried to form the net described by Ibson, but she was weak in the spark and couldn't create a net large enough to encompass the pile. "I do not know the pattern well enough to compensate for my lack of spark. I will have to practice on campfires first." In Ispirtu, Annarelle had been ridiculed for her weak spark, but Lucus had taught Sana and now Sana had taught Annarelle that you didn't need to have the spark of Brannon to be a great wizard, so long as you were a student of the patterns around you.

Ibson smiled at her. "The best wizards know their own limitations. I'll do the honors." He cast the net over the pile of bodies and sent a small amount of wizard fire into the base of the bodies. They caught fire, and it spread quickly. The fire grew to immense proportions. Ibson said, "This fire will burn the remainder of the day and through the night and no remains will be left behind. Then you can focus on rebuilding your town."

"Fractal's blessing to you, Ibson." The innkeeper said before turning to Rosana. "I assume this display of magic is intended to awe my simple mind so that I believe your story?"

"That would have been convenient, but no, that was not my intent. I wanted to demonstrate to you and the rest of the town that our intentions are true. We want to help you. We want to help all of Malethya. I wanted to demonstrate this before you discovered who I am." Rosana alternated her voice. "I am Rosana Regallo, but you probably know me as the Sicarius Headmaster."

The innkeeper jumped back at the sudden

transition in speech. "What trickery is this?"

"This is the necessary type of trickery, the type done with the best of intentions. I am the Sicarius Headmaster and I travel with Annarelle, a Sicarius Guardsman, and Ibson, the famed wizard. We search for Slate Severance, and we all wish to defeat Lattimer, the blood mage who rules our kingdom. We will expose him, and when we do, we will need the people of Malethya to recognize us for who we are… people trying to protect you. I'll ask you to keep an eye out for a man that enters this town shortly after we leave. He is an abomination who tracks us with the sole intention of killing us. If you see him, do not interact with him. Don't let anyone in town interact with him, or they will die. Please believe me before your town has another pile of bodies in its street."

The innkeeper hesitated, but the resistance in his eyes was gone. He heard the words that she said, but would need time to process the information. Rosana pulled out a stratego medallion. "This should be proof of my identity, as it bears the seal of Sicarius, but your serving girl can help you believe me as well. If you see the stranger following us, I will ask you to bring this medallion to the blacksmith in town and strike it through. When it breaks, I will know that Phoenix has reached Landon, and I will need to move to stay ahead of him. More importantly, I'll know that the people of Malethya have come to know the truth."

Her argument was just moving enough to convince the innkeeper. "I'll keep the medallion and look for this man. If he is the abomination you speak of, I will break the medallion as you request. Also, I can tell you where Slate went after he left town. He walked toward the town of Emry."

Rose hugged the innkeeper, which he accepted with reluctance after learning that she was the Sicarius Headmaster. "Fractal's blessing to you, innkeeper. I thank you for your help." Rose turned to leave the man with his thoughts.

As Ibson, Annarelle, and Rose left the town, she could hear the innkeeper mumbling, "Slate Severance, the Sicarius Headmaster, and Ibson? I'm going to have to think of a new name for my tavern. The Clean Slate just won't do…"

CHAPTER ELEVEN

OUT OF DARKNESS

They entered Emry as the sun set. The smell of fertilizer and sweat permeated the air, and songs drifted from the tavern. Sana didn't need the Stratego medallion to know that Slate was still here. If he had been found by Lattimer, the scent of another pile of bodies would have stopped any singing. Where would she find Malethya's most notorious criminal?

Sana scanned the town, analyzing potential hiding places. A stable behind a town building would be an obvious choice, but Slate hated horses. He didn't like to ride them, and she couldn't imagine him sleeping next to the gentle animals either. The rooftops were a favorite in Ravinai, but out here, the simple buildings didn't provide adequate cover. There wasn't really anywhere to escape notice in the village because it was built for the plain purpose of labor. Then the words of the serving girl came into Sana's mind, and she listened more carefully to the music being played in the tavern.

Stone doesn't bend, Stone doesn't break.
Darik will never tame the infamous Slate.
In Darik's land we dance,
But tonight we toast Slate Severance.

Sana had imagined Slate living in exile on the outskirts of the kingdom, sneaking from town to town and stealing food as he needed.

She tried to push down her preconceived notions of his exile. Apparently, it wasn't the meager existence she had believed.

Rosana didn't give Ibson or Annarelle the option of entering the tavern with her. "Slate's in the tavern. Join us for breakfast. I have some things I need to discuss with him in private."

"We'll be in the stable if you need us." Annarelle gave Rosana a hug and whispered, "If you end up neutering him, I won't blame you a bit." Ibson wanted no part of the conversation and wandered toward the stable.

The Sicarius Headmaster flashed a knife and gave a smirk before Rose confessed to her friend, "I don't know what to do. Every time I think of Slate, I'm pulled in a million directions. One moment, I want to grab the man by the shirt and kiss him, and the next moment I want to grab him by the shirt and slip a knife in his stomach."

Annarelle gently wrapped her hand around the hilt of the knife and lowered it. "You have every right to be angry with him, but Slate has a good heart. He saved me from Ispirtu, and I don't think he would intentionally hurt you. Hear him out before you decide. And if you do find out he was being a complete idiot, just remember, we need him to kill Lattimer." Annarelle looked into her eyes with compassion that rivaled Rose's, but then her eyes hardened again. "He should be able to do that without his balls."

Rosana laughed at the Sicarius humor of her friend. "I'll meet you and Ibson in the tavern for breakfast after I sort things out with Slate. If he shows up limping, you'll know the result." Annarelle left her, and Rosana looked

through the tavern window to the bright
interior.

Inside, the band played merrily while one of
the serving girls crafted a song on the spot.
People danced and spilled beer near the band
while the quieter patrons sat at the bar. In
this quieter section sat a hooded figure
hunched over his mug of ale, staring into its
depths in what looked like a search for an
answer to which he'd forgotten the question.
*This is the supposed savior of Malethya? Slate
doesn't look like he has the ambition to climb
the stairs to his room tonight, much less fight
a blood mage.* Despite the dejected figure
before her, Rosana's heart fluttered after
months of separation.

A curvaceous girl tried to get Slate's
attention by blatantly rubbing against him as
she passed by. Slate didn't even lift his eyes
from his cup before gently pushing her away.
His response to her advancements did little to
reduce Rosana's anger toward Slate. For some
reason, the serving girl bore the brunt of her
angst.

Stupid girl. Rosana knew that drawing a man's
attention was infinitely more effective than
trying to make someone notice. The two things
were entirely different and the former didn't
require exposed skin or well-placed curves.
That girl probably put on a year's supply of
makeup in the hopes that her rosy cheeks would
look different than the rosy cheeks of every
other girl. In reality, it made her look
inconsequential. Rosana decided she would give
the girl a lesson in drawing attention. She
would make every man in the bar drool over her
by simply shaking the dust from her clothes. If
Slate was still interested in her, he could

fight for her.

Rosana walked into the bar and stomped her boots to clear the accumulated mud from the soles. It drew the attention of every patron in the tavern. She ignored them all, including Slate, as she pulled back her hood and let her hair fall down past her shoulders. She ran her fingers through her hair under the pretense of shaking the dust from her travels and, with a slight head tilt, made every man imagine her washing her hair. She let their imaginations go from there. Convincing a man from a small village to think of an attractive girl naked was easier than losing a trade with a tribesman. *Where was Rainier anyway?* She scanned the leering eyes with disinterest, giving the men more time to let their fantasies take hold. Then she found and approached the innkeeper. "Do you have any rooms left?"

"I'm sorry, my lady, but we are all full. Do you care to sit in the tavern for a while? I can talk to a few of the travelers and try to convince them to share a room for a reduced rate so that I can accommodate you."

"There's no need. I'll find someone to share a room with and negotiate my own rate." She turned to the crowded room, which was still watching her with interest. "I need a room and a drink. Is there a man in here who could help me find either of those?"

A couple eager patrons hurried to the bar, but Rosana found what she was looking for in a back table filled with tough-looking men. They looked serious about their dice and more serious about their drinking. She pointed to the table. "One of you will do. Someone get me a chair and pour me a pint."

One of the men grunted in surprise, but

pulled out a chair for her based on curiosity alone. She sat facing Slate, but still ignoring the bastard who'd stolen her heart and left her emotions in a tangled mess. *What is my plan, exactly?* She wasn't sure, but she knew she wasn't going to pine for his interest like the girl she saw in the tavern window. She took a big swig from her glass and asked, "What are we playing?"

"First things first, do you have coin?" The largest man asked with skepticism.

Rosana unceremoniously dropped her heavy coin purse on the table, easily exceeding the wealth of anyone else. "Like I said, what are we playing?"

A low whistle came from one end of the table. "These stakes just got too rich for my blood. I don't care what game we play. Count me out, Brick. I'm getting a drink at the bar."

Brick, a large man who obviously led the group based on the size of the coin pile in front of him, smiled mischievously and said, "We play Broken Fractal and if you want in, you won't be leaving until that bag is emptied." Considering that one man had just left the game, it seemed Brick wanted to play by a new set of rules.

"I hope you aren't too attached to your coin. Let's play. Tell me the house rules." Broken Fractal was a common dice game in Malethya, but the rules varied widely. Generally, the objective was to chain together a recurring pattern amongst your dice. With six dice, a player would want to roll three fours and three ones, for example, giving them a pattern of 3-1-3-1-3-1 that could be looped and repeated. The roller had to lock into the pattern at least one die per roll and couldn't re-roll a die once it had been locked in. If the roller ending up needing to lock in a die that didn't fit the pattern, it was termed a Broken Fractal and the player's turn was forfeited.

"High roll finishes the pattern. Triples beat doubles. Hijacked patterns beat triples. Role until the pattern is broken. You pay the winner the difference." Brick passed her a set of dice before adding, "and we drink with each role… it keeps us honest."

Most of those rules were common variations. The person with the best starting roll got to go last so that they knew which score they needed to beat. Triples, like 2-8-3-2-8-3, were considered a higher point value than any doubles rolled, and hijacked patterns occurred when one player continued the pattern of the previous player. The drinking part was a new wrinkle. Apparently these men took their drinking as seriously as their dice.

"May your fractals be blessed and not broken. May they always rise to the occasion." Rose cringed at the crass reference, but the salutation drew laughs from the men as they raised glasses and drank. Slate undoubtedly heard the laughter and decided to come over. Sana expected him earlier.

"Sana—it's good to see you." Rosana ignored him, rolled her dice, and took her obligatory drink. 4-3-6-6-1-3. With a pattern of 6-3-6-3, Rosana had the second highest roll. Slate tried again. "What are you doing here?"

While she waited for her turn, she finally addressed Slate. "I'm drinking, playing dice, and looking for a room to stay in. If you take away the dice game, I have the same number of accomplishments as you do since leaving Ravinai. Am I wrong?"

Slate's face furrowed in frustration. *This obviously isn't the reaction he's hoping to get. Good.* "Yes, you are wrong. I've learned how to fight Furies. Lattimer sends his men for me, but I've figured out how to combat them."

Sana contradicted him and Rosana's affection couldn't keep cruel sarcasm from lacing her words, "You have wasted time and nothing more. Whatever tricks you've learned are miniscule compared to the power Lattimer has gained. Do you remember our friend Magnus—big guy, killed your parents? He can now command Furies, and he is training an elite group of Bellator Furies to attack without the blind rage you are used to seeing in these villages. While you fight without purpose, you are letting Lattimer win. You are failing the people of Malethya." She turned back to her dice game while Slate contemplated her harsh words.

Sana watched her opponents at the table. They played the odds fairly well, but the beer they had already drunk affected their judgment.

"I didn't know…"

The serving girl brought a new round of beers. "Maybe that's because you were too busy sleeping with every serving girl between here and Ravinai." She turned to the serving girl. "How were you planning on getting in his bed? You've already undone enough buttons on your blouse to make the town whore blush." The serving girl quickly averted her eyes and dashed away to find a safer table.

The men at the table offered a round of catcalls at her expense. "Don't listen to her, baby. You can undo as many buttons as you want!" Laughter filled the tavern.

Slate looked despondent. Rosana had anticipated defiance or anger, but not the sad red eyes she saw looking back at her. "After the attack on Brannon, I didn't think you would forgive me. My actions resulted in your father's death. The pain I saw in your eyes when I awoke in the catalpa grove will stay with me forever…"

Rose had been the one to grieve the loss of her father, while Rosana and her other selves simply blamed Lattimer. She had since come to grips with the events leading up to her father's death and no longer blamed Slate. "It's my turn to roll." She kept the sixes and threes from her original turn and followed it up with a long drink. This wasn't going the way she thought. Slate was the bastard who slept around. Rosana deserved to be angry with him.

She looked down at her two dice that were still in play and luckily rolled a six, which she kept and rolled again, giving her the opportunity to have another drink.

Why do I feel partially responsible for Slate's actions? Sana rationalized that Rose's comments could have led Slate to believe that she rejected him. It would also explain the heavy drinking he had been doing. Rose apologized to Rosana for causing her to be in such conflict, but Rosana's heart was still torn. In that moment, she determined what she needed to do about Slate. All the confusion she saw on his face, all the confusion she felt in her heart, could have been avoided. Her identities were her most personal, deepest secret. She needed to tell Slate, and it scared her more than any Sicarius mission she had ever conducted. She took another drink.

Her final die stopped rolling and landed on three. Curses arose from the table. "Of all the fractal-forsaken luck!" Her rolls took the lead and the last turn belonged to Brick.

Brick's initial roll was a 6-2-6-2-2-1, leaving him with the option to go for a 6-2-1 triple but only a single roll to win. Instead, he kept the sixes and rolled the remaining four dice, resulting in two fives. With a 6-5-6-5 combination, he was now in position to win with just another six and five. He rolled again and took a drink, but he casually reached inside his pocket with his free hand while drinking. Rosana detected his backroom bullshit as obviously as if he'd announced to the table, "I have a loaded die in my pocket." Brick got the five he was looking for, so he needed a six on his final roll.

The crowd at the table pounded their glasses in anticipation. "Get her, Brick! Show her how we do it in Emry!"

Brick smiled and blew on his die. "Thanks, boys, I'll need some luck on this one. If it's a six, I'll pick up the bar tab tonight!" He rolled the die and took a drink, surreptitiously slipping the regular die back into his pocket.

Rosana watched the die roll slightly unevenly across the table. She didn't need Sana to calculate the odds of a six coming up. They were much better than one in six. Under the table she grabbed a throwing knife.

The die landed on a six and the table erupted in cheers for Brick's victory. He accepted congratulations and reached for Sana's coin purse. She snatched it from the table before he could claim his prize, and the cheers stopped abruptly. She said, "I don't think I'll be paying you, Brick. Thanks for the game."

"You fractal-forsaken bitch! We don't take kindly to cheats in Emry." He pulled a knife, but before it cleared his pocket, the Sicarius Headmaster flicked her wrist beneath the table. Brick tried to stab Rosana in the chest, but he had no chance of reaching her. Slate moved quickly, and Slate could go from a standstill to a full sprint or, in this case a punch, with the blink of an eye. He grabbed the man's forearm with his left hand and slammed it to the table right before his right fist smashed the man's hand into a million pieces.

When Slate had fought in the tournament, Lattimer cast a spell that moved the iron in Slate's blood to his extremities to cause fatigue and rig the fight. Lattimer hadn't counted on Slate's abilities as a Perceptor to concentrate the spell into his fist and merge the iron with the bones of his hand, so that the match ended with a punch from Slate that destroyed a shield and Lattimer's jaw. With a direct blow from Slate's stonehand, the bones in Brick's hand would be pulverized to powder. Brick cried out in agony as he dropped the knife.

Rosana gave her best serving-girl smile to Slate and said, "Aww, you do care, but someday you will learn I can take care of myself." The Sicarius Headmaster pointed beneath the table, and Slate looked down to see Brick's foot pinned to the ground with a throwing knife. With his foot pinned, he didn't pose any danger to Rosana.

The other men stood up in anger, and Sana simply said "Sit down before you hurt yourselves." The seemingly idle threat took meaning as she cast her shockstick spell with an open hand. The spark it produced arced across her fingers, and the brave men wisely sat down even though their fists stayed clenched.

Rosana addressed them. "You won't be so mad when you realize that your friend Brick has a trick die. How long have you been playing with him? I bet it was his idea to initiate the drinking rule as well, because it provided him an opportunity to switch his die. Would one of you care to check his front right pocket? You'll find a normal die that he deposited there before his final roll. This die…" She picked up the final six rolled by Brick and gave it another toss. It landed on a six and she didn't need to finish her sentence. The attention of the drunks at the table shifted to Brick.

"She better not be telling us the truth, Brick. We've been playing with you at this table for years!" Brick was enduring too much pain to argue, and Slate still held the man's arm down to the table, so he couldn't prevent his pockets from being searched. Upon finding it, the man tossed it on the table, saw that it rolled true, and punched Brick in the jaw.

All the commotion and screams of pain drew the attention of the innkeeper. "Look at the mess you've made! There is blood and beer everywhere. Get him outside!"

Sana eased the man's concerns. "If Brick will allow me, I will heal his arm and his foot. Brick, do I have your permission?" Sana kept to the Wizard's Council's practice of asking permission to perform magic prior to casting a spell out of respect to Lucus.

The large man looked down to his crushed hand, which now appeared inflated and purple from the internal bleeding and nodded vigorously.

Sana cast a probing spell and searched his

hand for the tiny pieces of bone scattered throughout. With a fresh break, the pattern of his bones before Slate's punch was still dominant. Sana detected the pattern and then coaxed the bone chips back into their normal position. The bone that passed through the tissue of his hand caused enough pain that Brick almost passed out, but Sana didn't really care if he did. When the pieces were set, she used the pattern of a growing tree—taught to her by Lucus—to mend the pieces together. She left the tissue damage as a reminder of his failure. "If you are going to cheat, cheat well." Rose and the Sicarius Headmaster often conflicted over the morality of cheating, but they both agreed that if you were going to do it, you should do it well enough not to be caught.

With the bones of his hand mended, Sana unceremoniously pulled the knife from Brick's boot. Blood shot out of the wound. The Sicarius Headamster must have hit an artery. She heard a thud and looked over to find that the serving girl with an aversion to buttons had fainted at the sight. Rose momentarily felt concern for her, but Rosana reminded her that a passed-out half-naked woman would have plenty of attention and help in a room full of men. The headmaster just scowled in disbelief. This was Malethya. Even a serving girl ought to be comfortable with blood. Sana reached over and grabbed the towel the serving girl used for cleaning tables, pulled it clear of her collapsed body, and applied pressure to Brick's foot. "Brick, hold this towel." Then she repeated the probing spell and the healing process, this time focusing on closing the vessels and tissue to stop the bleeding and prevent infection. When she finished, she said, "Since you are holding the towel, clean up your mess. After you've cleaned up this nice innkeeper's floor, I'm sure your friends will want to talk to you outside. Do you understand me?"

Brick awkwardly crouched below the table in response and vigorously wiped the floor with his good hand.

Then she turned to the other members of the table. "I won't be taking the coin from the table, so whoever gives me their room for the night can have Brick's share of the coin." Finding no shortage of offers, she traded Brick's coin for a room key, and the Sicarius Headmaster addressed Slate to save Rosana from her conflicted feelings. "I don't know if you have more interest in the wench at your feet or me, but we have things to discuss. If we are going to defeat Lattimer, I need your help to accomplish this mission. There's a room full of blood that we need to find. Maybe we can bring the serving girl with us, and she can help locate it by applying her unique ability to faint whenever she nears blood." The crowd parted as she made her way toward the stairwell.

Slate followed after her closely and with deep confusion. Rosana knew her changing personas this evening left Slate thoroughly confused, but the headmaster was right. They had a mission to fulfill, and she needed to deal with that before discussing personal matters. Annarelle had reminded her off this fact prior to entering the tavern, albeit with her own unique sense of humor.

She entered her room and found it to be small but practical... practical, at least, if you didn't need anywhere to sit and only needed one bed. The bed was a distraction to Rosana, so she chose to stand.

Slate closed the door and stood before her, a darkened shell of the hero she'd fallen in love with. He started the conversation on safe grounds. "Tell me about this room full of blood."

"Lattimer requires the blood of his involuntary subjugates to control their minds, as you know well. I thought he just needed the blood to cast the spell, but that isn't the case. He needs to preserve the blood for the spell to remain active."

"You are telling me that I can be free from Lattimer's control by destroying the blood in this room?" The darkness that surrounded Slate lifted slightly.

"I don't think it will be easy, but yes, I think that is the case."

"How did you find this out?" Slate asked in disbelief.

"I'm the Sicarius Headmaster." The headmaster thought that was reason enough, but Sana provided a more thorough explanation. "I deduced that Ibson faked his mental illness to remain in the infirmary, so I kidnapped him and…"

Slate interrupted her. "Ibson is ok?" Ibson had suffered his injuries while investigating Slate's Tournament match and the appearance of his stonehand. Rose's empathetic nature had always sensed that he carried the burden of Ibson's accident with him as further evidence of his failures.

"Yes, he is here with me. I've brought Annarelle as well." A further weight lifted off Slate's shoulders upon confirmation of Ibson's health. Rosana started to see the first glimpses of the real Slate crack through his depression. "We went to Minot and discovered that Lattimer has built a large base on the ashes of the tiny town. He is running a mining operation of sorts, except he isn't digging for stone like the people of Pillar. He found a hidden library—no, a hidden city—that catalogs all the learnings from the days of Cantor and the blood mages."

"Then his power grows even more quickly than I feared. You were right to condemn me before. I should have acted sooner." The cloud over him grew a little darker and Rosana wouldn't have it. She slapped him.

"Slate Severance, you are a fractal-forsaken tournament champion and our only hope. You resisted Lattimer's attempt to subjugate your mind and continue to do it to this day. Now you are so wrapped up in your own mind with thoughts of failure that you are defeating yourself. How do you expect to save everyone in Malethya if you don't have the mental fortitude to escape your own demons?"

Slate slowly nodded. At some point everyone needs a slap in the face. "You are right…"

This time the Sicarius Headmaster cut him off. "I know I am." After wiping some of his regrets away and then shocking him back to reality, Slate needed a purpose. The headmaster had exactly the mission for him. "We need to find this room full of blood and destroy it. You will be completely free from Lattimer's control and half of his army will be freed, hopefully weakening him enough for a direct attack. There's only one problem. This room full of blood will be heavily guarded. All of Lattimer's generals have sworn to protect it. Magnus is one of them. Phoenix is another.

There may be others…"

"Phoenix?"

"A fallen Sicarius Guardsman named Phoenix now runs information networks for Lattimer and is currently tasked with tracking and killing me."

The dark cloud around Slate slowly disappeared and he began to transform before her eyes. It was a little like Rose staring into the mirror and seeing herself transform into Rosana. The man staring back at her wasn't a drunkard staring into the bottom of his cup. He wasn't a hero yet either, but the seed of purpose had been planted. The cloud would slowly disappear, and Slate would emerge again. He promised, "I won't let him. Let's see if he can withstand a blow from my fist."

Sana gently chided him without being too harsh. He was making progress after all. "Didn't you learn anything from the incident downstairs? If I wanted to kill Phoenix, he would be dead by now. He's alive because I still have a use for him." Then, with Slate officially signed up for the mission ahead, Rosana could no longer withhold her concerns any longer. She wanted answers. "Now tell me why you've been sleeping with every girl between Emry and Ravinai."

The sudden change in direction of conversation caught Slate off-guard, but he knew the subject would be broached eventually. "I thought I lost you. You asked me to trust you before we broke into Ispirtu, but you asked as the Sicarius Headmaster. I didn't see you again until you appeared at Brannon's side, except even then I didn't know if I could trust the headmaster. During the battle, I hung back and watched, trying to decide who the blood mage really was. The Ispirtu wizards turned to Furies and Brannon didn't attack them, so I figured he commanded them. I chose wrong. If I had known that you, Sana—my Sana—the girl I fell in love with, was the Sicarius Headmaster, I would have fought at your side. I wouldn't have killed your father, and I wouldn't have lost you. I'm sorry. I was lost in my regrets."

Seeing his earnest regret and lingering confusion, Rosana wanted to comfort him, but she held back. Then she took a deep breath and gathered her courage. If she wanted things to work with Slate she had to tell him the truth about herselves. She feared rejection, but she had forced Slate to live in fear of her own rejection for months.

"Do you remember when we traveled to Pillar and you smashed your hand against a branch in a foolish attempt to learn about the capabilities of your stonehand? We went for a walk that night…"

"Of course I remember. You healed my hand. I hugged you, and you pushed me away."

"Then I told you that my life was complex."

"I didn't realize you were talking about your life as the Sicarius Headmaster." Slate reached for Rosana's hand. "If I had known, it wouldn't have changed my answer."

"There's more." Slate remained silent while she paused. Slate continued to hold her hand and gave her the strength to go on. "My name is Rosana Regallo, and I love you, Slate Severance. I am the girl you walked with in the woods. I am the girl you flirted with, and I am the girl who met you with a picnic basket in hand after you returned from Minot." Having said the easy part, she rushed through the rest.

"I am also Sana, the wizard who healed your wounds and covered your feet with moss in Pillar. I devised the plan to help you win the Bellator competition and conducted the testing on your hand. I don't love you, and I have witnessed your good intentions sabotaged by your lack of strategy." Slate was taken aback by Sana's summary of her feelings for him but the Sicarius Headmaster introduced herself before Slate had a chance to speak.

In her alternating voice, she said, "I am the Sicarius Headmaster, the Shadow in the Night. I do what must be done to protect the people of Malethya, regardless of personal cost. I have given you your missions and fought by your side on several occasions. When it comes to matters of love, I abstain from having an opinion. On several missions I have needed to use seduction as a means to gather information, and I find your practice of sleeping with serving girls without obtaining any useful information to be beneath the standards of a Sicarius Guardsman."

Rose finished the introductions. "I am Rose Regallo. I am the little sister of Lattimer and the daughter of Brannon. I don't care for the bloodshed the headmaster sometimes deems necessary, and I don't agree with Sana's assessment of you. In you, I saw the same passion and fearlessness that I saw in my father. It was I that gave Rosana permission to pursue her interests in you. I judge you to be a good man, recent transgressions notwithstanding."

Rosana stood sheepishly in front of Slate, feeling more exposed and endangered than at any point in her life. After painstaking moments of silence, Slate formed his thoughts. "You may have just introduced yourselves to me, but I already know you, even if I didn't know your names. I may not know all of you as well as I know Rosana, and if what you told me about this room full of blood is true, we might have a large need for the Sicarius Headmster in the coming days, but I want to know all of you." Slate laughed as he said, "Fractal's clarity… now I can see why I've been so turned around when I talk to you!" Then he got serious again and said, "When I left the infirmary after being whipped within an inch of my life, you are the person I wanted to see. I need you in my life. Will you give me the chance to know all of you? Will you take me back?"

Slate's comment about needing more of the Sicarius Headmaster, even if it was made in jest, troubled Rose. The Sicarius Headmaster had demonstrated her effectiveness in Minot and urged her other selves for more missions, more action, and more control. The prospect scared her, because balancing her personalities was a tenuous equilibrium, but Slate might be right. Maybe Malethya did need the headmaster right now. She struggled with her thoughts, but kept them to herself. She didn't want to spoil Rosana's moment.

Rosana had heard enough from Slate. Relief overwhelmed her and she refused to overthink things. Slate could make amends with Rose and win over Sana and the Sicarius Headmaster later. For now, it was enough that he accepted them. Rosana pulled him in for the kiss. Into that kiss, she put the passion born from the months apart from the man she loved and found every feeling returned from Slate.

Afterward she said, "I guess I was right about you. You can handle a little complexity in your life."

Slate laughed and it was a beautiful sound. Rosana had a hard time imagining the last time Slate laughed. "I thought dating one girl was difficult. I don't know if I should sign myself up for the four-in-one package…"

Now it was Rosana's turn to laugh. "Well, tonight you have only Rosana, but I expect you to exert four times the energy you used on any mere serving girl. Get over here. I've missed you."

CHAPTER TWELVE

THE MORNING AFTER

"You look chipper this morning, headmaster." Annarelle greeted her mentor when she walked down the stairwell to the tavern for breakfast. "I started to think we'd be waiting here all day."

"Yes, Annarelle. Slate kept me up late, and then we slept in even later."

"I take it you didn't need your throwing knives, then?" Annarelle twirled a couple throwing knives around jokingly.

Rosana playfully slapped Slate in the arm. "Slate can keep all of his body parts intact… but keep the knives handy. If he slips up again, I might give you a mission and let you use them."

Slate grimaced in mock pain before giving Annarelle a hug. "It's good to see you again. The headmaster tells me your training is coming along nicely."

"It wouldn't be if you hadn't saved me from the halls of Ispirtu. It's great to see you again, as well." She returned the hug.

Ibson stood from the table and said, "Fractal's blessing, Slate." From the formal greeting, Rosana could tell the elderly wizard was unsure of Slate's expected reaction. Even Rosana wasn't sure. Would Slate's relief regarding Ibson's well-being overcome the cowardice of Ibson's hiding in the infirmary?

Slate extended his hand, apparently giving the wizard a second chance. "Fractal's blessing, Ibson. I'm glad to see you with all your faculties intact. I'm even happier seeing you take action to stop Lattimer. I was filled in on some of the trouble the three of you caused in Minot, but from what I can tell, I have a lot to catch up on. What happened, and what did you find?"

"Ibson saved my life." Annarelle mentioned first before giving a mission report. "We infiltrated the Bellator barracks in Minot to search for information. Ibson and I sorted through the command center while the headmaster searched the rooms of Magnus and Cirata."

Ibson continued as their breakfast arrived. "In the command center, we found a large map describing the locations and magnitude of Lattimer's forces under the command of Magnus. I committed the details to memory. The headmaster has kept meticulous maps of Malethya as well, so I added the information for future use."

"You are telling me that we know where all of Lattimer's troops are?" Slate was astounded, but Sana brought him back to reason.

"Ibson said we know where the troops under Magnus' command are located. The map didn't contain knowledge of the Ispirtu deployments, but at least we'll know where Magnus' troops are stationed and in what capacity. I'm sure Lattimer has a few surprises that he hasn't shared with Magnus as well." Sana then let some pride show in her apprentice's work. "What it reveals are some of the locations that Lattimer values. Unless Villifor, Jak, and Tommy have recruited enough men to wage war against Lattimer and his troops, we won't be facing them head on. We'll fight the Sicarius way, by infiltrating buildings or organizations and taking out their command. Now I know what to expect in terms of resistance."

Ibson wasn't done with his findings though. "After memorizing the map, we searched through the Bellator reports, and we found something of interest. Did the headmaster mention what she found in the hunter's cottage? Did she tell you about my connection to it and to Lattimer?"

"She said something about it housing a library and a hidden city that contain the secrets from the days of Cantor. She did not speak of your connection to the cottage." The words sounded crazy even to Sana's ears, and she had seen it with her own eyes.

Ibson nodded. "Yes, the city is protected by a wall that Lattimer can't breach with magical or physical means. Magnus calls it the vault. As for my connection, I knew of the library's existence and value to a blood mage. But I couldn't speak of it to you, and thought the best course of action was to hide myself within the infirmary so that I couldn't be used to locate the cottage. It is only recently that I have been convinced of Lattimer's rise in power and deduced that the library was discovered."

"What do you think is inside the vault?" Annarelle asked.

"My bonds prevent me from discussing that which you haven't already discovered." Ibson said apologetically.

Rosana kept Slate up to speed. "Ibson was able to direct us toward Minot based upon logic from your previous mission to the town without directly mentioning the cottage. Once we'd discovered it, he became quite useful. For instance, he described the library and the city as a space created from the foldings of a four-dimensional fractal. We have no chance of practically implementing anything with that knowledge because I have no idea what it means, but it does provide some measure of the extent of his knowledge. I don't know what bonds hold him, but they are strong and immune to physical torture. Our only hope of using Ibson's knowledge is to find out more information and hopefully free his tongue in the process."

Slate didn't want to dive into Ibson's complexities since he was still trying to get up to speed on more pertinent matters. "You are full of secrets, aren't you, Ibson? Please continue. If you can't share information about the vault, then share what you can about the library."

"Cantor was the most famous wizard to ever walk in Malethya. He developed spark-based magic, which created a time of prosperity called the Golden Age. During this time, his students built upon Cantor's knowledge. Namely, Koch and Julian, who were Cantor's most prodigious students. Their accomplishments made them very powerful, and their competition led to a devastating war with all the students siding with either Koch or Julian. The breadth of the war's destruction earned them the name blood mages. Seeing his advancements in magic used for personal schemes and advancement, Cantor called all of his former students together and killed them at dinner. Then he supposedly destroyed all knowledge of spark-based magic, but that part of the story isn't true. He merely hid his research. He hid it in the library. I suppose you could call me the caretaker of the library, or at least I was before Lattimer discovered it."

"So Lattimer has all the information he needs to become as powerful as the blood mages from the days of Cantor?" The smile on Slate's face disappeared, and Rosana knew the conversation had just taken a serious turn.

"More than that… he also has access to all of the magical artifacts from the days of Cantor. They are kept in a portion of the library simply called storage. The name contradicts the complex reality of the storeroom. It is a stony desert of infinite length and infinite storage capacity, also created from a four-dimensional fractal." Before Slate could ask any more questions, Ibson pushed on. "With our successful raid of Magnus' command center, we found the list of artifacts stored within this barren wasteland and the number of items recovered by Lattimer."

Ibson pulled the list from his pocket with a triumphant flourish and splayed it out on the table for all to see. Sana scanned the list and found that the artifacts were meticulously labeled with diagrams and a list of known properties or functions of the artifact. Some were highly technical and some were borderline comical. Apparently when blood mages weren't trying to take over the world, they spent their limitless power to create objects of questionable use.

Tiny wooden elephants	They step with the force of a normal size elephant — purpose unknown.	In storage
The Closed Door	Pass through the threshold and travel to your heart's desire. Door can't be opened.	In storage

Vial of enchanted slippery water	Applies the properties of a water/glycerine mixture to whatever it touches. Note: Use with care. Effects are temporary but cleanup is impossible.	In storage
Footstool of the Diminutive	Obtained from the stores of Hector "Colossus" Hegemon. Function unknown.	In storage
Pendant of the Patriarch	Fertility charm. It can also be used to deny claims of fatherhood or impropriety.	In storage
Blighted Knife	Black etchings of catalpa trees adorn the hilt. Extremely dangerous. Both librarians that touched this object died after it was catalogued and stored.	In storage

Rosana stopped scanning the list at the mention of the Blighted Knife. The drawing matched the etchings of her throwing knives perfectly. *How is that possible?* Sana was in disbelief. *It doesn't have a listed function, but it obviously does something if it killed the wizards who touched it.* She continued to contemplate the knife and its significance as the others discussed objects that interested them.

"Can you imagine if Lattimer had access to some of these things? What if he had the Closed

Door and used blood magic to open it? He could go anywhere and attack at any time. Even if we did get close enough to attack, he could just escape through the door!" Annarelle thought aloud.

"These tiny elephants interest me. They could be used to speed construction by leveling a foundation or be placed inside of a battering ram to produce a siege weapon of immense power." Ibson contemplated the function of the artifact.

"You aren't fooling us, Ibson. I know you just want to see a tiny wooden elephant walking around." Annarelle teased the old wizard.

"Do you see the right-hand side?" Slate asked eagerly. "They haven't found any of the artifacts."

Annarelle said, "Yes, apparently some measure of luck or a fractal's blessing has been on our side."

Ibson disagreed. "The desert storage facility is vast, if not infinite. They can dig forever and never find a single artifact. It is simple probability. People attribute too many logical outcomes to fractal's blessings and grace in this world." Sana couldn't agree more, but her mind still focused on the blighted knife and she didn't join the conversation.

"Look at this one, Slate. Do you have any need for the Pendant of the Patriarch?" Annarelle referenced his recent exploits.

Slate took the comment light-heartedly but didn't try to hide his embarrassment. His reaction furthered Rose's initial assessment that he was indeed a good man worthy of Rosana. Slate turned the conversation back to more serious matters. "So to summarize, there is a walled city that we can't break into and a bunch of artifacts that we can't obtain, but the good news is that Lattimer has failed on both counts as well?"

"That's an accurate summary." Annarelle reported dutifully, cutting off one of Ibson's long-winded responses.

"Ok, then tell me about this room full of blood. What did the headmaster find in Magnus' room to suggest this place exists?" Slate asked the group.

"The room full of blood is a phylactery of a grand scale. A phylactery is typically a small vial or bottle containing a magical specimen, but Lattimer took the idea to new extremes and built an entire room to store his collection. With this room secure, Lattimer can maintain an existing spell that utilizes the samples. The Sicarius Headmaster has informed me that Lattimer is capable of using someone's blood to subjugate their mind against their will and turn them into a Fury. He will store the blood used to create these subjugates in a phylactery. My understanding is that this technique was also used to subjugate King Darik." Ibson corrected Slate's choice of words and then further corrected the means with which the information was obtained. "Also, the headmaster did not find the evidence of a phylactery in Magnus' room. She found it in Cirata's collection of artwork."

Ibson pulled the painting from his travel sack and spread it on the table. The drawing clearly showed Magnus and Cirata killing Slate and Sana in a room full of blood—the phylactery Ibson referred to. Slate examined it and said, "When they find this painting missing, they will know our plans."

Sana agreed, but she grabbed the painting in

case any of the details provided clues to the phylactery's location. "That's true, but I already knew it would be well-guarded. The difficulty of our mission remains comparable, even if they expect us."

Sana elaborated on the difficulties she expected to encounter. "When I raided Magnus' quarters, I found a plaque that stated Magnus' responsibility as a general was to 'command the mindless and protect the blood.' I have seen Magnus command Furies with the aid of an artifact he keeps in his pocket, and the direction to 'protect the blood' is an obvious reference to the phylactery that Ibson described. Additionally, I have seen Phoenix also exhibit the ability to control Lattimer's troops, so I believe he is also a general in Lattimer's army. When I combine all this information, it is only logical to assume the phylactery will be guarded by Lattimer's most loyal and dangerous supporters, and that they can summon the aid of Furies at a moment's notice."

Slate smiled and his eyes sparkled, the red glow making him look as crazy and scary as the stories told about him. "So we face difficult odds with a low probability of success? It sounds like you need someone good at improvising if your plan falls apart…"

Sana didn't argue. She was excellent at providing a strategy, but she couldn't match Slate's creativity in the heart of combat. "Let's hope it doesn't fall apart, but if it does, I'm glad you will be fighting at our side."

"So what is the plan? You said you wanted to keep this Phoenix character alive. I'm assuming there is a complicated reason buried within an equally complex plan?" Slate teased Sana, much to the delight of Rosana and Rose.

Sana was going to answer Slate when she felt a shock in the pocket of her traveling clothes. She pulled out a stratego medallion. "I'm afraid I will have to answer your question on the way to Ravinai. This is the other half of the medallion I gave to the innkeeper in Landon. I asked him to break his medallion when Phoenix appeared in town. We must leave for Ravinai. I will explain the plan on the way there."

Everyone finished the remainder of their last hot meal in a hurried fashion and left the village through the forest, where Sana's training under Lucus gave her an advantage over Phoenix. She wanted Phoenix to follow her to Ravinai because her plan depended upon him, but she needed to do it in a manner that still slowed him down while not appearing to be too obvious. In the end, she decided to periodically cover their feet with moss for short distances through the forest, using the same spell she had used on Slate and Rainier in Pillar. The moss left no tracks as they walked through the woods and would force Phoenix to spend an inordinate amount of time finding where the tracks picked back up. The walk back to Ravinai also gave the group time to consider and refine Sana's plan. By the time the group completed a scrub run within the city to ensure that Phoenix couldn't follow them, they knew their roles and were prepared for anything… anything except the smell of rotten fish that met them in the headmaster's safe house.

CHAPTER THIRTEEN

THE HEADMASTER'S MASTER PLAN

"What is the time scale for this phase of the mission?" Sana quizzed her friends as they shared a small dinner in the cramped safe house. The table was arranged in a re-creation of her war room. The team had mapped out their plan in exact detail on the wall before them.

"Two days." Annarelle answered her headmaster even though they had been over the information countless times.

"Why do we need to be ready in two…" Sana began to ask but Slate cut her off, having heard the question too many times.

"We believe it will take Phoenix five days to act, so we will be ready in two."

Ibson preempted the next question and continued. "Phoenix will know we are in Ravinai. He will look for clues to our location and stake out locations he expects us to be at. When he doesn't find us, he will activate his field assets."

"Right. He believes Lady Highsmith is one of those field assets. We need to use her to accomplish our mission and ensure her safety once she is burned. She is risking her life to help us." Nods surrounded the table, which is as much as she expected from the group. Sana knew that the repetitive conversation bored her friends, but when she executed a complex plan she ingrained every detail to memory. When the details of a plan became second nature, they could improvise and get back on track when something went awry. Something always went awry.

"Annarelle, have you used the medallions to track Villifor, Tommy, and Jak?"

"You and I will travel to them." Annarelle nodded in an attempt to mask her enthusiasm at seeing Tommy again. Rosana didn't blame her one bit. "Slate, do you remember the location of Rat Roost?"

"Yes, Sana. It is located below the Moonlight Rooster. I will make an appearance at the tavern tonight but will not show my face. It will be just enough to start rumors of my presence for anyone listening closely."

"Good. How's your head?" The last time Slate encountered Lattimer, Lattimer reduced Slate to a quivering mess. He fought such an intense battle in his head that he became incapable of fighting. Slate deserved respect for preventing Lattimer from taking over his mind—likely the result of his ability as a Perceptor to influence spells against him—but he didn't escape the experience unscathed.

"I've got a headache, but it's tolerable. The closer I get to Lattimer, the more painful it is. I think if Lattimer stays in the Ispirtu tower, I'll be ok." Rose wanted to comfort him and ask Sana if she could ease his pain. Instead, Sana remained preoccupied with her preparations and moved to question Ibson.

"Ibson, you are a master of defensive magic. What is your role?"

"I have already cast spells to protect the three of you from arrows and wizard's fire. I will stay here and hold the spells until the rest of you complete your mission."

Sana looked around the table and set down her fork. "We are ready. Perform your parts, and we have a chance. The plan will get us close to our goal, but the plan always requires modification. Stay focused but not inflexible, right, Slate?"

"There is some wiggle room in every plan." Slate smiled at Sana, and she couldn't help but appreciate his ability to conform to any situation. It was a trait that Rosana held and Sana did not, but she was learning the value of incorporating it into her plans. This plan, in particular, relied heavily on Slate for success. Maybe the man did have some usefulness to him after all… she'd have to tell Rosana.

When their meal finished, the team left to complete their various tasks. They staggered their exits by several minutes to make sure they didn't attract any unnecessary attention on the streets. Slate left but not before Rosana kissed him and said, "Stay alive." She didn't bother to tell him to stay away from serving girls because it was encompassed in her simple message. If he messed up again, the Sicarius Headmaster would kill him for her.

Sana was left with Annarelle after Ibson sought some privacy within the tiny safe house. She scanned the wall of the war room one last time and then took down all of their carefully crafted plans. If their hideout was discovered, it meant their plans had already failed, but old habits died hard. As she took the plans off the walls, she exposed the names of the previous headmasters that Annarelle had etched into the wall at her command. The reminder of her own mortality gave her pause. Did she account for every possibility or would she join the list of headmasters who had given their lives to Malethya?

"It will work, headmaster. No one could have

devised a better plan." Annarelle read her friend's thoughts and tried to comfort her.

"It is a good plan, but no plan is perfect. Will it be good enough?"

Annarelle smiled at the possibility of death in a manner only a Sicarius Guardsman would understand. "The prospect of death isn't anything new to Sicarius. The headmasters on that wall taught us to operate independently and control every situation. It was the Sicarius way, and it made us shadows in the night, but it left us isolated and vulnerable. You are different from them. You have taught me the strength of Sicarius but also the power of Ispirtu and the teamwork of Bellator. Our team is small, but we are strong. We will not fail."

Rose almost hugged Annarelle for the encouragement, but the Sicarius Headmaster would not allow it. Instead, the headmaster said, "Let's cage a Phoenix." She threw on a coat that would disguise her as they walked through Ravinai and left with Annarelle in tow.

They headed for the center of Ravinai's business district, where the medallion indicated Tommy was located. Sana couldn't guess why Tommy would be in the business district of Ravinai, but she trusted soldiers to know where and how to recruit other soldiers. Sana and Annarelle weaved through the foot traffic that traversed the city after dark while Sana periodically pinged Tommy's stratego medallion to keep their bearings. The medallion led her to a large merchant's shop that was closed for the night. As she walked past the front of the barred doorway, she pinged the medallion again and sensed Tommy was actually underground. What could he be doing?

"We need to scout the area in more detail."

She whispered to Annarelle as they casually strolled past the building.

Annarelle found a vendor selling food to late-night patrons, bought two sweet rolls and handed one to Sana. "There's a bench across the street."

The two enjoyed the fresh, heavily sweetened rolls from the bench and absently chatted while they kept an eye on the building from which Tommy's signal originated. It only took a minute or two before a wealthy nobleman turned into the alley of the merchant building. "How often do you see a nobleman enter an alleyway for any reason?"

Annarelle answered without a care in the world showing upon her face, despite the serious thoughts going through her head. "There aren't too many things I can think of that would entice him enough to dirty his appearance… women or money?"

"If its women and Tommy's involved, I'll lend you my knives." If Tommy had a following of serving girls like Slate, he would learn the consequences.

"Thanks, but I've got plenty of my own. Let's go find out what Tommy has in common with a rich nobleman. It should be easy to enter. If Tommy's secret has found its way to nobleman's ears, than it's no longer a secret."

By the time they finished their sweet rolls, three more people had entered the alleyway and each displayed varying amounts of wealth. Whatever was going on didn't adhere to Ravinai's well-established societal hierarchy. Noblemen were mixing with commoners and peasants. Rosana and Annarelle got up from their bench, crossed the street, and entered the alleyway.

Halfway through the alley, they came upon a cellar door. Without bothering to knock, Annarelle opened the door and was met by the roar of a crowd. Rosana took in the rich nobleman standing shoulder to shoulder with commoners who shouted and yelled in anticipation. Before Sana could synthesize the observations, a large man in an oversized hat stepped into the circle. The hat stood out against his tattooed chest and colorful suspenders. Altogether, the odd collection was half-clown and half-Bellator Guardsman. Shouts of "Ro-nin! Ro-nin!" filled the market cellar.

"Ladies and gentleman, boys and girls of all ages..." The man managed to raise his voice above the bawdy crowd. "Welcome to the finest form of sport in all of Ravinai. King Darik gives you the tournament once a year. People flock to the arena to witness half-trained soldiers fight with dulled blades." Boos filled the room. "You won't find that here. This is Malethya at its finest! This is where grown men and dangerous women come to hone their skills in intimate fashion. We don't do it with dulled blades—we use fists. We don't do it once a year—we do it every week. We don't fight for some nameless king—we fight because it's in our blood. We will spill it willingly on the ground upon which I stand! This is the Underground!" Ronin whipped the crowd into a frenzy, making it impossible to talk to Annarelle.

When the crowd quieted slightly, he announced the night's billing. "Our first contestant has been the champion of the Underground ever since Magnus left our ranks. You know him as Titan! Witness his dominance!" A colossal man wearing shorts with enough fabric to make a dress stepped into the ring to deafening cheers. His body bore the scars of experience, and his experience taught him not to waste energy acknowledging the crowd. Instead, he stood with arms folded in intimidating fashion.

Ronin then openly mocked the next contestant. "The second entry into this contestant is a newcomer to the Underground." Laughter filled the room at the bloodbath they were about to witness. "I know, I know… but bear with me. I always strive to give you nothing but the best of Malethya's fighters, but this is no ordinary fighter. He claimes to be personally trained by the legendary Vilifor!" A sinking feeling settled in Rosana's stomach. "He demanded to fight our very best! With such lofty credentials, I happily fulfilled his demands. Let's watch this bastion of Malethya face the lowly champion of the Underground. I didn't bother to learn his name, so let's call him Bastion!" Rosana looked over to Annarelle and saw worry cross her face.

Tommy stepped into the ring. Jak had obviously introduced him to his training regimen, because he had gained several pounds since his Ispirtu days, but he still had a considerable disadvantage compared to Titan. He kept his face the picture of confidence and lifted his sword high in the air to calls of ridicule that rained upon him from the crowd. He handed his sword to Ronin, who curtsied in mock respect to the laughter of the crowd.

Ronin addressed the crowd, "Last call for bets! Once the bell rings, all bets are closed and the fight begins. We don't stop until one of these men"—Ronin paused to pat Tommy on the back—"lies flat on his back and tastes his own blood." He walked to the edge of the circle, rang a bell, and yelled, "Let the games begin!"

Tommy and Titan circled each other, and Rosana saw Annarelle finger the hilt of a throwing knife hidden in her pockets. Rose grabbed her hand in calming support, and they watched the fight in trepidation. Sana prepared a spell in case it was needed.

Titan tired of circling Tommy, and he closed the distance with a bull rush, knowing that Tommy would have little chance in close quarters against the larger opponent. But Tommy was prepared. He dove to the side while simultaneously wrapping Titan's leg and twisting. The twisting motion worked with Titan's aggressive approach, and he fell face first in the dirt. Tommy quickly transitioned to an arm bar and threatened to break the larger man's arm. Titan called for mercy, and Tommy stood up in victory with his arm raised.

Before Annarelle and Rose could release sighs of relief, Titan kicked Tommy's knee, and he nearly toppled, barely managing to transfer his weight to his good leg as Titan stood. Ronin laughed, "Did you think this was the tournament, Bastion? If you wanted to play tag, go find some kids in the street. This is the Underground!"

Titan didn't waste his advantage and closed on Tommy, who couldn't move quickly enough with one good leg to escape the giant man. Titan hammered Tommy with blows from above that he tried to block with his arms, but the best he could hope to do was deflect and absorb. Just when Titan fell into a rhythm of punishment, he switched tactics and enveloped Tommy in a bear hug that prevented him from breathing. With his arms pinned, Tommy was defenseless, or at least he should have been. Instead of panicking, Tommy got a look of concentration on his face.

...*1* Tommy's face turned bright red ...*2* The veins on his head popped out in protest. ...*3* Titan threw his head back in a victorious laugh. ...*4* Tommy looked like he was going to pass out. ...*5* Tommy released a pressure waved that extended in all directions from his body, throwing Titan to the ground. The pressure wave dissipated a few feet from Tommy's body and was extremely weak by wizard's standards, but Titan would beg to differ. The pressure ruptured his eardrums and the sinus membranes in his head. Blood flowed freely from his ears and nose. The Sicarius Headmaster knew from her studies of the third tenet of torture that ruptured eardrums were excruciating. Titan clutched his deafened ears and tried to curl into the fetal position, but Tommy stood over top of him, placing his boot on Titan's chest. He bent down to wipe blood from the man's nose and smeared it across his lips. "He is on his back and tastes blood upon his lips." He hobbled over to Ronin and took his sword from the man.

Before he thrust it into the air, Ronin exclaimed, "You used magic! You can't..."

Tommy cut him off. "Did you think this was the tournament? I tried to beat Titan honorably, and you mocked me. Now I have beaten him by your own rules and still you argue. I will not have it." He extended his arm into the air and was met by the shocked silence of the room still trying to come to grips with the fight's events. "I have won this match, and I am not Bastion of the Underground. I am not a wizard of Ispirtu or a Guardsman of Bellator. I fight an enemy that is so dangerous that none of you even know he exists. For those of you that truly want to make a difference in Malethya instead of playing games in basements, follow me tonight. You will train with me under Villifor, the most famous war hero in our nation's history. A battle approaches. If you come with me, you may die. If you don't come with me, you face a fate worse than death." A group of three men and two women volunteered. Before leaving, he turned to Ronin, "I'll also take my cut of the winnings. I believe the odds were 10:1? Pay up. I need to fund an army." Ronin's face morphed into an expression that rivaled the pain of Titan's current state, but he handed over a heavy bag of coin.

"Nice speech, you cheating coward!" Annarelle yelled in the alternating voice of the Sicarius Headmaster. The silent crowd grew petrified at the sound of her voice. Everyone feared for their lives, except for Tommy.

His face lit up, and Annarelle rushed toward him. She jumped into his arms with no regard for the watching crowd or the man's wounded leg, but Tommy was so lost in the moment he probably wouldn't have noticed if Titan had kicked him again. They whispered to each other words that Sana couldn't hear, but that's how things were supposed to be. She followed Annarelle into the ring and spoke to Ronin.

"I will heal Titan. I do this for the sake of Tommy. He tried to fight fairly, and I know his conscience will be troubled that he needed to permanently impair his opponent."

Ronin nodded dumbly, probably still mourning the loss of the coin he handed to Tommy.

Sana probed the ears and sinuses of Titan's head and carefully mended the delicate membranes, which restored his hearing instantaneously. More importantly, it stopped his pain, and he looked upon Sana like she was fractal-blessed. As for Tommy, she would heal him later. She didn't want to interrupt his reunion with Annarelle. Instead, she addressed the crowd.

"Tommy also fights with Slate Severance and the Sicarius Headmaster. We battle a blood mage. Come with us now." The small group of recruits tripled, with Titan and even a few rich nobleman among them.

Ronin exclaimed, "You can't take Titan! He's my champion!"

"The choice is his." Sana proclaimed.

"I fight with her." Titan decided.

"Ahh, shit. I'm ruined then. I might as well come with you, too." Ronin put on his hat and joined the group.

Rosana walked over to Tommy. "Nice to see you, Tommy." She patted him on the back teasingly. "You fight well, but your recruitment pitch is piss-poor. I hope you took notes when I was talking. That's how you give a speech. Now, let's go meet your other recruits."

"Recruitment pitches are Villifor's department," Tommy explained and then warned, "and I don't think he'll be happy with your efforts…"

CHAPTER FOURTEEN

UNDERGROUND RESISTANCE

"Welcome to the Resistance! My operation is small, but we are growing," the man Malethya knew as Villifor greeted Rosana.

In reality, Villifor had assumed the identity of Slate's father, a famous war hero from the Twice-Broken Wars after betraying the real Villifor to King Darik. He offered his sword to Slate as a means to atone for his past deeds, and Slate ordered him to continue using the name of his dead father as a reminder of the man he needed to be.

"I didn't realize this was your operation. I thought you were here carrying out the orders of Slate. Have you taken matters into your own hands?" Rosana spoke just loud enough for Villifor's ears since recruits assembled a short distance away. Slate had forgiven Villifor's transgressions, and Rosana tried to trust him as Slate did. As the former Bellator Headmaster, he was a valuable ally. Her other selves had a hard time getting past his history. The Sicarius Headmaster did not trust Villifor. *He is the man who carried out King Darik's orders to eliminate the Sicarius Guild. Such an atrocity is unforgivable.*

Villifor whispered, "Of course I'm still following Slate's command, but Slate is the most feared criminal in the kingdom. The people of Malethya need something more tangible to rally behind than a red-eyed ghost that doesn't bleed. They need a cause, and I will give it to them."

Sana begrudgingly understood the shrewdness of Villifor's words and refused to let her ego, or the ego of any of her other selves, undermine his efforts. Sana whispered back, "Show me your operation and then we'll need to talk in private."

They met in an upscale restaurant called The Royal Boar, an establishment that Villifor frequented during his days as Bellator Headmaster. It might serve for a hideout, but it didn't have the necessary infrastructure to recruit and train an army.

"In due time, headmaster. First, let me address our new recruits." He turned away from Sana and looked toward the newcomers with his typical exuberance. Through the façade of his oversized personality, Rosana saw his eyes rest on Titan and Ronin. He tried to cover his anger at their presence, but Rosana was too skilled at reading people to miss it. He spoke, "Thank you all for joining us here today. You will all have the option of leaving after my talk, but if you choose to stay, you will be under my command and expected to follow through on your orders. Do you understand?"

The recruits nodded and one even gave an enthusiastic, "Yes, sir!"

"Good. You know me as Villifor and if you don't know me, then I assure you that your parents do. During the Twice-Broken Wars, the Disenites invaded. They overpowered all of our defenses and marched unencumbered toward Ravinai. I watched nobleman trot out their troops onto a field of battle and get blasted away by Disenite cannons. They led the people of Malethya to their deaths. I watched these battles and knew we had to fight differently.

We couldn't face them head-on, so we let them
march wherever they wanted to go. We just
didn't make it easy on them. We picked off
scouts and officers with our arrows and raided
supply caravans coming from the port cities.
When they tried to chase us down, we
disappeared into the countryside. Without
armor, we looked no different than the peasants
and farmers they passed every day. I taught our
soldiers to help the farmers in their fields
and to smile and wave at the Disenites that
walked by during the morning, but to be ready
for orders to set an ambush by lunch. We were
small, we were flexible, and we were lethal."

Villifor looked into the eyes of each recruit
as he gave his speech. Rosana had to give the
man credit. He sounded passionate, honest, and
the history lesson served to underscore his
credibility. Now she waited for the hook to win
over the captive audience.

"The Disenites will return and this time we
will be ready. You will be my soldiers. You
will save Malethya." Rosana noticed Jak
shifting his weight ever so slightly during the
speech. *He must not be totally comfortable with
the lies Villifor told in his speech.* "When
will they return? They are already here… maybe
not their armies, but they have already
infiltrated King Darik's circle. That person is
Lattimer Regallo, the new headmaster of the
Ispirtu Guild. The Disenites taught him
powerful magic that he used to kill his father
and take command of Ispirtu. That same magic
allows Lattimer to control King Darik's mind.
He controls the kingdom through King Darik, and
the people of Malethya are not even aware of
the threat he poses. He works from behind the
scenes to prepare for a successful Disenite

invasion. I need to stop him before they come. Will you"—he paused to look each of them in the eye and personalize his message—"help me stop him? Will you help me save Malethya from the ineptitude of King Darik and the pending threat of the Disenites? If you won't answer my call, then you know where the door is. All I ask is that you keep our existence and our knowledge of Lattimer a secret."

The ineptitude of King Darik? Where did that come from? The King Darik I know would meet the Disenites at the shores of Malethya with his sword raised and probably jump into the water to attack their ships by himself. Sana pondered the question but the message resonated with the recruits. Most of the recruits nodded silently or gave quiet confirmations while a few of the uninspired stood up to leave. One particularly adamant recruit voiced his displeasure to Villifor. "I've been hearing stories of the imminent Disenite invasion since my youth and guess what? They never came. They aren't here now, and they aren't coming. You can throw your lives away fighting Lattimer if you want, but I'm going home."

"I'll shed a tear when I come upon your corpse, trampled by the Disenite armies." Villifor countered the objection from his recruit, and no others dared to argue with him. When the door closed for the last time, a strong majority of the recruits remained, including Ronin and Titan.

"You are now soldiers of the Resistance under the command of Tommy. He is one of our squad leaders and will issue you orders, establish your training regimen, and activate you for missions when required. If you fail to execute a single order, you will be thrown out of the

Resistance. If we find out that you have spoken of the Resistance to anyone outside of the organization, the punishment will be more severe. We can't let an individual jeopardize our cause, not with the fate of Malethya hanging in the balance. Do you understand?"

"We understand." The reply came in unison.

Tommy corrected the group, "We understand, sir!" He then took over the orders from Villifor. "Each of you will return to your homes. You will carry out your lives as if tonight never happened, but when you receive a message from me, you will follow the instructions exactly. You won't be five minutes late, and you won't forget. I don't care if you have to leave your own wedding to carry out my orders. Do you understand?"

"Yes, sir!"

"Good. Write down your name and place of residence. Your training will begin tomorrow. Now get out of here before your husbands and wives wonder why you haven't returned home."

The eager recruits followed Tommy's orders, and he shook each of their hands before they left. The only exceptions were Titan and Ronin, whom Villifor pulled to the side. Rosana joined the conversation without an invitation from Villifor.

"Ronin, I haven't had the pleasure of meeting you in person, but I am familiar with your profession. I did not expect to see you or Titan here tonight. What happened?"

"Tommy wagered heavily upon himself to win," Ronin said. "I don't normally take that large of a bet at those odds, but I didn't really believe that he trained under your tutelage. I thought it was free money. When he won, I paid up out of fear of Tommy. He won his match with magic, and I don't mess with that. The loss of money was crippling to my organization. Then the Sicarius Headmaster spoke up and most of my patrons became recruits. It would have been nearly impossible to keep the Underground afloat without money or patrons, so I folded up shop and am at your disposal."

Villifor turned to Rosana. "You wanted to know about my operation? Congratulations, you've just ruined it." He muttered a couple fractal-forsaken curses beneath his breath and then explained. "The Underground was the perfect breeding ground for recruits to the Resistance. They already operated out of sight from King Darik's men, taught men to fight, and most had a grudge against King Darik, the army, or both."

"Where do your men train after they are recruited?" Sana asked in an effort to fix the situation.

Villifor grunted and then said, "Jak or Tommy visit small groups of recruits, run a training session, and then give training plans for individual use. It's sporadic and far from ideal."

King Darik didn't support the Underground, but he wasn't running Malethya anymore. *What would Lattimer do?* Rose thought back to her childhood memories. Lattimer had always enjoyed going to the Tournaments, and he admitted to joining the Underground to train for his own entry in the Tournament. That's where he met Magnus. *If we use that history to our advantage and play off my brother's ego, then maybe…*

"Would you still want to run the Underground even if it were under the control of the Resistance?" she asked Ronin.

Villifor looked at her questioningly but

Ronin's response was immediate, "You want to be my backers? Yes, I would run the Underground with you as partners. You've already shown you can be discrete."

"It would take a great deal of our meager resources to run an operation outside of the Resistance," Villifor argued, but Sana kept voicing her train of thought.

"The problem with your current operation is that if you get too large, you run the risk of Darik shutting you down. Our problem is a lack of resources to fund the Resistance and a lack of facilities to train our recruits. We can solve all those problems if we do things a bit differently."

"What do you have in mind?" Ronin asked, and even Villifor looked interested.

"Darik no longer runs Malethya. Lattimer does, and Lattimer used to be a part of the Underground. I don't think he has a vested interest in shutting it down, because it holds a special place in his heart. To you, he was probably just another fighter who came and left. To Lattimer, the Underground gave him an identity. He was no longer Brannon's son, born under the expectations of magical greatness." She put an edge to her voice as the wandering thoughts coalesced into commands. "Keep your fights secret as you have done, but quietly build them to be more frequent and spread over a larger area. At every fight, honor Lattimer and Magnus as former members of the Underground and aspire your fighters to one day meet their level of accomplishments. If we do that…"

Ronin continued her thought, "…we won't need to operate the Underground in fear of Darik's armies…" and Villifor finished it, "and we can bring in coin to fund the Resistance."

Sana didn't have to ask the two men if they would agree to work together. Instead she finished her plan with the knowledge that they would eagerly carry it out. "If you grow the Underground, you will need more fighters. Our current recruits will use the Underground as training and Titan will remain the champion. It will also give us an organized way of communicating orders to the recruits. You will no longer be just the Underground. You will be the Resistance's Underground network for training and information. You will operate in semi-secrecy to maintain the allure of the Underground but without trying to hide your presence as you have done in the past. Lattimer will learn of your fights and learn that you honor his name before every match. His ego will allow you to continue, and we will take him down by training Resistance recruits right under his watchful approval."

A slow smile spread across Ronin's face and Villifor counted the gold coins in his immediate future. Ronin said, "It looks like the Underground is going mainstream."

Villifor shook his hand and said, "Make plans and we'll talk later. I have a feeling that the Sicarius Headmaster has more ideas to discuss with me." Ronin and Titan left the restaurant in eager discussion of their future fame.

Their departure left only Villifor, Tommy, Jak, and Annarelle in the restaurant with her. Rose spoke to Villifor to clear the air about something that bothered her. "I do have plans to discuss, but first I want to know why you lied to these people."

Villifor pushed down his anger that Rose questioned his methods of operation and managed to answer with only partial contempt, "You know a lot about slinking around in the middle of the night, but you have no idea how to motivate. Should I have told them to come and fight with you? Half of those kids grew up hearing horror stories about you. They locked their windows and doors to keep the Sicarius Headmaster from sneaking in during the middle of the night." Rose was going to defend the actions of the Sicarius Headmaster, but Villifor was just getting started. "No... if you want to motivate someone, you start with something they believe. You confirm what they know, and then use what they fear to push them into action. Your father was fond of saying that the best lies are half-truths. That egomaniac was only half right. The best lies get results and a half-truth is simply the most effective way of achieving those results. How you convince someone to act is immaterial."

Tommy, Rosana, and Sana didn't argue with the speech because they had just witnessed the effectiveness of his techniques. Annarelle and the Sicarius Headmaster wholeheartedly agreed with Villifor's assessment, while Jak looked uncomfortable at the words. His concern resonated with Rose. She felt strongly enough to overrule her other selves and challenge Villifor. "Slate ordered you to live up to the name of his father. Your lies disgrace the name of Villifor."

Villifor threw his head back and laughed in genuine amusement. "You think I disgrace the name of Villifor? I may not be the original Villifor, but I was his friend during the Twice-Broken Wars. I was with him when we recruited troops to fight the Disenites. We told them anything they needed to hear in order to pick up arms and join our cause. If they were drunks in a bar, we would pay in liquor. If they were bandits, then they would get a portion of each raid. If they were womanizers… you get the idea."

Rose revised her opinion of Slate's father and kept her thoughts to herself, but Sana still had a question for the man. "You promised a Disenite invasion to the recruits. What will happen when they realize there isn't one coming?"

Villifor countered, "How do you know there isn't an invasion coming? I may have told them the truth." His smile left no doubt on his thoughts regarding the likelihood of a pending invasion. "When the invasion doesn't come, then we will tell them that the Resistance's efforts are having an effect. We will ask them to redouble their efforts against Lattimer to keep the evil foreigners from our soil." Jak looked repulsed.

Villifor had thought through his lie. Sana had to give him that. "What about the recruits you didn't convince? Some walked out the door after hearing your speech. They won't be able to keep a secret like the Resistance to themselves."

Now Villifor truly smiled. "I know that they won't. They will tell everyone they know in half-guarded whispers exactly what I just told them. Rumors will spread of Lattimer's allegiance to the Disenites and the blood magic they bestowed upon him. Every time I speak to a group of recruits, I hurt Lattimer on two fronts. I gain soldiers to fight him, and I spread dissent throughout the land. Villifor would be proud."

No one contradicted him. After all, he was the only person in the room who had known

Slate's father when he was alive. Even Slate didn't hear his father's stories from the Twice-Broken Wars.

Jak brought the group back to task, and Rosana assumed he was eager to cleanse the dirt of Villifor's manipulations from his palate. "Sicarius Headmaster, why is it you have chosen this evening to visit us? How can we help you? How can we reach Lattimer?"

"We won't be able to reach Lattimer… at least not yet. He has become too powerful. However, I have found a way to free his hold upon Slate's mind and weaken his army in the process." Sana struggled with where to begin her story, so the Sicarius Headmaster jumped in and provided the mission-critical information. "Lattimer maintains all of the involuntary subjugates in his army by using their blood as a medium to cast his spell. He needs to keep that blood safe or his spell is broken. He stores all of these samples of blood in a single location called a phylactery, and it is guarded by his most trusted and powerful allies."

"So you know where this phylactery is, and you need to devise an assault?" Jak had always been Professor Halford's best student in battlefield tactics, and it didn't take Rosana's skills at reading the subtleties of body language to know he was itching for the opportunity to demonstrate them.

"No, I know there is a phylactery and have a plan to determine its location so that we can destroy the phylactery. With our combined efforts and Slate's help, we might be able to pull it off."

Villifor laughed at the headmaster. "You want to destroy this phylactery, and you haven't even found out where it is located? Soldiers need to know where to attack."

"And that's why this isn't a job for the Resistance yet. This is a Sicarius mission, but I'll need your help to uncover the information we need. If you all play your roles, we can control the actions of our adversaries, and they will lead the Shadows of the Night right to the phylactery. Then I'll know where to point your soldiers."

Before Villifor could argue, Jak answered and saved the Sicarius Headmaster some arguing. "I'm in. What do you need from me?"

Tommy echoed the sentiments. "I'll play any role you need me to play if it means a chance to attack the phylactery. It's our best chance to damage Lattimer's control since he took power."

Rosana delivered a challenging stare to Villifor, who realized his objections had fallen on deaf ears. He recovered some dignity by posing a question after his acceptance. "Of course we will help you, headmaster, if it means reducing the number of soldiers in Lattimer's army. I would assume that our success would bring a large number of the freed soldiers to the doors of the Resistance. What roles do you need us to play?"

"Villifor, this is your chance to prove your dedication to the Resistance. The entire operation depends upon you, so I feel the need to restrict your role from the ears of the others in case they are captured. Make it convincing, and be prepared to act on a moment's notice. If you don't, the mission will fail. Annarelle will fill you in on the details." Annarelle dutifully led Villifor to the far corner of the restaurant. He allowed Annarelle to lead him away while delivering a questioning look to the Sicarius Headmaster. She hoped the man did his fractal-forsaken job. The two of them started whispering quietly at a table, and the headmaster issued orders to the others.

"Tommy, your job is to prepare a small group of your best recruits for an assault in two days' time. When we determine the location of the phylactery, we will need to act immediately before Lattimer has a chance to move its location. Annarelle will stay with you for the next two days to coordinate as many scenarios and outcomes for this mission that we can imagine. Your job will be to plan for as many of these mission outcomes as possible and determine the best plan of attack for your Resistance troops." The work was necessary and had the side benefit of reuniting Tommy and Annarelle for a few days. The Sicarius Headmaster trusted her student to maintain her professional commitments to the mission, but there would also be time to be unprofessional, and Rosana knew Annarelle deserved that opportunity before a dangerous mission.

Tommy apparently saw the benefits as well and would have enthusiastically agreed, but Jak spoke first. "With all due respect, headmaster, I have extensive expertise in that area…"

The Sicarius Headmaster hated when people questioned her orders and she snapped her response in the form of rhetorical questions. "You and Villifor have been teaching Tommy the ways of Bellator, correct? Have you taught him sufficiently to trust him in this capacity?"

Jak struggled internally with his desire to demonstrate his own abilities, but he didn't let his desires affect his response. "Tommy is an excellent student and a fine strategist. He will perform admirably."

Tommy nodded appreciatively to Jak as the Sicarius Headmaster finished giving orders to the heavily armored soldier. "He will succeed, and so will you. Your portion of this mission starts now. Get out of that armor and try not to look like a soldier." Sana pointed to a bundle of nobleman's clothing they had brought for just this purpose. They would need to hurry to arrive at the appropriate time. Most patrons arrived after bar close. If they arrived too early or too late, they would attract attention.

Jak removed the armor but failed miserably at removing the soldier. It was too ingrained in his personality, and even dressed in nobleman's clothing, Jak still looked and acted like a soldier. Rosana studied him and took some mental notes. "It looks like we'll have our first lesson on the way there."

She left the others in the care of Annarelle, confident in her students' abilities to carry out the plans they discussed. If everything went according to plan, she would see Annarelle and the others in a few days. Jak the Nobleman followed her into the street.

"Where are we going? Why am I dressed like someone who wouldn't know a sword from a stick?" Jak asked, and Rosana just laughed.

"Trust me, the person you are about to meet is well-versed in swords and sticks." She proceeded to inform him of his role and the manner in which she wanted him to act. "Before you meet her, you will need to become an entitled nobleman with too much coin and too few morals to worry about things like fidelity." She tossed him a large sack of coins. "This should last you a few nights."

Jak looked confused, which suited Rosana just fine. She started walking into the heart of Ravinai. While they walked, she critiqued him on his apparent nobility. "Keep your posture, but don't be rigid. You need to project authority without training. Nobles are born into their roles. The only training they get is through interactions with other entitled children and the presumption that they can perform their father's function better than he does."

Jak tried to walk according to Rosana's description and failed miserably. "You look like a peacock with his chest puffed out." She thought of an analogy to help him understand. "Imagine you are training a new recruit. You know you have to execute your forms precisely to properly train the soldier, but in your mind you know the recruit is beneath you. You could face five opponents of the recruit's skill level and leave without a scratch. Now take that mentality and project it to all the people around you. They are less valuable than you. Their collective thoughts are worth less than your own. They need you to teach them. Act the part."

Jak may not have understood nobility, but he was an accomplished soldier who understood how to train new recruits. He gathered from his experiences to project the infallibility that Rosana described. The effect on Jak's appearance was immediate. His bulk was too immense to fully fit the bill, but it was passable. Sana complimented him, "You train well. Keep up that persona throughout our walk." The rooftops were the Sicarius Headmaster's preferred method of travel, but Jak wasn't built for stealth. Muscle and mass helped soldiers in battle, but it didn't help them leap quietly across rooftops. They took the streets and soon arrived at their destination.

"Where are we?" Jak asked as they stood within sight of a balustraded building.

"That is the target of your mission. It is frequented by Ravinai's nobility but known throughout Malethya. That… is the Lustful Lord."

Jak appeared instantly concerned, "And what is it you expect of me? There aren't too many of Lattimer's men in a brothel."

Rosana smiled at him. "You won't need the skills of a soldier for this mission." The Sicarius Headmaster then described her expectations. "You will walk into the Lustful Lord and request an evening with Lady Highsmith. She doesn't normally take clients, but you will give her this purse of gold and use this exact phrase: 'The purse contains a tenth of a week's profits as payment for invaluable service.' She will recognize the statement from a previous conversation and bring you to her room. Complete the transaction and devise a method to extricate her in two days' time. Villifor and I will come to Lady Highsmith at that time and battle a man named Phoenix who possesses Sicarius training. You can expect Bellator soldiers and Ispirtu wizards to participate in the attack at some point as well. Lady Highsmith is a valuable asset of mine, and I have promised to protect her safety. Can you extricate her and keep her safe from Lattimer's men? Annarelle will be waiting for you and can lead you to safety once you leave the Lustful Lord."

The wheels in Jak's head spun quickly with

all the new information. In the end, he asked a question about the night's activities before progressing to main event. "You mentioned that the transaction would be completed. What did you mean by that?"

Sana answered the question. "I need to assume that the Lustful Lord is being watched. I can't enter Lady Highsmith's room without potentially jeopardizing the mission. You, acting as just another nobleman with too much money in his pocket, can enter without notice. You can deliver the message that could save Lady Highsmith's life, but it will only work if you complete the transaction. If someone is watching, they need to see what they expect to see."

Jak visibly struggled with his own morals, and for a second Sana thought he would reject the mission. Instead he asked more questions. "What message do I need to tell her?" He was obviously buying time before making a decision about participating.

"You will run your hand down her side. When your hand reaches her hip, you will stop and say, 'The business of Malethya is changing. It is time for you to stop creating fantasies for others and rediscover yourself.' She will understand. At that point, tell her you have matters to discuss in the manner of lovers. She will do what she does best, and then you can devise your strategy." Rosana couldn't help but add a comment. "It will be the most enjoyable mission you have ever undertaken." She smiled at Jak, but he didn't return the smile. He was still wrestling with his own morality.

The Sicarius Headmaster didn't have any pity for him. There was a mission to complete, and he needed to do what was necessary. Rosana didn't allow Slate to undertake this part of the mission for obvious reasons, and Tommy was excluded out of consideration for Annarelle. Jak was the final option. Sana hadn't counted on him being the last person in Malethya with morals strong enough to prevent him from visiting the Lustful Lord.

"If I do this and pass along information to Lady Highsmith, why is she worth saving?"

Ah… now Rosana saw the dilemma. If Lady Highsmith were just the owner of a high-priced brothel, she wouldn't live up to Jak's visions of saving a damsel in distress. She needed to convince him. "Lady Highsmith is a true patriot. She has passed along information to me, information that saved countless lives, and now she is in mortal danger. She has sacrificed herself to protect others. You will repay her service, and you will do it as recompense for the sacrifices she has made on my behalf."

Jak weighed Rosana's words and found enough merit in them to continue. "I will deliver your message in a convincing manner, but I will not sacrifice her honor for the sake of the mission. Then, I will devise an escape plan. When do we meet next?"

Rosana wanted to breathe a sigh of relief that he hadn't rejected the mission outright. Who would have thought that convincing a single man to visit the Lustful Lord would be difficult? "Good. The action will start two nights from now. Meet me in the lobby of the building below us, dressed as a businessman. Lady Highsmith can procure you suitable clothing. Now act like an arrogant nobleman and go in there for the good of Malethya." She bounded away and scaled a building before yelling down at Jak, "And be convincing!"

From the rooftops, she watched Jak walk into the Lustful Lord, drop the heavy purse on the counter, and ask to talk with Lady Highsmith. A few moments later, Lady Highsmith accompanied Jak to her room. From there, the pride of Bellator acted more like a soldier who had never held a sword than an entitled nobleman who expected women to drop their clothes at the sound of his name. Rosana thought she should have given him more extensive lessons in the tendencies of nobility as Lady Highsmith easily saw through his poor disguise.

She approached him demurely and then slipped a knife against his stomach, demanding answers. Rosana couldn't hear Jak's words but she imagined they came out something like, "I… umm… the Sicarius Headmaster…" *How could a man be so accomplished on the battlefield and so inept in the bedroom? Both skills require the ability to read your opponent and the decisiveness to act. Maybe Jak wasn't the best choice for this mission.*

The Sicarius Headmaster was about to leap from her rooftop perch onto Lady Highsmith's balcony to save the situation when Jak slid his hand down her waist and recited the words Rosana had given him. The scene changed dramatically. Lady Highsmith took charge and compensated for any awkwardness Jak projected by pushing him onto the bed. When he tried to lean up, she pushed him back down and unbuttoned his shirt. Confident that this portion of the mission would progress convincingly, the Sicarius Headmaster fled the rooftops, leaving Jak in Lady Highsmith's capable hands.

CHAPTER FIFTEEN

A PLAN COMES TOGETHER

Rosana hated waiting. She looked around the rooftop perch that had been her home for more than a day now and took inventory of the less glamorous tools of her trade. A looking glass lay next to throwing knives which lay next to covered jugs for taking care of life's biological necessities. When she recruited for the Sicarius Guild, her sales pitch didn't include a stakeout. Even Villifor's motivational talents couldn't spin the smell permeating the enclosed space into anything short of unpleasant.

From within her blind, Rosana had a clear view of the Moonlight Rooster and the surrounding buildings, but she hadn't chosen this location to watch the Moonlight Rooster. Instead, she had chosen this spot because it gave her a clear view of where she presumed someone else would watch the Moonlight Rooster. She wanted to watch the watcher. Unfortunately, that meant she had to start her stakeout extremely early to avoid detection, hence the unpleasant aroma surrounding her.

Last night, she saw Slate enter the Moonlight Rooster according to plan. Once he entered, she couldn't see him drink quietly at the bar and let rumors spread of his arrival. She couldn't see informants leave messages for Phoenix at various drop locations, but the thought made Sana smile. *Did a bar patron drop a sealed correspondence through the floorboards and into*

*the compromised drop-box known as Rat Roost at
this very moment, unknowingly contributing to
Phoenix's demise?*

Rosana silently celebrated when the sun set
and the Moonlight Rooster began to fill in,
signaling the approaching end to her day-long
vigil. She refocused on the task at hand and
promised to retain every detail around her.

The fading sun glinted off a distant rooftop,
but a cloud blocked the sun and revealed a
harmless bird coop.

Clunk. Something hit a rooftop and slid down.
Some kids rounded the corner and picked their
ball up off the ground. They continued their
game and threw the ball onto the rooftop again,
trying to catch it as it rolled off.

The wind picked up and blew some clothes on a
rooftop clothesline. A bed sheet drew her
attention. She pulled out her looking glass,
careful to shield the lens from the sun's rays.
All the shirts and robes blew freely in the
breeze of the rooftops, except for the bed
sheet. It softly wrapped against a figure
crouching behind it.

Relief and disappointment mixed within Sana
in a rather unsatisfying way. On the one hand,
Slate's efforts to visit the Moonlight Rooster
had drawn the attention that Sana's plan
required and she should be happy. Phoenix had
sent a member of his Sicarius Guardsmen to
scout the location. However, the Sicarius
Guardsman that the headmaster spotted had made
a profound mistake by Sicarius standards.
Choosing a location was a difficult task, but
one learned early on to take into account
changing weather conditions while assessing the
quality of a lookout. Phoenix wouldn't have
made that mistake, a pity since his presence

would have simplified the complexity of the mission.

Rosana split her time watching the location of the Sicarius Guardsman, scanning for additional threats, and watching people enter the bar. After an hour passed, the time approached for the action to begin. *Sana loved this part of the mission—the cadence of a well-executed plan coming together from seemingly random actions into a pre-described outcome.*

A hooded figure approached the Moonlight Rooster and leaned an arm against the doorframe, as if he searched for a friend inside the bar. In actuality, the subtle gesture alerted the headmaster. Slate had arrived. Rosana imagined him quietly strolling to the bar and sitting down. No one would pay him any attention until he lowered his cloak.

The crowd noise from the bar dropped dramatically. The appearance of Slate Severance in a bar would do that. Slate would ignore the stares from the crowd and order a drink, which no one would deny him.

Informants scuttled from the bar like cockroaches fleeing the light. The informants would communicate with Phoenix. Sana relied upon these informants to perform their duties with expedience.

The Sicarius Guardsman that Rosana stalked remained in his position because he lacked enough information to act. The diminished crowd noise alerted him, but he'd only seen a cloaked figure enter the bar. Sicarius protocol required him to identify the man before acting. Villifor would give him the opportunity.

The war hero arrived at the perfect time—long enough after Slate's arrival to allow the informants to leave but too soon for them to reach Phoenix. A visibly drunk Villifor walked down the street with great fanfare, shaking hands with citizens he met on the street and collecting an entourage that followed him to the Moonlight Rooster's door.

Villifor threw open the door of the Moonlight Rooster to announce his arrival with the subtlety of a raised flag on foreign soil. "Tonight we will drink in honor of all my countrymen that I could not save during the Twice-Broken Wars! King Darik has labeled me a traitor after all of my service, but the people know the truth. You are my people! Let me drink with you. Who has a drink for me?"

Cheers came up from the bar and Villifor's voice easily carried through the night to the Sicarius Guardsman watching the bar. Even if the young guardsman had been sent to watch for Slate Severance, Villifor's name would draw his attention. The only question was how the guardsman would respond.

The Sicarius Headmaster would ensure the proper response. She grabbed a throwing dart, dipped it in a small vial reserved for just such occasions, and left her blind to circle behind the guardsman's location.

People spilled from the bar in droves as Villifor yelled from within the bar, "You picked the wrong bar to stumble into tonight, Slate Severance! You have terrorized the people of Malethya for too long. I, the people's champion, will fight in their name!" Slate stepped out of the bar as the Sicarius Guardsman readied his bow. He pulled the string back to a full draw.

The Sicarius Headmaster's dart embedded in the guardsman's neck and ended the cadence of another successful phase of the mission. The guardsman collapsed on the rooftop and the headmaster jumped down to rip the Sicarius mask off the fallen but still-awake guardsman. Terror filled his eyes. In alternating speech, she said, "You do not deserve to wear the mask of the Sicarius Guild." A member of Sicarius could never let his emotions be controlled by terror and the fear in the guardsman's eyes disgusted the headmaster.

Sana explained why the guardsman's body betrayed him. "The dart in your neck contains a liquid that blocks the connection between your nerves and your muscles. Your muscles still work, but they can't receive the signals they need to respond to the desires of your brain." The headmaster picked up the guardsman like he was a baby and propped the defenseless man up so that he could see the fight below. Villifor had followed Slate into the street, and Slate finally responded to Villifor's drunken challenge.

"I am not a traitor to Malethya. That honor falls to Lattimer Regallo. I do not wish to fight you." Slate removed his traveling cloak and his ghostly white skin accentuated his muscular physique against the darkness of the night. Rosana tried to control her emotions, unlike the the Guardsman propped up next to her. *I love seeing my man in action.*

Villifor taunted Slate. "Of course you don't wish to fight me! You only passed your first round of training in Bellator. I could beat you with one-hand tied behind my back."

"I think I will be a more difficult challenge than you assume. There are reasons that stories are told of me." Slate spoke loudly but without boastfulness.

"Enough… I will eliminate one more threat to

the people. Die, demon." Villifor ran toward Slate in a drunken charge of glory. Slate stood stoically until the last second and then sidestepped the blow with remarkable speed. He flicked his staff at the wrist of Villifor and caused him to drop his blade. He could easily have crushed his arm with that blow, but Slate had learned to control his strength and didn't leave any serious damage.

Villifor, swordless and confused as to where his enemy went, turned around to find Slate with a knife next to his neck. Slate said, "You are not my enemy. You are a hero of the people, even with impaired judgment. I will let you live. Do not mistake this gift for weakness. Do not attack me again or my knife will find blood." Slate removed the knife. Villifor rubbed his hand against his neck and found that his skin was still intact. With his ego bruised and his life preserved, Villifor cut his losses.

The people stood in silence as their beloved war hero picked up his sword and walked away in complete defeat. During Villifor's long, awkward walk down the street, the guardsman next to her started to stir. The Sicarius Headmaster told him his options. He only had one.

"You came here tonight to find Slate Severance. You will not have him. He is mine." She picked the guardsman up and slapped him in the face a few times to awaken the muscles enough to speak. "You are leaving without your Sicarius mask and must report back to Phoenix. I can only imagine the punishment for someone who failed his mission and lost his Sicarius mask in the process." The Sicarius Headmaster didn't wait for a response; they both knew

Phoenix would kill the man. "You can try to follow Slate. If you do, I will kill you. You can go back to Phoenix empty-handed. If you do, Phoenix will kill you. If you delivered Villifor to him…" The headmaster let the guardsman finish the thought process and arrive at the obvious conclusion. If he wanted to live, he needed Villifor.

"Why are you doing this?" The guardsman said with much effort as his mouth and brain reacquainted.

"Slate Severance has earned my protection, but Villifor's crimes have gone unpunished for too long. I do not trust the man, and therefore I have no use of him." The Sicarius Headmaster slapped the guardsman so hard his teeth rattled. "Now, do not ask any more questions. Your time is short." She pointed toward Villifor disappearing around a street corner in defeat.

The guardsman clumsily shuffled along the rooftop and barely cleared the alleyway on his jump to the adjacent building. Sana wondered if she should have lowered the dose of poison. She started thinking of the next stage of her plan when she heard a noise in the alleyway. She turned her head to look and Slate appeared next to her. She barely had time to draw a knife. *Damn, this man is fast.*

"How did we do, Sana?" He knew who made the plans and asked Sana directly. Rose and Rosana appreciated the personal gesture.

Sana removed her Sicarius mask and recounted her activities. "Phoenix sent a junior guardsman to watch the Rooster. I poisoned him. He is now too impaired to fight Villifor directly, even in his drunken state. He will follow Villifor and report back to Phoenix.

When Phoenix tortures the guardsman to verify his story, he will hear of my mistrust for Villifor. Phoenix knows of Villifor's previous betrayals and should believe the information. With Villifor isolated and impaired, he will see an opportunity to attack. He will act."

"I'm glad I'm not the target of any of your plans." Slate smiled at her.

Rosana smiled back and said mischievously, "How do you know you aren't?" She ran her hand down his face and gave him a quick kiss on the cheek with a wink. Before he could respond, she switched personalities. The headmaster turned away and flipped the Sicarius Guardsman's mask to Slate. "Wear this. You are on a Sicarius mission, not some Bellator fistfight."

The headmaster sprinted ahead and jumped gracefully across the rooftops of the city as Slate took off to follow her. Rose felt the crisp night's air and sighed in satisfaction at the freedom she felt in this moment. Rosana was reunited with the man she loved. Sana was neck deep in the strategy of a complex plan that was going perfectly so far, and the headmaster had an important mission to carry out. In this moment, all of herselves were complete.

The moment passed as they approached their destination, and the Sicarius Headmaster made sure to get her other selves back to the task at hand. The events at the Moonlight Rooster simply set off the rest of the evening's activities, and she needed to be sharp. She needed everyone else to be sharp too. She turned to Slate, "Are you ready?"

"I know my role and will complete my mission." He sensed that he was talking to the headmaster and answered seriously. Then he changed his demeanor and gave her an impromptu kiss. "Give that to Rosana for me. Keep her safe, headmaster."

Rosana blushed before the headmaster got her back in line. "She appreciates the sentiment." The headmaster departed before Rosana made her pass along any more messages. From the next rooftop over, Sana called back to Slate. "Stay with the blood."

Alone, the headmaster descended into the alleyway and found a package provided by Annarelle in the exact location she had specified. She opened it up and found the clothing of an affluent businessman inside, which she put on quickly but fastidiously. Where she was going, noblemen would be present. Rosana knew that noblemen took their fashion very seriously. If she showed up with a single cufflink out of place, she might as well announce her arrival.

Rosana used a side entrance to an affluent apartment complex. With the Sicarius mask in place, she would appear completely natural within the building to the casual observer. Inside, she was ignored by several people, including the person she had come to meet. "Hello, Jak."

The large man suddenly became aware of her presence, but he had trouble looking up from her feet due to the effects of the Sicarius mask. "Good evening. Is our buyer ready?" The question really meant: *I'm ready and prepared. Is the mission a go?*

"There is interest, and I never keep a buyer waiting." Translation: *We need to hurry.*

They left through the front door to avoid attention. Affluent businessmen very rarely exited from alleyways. Outside, the two businessmen walked a few blocks until their destination came into view.

Glowing orbs lit the grand architecture of the Lustful Lord and highlighted its beauty at night. Rosana always thought the building was a perfect representation of what the business offered within. The beautiful columns matched the beauty of the women that worked within its walls while the orbs, a symbol of status within Malethya, discouraged those without copious amounts of coin.

Jak walked straight into the front doors, through a dazzling display of beautiful women lounging in alluring manners, and up to the front desk. Rosana intermingled with the other patrons in the lobby but positioned herself close enough to hear Jak speak with the girl at the front desk. He said, "I would like one of your finest, please." Anyone not named the Sicarius Headmaster needed an escort to go upstairs. Jak needed to purchase his admittance like everyone else.

The sound of the heavy bag hitting the counter thoroughly captured the attention of the Lustful Lord's proprietor and Lady Highsmith joined the conversation. "For that much coin, you can pick your flavor…" She emerged from a back office and guided Jak toward the women, leading him by the elbow. "What suits your fantasy this evening?"

Women stroked his arm and pursed their lips in the manner that had tantalized men since the beginning of time. "It is a beautiful night, and we live in a beautiful city. I see no reason why I shouldn't be able to enjoy both during this evening's activities."

The proprietor tried to close the sale. "I will offer you my personal suite. It should suit your desires perfectly." She paraded a steady stream of girls past Jak. As a demure brunette walked by him and gave him a playful squeeze on his arm, Lady Highsmith tapped the inside of Jak's elbow. Jak promptly put a hand around the brunette's waist to stop her.

"With a smile like that, I might not even notice the beautiful evening." Rosana was impressed that Jak managed to untie his tongue long enough to display some wit. Based on his reaction the first time he came here, she had been worried about his performance.

"With arms like that, I would have offered a discount…"

Lady Highsmith, the experienced proprietor, jumped in before any talks of discounts continued. "The stairs are this way. Veronica will lead you up to your room, sir." Veronica disappeared with Jak up the stairs almost as fast as the proprietor disappeared with Jak's money.

Rosana waited a few minutes for a nobleman to choose his night's conquest and followed the couple as they walked up the stairs. No one made it up the stairs alone, but groups of people did on occasion, and Rosana's Sicarius mask didn't draw attention from bouncers standing guard at the foot of the stairwell. The headmaster could have easily incapacitated them, but not without drawing attention. The couple ahead of her turned into a room, oblivious to her presence as she continued down the hallway.

Up ahead, she saw the door to Lady Highsmith's room. She removed her lock picking tools from a pocket of the merchant's clothes and worked the lock for a few seconds until a click signaled the lock's forfeiture to the expertise of the headmaster. She pushed the door open.

Inside, Veronica had her hands on Jak's broad chest. Jak grabbed her wrists gently and tried to explain the situation in an attempted protest. The Sicarius Headmaster didn't waste time with pleasantries. In alternating tones that froze Veronica to the floor, she said, "Tonight won't be that type of evening." The door slammed behind her, and she closed the shades leading to the balcony.

Jak finally got a word in edge-wise with the woman who mistook his inaction for shyness. "I tried to tell you. I picked you for a very specific reason. Lady Highsmith considers you a friend. We are here to save her life. After tonight, you will never see her again."

Veronica dumbly repeated Jak's words as the shock had yet to wear off. "Save her life? Never see her again…"

The Sicarius Headmaster didn't want to wait for Veronica to shake off her fear, if she ever did. She grabbed Veronica's chin, forcing her to look at the Sicarius mask. The mask had an unsettling effect on people that made them look away. For shock victims forced to look at the mask, it had the effect of breaking their minds from their endless loop of thoughts that they were stuck in. When Veronica started to fight to look away from the mask, Rose knew that its effects had brought her back to the present.

Rose spoke gently. "It's understandable that you are confused, but we don't have much time. Lady Highsmith has been my informant for many years. In several minutes she will bring Villifor up to her room and shortly after, she will have some very dangerous visitors."

Jak said, "I made this plan with Lady Highsmith. Your role was to get me up to her room, which you have done, and then to stay out of the way. I'm going to tie you up in the bathroom."

Jak walked Veronica into the bathroom and started tying her up with rope when she surprised Sana by saying, "I can help!"

Sana gave her a quizzical look, which caused Veronica to burst out a more lengthy explanation. "There is a room where you can safely hide. If what you say about Lady Highsmith's safety is true, then I want you to be watching her and protecting her."

Sana quickly calculated the improved odds of mission success and risked a few precious seconds before Villifor arrived. Slate's voice sat somewhere in the back of her head, reminding her to be flexible in her plan. She decided to follow his advice. "Tell me about this room."

"Lady Highsmith might not take clients, but her room still has all the features of the other rooms in the Lustful Lord. Have you heard of a voyeur room?" Rosana had, but Veronica explained for Jak, Rose, Sana, and the Sicarius Headmaster. "Some of our clientele prefer to watch. They enjoy it more if they believe we don't know they are watching, so we built rooms specifically for them. They are our favorite clients because we get paid and never even have to see them."

Jak had heard enough. "Where?"

"In here, the bathroom. Where else would creepy guys feel at home spying on women? The linen closet has a false back."

"Thank you for your help, Veronica." The Sicarius Headmaster held out her shockstick and Sana sent a few volts through her. She dropped unceremoniously to the floor and Jak frowned at the headmaster.

"That wasn't part of the plan. She is Lady Highsmith's friend."

"And now she is a friend who won't make any noise," the Sicarius Headmaster said. She needed no other explanation.

Jak didn't appear satisfied with the result of the conversation, but he recognized that it was over. In the darkened room, he retrieved his armor from a trunk he had stowed in anticipation of the night's events. The awkwardness Jak showed in a nobleman's clothing disappeared as he put on his armor. Some people were meant to be soldiers. The Sicarius Headmaster searched for the voyeur room.

She ran her hands across the smooth back of the linen closet, found a latch, and threw it open. The false back of the linen closet swung open to expose the cramped space within. The headmaster scanned the room while Rose tried not to think of the people that made the construction of such a room necessary. The headmaster said to Jak, "There is a slot at eye level that you can slide to the right. It will give you a clear view of the activities in Lady Highsmith's room. The only downside is that your response time may slow since you'll have to exit through the bathroom."

Jak took his place in the cramped room and knocked softly on the wall in front of him. Then he gave a sly smile, "I wouldn't worry about that. This is perfect. We'll have to thank Veronica if we ever see her again."

"We can thank her by saving Lady Highsmith's life. I'll be in the slatted closet across the room." The headmaster closed Jak into the voyeur room and made her way over to the slatted closet she had used previously, and tucked herselves between various garments. She closed the door and waited, ceding control to Sana. This part of the plan required patience, a virtue that didn't exist in the headmaster's arsenal of skills.

Footsteps in the hallway preceded the opening of the door, followed by Lady Highsmith's prearranged words to signal that the night's activities were still going according to plan. "Welcome to the Lustful Lord, where your desires are only limited by your fantasies and the depth of your pockets."

Lady Highsmith ushered Villifor into the room while an attendant filled the room's fixtures with orbs that bathed the room in light. Villifor commented in heavily slurred speech, "Now I know why the boys in Bellator spend their last dimes to come here. I never thought I had the need. Pints of beer and women at the bar are two privileges of a war hero." He then looked around the room and settled his eyes on Lady Highsmith. "Maybe I should have believed the men's stories and made the trip long ago…"

Lady Highsmith purred as she placed her hand on his chest. "I don't normally take clients, but when the famous Villifor walked through the doors of my establishment, I decided to make an exception…" Villifor took her words as an invitation, letting his hands wander. The attendant left the room, freeing Lady Highsmith to speak openly even if she had still had to act the part. One never knew who was looking in the window. "The plan calls for us to be realistic, but that doesn't mean we need to be overly enthusiastic. You will pick me up and place me on the bed with the affection of a long-lost lover." She slowly slid his groping hand to a safer location and continued her instructions. "At the bedside is a vase of roses. You will take one of these roses and trace it along my body in anticipation of the night's events. Those events will not happen and you will take your time exploring every inch of me with the rose. According to the Sicarius Headmaster, we should expect visitors shortly. Do you understand me?"

Villifor picked Lady Highsmith up and brought her to the bed as if he were carrying her across the threshold and gently laid her down with more tact than Rosana would have given him credit for. As he reached for the bedside rose, Villifor responded. "I'm more of the get-her-drunk-and-throw-her-on-the-bed type, but you are the expert. I will try to make it convincing."

The rose petals gently caressed Lady Highsmith's neck and worked their way slowly down her shoulders and arms. Lady Highsmith continued her conversation as if it were the typical banter with a client. "The only type of person you need to be tonight is the type that saves Malethya. I'm sorry if the task requires more restraint than your typical evenings."

Before Villifor could respond, a dart embedded in his neck. He reached for it in slow motion as his eyes went wide. Lady Highsmith screamed as Villifor collapsed on top of her. She struggled to get out from beneath him. As she sat up in bed, Phoenix stepped into the room from her balcony.

Sana breathed a sigh of relief. The entire night's activities up until this point were meant to bring Phoenix here in person. The lure of Villifor had been enough to entice him into action, but she hadn't counted on him incapacitating Villifor at the onset. They

would have to improvise from their original
plan. She looked across the room to the section
of the wall where she knew Jak watched
anxiously. She willed him to stay patient and
to choose his moment wisely.

Phoenix walked casually toward the bed,
ignoring the hysterics of Lady Highsmith. "The
great and mighty Villifor has fallen without
even having his sword in his hands. Maybe I
should have waited a little longer to catch you
with your pants down and further your
embarrassment." Phoenix propped Villifor up on
the bed as he glanced toward Lady Highsmith. "I
thought you were just the proprietor of the
Lustful Lord. If I had known your services were
for sale, we could have come up with an
alternative method of payment."

He laughed and took off his Sicarius mask to
expose his deformed face. Then, he stared into
Villifor's frantic eyes. "Earlier tonight, some
of my men witnessed your encounter with Slate
Severance. You are getting old, slow, and
drunk. One of my guardsmen tracked you to this
location and informed me immediately. Upon
questioning him further, I found out my
guardsman had an encounter with Rosana Regallo.
She hit him with a dart that temporarily
paralyzed him, stripped him of his Sicarius
mask, and sent him after you. You have been
betrayed by Rosana just as you betrayed King
Darik." He plucked the dart from Villifor's
neck. "I thought it would be fitting to use a
similar dart on you. I won't kill you because I
have a need for you still. Your name still
carries weight in this kingdom and you can use
it in service of the Great Redeemer."

Phoenix drew a knife with one hand and gently
lifted Villifor's paralyzed chin with his

other. Then, he took the blade and expertly
traced a shallow cut along Villifor's hairline.
The wound was purely cosmetic but produced a
steady stream of blood that soon ran down into
Villifor's frantic eyes. He then pulled out a
bottle with a stopper on the end, which he
removed to collect the free flowing blood.
"With this blood, your loyalty to the Great
Redeemer will be ensured. You will soon know
Lattimer as your rightful ruler." Sana turned
her attention to Lady Highsmith, still sobbing
hysterically in the bed next to the two men.
Between gasps of fear, she reached her hand
beneath the pillow at her side. The Sicarius
Headmaster, sensing the time for action neared,
took out a specially prepared stone. The small
pebble fit perfectly into the blowgun she used
for her darts.

Phoenix let go of Villifor so he could
stopper the bottle. As he glanced down, Lady
Highsmith struck with her hidden knife. She
stabbed into the muscles of Phoenix's leg and
screamed, "You bastard!"

Phoenix didn't even flinch. Without the
burden of pain, he finished the menial task of
closing up the bottle and securing it within
his pocket. "I'm going to have to get that
mended," Phoenix said as he removed the knife
from the flesh wound. He then looked at Lady
Highsmith and hit her with the hilt of the
knife, sending her sprawling across the floor.
"You are inconsequential. Your service is at an
end." He stood with the intention of tying up
loose ends. With his back to the closet, the
Sicarius Headmaster slid the blowgun out of the
slats. She didn't have the shot she needed
unless Phoenix turned.

The wall across the room from Rosana exploded

outwards as Jak pushed himself through the thin wall. He rushed outward in full Bellator armor and drew his broadsword, yelling, "For Malethya!" Phoenix pivoted toward the new enemy and flicked the knife in his hand toward Jak, but the knife bounced harmlessly off Jak's armor. He charged and Phoenix suddenly found himself at a disadvantage. Sicarius Guardsman weren't trained to engage in direct combat with heavily armored opponents. Phoenix's knives and darts needed exposed skin to be effective, and without the ability to affect their flight like Sana, it would take a miracle throw to find the soft spots in Jak's armor while he was charging.

Phoenix clearly understood his situation and flipped backwards to gain room. During his flip he reached into a pocket to grab an orb that he broke against the floor. Smoke instantly spewed forth and filled the room. The smoke screen slowed Jak's charge as he lost sight of his opponent. A moment later, she heard a door open and a voice from the balcony.

"I didn't give Villifor enough credit. I didn't think he would assign one of his troops to guard him on his drunken march through town. Or, maybe you were sent by Rosana as part of one of her schemes? If so, you can tell her of your failure. I came for some of Villifor's blood. I claim him in the name of the Great Redeemer." Jak rushed toward the location of the voice, but Rosana didn't need to look through the smoke to know that Phoenix would already be gone.

The whole encounter with Jak took less than a minute, with the highly trained responses of Jak and Phoenix happening in a rapid succession of seconds. They were impressive, but not as impressive as the Sicarius Headmaster. The Sicarius Headmaster had completed this phase of her mission before Jak took his first step.

When Phoenix had pivoted to face Jak, the headmaster had a clear view of the knife wound in Phoenix's leg, and she released the small stone on a perfect path to embed in his muscle. Without the sensation of pain, Phoenix failed to notice. Jak had been the perfect diversion, but Sana knew the complexity and danger of the mission she had just accomplished. She took a moment to reflect on the whirlwind of events.

This is a dangerous mission, more dangerous than any other. Would the previous Sicarius Headmasters have completed the mission? Sana didn't believe so. It was too much happening in a short period of time for a single person to respond appropriately. Rose's sacrifice to split herself into her other selves had made the difference between mission success and potentially adding her name to the list of headmasters burned into her memory.

When Jak crashed through the wall, a normal person's natural instinct would be to look in that direction. Rosana was able to watch the scene develop and fill that role, but when she heard the noise, she was overruled by the determination of the Sicarius Headmaster. The headmaster needed a moment in time to shoot the stone into Phoenix's leg. She didn't allow any of her other selves to divert her attention, knowing that if Rosana saw something that put her in mortal danger, she would act. Sana had been holding a spell to guide the flight of the stone, but she never had the chance to use it. The Sicarius Headmaster sent the stone flying through the air the moment that Phoenix exposed his wounded leg, without any magical enhancements, in the briefest of moments before the battle began. Sana did not respond quick enough to aid the headmaster, and afterward she marveled at the headmaster's actions. The odds of hitting such a small target while Phoenix was engaged in battle were miniscule. The headmaster had saved the mission, and quite possibly Villifor's life.

Maybe Slate is right. Maybe Malethya does need more of the Sicarius Headmaster right now. How can I give more of myself to the headmaster though? The headmaster needed Rosana. Rosana was the master of her environment. She could sit next to her own mother and not be noticed if she wanted. The headmaster needed Sana. Sana provided the logic and strategy for the headmaster's plans. She had to give up some of her innocence.

Rose gave more control to the headmaster. She might have cried, but the headmaster didn't allow it.

CHAPTER SIXTEEN

FALLEN PHYLACTERY

The headmaster stepped out of the slatted closet before the smoke cleared. Jak tended to Lady Highsmith while blood streamed down Villifor's face. His mind couldn't find the right connections with his muscles to make them move and wipe it away.

"Did we succeed?" Jak asked. Sana had only told him the portion of the plan related to him and Lady Highsmith. He knew Villifor would try to land a wound on Phoenix. Lady Highsmith was tasked with feigning fear. She was also the backup to Villifor, and his responsibilities fell to her when he was incapacitated. Jak needed to engage Phoenix before any harm came to Villifor or Lady Highsmith, but only after the wound was landed.

"This portion of the mission is a success. You all performed beautifully." They all breathed a sigh of relief, but it was Villifor who had the most pronounced reaction. His eyes lost some of the frantic fear he'd displayed during the encounter, which was entirely understandable from someone who would soon be enslaved by a blood mage.

"What happens next? What did we accomplish?" Lady Highsmith asked.

"I'm afraid I can't tell you that. We aren't entirely safe yet, and there will undoubtedly be soldiers sent to secure Villifor. If you get captured, you will be tortured, and I can't risk knowledge of our plans falling into

Phoenix or Lattimer's hands. I'm sorry." Jak nodded. His training in Bellator gave him a thorough understanding of the phrase "need-to-know" and he could carry out his orders when needed.

"Let's hurry," Villifor slurred, and he rose on staggering feet as the effects of Phoenix's dart started to wear off. Sana had taken the time to explain the full plan to Villifor, since she needed his name to draw Phoenix from hiding. His blood would be brought to the phylactery. If Lattimer got hold of it before they destroyed the phylactery, then Villifor would lose his mind and become one of the many subjugated to the blood mage.

After making sure she wasn't seriously injured, Jak asked Lady Highsmith, "Should I go get Veronica?"

"This isn't the first time she's been tied up and left in a room. She'll be ok."

Jak shrugged and instead threw Villifor's arm over his shoulder and dragged him toward the door. For his part, Villifor tried valiantly to make his legs work again. Lady Highsmith led the way toward the lobby just as they heard a commotion downstairs. Phoenix's soldiers had arrived. "Are there any other exits?"

"Of course. We've had to sneak a few patrons out of the building when their wives came looking for them." She led the way down a side stairwell but Villifor stopped her.

"They will have surrounded the perimeter of the building before entering. We are trapped." Villifor spoke as a seasoned soldier who understood the standard protocols for raiding a building.

"Then we fight." Jak said with conviction.

An explosion rocked the building. Sana tried

to shout over the ringing in their ears, but it didn't help. Her friends would have to read her lips. "Annarelle is outside waiting for us." She must have reached the same conclusion and released her exploding orbs, trying to thin the herd. "I'll provide cover and weaken the guardsmen inside. Lady Highsmith, you help Villifor and stay on Jak's heels. Jak, punch a hole." They had to hurry. Everyone in Ravinai would hear the explosion, and guardsmen would be rushing to the Lustful Lord in force within minutes.

The headmaster jumped ahead of the group now that resistance was inevitable and stormed down the stairs. With throwing knives at the ready, she erupted into the main lobby in a whirlwind of death. The Bellator soldiers held their shields high to block her knives, but the headmaster preyed on wizards first. She ordered Rosana to scan and locate while the headmaster sent throwing knives screaming across the room, propelled by a spell from Sana to fly fast and straight. Rose prayed for the dead.

The headmaster's aggression was dangerous, but it felt good to be on the offensive instead of lurking in the shadows. Besides, her opponents weren't Furies. Without Phoenix around to command them, their eyes stayed white until they rolled back into their heads. Three dead wizards later, she flipped over a couch for cover and had it erupt in flames that dissipated before they reached her. Rose whispered a silent thanks to Ibson for his defensive spells and then the headmaster launched into another round of killing. The remaining wizards fell to her knives, starting with one who'd had the audacity to cast the fireball at her. With the main threat to Jak out of the way, he charged down the stairwell and headed for the door.

The Sicarius Headmaster changed tactics to weaken Jak's opponents. She sent one throwing knife at the neck of a guardsman and rolled to pick up his sword when he fell. She wasn't a soldier and had little use for the sword in a conventional fight, but she didn't plan to fight fair. She danced from soldier to soldier, swinging her sword. The second they blocked or parried her blow, Sana released a small spark at the headmaster's command. It traveled through her sword and easily jumped into the metal swords, shields, and armor of the guardsmen she fought. Sana's spell was a weak one, not nearly enough to kill but with such close contact to the soldiers, it didn't have to be. They became disoriented as the spark passed through their bodies, and then the headmaster moved on to the next opponent, clearing a path toward the door. Rose gave silent thanks that Lattimer's shock-proof enchanted armor hadn't made its way to the troops of Ravinai yet.

Rosana glanced back to see how Jak fared, and he was nothing short of impressive. The large man dispatched disoriented soldiers with broad swings of his sword without breaking stride. Some of the soldiers that Sana didn't reach tried to converge on him, but Jak swung a mighty blow at the oncoming soldiers and then abruptly followed it with an armored shoulder, sending the soldier sprawling across the floor toward the shrieking women of the Lustful Lord who cowered in the corners. Jak was a big man, and he knew how to use his weight. He would not be stopped. He barreled through the front door. Lady Highsmith strolled untouched in his wake and Villifor limped beside her under his own power.

Outside, Annarelle jumped from a nearby balcony and motioned her friends toward an alleyway. They hurried over while the headmaster threw knives at anyone who dared follow. In the alleyway, Annarelle had set up a pulley lift like they used when kidnapping Ibson, and it hoisted them to the relative safety of the rooftops.

On the rooftop, Annarelle smashed open a ceramic lid to a hidden cache of supplies and then gave her report while the headmaster restocked her weaponry. Annarelle said, "Tommy and his troops are ready and awaiting orders. I watched the perimeter of the building during tonight's activities and witnessed one person enter Lady Highsmith's room and one person exit, heading to the east. Shortly thereafter, a group of wizards and soldiers came down the street and began to enter the Lustful Lord. I released my spell when I thought my exploding orbs would do maximum damage, but some of the soldiers made it inside, as I'm sure you know. I then finished off the remainder out here with some thrown exploding orbs and a few arrows."

"You did well, but this place will be swarming with more soldiers very shortly. Is your escape route planned?"

"Yes, headmaster. I have left one more ring of exploding orbs on this roof in case we are followed. I will then lead Lady Highsmith, Jak, and Villifor on a scrub run as planned and meet you back at the hideout. Does the mission proceed successfully?"

"The first two phases of the plan are a success. Did you bring the item I requested?"

"Yes. I didn't risk leaving it in the cache."

Sana turned to Jak. "I will consult alone with Annarelle for a moment. Can you keep an eye on the streets below and alert us if we need to leave?"

"I'll keep watch." He headed to the edge of the roof and was joined by Lady Highsmith and Villifor, who wanted to give the headmaster her privacy.

Annarelle led Sana a short distance away and pulled out her box of maps and stratego medallions. Inside, there was a small stone identical to the one embedded in Phoenix's leg. She picked it up and cast a probing spell. The spell sensed the stone's counterpart, and from this distance, Sana could locate Phoenix's location to the exact building. She pinged it several times, and when she was convinced that it stopped moving, she looked up to Annarelle. "He's at the infirmary. Have Tommy send the Resistance troops on several diversionary missions and then hit the target. Keep the wizards engaged but try to minimize losses and always leave a route to escape."

"Yes, headmaster. I can deliver the message before the scrub run. He is awaiting word and is ready to attack."

"Well done." Sana then picked up Slate's stratego medallion and pinged his location. "Slate is tracking Phoenix. I'll take both of these stones with me when I meet up with him." She pocketed the medallion and the small stone that tracked Phoenix. They could still tell her a direction and distance, even without the maps, and would make her rendezvous with Slate that much easier. "Let's get the others to the hideout."

Sana and Annarelle rejoined the group and Jak reported back, "Soldiers are forming up the street, but they don't appear to have clear direction. I think the heavy casualties they sustained made them lose their chain of command. We should have a clean getaway."

Annarelle spoke, "Then we will take advantage of our opportunity. We will travel a few buildings to the south via the rooftops and then take the time to change out of our clothing for a quiet walk back to the docks. Jak, I picked this route because of the close distance between rooftops. Can you manage in your armor?"

"If I can't, I can always take a few pieces off and toss them across. Don't worry about me."

Before they left, Rosana wanted to give some praise to her friends. A good commander always kept up morale, even if praise wasn't the headmaster's strong suit. "You all performed admirably back there. Lady Highsmith, it took a lot of bravery to stab Phoenix. Jak, your timing was perfect for breaking through the wall, and it was impressive to watch you barrel through the lobby. I'm glad we are on the same team."

Lady Highsmith was the one that answered, "You can call it bravery, but I just call it being a Malethyan. I did what I needed to do." Then she sauntered over toward Jak. "As for Jak's performance, his entire stay with me has been impressive. I'm used to men only looking for one thing. It isn't often that a true gentleman comes to my door…" Then she kissed him on the cheek and Jak turned bright red from embarrassment.

Villifor wasn't in the mood for small talk. "Yes, we're all very impressive people. Now, can you get to this phylactery place and kindly smash the bottle of blood with my name on it before I turn into Lattimer's man-slave?"

"We'll do everything within our power to find it and destroy it. I promise." The Sicarius Headmaster offered, and the promise of the headmaster was as good of a promise as anyone could get. Before she left, she pulled Jak aside. "When you get back to the hideout, tie up Villifor. If I do fail, he'll need to be restrained until we find a way to make amends." She left her friends before they could contemplate the consequences of failure. A bound Fury was a dangerous pet to keep hidden. Rose wanted to think they could find a way to help Villifor if he turned. The Sicarius Headmaster knew the best course of action for dealing with a rabid pet was to put it down.

While the headmaster and Rose argued over the morality of the hypothetical situation, Rosana sped across the rooftops toward the infirmary, guided by Sana's periodic probing of Slate's medallion. She slowed as she neared the infirmary grounds, but it didn't take the keen observations of Rosana to find where Slate had taken up watch. A large bell tower graced the skyline on the western edge of the infirmary. It tolled every time a life was saved by the deeds of the wizards within its walls. It was also very steep and impossible to climb, even for someone who grew up in the rocky terrain of Pillar or had the practiced skills of Rosana. Slate, with his stonehand, wasn't limited by such constraints. He just punched the wall to make a handhold and then jumped higher and did it again, making his own ladder as he went. The only problem for Rosana was that he jumped so fractal-forsaken high that she couldn't follow suit without terrible risk. She could break

into the tower and climb the stairs to surprise
him, but this wasn't the time to let her ego
get the best of her. Instead, she made the call
of the night owl, "Whoo, Whoo-hoot".

Slate returned the call and climbed down the
backside of the bell tower, out of sight from
any watchful infirmary eyes that Phoenix
employed. "Need a lift?"

The headmaster couldn't bring herself to
acknowledge his aid, but she allowed Rosana to
climb onto his back. "Are you trying to impress
me with schoolyard tricks? We have a mission to
fulfill." She chastised him for the sake of the
headmaster, but there was no anger in it. She
liked seeing her man in action.

Slate leapt up the wall of the bell tower at
amazing speed. "…and there is no better place
to watch than from up here." Slate reached the
top of the tower and waved his hand over the
view of the infirmary. "I can see the entire
complex. Phoenix won't leave without me seeing
him."

"What did Phoenix do after leaving the
Lustful Lord? Did he know that you followed
him?"

"He headed straight here. Either he didn't
think he would be followed…" Slate started.

"…or he didn't care if he was." Rosana
finished his thought. She tried to keep Sana
from contemplating the different scenarios of
what that could entail. "Where did he enter?"

"Do you see the door over there?" Slate
pointed toward the door through which she had
escaped with Ibson.

"I know it well." There was no point in
elaborating to Slate that she'd been clinically
diagnosed as a schizophrenic by Master Meikel
during her kidnapping of Ibson. It was simply a

necessary part of the mission.

"He entered there. I saw him speak with one of the infirmary wizards at the door, and then he disappeared. Infirmary wizards patrolled the halls on a regular basis before Phoenix arrived, and they have increased their frequency since." This must be the right place. Wizards wouldn't be guarding the hallways if there wasn't something to guard.

"The phylactery is here. Now we just need to find it. Would you recognize the wizard Phoenix spoke to?" Slate nodded and the headmaster felt foolish. Of course he would recognize the wizard. She had trained him in the ways of Sicarius, but that didn't put Sana's mind at ease. She hated this part of the plan. Everything else was laid out in exacting detail so that they could coerce Phoenix to show up at the Lustful Lord, take Villifor's blood, and lead them to the phylactery. Now that they were here, she had no idea what to expect and no plan to follow, with the exception of finding the nameless wizard that Slate mentioned. At least she knew the layout of the mental ward well. That provided some advantage.

"Do we go in now or wait for Phoenix to leave?" Slate asked.

"We wait. He will leave to inform Lattimer that he has collected Villifor's blood. That will leave us a window of time to infiltrate the infirmary and give us one less opponent to deal with. I don't know what surprises Lattimer has in store for us when we attack the phylactery, but it will be easier if Phoenix isn't around to command his troops. I would prefer not to fight Furies if we can avoid it." Rosana couldn't help but ask Slate, "How's your head?" because the infirmary was closer to the

Ispirtu tower than the docks.

"I've got one fractal-forsaken headache, but I can manage. If this goes well, Lattimer's hold over me will disappear and the headache should go away entirely, right?"

Before she could answer, Phoenix appeared in the orb-lit hallway of the infirmary. He walked purposefully toward the courtyard door and strode across the infirmary grounds in the direction of Ispirtu. Once Phoenix left the vicinity, Rosana finally answered Slate's question. "That's the idea. Let's go find out if I'm right before Phoenix and Lattimer return."

Slate didn't need any encouragement and didn't bother to ask Rosana's permission as he threw her over his shoulder and quickly climbed down the far side of the tower from the infirmary, again using the structure to remain hidden. At the bottom of the tower, they waited until the infirmary wizard made his rounds in the hallway. When he passed, the Sicarius Headmaster ordered Slate, "Pick me up and flash to the entrance." Slate raised an eyebrow questioningly. The Sicarius Headmaster wasn't one to ask for anything. She explained tersely, "There's a lot of ground to cover between here and there. You are quicker. Don't make me ask again."

Slate grabbed her and accelerated to top speed within his first two steps. The sudden acceleration jolted Rosana's stomach. Slate's ability was useful, but it would take some getting used to. He flashed from the tower to a tree trunk to a bush to various other forms of natural cover found in the infirmary gardens, quickly making his way to the door, where he unceremoniously dropped her to her feet. She got to work, pulling a set of lock picks from her pocket. The headmaster made short work of the lock and they stepped inside.

She sprinted to the end of the empty hallway, sacrificing stealth for speed. Not a single gold coin or drop of magic had been spared in the construction of the infirmary, and its well-lit halls provided no cover. Thankfully, all the doors in the mental ward opened from the hallways, so patient rooms provided abundant locations for hiding or stashing bodies. She peeked around the corner and saw a group of wizards talking in the middle of the hallway. She tapped Slate's shoulder, and he took a look.

"Is the wizard you saw in that group?"

"Yes, the tall one with his back to us. It was him." Sana would have smiled if the headmaster allowed it. If they weren't going to have a plan, they would need some luck. It appeared to be with them.

The headmaster pulled out two poison-tipped darts and Sana readied the spell. "You grab him. I'll take care of the other two." She turned the corner and threw the first dart while Sana cast a spell to ensure it flew straight. Before it struck the neck of the wizard, she released the second dart and and it flew halfway to its victim. Slate flashed toward the remaining wizard and grabbed him before his coworkers crumpled to the ground. The wizard didn't even have time to react. Slate reached into his pocket and pulled out a bottle of wormroot. He forced the wizard's head back while pouring the contents into his mouth and plugging his nose. The wizard was so surprised that he swallowed before understanding what was happening to him. The

Sicarius Headmaster caught up to Slate and pushed open one of the patient's doors in the mental ward, dragging the two unconscious bodies with her. Slate roughly pushed his captive into the room and closed the door.

Inside, Rose took the time to calm the frightened patient whose room they had just entered. Then Rosana turned to ask some questions of the wizard and saw his face for the first time. It was Master Meikel, the wizard who had wanted to administer treatment to her during her stay in the infirmary. The headmaster pushed the coincidence from her mind, knowing that her identity was safe behind her Sicarius mask. It was inconsequential to the mission and familiarity would only stand in the way of the third tenet of torture if it became a requirement.

Rosana got back to task and addressed Meikel in alternating speech. "Master Meikel, we know that you spoke with Phoenix a short time ago and let him enter the infirmary. He had in his possession a vial of blood. Where did he take it?" While she didn't want to have the familiarity limit herself, speaking in the familiar to a captive could loosen their tongue.

Meikel's eyes darted around the room franticly and his words came out in fragments. "Phoenix? I don't know him. He had the seal of King Darik… just doing my job. I… I… I don't know anything about a vial of b-b-b-blood. I just deal with b-b-b-brains." He acted quite differently when he wasn't analyzing someone from behind the safety of his clipboard. Rosana wondered if Master Meikel would have diagnosed the man in front of her with a mental illness if he had been observing himself in his current state.

The headmaster grabbed his chin and forced him to stop looking around the room. "Focus. Phoenix would have taken the vial of blood to a room whose sole purpose was to store blood. Do you know where that would be? It is probably heavily guarded."

"Well, yes, we store all of our blood in the same location and call for it when one of our patients needs advanced forms of healing. It needs to stay cool to remain effective during the spell, so it is more efficient to only cool one room. We devote a group of wizards to maintain the temperature around the clock."

Slate interrupted the lecture on the storage of blood by roughly pushing Master Meikel out the door. "Show us this room."

They walked down several empty hallways before rounding a corner and encountering a wizard. At the sight of the masked intruders the wizard concentrated, preparing a spell. Yelling for help would have been more productive; he didn't have a chance to cast anything. Slate left Meikel and flashed forward while grabbing his staff from his back. He tapped the staff on the side of the wizard's neck, rendering him unconscious, and shoved him inside of a patient's room before Sana even counted to one. Then he flashed back and pushed Meikel forward again.

When Meikel led them through the doors that marked the end of the mental ward, Sana began to question his directions. "Where are you taking us? Phoenix entered the door in your department. He wouldn't have entered there just to trek halfway through the infirmary."

Slate didn't appreciate being tricked and he didn't wait for an answer. He simply broke the wizard's finger with a quick snap of his stonehand. Meikel grimaced in pain, but he remained resolute. "You fools, the Great Redeemer will be here in minutes. Did you really think I would just point you in the direction of the Phylactery? I have spoken my oaths. I will not break."

Slate broke another finger. "You might not break, but you've got plenty of bones that will." A third finger snapped in half. Meikel's tortured scream was silenced by an exploding orb detonating outside the complex. Tommy had arrived with his band of Resistance fighters.

Tommy would be outside the complex, attacking the infirmary and harrying any defenses that the wizards of the infirmary employed. His job was to keep the guards occupied with activities outside the building, so that Slate and Rosana were free to explore within. Hopefully, the strategy would also distract Lattimer and Phoenix when they returned from Ispirtu and buy them a little more time.

A security orb triggered within the infirmary when the exploding orb detonated, so Sana signaled Slate to pull Meikel into one of the patient's rooms again to avoid unnecessary confrontation. Inside, they waited impatiently as wizards responded to the alarm. Every few seconds, an exploding orb would detonate. The distinctive sound of wizard's fireballs followed shortly after. Between the sounds of battle, Sana ran through scenarios with Slate.

"We can't trust Meikel, but he may have unknowingly helped us. He said the blood needs to be cold and that they used a significant number of wizards to control the temperature. If that's true, they'd probably place the Phylactery close to other departments that need cooling."

Slate snapped another finger on Meikel's hand as punishment for the lie and responded, "Sure, but what departments are those?"

Sana had collected plenty of anatomical specimens from the infirmary in the past. They were all frozen. "The morgue, Slate. I know the way." It was right next to the mental ward, so it made sense for Phoenix to use that point of entry if the Phylactery was close by.

Meikel spoke, "You are too late. You have already lost."

Slate easily snapped the last intact finger of Meikel's left hand. "You just confirmed the Phylactery's location. I guess an oath doesn't tell you when to shut your mouth. I'll bring you with us and see if you divulge anything else useful."

The headmaster opened the door even though she heard footsteps approaching. A flick of her wrist silenced the footsteps with a thud as the body collapsed to the floor. The headmaster stepped over it without bothering to dispose of the body. With a battle raging outside, they were past the point of stealth. She ran down the hallway in the direction they'd come with Slate and Meikel following closely behind. Any wizards she saw received a greeting from a throwing knife, but the resistance was surprisingly sparse. When they passed the door to the infirmary gardens, Rosana understood why.

Wizard's fire destroyed the painstakingly manicured courtyard, razing it to the ground. Rose thought, *There goes the infirmary's efforts to promote holistic healing.* The infirmary wizards spread out amongst the grounds and set aflame any object that could provide cover to the unknown attackers. The infirmary wasn't designed for defense, but the strategy was sound. By clearing everything away from the building, they created a killing zone for their fireballs to do maximum damage. It would be a difficult place to attack, if she was attacking it with Bellator techniques. Sana hoped Tommy heeded her advice and kept clear of the complex, but then she refocused her attention on the mission. They neared the morgue.

Sana stopped Slate and said, "The morgue is through these doors. I don't know where the Phylactery is, but it must be close." A subtle but palpable heat came from the door. Sana wasn't sure what it was, but the headmaster told her not to worry about it. She would find out quickly enough.

"Good, then we won't need him anymore." Slate gestured to Meikel.

Rosana thought back to her time in the infirmary and Meikel's planned treatment of her mental illness when Caitlin Regallo's words rang through her head. "Lattimer has made great strides in the care of patients at the infirmary and several of the infirmary wizards have been visiting Ispirtu to learn his techniques *Was Meikel planning to scramble my head as part of some blood magic-enabled concoction for Lattimer?*

"Allow me to dispose of him." She pulled off her Sicarius mask and saw recognition spread across Meikel's face. "I am Rosana Regallo, and you have had the pleasure of meeting all of my selves, although you didn't know my name at the time. I don't appreciate the fact that you wanted to scramble my brain. Lucky for you, I don't kill unnecessarily, and you are defenseless with wormroot in your system. I am, however, interested to see if you'd like your own experimental techniques applied to you. How did you say this worked? Application of a probing spell at high frequencies? Let's try it with some spark." Sana cast a spark that arced across her fingertips. She put her hands on either side of Meikel's head as fear spread across his face. She said, "Keep that thought in mind the next time you plan to experiment on people's brains." She released her typical spark spell and he crumpled to the ground. She explained to Slate, "It was a simple shock spell. He'll be awake in a few minutes. I just wanted him to realize the fear he put in his patients with his techniques."

Slate rubbed his neck, reminding Sana of her first encounter with him, and said, "He might wake up shortly, but he'll have a headache for much longer."

The headmaster had had enough distraction. "Let's get going. Sana doesn't have a plan past this point, so it's time for action."

Slate smiled and said, "Don't worry about having a plan. A simple rule will help us find the Phylactery. Go in the direction of the fireballs. They will have the most defenses surrounding the Phylactery. I'll draw their attention and get them to engage me first. Kill as many as you can before they cast their first spell. If they turn to Furies, try to listen for the song of the battle and time your attacks with mine." He pulled out his staff and twirled it in preparation.

Song of the battle? What in the name of a fractal's length is Slate talking about? Sana was bursting with frustration while Rose and Rosana tried to calm her.

The headmaster grabbed a smoke orb and a throwing knife and ordered Sana to ready a spell. Then Slate kicked in the doors to the morgue and chaos erupted.

Inside the frigid room, ten wizards stood in a circle facing outwards. They maintained a spell that pushed heat away from them, cooling the room to near freezing temperatures. *That explains the heat outside of the doors.* When the doors kicked open however, the wizards were prepared. The security orb and the sounds of battle outside served as a warning and all the wizards held spells at the ready. They released multiple fireballs and pressure waves at one time.

The headmaster barely had enough time to dive away from the doorframe before it exploded where she had been standing. She wasn't sure if she was saved by her own reflexes or by Ibson's defensive spells, but the end result was the same. She wouldn't be adding her name to the list of deceased Sicarius Headmasters quite yet. She started to count.

...1

The headmaster jumped up and threw the smoke orb, despite the ringing in her head from the noise of the explosion. She flicked her throwing knife at a wizard while Sana released her spell that ensured it met its mark. The wizard collapsed to the ground with the hilt protruding from his neck.

As fast as she was, Slate was faster. While the headmaster had jumped away from the doorway, Slate jumped inside the room and used his staff to vault past the fireballs. He landed on his feet, dealing death before the smoke orb released its first fumes.

...2

Slate's staff flourished in a series of lethal strikes, collapsing lungs, breaking necks, and stopping hearts. *Slate is unbelievable. I'll never again chastise him for his time 'wasted' in the northern villages.* The headmaster reached for another throwing knife and tossed it at the last standing wizard. The blade reached him a split second before Slate dealt a lethal blow.

"That last kill was mine." 2 to 8 was a poor enough count. She wasn't going to let him claim nine of the ten kills.

Slate chuckled. "I don't count unless their eyes turn red." He started looking around the room for signs of the Phylactery. He didn't have much time to look before they were interrupted.

Bellator Guardsmen came rushing through a side door, with wizards in tow. Slate immediately engaged the guardsmen, counting on the headmaster to take care of the wizards in the rear with her knives. She jumped in the air to get a clear line of sight above the Bellator soldiers and threw two knives in quick succession, leaving only a single wizard left standing. She landed and rolled along the ground, utilizing the billowing smoke from the smoke orb to obscure her location. While she rolled she grabbed another knife and popped up ready to throw. She was too late.

The last remaining wizard had a fireball prepared, and he sent it straight at Slate, without caring about the damages to any of the Bellator troops in front him. They burned as their metal armor became engulfed in flames, but as it approached Slate, it dissipated. Slate finished off the remaining guardsmen and looked back at her. "Remind me to thank Ibson when we get back to the docks. I could get used to fighting with defensive magic protecting me."

Rosana answered, "Let's not test the limits of his skills. Try not to get yourself burnt to a crisp." She pushed over a soldier's armor that was still standing with its owner's charred remains inside, hoping the sight would inspire a small degree of self-preservation in Slate's attitude. Then she said, "What did you mention next? Follow the direction of the fireballs?" She pointed toward the side door through which the guardsmen had entered.

"Yes, but there is one thing you should know."

"What's that?"

"Lattimer is coming." Slate grimaced and felt his head. "I can tell he's getting closer."

"Then let's spill some blood. Let's empty this Phylactery."

Slate shook his head in an attempt to clear it and then kicked the door so hard it flew off its hinges, knocking into Bellator Guardsmen on the other side. Slate flashed toward the distracted guardsmen and finished them off before they recovered from the surprise. The lone remaining wizard glanced around the corner, and the Sicarius Headmaster threw a couple of knives to keep the wizard under cover while Slate flashed behind him and delivered a blow from his stonehand.

The destruction was so complete that it didn't even disturb the blood on the shelves. Stacks of blood-filled vials lined shelves that spanned from floor to ceiling. Row after row of shelves stretched the length of the room. They had found the Phylactery.

Rose immediately noticed the meticulous

labeling and was reminded of her brother's attention to detail. She scanned the labels and realized they were alphabetized within their guilds. "I bet you are in the Bellator group… Lattimer never really considered you a member of Ispirtu."

Slate gripped his head and walked in the direction Rose pointed. "I'm having trouble concentrating enough to read the labels." Slate's pain was increasing to unbearable levels as Lattimer neared. She needed to find Slate's blood and destroy it quickly.

Rose raced down the aisle searching for Slate's name. She scanned the vials of blood in the S's and stopped. There was an empty spot on the shelf where Slate's blood should have been stored.

"If you are looking for Slate's blood, you won't find it here." Rose looked up to see Meikel standing in the doorway, surrounded by guardsmen and wizards. He painfully reached into his pocket and grasped an object with his broken fingers. In an instant, Sana realized her mistake. *Meikel is a general in Lattimer's army.* He held it in the air and commanded, "Attack! In the name of the Great Redeemer! Protect the blood!"

The eyes of all the wizards and Bellator Guardsmen surrounding him turned red, and he continued to speak. "You called me defenseless, but you failed to realize my greatest defense is my loyalty to Lattimer. He has given me the power to command his troops."

Slate jumped into action, drawing their attention away from Rose as he had promised. The highly trained soldiers tried to encircle Slate. They managed to get a few glancing blows when he broke through their ranks. When the swords pulled away, only a slow trickle of blood oozed out, and Slate continued to fight through the pain. He cut down soldiers and avoided spells as he flashed around the room, but there were simply too many enemies in a small space. Even with the wizards only casting small, localized concussive waves so that they didn't destroy the bookshelves, Slate wouldn't last long if Sana couldn't turn the odds in their favor. She couldn't free Slate's mind, but maybe…

She pushed against the heavy shelving and felt its weight tip. Gravity took over as hundreds of vials of blood crashed against the phylactery floor. The Sicarius Headmaster ran to the next shelf and lowered her shoulder into it as Rosana watched the battle in front of her. One of the Bellator Furies stopped fighting when the blood crashed against the ground and shook his head in confusion.

Will he run away like Josef or will he fight?

He looked up to Meikel, the man whose orders to kill overpowered his brain, and his face twisted in rage that would make a Fury jealous. With his own free will, the man decided to end Meikel's life. He released a guttural scream and rushed toward Meikel, who, without the ability to perform magic, had only one defense. He raised his hand in the air, gripping whatever he used to command the Furies, and said, "Protect me!"

The poor soldier's freedom was short-lived as he became a pin cushion for the swords of the Furies around him, but the Sicarius Headmaster didn't sit idle while the man died. She toppled shelf after shelf of blood. Her strategy became more effective the deeper the blood ran, as soldiers regained their freedom and entered into battle with the Furies surrounding them.

Slate turned from a man running for his life into a man that extinguished the life from others, his staff whipping through the chaos at astounding speeds. Seeing the tide turn, the Sicarius Headmaster grabbed throwing knives and let loose at the unarmored wizards. Just as it turned into a rout, Slate dropped to one knee.

Slate clutched his head and began to shake. Fear clouded his eyes as he fought a battle inside his head for his own free will. Lattimer was very near, and Slate was rendered useless.

The headmaster dropped the wizards surrounding Meikel with a combination of kunai and throwing knives and ordered Sana to prepare a spell with what was left of her spark. Sana did as commanded and released an arc of electricity into the armor of the closest Bellator Fury. It traveled through the combatants instantaneously. They dropped beside their Ispirtu and infirmary brethren and the chaos of battle turned to the silence of death. Rose's heart ached for the men and women who had just gained their freedom and now died at her hand, but Sana couldn't control where the spark travelled after it left her fingertips. Her spark spell killed indiscriminately and she used it as a last resort, only casting it at the command of the Sicarius Headmaster. It was her job to make the tough decisions and to do what needed to be done. Rosana looked over to Slate and saw him still shaking. She silently willed him to keep fighting.

The headmaster didn't waste time worrying about the souls of the bodies on the ground or Slate quivering in the corner. She strode toward the only man left, Meikel, and put a knife in his gut. "Start talking or I'll twist the knife. By the time I leave there won't be enough pieces for the infirmary wizards to put back together." She took off her mask to ensure he saw the seriousness in her eyes. "Slate's blood wasn't in the phylactery. Where does Lattimer keep it?"

Fear filled Meikel's eyes, but his tongue would not betray him. "I have spoken my oaths to the Great Redeemer and will protect the blood. You are a fool. You can destroy every vial of blood in this room and Lattimer's army will be replenished in a month. Your actions today are inconsequential compared to what the Redeemer has already accomplished with Slate's blood. It is far too valuable, far too powerful, to sit on a shelf." Meikel clenched his fist as he spoke the words. Most people would have missed the slight movement but not Rosana. She was a master of her environment and knew its meaning. He associated Slate's blood with power and subconsciously gripped the object in his hand that allowed him to control the Furies. Whatever he held in his hand had something to do with Slate's blood. Meikel said, "I will tell you nothing."

The Sicarius Headmaster leaned close and whispered, "You already have." She turned the knife in his gut, and he collapsed to the ground. The bleeding from the wound would kill him quickly, but he would remain alive long enough to witness his failure.

The headmaster peeled open the dying man's hands to reveal a hollowed-out wooden totem. Intricate carvings and writing were inscribed around the totem, but she would take the time to read the words later. What interested her at the moment was the tiny vial of blood housed within the totem's cavity. She stabbed her knife into the vial of blood, spilling its contents. Meikel closed his eyes for the last time as the blood hit the ground. The Sicarius Headmaster dropped a note on the chest of Lattimer's loyal servant for her brother to find. It promised that the blood would continue to flow until Lattimer's stopped.

In the corner, Slate looked up. "My head…" He got to his feet but stumbled.

"You aren't better yet, are you?" If Meikel had been given a portion of Slate's blood to command the Furies, Lattimer's other generals would have some of Slate's blood as well.

"Not completely. The pain decreased significantly, but…"

"Do you feel well enough to escape this place?" Carrying Slate significantly decreased the probability of escaping the infirmary.

Slate grunted and gave a twisted smile. "Lead the way." In his carved up, blood-covered state—even if most of the blood belonged to the people on the floor—Slate looked downright demonic. The smile against his ghostly pallor didn't help matters. Rose wanted to get him to the hideout and give him a bath. Rosana seconded the thought.

Sana issued orders that maximized their chances of escape. "Knock down the remaining shelves, starting with the blood grouped in the wizard category. Hopefully some of the wizards defending this place will be freed and hide our escape." If they had the same reaction as the freed Bellator Furies, the infirmary Grounds would be a complete mess of fireballs and crispy wizards. "At the very least, it will slow Lattimer upon his arrival if the infirmary wizards are battling themselves. It will take time to sort through the confusion."

Slate didn't need to be told twice. He flashed through the room knocking over shelf after shelf of blood. The headmaster ran toward the Bellator section and searched in the V's, taking only a minute to find Villifor's blood. She smashed it to the ground, much to the satisfaction of her other selves. *Regardless of the rest of the evening's outcomes, I have succeeded in preserving Vilifor's mind. He has proven his loyalty to Slate through his actions, and we have rewarded his trust by recapturing his blood. Villifor will not be one of Lattimer's mindless minions.*

Her momentary reflection was cut short as Slate pushed over the shelf in front of her. She looked up to see the entire room leveled. *Man that guy can cause some damage.* Splintered shelves bobbed on the ocean of blood surrounding islands of armored bodies. The floor of the phylactery turned into a pool of defiance toward Lattimer's reign.

Outside, the sounds of battle changed dramatically. What had once been a coordinated defense sounded much closer at hand and intimate. Slate said, "The infirmary wizards are fighting each other. This is our window to leave."

The headmaster tolerated Rosana's love for the man, but he had a terrible habit of stating the obvious. "The morgue has a crematorium for disposing of remains. The chimney will be a discreet means of exit." She stepped over dead bodies and reentered the morgue before Slate had a chance to think about what they would be climbing through.

Inside the morgue sat a brick oven large enough to hold several bodies. The infirmary wizards cremated bodies within the oven using wizard's fire. The flame shot through the flue and into the night sky, giving the neighbors a spectacular display on the evenings of cremation. The headmaster climbed into the oven and looked up the flue.

"I normally bring rope to help climb, but would you do the honors?" Rosana asked Slate with a grin, as if they were on a date and she asked him to hold the door for her.

Slate rubbed a finger against the walls of the flue and it came back black. "Is this what I think it is?"

The Sicarius Headmaster answered without any playful banter. The mission wasn't done yet and she spoke in alternating tones, leaving little doubt as to which one of herselves was speaking to Slate. "They are the charred remains of Malethyans burned within this oven for decades upon decades. You might have a speck of your great-great grandfather on your finger. Now quit asking dumb questions and do what needs to be done. You just carved through dozens of people and now you are hesitant to climb a chimney full of dust? Pick me up and get us out of here now, guardsman."

Slate wiped his hand on his pants and threw the headmaster over his shoulder, rather roughly Rose thought. Then he climbed the flue quickly, punching with his stonehand to form a grip and then launching himself up to do it again. At the top of the flue, the Sicarius Headmaster stood on Slate's shoulders to survey the battleground below.

Immediately below her, the roof of the infirmary was a catastrophe of a magnitude that only battling wizards can produce. Pockmarks and cave-ins riddled the roof where errant spells hit, and a crater marked where a Fury turned his dying body into shrapnel by exploding himself to kill his opponent. Wizards with freshly freed minds still fought the Furies that had given their minds to Lattimer of their own accord. He didn't require their blood to subjugate their minds, so even the destruction of the phylactery could not save them.

On the scorched earth formerly known as the infirmary grounds, nothing moved. Every tree and bush had been burnt to establish a clear line of sight and a killing zone. Rose pitied any squirrel or rabbit that attempted to traverse the barren landscape in search of a new home. Anything that moved became a target for a wizard's fireball.

The headmaster looked toward Ispirtu's tower. Fires speckled the scene where the Resistance had struck targets to distract the King's army or Lattimer's men. While the effort undoubtedly provided them some time, its usefulness was at an end because a full battalion of soldiers emerged from the city on a march toward the infirmary. Lattimer was in the lead, with Phoenix at his side and Ispirtu wizards flanking them. Lattimer held the scepter he claimed from her father's dead hands and wore the same resplendent robes that Brannon favored.

Rose could easily imagine her father walking onto the battlefield of the Twice-Broken Wars, but Rosana knew the similarities between Brannon and Lattimer ended with their appearance. Her father had tried to protect the kingdom and placed his own personal affairs—even his duties as a father—aside to serve Malethya. Lattimer chose a different path, resorting to the most repugnant form of magic to achieve his gains. Blood magic was a shortcut. It gave power to those willing to sacrifice their families and friends, and it corrupted the morality of anyone who used it, regardless of their intentions. Rose would order the headmaster to put a throwing knife through her brother's heart, but she already knew his defensive magic would protect him from her knives. Besides, Sana was running low on spark, and she still needed to reach her hideout before she escaped danger.

She pulled her gaze from her brother, aided by the knowledge that a throwing knife would fail to pierce his defenses. She had already tried that once. Instead, she looked in the opposite direction and saw Tommy's band of Resistance fighters huddled on the far end of the infirmary grounds, out of range from the wizard's spells as she had commanded. Tommy had performed his duties to perfection by distracting the infirmary wizards from her presence within the infirmary and avoiding the side of the infirmary closest to Ispirtu. Sana didn't want Tommy and his fledgling Resistance fighters engaging directly with Lattimer and his men. It would be a bloodbath. Sana summoned some of her remaining spark and sent a light shooting over the heads of Tommy's men.

"I've signaled Tommy to retreat," she told Slate. "There is chaos surrounding us, but if we can get past the wizards on the roof, we should be safe."

Just then, a series of explosions detonated between Lattimer and the infirmary. The blast dissipated as it reached Lattimer. Whatever defensive magic he maintained protected him from the blast, but the explosions did draw the attention of the wizards on the rooftop still tasked with defending the infirmary. They rushed to that side of the building. Rosana looked toward Tommy and saw that smoke filled the air in the direction of their retreat. To a member of Sicarius, a smoke-filled escape route was like someone setting a warm bowl of soup on the table for you after a long day of travel through the rain. Rose whispered a fractal's blessing.

"Tommy has masked our escape. Go now!" The headmaster commanded Slate.

He vaulted out of the flue and onto the rooftop. The headmaster threw a couple of darts at wizards that took notice of them, and Slate flashed into the safety of the thick smoke. He moved forward quickly but carefully, tapping his staff to find the edge of the rooftop. Once he located it, he punched his way down the side of the building while carrying Rosana on his back. They rushed toward the safety of Ravinai as the sounds of battle diminished behind them.

In a darkened alley marking the start of the preplanned scrub run, the headmaster finally let Rosana breathe a sigh of relief. She thought back to the names of the Sicarius Headmasters burned into her memory. Tonight would not be the night she added her name to the list. Surviving this mission made her feel alive with emotion, and she threw all of it into a kiss. Slate returned the gesture after a moment of surprise, but the headmaster pulled back without explaining herself.

The mission wasn't complete until they safely reached the hideout. Any displays of emotion would have to wait until then. The headmaster would let her other selves enjoy the company of her friends tonight, but her next mission would start in the morning.

J. Lloren Quill

Malethya needed the headmaster more than ever. Her other selves would have to wait.

CHAPTER SEVENTEEN

A PLAN FALLS APART

A greater reunion never occurred in a darkened basement that smelled of fish. In the tiny hideout near the docks, the small group came together as one for the first time since Brannon's death. As expected, Slate garnered the most attention, since he had been the person who'd originally formed their little group. Rosana happily stood to the side to give her friends time to say their hellos, and the Sicarius Headmaster waited impatiently for the trivialities to end.

"Slate! Your time away hasn't made you any prettier. I'd hang on to that one if I were you!" Jak gave his friend a ribbing while pointing toward Rosana. She blushed, to the dismay of the headmaster.

"Hey, big fella! I could say the same for you, but the beautiful lady on your arm is a good distraction for anyone that has to stare at your ugly mug. Who is she?" Slate asked about Lady Highsmith.

Now it was Jak's turn to blush, which drew laughter from the entire room. Lady Highsmith didn't wait for Jak's introduction and stepped forward to meet Slate. "I am Lady Highsmith, former proprietor of the Lustful Lord and former informant of the Sicarius Headmaster. Now I am… redefining myself. Jak told me I am under his protection, but we'll see. He might like it better when I am on top." Jak turned every shade of red imaginable. Lady Highsmith stroked his arm comfortingly. She obviously enjoyed watching the big man blush. "After being in the business a few years, it's hard not to pick up a few jokes along the way."

Villifor interrupted from a chair in the corner, where he had been tied up until Slate and the headmaster's arrival. "I've got some ropes you two lovebirds can use. Cut me out of these fractal-forsaken things and go tie yourselves up somewhere." Bellator humor was crude, but Villifor was mild compared to Hedok.

Rosana walked over to him, "Let me do the honors." With a couple quick flicks of her knives, Villifor was freed.

"I take it you found my blood and destroyed it?" Villifor asked Slate while giving Rosana a hug. Rose squirmed a bit at the gesture, but she assumed he was caught up in the moment.

"We destroyed yours and a few thousand other vials." Slate smiled.

Tommy walked down the stairs to more cheers from the group. Annarelle planted a kiss on him, and he looked over at the sight that was Slate Severance. Half-dried blood covered his body but most of it was either his victims or spillage from the destruction of the Phylactery. "From the looks of you, there is more to the story then a quick sneak into the infirmary. Do we get to hear the whole story?"

Ibson, the lone stranger to some of the members of the group, also chimed in, "Yes, I felt the defensive magic I placed around you being challenged. I would like to know what happened as well."

Slate looked over to Sana, "It was your plan to execute, so it is your story to tell. I couldn't have pulled together a mission that complex…"

"No one else could!" Annarelle exclaimed with pride in her voice. Now it was Sana's turn to blush. She wasn't accustomed to praise from her friends.

Slate then pulled out a stash of drinks. "The only plan I have ever pulled together to outwit Sana was to smuggle some drinks into the hideout while she was on stakeout at the Moonlight Rooster." He passed the drinks around the table. "Here's to Sana—a beautiful piece of a beautiful person." They all cheered and tipped their cups.

Damn that man. He is rapidly learning how to charm all of my personalities. Rosana buzzed with excitement and the Sicarius Headmaster assumed responsibilities for the debriefing, so that Slate wouldn't see his efforts toward Sana making headway. The headmaster needed Sana to remain logical while strategizing future missions. She couldn't let Sana's emotion start clouding her judgment. Regardless, some of the mission's participants didn't know how their contributions fit into the overall mission. They deserved to hear the story.

"We destroyed the Phylactery and completed the mission, but our job is not finished. The plan fell apart in the end, as you will hear." The joy in the room tamped down considerably with the Sicarius Headmaster's opening remarks. Her temperament wasn't suited for joyful occasions. "While prep work has taken considerable time, the mission got underway when Slate entered the Moonlight Rooster. Phoenix had planted informants in the bar, and they left immediately to tell him of Slate's presence, leaving the bar clear of informants for Villifor's performance. He appeared precisely on time and challenged Slate to a duel. The commotion he made entering the bar revealed the position of one of Phoenix's Sicarius Guardsmen. I paid him a visit and presented him with a choice following Slate's defeat of Villifor. He could either be killed by Phoenix for failing to track Slate, or he could follow Villifor and hope the war hero's name would redeem his failures. He chose to follow Villifor."

"How did you know the Sicarius Guardsman wouldn't just kill Villifor?" Annarelle asked her headmaster.

"I administered a toxin that would have made battle difficult while its effects were still in his system. I also relieved him of his weapons." In truth, Sana had feared the guardsman would attack Villifor and the mission would end before it began, but there was always risk in a plan. Villifor didn't need to know that the Sicarius Headmaster had considered the probability of his death an acceptable risk. "Villifor entered the Lustful Lord, presumably to massage his bruised ego—"

"I think he wanted something else massaged, and it wasn't as big as his ego." Lady Highsmith interjected to stifled laughter.

"I've never heard any complaints…" Villifor said defensively.

"I bet you haven't heard any compliments either."

The headmaster continued her report before Lady Highsmith and the drinks degraded the conversation too quickly. "Villifor entered Lady Highsmith's room, where Jak and I hid in preparation of Phoenix's arrival. He showed up and temporarily paralyzed Villifor so that he could easily obtain some of his blood, leaving it to Lady Highsmith to stab Phoenix." At this point, those unfamiliar with Lady Highsmith's part in the evening's activities gave appreciative nods and a closer look at the swelling of her face where she'd been struck by Phoenix. "Jak entered the battle—"

"By bursting through a wall!" Lady Highsmith interrupted.

The Sicarius Headmaster ignored the commentary and continued, "…and Phoenix fled with Villifor's blood. He left thinking he had captured a new subjugate for Lattimer and had no idea I'd tagged him with a tracking stone. Without the ability to feel pain, he didn't know the stone penetrated the flesh of his wounded leg."

"That tracking stone is a clever bit of magic." Ibson complimented the spell, to the delight of Sana. She hadn't completed her formal Ispirtu training or her apprenticeship under Lucus before his death. At times, she felt like an amateur, but her lack of training also led her to experiment with magic differently than others. Having a famed wizard like Ibson compliment her tracking spell gave her a sense of validation.

The Sicarius Headmaster condemned the need for validation as weakness and continued her debrief. "Outside the building, Slate watched for Phoenix to exit and discreetly trailed him to the infirmary while Annarelle covered our escape with a well-timed release of exploding orbs. Once we escaped harm's way, I used the tracking stones to locate Phoenix and Slate. Annarelle communicated with Tommy that the attack would concentrate on the infirmary. Annarelle, Villifor, Jak, and Lady Highsmith returned here after a scrub run. I met up with Slate."

The headmaster looked to Slate as a cue to pick up the story. He continued, "I saw Phoenix enter the infirmary, speak with Master Meikel, an infirmary wizard, and then promptly leave, presumably to get Lattimer after securing Villifor's blood in the Phylactery. We discreetly entered the infirmary, detained Master Meikel and forced wormroot down his throat. Unfortunately, the wormroot didn't stop his tongue from lying and he led us away from the Phylactery. Sana's deductive reasoning got us back on track, and she led us toward the morgue. Around this time, Tommy and his troops attacked, and the infirmary wizards mobilized to defend the infirmary grounds. With the wizards' attention diverted to the infirmary grounds, the hallways cleared for us."

Annarelle squeezed Tommy's arm in appreciation of his efforts, and Slate got to the important part. "We fought our way through a group of infirmary wizards and Bellator soldiers to get past the morgue and into the infirmary. It was at this point that your defensive magic saved me from a fireball… thank you, Ibson." Ibson nodded in response. "Then we entered the Phylactery and searched for my blood. We didn't find it. Instead, Master Meikel returned with a host of wizards and soldiers. He commanded them to attack me and turned them into Furies. I fought them off as long as I could, but then my memory gets a bit hazy."

The Sicarius Headmaster filled in the gaps in Slate's recollection of events. "Slate occupied the soldiers, which gave me the opportunity to knock down some shelves of blood. The resulting chaos created some infighting between the soldiers who were freed from Lattimer's control and the remaining Furies, allowing us to take the offensive."

The Sicarius Headmaster had been conflicted about telling the next point in her story. Ibson didn't know about Slate's handicap when it came to fighting Lattimer, and the headmaster hated giving out information unnecessarily, but ultimately her other selves decided that Ibson had earned their trust, so the headmaster appeased their wishes. "At this point, Lattimer neared the infirmary and his proximity to Slate made him kneel on the ground as he fought the internal struggle against Lattimer's blood magic in his head."

"Slate isn't free from Lattimer's blood magic? I thought he escaped the battle with Brannon. Why haven't I been told this?" Ibson demanded as he looked at Slate with concern evident upon his face.

"We all have our secrets and our bonds, don't we, Ibson?" Rosana referenced Ibson's inability to share his knowledge regarding the vault or details of the hunter's cottage. She then mollified him by saying, "Now you know the whole truth. Lattimer tried to subjugate Slate's mind using his own blood. We escaped before Lattimer could take control of his mind, but it took Lucus' life in the process."

"How did you stop the spell?" Ibson looked squarely at the headmaster.

"I drained some of Slate's blood into the catalpa trees and replaced it with my own. The trees absorbed the blood magic, but they couldn't contain it."

"The magic of catalpa trees is very old and not well-understood any longer. That spell could only be cast with a very weak link. Some might even call it blood magic." Ibson's eyes narrowed. "You caused the blight." The Sicarius Headmaster refused to drop her eyes from Ibson's stare despite Sana's shame. She had made a tough decision and had to live with the consequences of her actions, but she had chosen the best she could in the given situation.

"She saved my life." Slate defended her.

"You are right, and her efforts may end up saving us all from Lattimer, but there is always a price with blood magic." Ibson dropped the subject and looked to Slate. "I want to probe your head, Slate, if you will allow me."

"I'll allow it, Ibson. Thank you for asking."

Ibson laid his hand on Slate's head and closed his eyes. The room waited in silence for several minutes as the elderly wizard investigated the internal conflict within Slate's mind. Sana knew he was done when the wounds on his body started to close up. After repairing Slate's nearly bloodless wounds, he opened his eyes in bewilderment.

"You are remarkable, Slate Severance." He expressed his findings with incredulity. "The blood magic runs throughout your body, with one exception. Your mind is preventing the tainted blood from entering into it. I wouldn't have thought it possible, but it must be. Your abilities as a Perceptor have allowed you to fight Lattimer's spell within you. It becomes more difficult to fight his spell the closer you are to him because his spell strengthens as he nears. It is very similar to any other spell, like healing. It is easier to heal if I have direct contact with you while I cast my spells." Sana could see Ibson's brain spinning with ideas, and then his face darkened in realization. "If you are still actively fighting Lattimer's spell, then he is still maintaining it. He still has your blood and is trying to turn you into one of his subjugates. Is that the real reason you went to the Phylactery?"

Rosana wanted to answer with emotion, but she knew he would respond better to an argument from Sana, so she held her tongue. "It was *a* reason, but not *the* reason for the mission. The mission freed the minds of all the involuntarily subjugated people in Lattimer's army. We have significantly weakened his efforts and would have conducted the mission even if there wasn't benefit to Slate." Rosana couldn't help but add in a final statement, "However, I would have conducted the mission even if the sole purpose was to help Slate. We need him." *I need him.*

The darkness disappeared from Ibson's face, "I would have conducted the mission as well. Now that I have seen inside his head, I understand how important he is."

"We knew Slate's importance without having to use magic. Slate saved me and Tommy from the halls of Ispirtu. You should trust your heart more than some spell." Annarelle spoke of her own experiences, but everyone around the room felt the same way about him. They would follow Slate anywhere, regardless of what Ibson found with his spell.

"I guess I needed a bit more convincing, but I am convinced now." Ibson offered as a small amount of recompense. "He can stop Lattimer if we stop the spell in his head and get him close enough to finish the job. Please, continue your story. Slate was out of commission…"

"Yes, Slate was out of commission due to Lattimer's presence, but I killed the remaining Furies with a few throwing knives and a spell.

That left Meikel alone and doped up on wormroot. He was at my mercy." Rosana paused and let the Sicarius Headmaster finish the sentence. "I showed him none."

"So you didn't question him? I personally know you have a host of skills at your disposal to obtain answers." Ibson referenced his near-exposure to the third tenet.

"And I would have used them, but he was under Lattimer's control. He refused to answer my questions. I killed him, and we escaped through the flue of the crematorium's furnace. I signaled Tommy to fall back as Lattimer and his troops marched toward the infirmary. He detonated some well-placed smoke orbs to mask our escape."

Tommy smiled with pride but gave the credit to Annarelle, as a good boyfriend should. "Annarelle rigged up a complex series of smoke orbs to all detonate with a single trigger orb. It was fairly straightforward to place the smoke orbs on infirmary grounds prior to the attack. The infirmary wasn't on high alert yet, so I just had a member of the Resistance dress as a patient and walk the grounds on a moonlight stroll, casually hiding orbs under the cover of darkness. When I saw your signal, I jammed a sword into the trigger orb."

"That was some good thinking, Tommy." Villifor complimented his student.

Jak asked a follow-up question. "How did the retreat go?"

Tommy answered, "There were small skirmishes when we encountered groups of the King's army, but Lattimer's men were marching toward the infirmary, and we had a large enough head start that we avoided engagement. By the time they looked for us, the Resistance had already disappeared. They are tucked safely away in their homes, or in the homes of their parents, and are completely unrecognizable from the neighbors that surround them." Villifor smiled condescendingly at Rosana for questioning his methods earlier. Rosana had to admit that his Resistance had proven to be quietly effective tonight. Rather than acknowledge the man, she finished her debriefing.

"Slate and I completed a scrub run, as I trust all of you have done, and returned to the hideout to celebrate the success of our mission."

"How much success did we really have? We went to all this trouble, and we aren't any closer to finding out how to stop Lattimer." Villifor's condescension remained openly visible. It was time to shut him up.

"I told you all that Meikel didn't answer my questions. I didn't say I left without answers." The Sicarius Headmaster rolled the totem to Villifor that she had taken from his lifeless hand. "Meikel used this to control the Furies. It housed Slate's blood, the blood of a Perceptor, inside. I spilled the blood on the floor and Slate's condition immediately improved. I'm not sure how it works, but there is an inscription on the outside. Read it."

Villifor turned the totem in his hands, reading the inscription with a mixture of fear and reverence.

The mind remains,
Yet still obeys,
When called upon,
A Fury slays.

Silence filled the room as the weight of the

words sunk in. Jak spoke first, "Lattimer has created these totems that gift the ability to control Furies to whomever holds them."

Rose knew her brother too well. "Lattimer would never relinquish that kind of control freely. I don't think the power to control Furies passes to whoever holds the totem. Meikel was a general in Lattimer's army. Whatever oaths Meikel swore when he accepted the title from Lattimer would have been lock-tight."

"So all of Lattimer's generals presumably have a similar totem..." Lady Highsmith surmised. She caught on quickly.

"I have seen Magnus and Phoenix command Furies with such totems. I have no idea how many more generals Lattimer has recruited."

"That, my dear, is likely limited by the amount of Slate's blood that Lattimer has at his disposal. Do you know how much blood he took from you?" Ibson asked Slate.

"He took my blood after I was whipped by Master Primean. I bled a lot, but that experiment initiated the nickname 'Slate the Bloodless,' so I probably bled less than I imagine. My memory of that evening fades as the experiment drew to an end. I'd guess that the blood I lost was mostly soaked up by the sawdust on the floor."

"So let's assume he doesn't have pints of the stuff," Rosana pondered. Then Rose drew upon her childhood experiences to extrapolate Lattimer's actions. "My brother would want to keep the majority of the blood, so that overall control of his armies remained within his possession."

"Having more of Slate's blood in his possession might also make it easier for

Lattimer to overrule any orders given by his generals during battle, if he felt the need. I believe your logic is correct." Ibson complimented Rose. Sana was used to getting the compliments about logic, but she did split from Rose's mind after all.

"Theory may satisfy inquisitive minds, but it doesn't get us any closer to freeing Slate," Villifor said. "Magnus and Phoenix are two of the most dangerous people in Malethya. Assuming we can kill them, somehow, Lattimer still holds most of Slate's blood. Slate is our best chance of getting close to Lattimer, but he can't get close to Lattimer while Lattimer holds Slate's blood. Practically, we are screwed." The Sicarius Headmaster agreed with his assessment of the situation, but she would not allow herself to wallow in despair.

Jak deferred to Slate, "It is your blood that he is using. What do you want to do?"

"I'm going to kill Phoenix and Magnus. Then I'll kill Lattimer or die trying."

Villifor just laughed, "Fractal-forsaken odds and a death wish. I don't know who the bigger fool is—you for thinking you can beat Lattimer or us for following you."

The comment broke the tension in the room and everyone remembered their drinks, with quite a few glasses promptly emptying. Tommy finally asked Slate, "So who gets to die first, and how are we going to kill him? Is it that raven-picked, half-dead guy pretending to be the Sicarius Headmaster or the mountain disguised as a man that does his thinking with an axe?"

Slate deferred the question by saying, "We might face long odds, but we wouldn't even know where to point our swords if it weren't for Sana. You've gotten us this far. What's next?"

Maybe Slate did have some sense in that brain of his. He was wise to let Sana do the planning. "Phoenix continues to follow me, but if we wait for him to find us, we will fight him on his terms. I never enter a battle without choosing the battlefield." All the Bellator-trained soldiers nodded approvingly. "Magnus will be our target. We know we can find him in Minot, and we know the layout of his barracks. That will help us a little bit, but our biggest advantage will be timing. We've just turned some of Lattimer's army against him, and some of those bottles of blood had to belong to soldiers or wizards in Minot. The place will be in chaos." The last word drew a smile to the headmaster's face that she felt the need to explain. "The only thing more attractive than a moonless night to a Sicarius Guardsman is chaos covered by darkness. Enjoy your drinks tonight. The next mission starts tomorrow. We attack tomorrow night."

CHAPTER EIGHTEEN

MASTER OF CHAOS

"Annarelle, describe the town of Minot." They all sat around the same table, but morning headaches and the seriousness of the day ahead replaced the joviality of the night before. As the Sicarius Headmaster expected her to do, Rosana held herself back from the night's festivities so that Sana's mind could clearly formulate a plan. Others had not shown the same restraint and lay strewn about the tiny room in various stages of consciousness.

Annarelle looked up with bleary eyes that contradicted the focus she willed upon herself. A Sicarius Guardsman knew when it was time to act, even if the mind and body had other priorities. Annarelle leaned over a scaled model of the town that Rose had constructed while the others slept—she always liked a good craft project—and described the main features.

"Minot was a small village nestled against a large rock outcropping. It burned to the ground. In its place, Lattimer constructed barracks to house his Ispirtu wizards and Bellator soldiers." As she spoke, she pointed to the buildings in Rose's model. "This derelict structure houses ex-prisoners. They pledged their lives to Lattimer in exchange for stays of execution and now spend their days mining for long-lost magical artifacts."

"I feel like I just did this. Are we prepping for the infirmary again?" Slate rubbed his eyes and tried to pay attention. *Of course we are prepping again.* Sana wanted everyone to go through similar motions in preparation for today.

"It worked once, so we might as well do it again." Annarelle said, and the simplicity of the statement wasn't far off. *Repetition minimizes mistakes. Repetition of a successful mission breeds confidence.* Sana wanted all of her friends to feel like they could succeed in this mission. It had a low probability of success, and the only thing to counteract that was preparedness and trust in each other.

"Mining? Where do they mine in Minot?" Villifor asked alertly, at least in comparison to the others in the room. He had foregone the morning hangover in favor of a morning drink. Rosana didn't condone the practice, but she had to admit he seemed in better shape than most.

Annarelle pointed to the tiny hunter's cottage hidden in the woods. "They mine here, in this hunter's cottage."

Villifor looked at the drink in his hand, "Either this stuff is stronger than I thought it was, or you aren't making any sense."

The Sicarius Headmaster hated repeating conversations, but not everyone in the group had been present when they'd discussed Minot with Slate, and the refresher course would hopefully engage some of the less alert members of the group. "Ibson, please describe the purpose of the hunter's cottage to Villifor."

The old man slept in his chair with his chin resting against his chest, but he roused at the mention of his name. "The, um, hunting cottage is neither for hunting nor is it a cottage. It is a feat of complex magic from the days of Cantor, possibly even constructed by Cantor himself. Inside this tiny cottage is a library housing all learnings of spark-based magic, preserved throughout time for Lattimer to now read at his leisure."

"You mean Cantor brought an unprecedented scope of destruction to Malethya in the form of blood mages and then decided to keep hidden instructions for Lattimer to recreate it? I thought this guy was supposed to be smart?" Tommy voice arose from beneath the table. He crawled out to join the living.

"Vanity is a powerful thing. I'm sure he wanted some good to come of his life's work." Ibson conjectured. "Within the hunter's cottage, there is also a storage room in the form of an endless desert. The magical artifacts are buried in the sand. It is here that the prisoners spend their days mindlessly digging, only to return to Minot with their minds erased of the day's activities, doomed to repeat the process the following morning."

"So we might be facing enemies wielding magical weapons?" Jak asked as he sat up, carefully enveloping Lady Highsmith as he did so. He had spent the night on the floor serving as Lady Highsmith's bed. For her part, Lady Highsmith looked refreshed after a good night's sleep.

Annarelle jumped in and said, "Magnus has been given armor enchanted by Lattimer to be impervious to the headmaster's shock spell, but we aren't aware of any enchanted weapons. We recovered this list of artifacts during our raid of Minot. None have been recovered from the storage room."

Annarelle laid the list on the table and jokes began surrounding the descriptions of some of the less pertinent items. Lady Highsmith got a particular kick out of the

Pendant of the Patriarch. Her jokes related to stories from the Lustful Lord and she spared no detail.

The headmaster let the jokes continue because the crassness helped awaken their minds. Rosana, meanwhile, had a passing interest in the Closed Door. It would be highly advantageous to possess an artifact that allowed one to travel anywhere in Malethya instantly, but the fact that it couldn't be opened limited its practicality greatly. No, there was only one item on the list that really drew her interested—the Blighted Knife. Ever since she had read the description, she had trouble keeping it from her thoughts. There was a knife with black etchings of catalpa trees on its hilt that was deadly to those who touched it. What were the chances that an artifact from the days of Cantor existed that precisely matched her throwing knives and that the artifact brought death wherever it went? *I am the Shadow of the Night. I deal death to all those that stand in my way. The knife is destined for me...*

She shook herself from her thoughts and interrupted the group's rapt attention to Lady Highsmith and her stories. "The last part of the hunter's cottage is called the vault. It is an entire city buried within the depths of the cottage and surrounded by an impenetrable magical wall. Ibson can speak of the construction of the Hunter's cottage, but he can't speak of the vault due to bonds from his past." *What bonds could they be? Malethya has too many mysteries and I don't have time to solve them all.* "Please give the short version of how such a structure could be constructed." She found it highly unlikely that such knowledge would aid someone like Jak in the mission ahead, but there was no point in withholding it either. She just hoped Ibson could avoid a lecture in the nuances of fractal lore.

"The hunter's cottage and the vast space of the store room are constructed using the pattern of a four-dimensional fractal. It has infinite volume that can be folded or unfolded to create objects within our three dimensional world." Ibson began.

The Sicarius Headmaster deemed the summary sufficient for the group's purposes and interrupted before he continued, "Are there any questions for Ibson?"

No one asked a question. Cutting Ibson off so abruptly was rude even by Malethyan standards. Villifor stared at the bottom of his glass, wondering where all his drink had gone so quickly and hoping the conversation changed from fractals and awkward silences. The Sicarius Headmaster brought them back to more pertinent matters. "While the cottage is undeniably intriguing, our target will be the Bellator barracks. Magnus resides on the top floor, and we are familiar with the layout. Bellator men, how would you attack the target?"

"The woods provide excellent cover and the rock outcropping is a strategic advantage if it isn't defended." Jak spoke to the terrain. "Archers could do some real damage from atop that rock, but catapults would be my weapon of choice."

"We won't be bringing siege weapons or catapults with us if we intend to leave Ravinai today, but we have bows and arrows." Villifor reasoned.

"We can expect the Minot wizards to respond

similarly to the attack at the infirmary. They'll head to the rooftops to give themselves an advantage. We could use the rock outcropping to launch some of Annarelle's smoke orbs toward Minot's Ispirtu complex at the start of the attack to handicap their response." Tommy added from his recent experiences, and Annarelle glowed with the recognition of her talents.

"And we can anticipate that Magnus will deploy troops using standard protocols from Bellator. Villifor had me watch him. His execution is superb, but he lacks of creativity." Slate nodded in acknowledgment of the lesson Villifor taught him on his first trip to Minot. It seemed so long ago.

Jak, who had studied Bellator strategies extensively, said, "Magnus will hold his position in an effort to occupy us. Then he will send troops up the back side of the rock formation in an attempt to smash us between two opposing forces."

"We should set up small groups of harrying forces in the woods in anticipation of the maneuver. In those dense forests, we could thin out quite a few of them before we engaged on the rock formation," Villifor strategized.

"If there will be fighting in the woods, I have a trick or two that could be helpful." The vines Sana had enchanted on their last visit had proven surprisingly effective.

Slate gave the final approval. "I like this strategy. We claim the high ground, debilitate the wizards with smoke bombs, reduce Magnus' numbers as they go through the woods, and then strike the Bellator complex. Any infiltratration that Sana plans will then be done under the cover and confusion of a Bellator attack."

Sana spoke up, "I have a few ideas, but I need to run through the contingency plans before choosing the best one. Now I know your plan of attack and can try to make my efforts coincide as best as possible. I trust you can formulate your plans and be ready to stage an attack this evening?"

Her statement about choosing a plan was only partially true. The whole truth was that Sana had made plans for so many different scenarios that it would have made Jak's head spin. Some of them she didn't want to share with the group. Once the mission started, the Sicarius Headmaster would do everything in her power to kill Magnus and free Slate's mind a bit further. *My friends cannot learn how far I am willing to go to accomplish this task.*

"We will be ready. I take it you want a small force? You seem to prefer a quick silent attack in most instances." Jak promised, and Sana could see his eagerness to join the fight after missing out on the battle of the infirmary.

"I can make it work either way. Choose what you think will be most effective. Just make sure that you can get to Minot undetected. An army of soldiers will be scouted and intercepted before we can carry out our plans." Jak nodded his agreement, so she turned her attention to Annarelle. "How are we doing on supplies?"

"We went through a lot of orbs and knives yesterday. We can make it through another assault, but then we'll need to stock up."

"Our efforts last night have left Ravinai in disarray, which is a prime opportunity to obtain supplies. I have a very specific target in mind. There is a man named Mr. Radcliff who runs an import/export business. He framed a friend of mine for murder and now Josef is under Lattimer's control, digging in the storage room mindlessly for the rest of his days. I think Mr. Radcliff should share his hardship." Sana had been searching for a way to bring justice to Mr. Radcliff ever since she'd met Josef in Minot. This seemed like the right opportunity. Rose just wanted to help Josef, but she recognized she might not be able to free him from his current predicament. Rosana served as the deciding vote. She bore no good will toward the pig who tried to pay his way into the bedroom of a simple serving girl. She would take what he cherished most. "I want you to steal anything of value that comes onto the docks with Radcliff's company stamp on the crates. If we don't have a need for it, dump it in the damn river. I want him to wake tomorrow without any inventory and a host of people demanding their merchandise. Mr. Radcliff likes to import illicit goods, so I'm sure his clientele will make his life difficult… not as difficult as the life Josef faces, but difficult nonetheless."

"I'll give the orders to the Underground this morning and join up with Jak later," Tommy promised. "As for Mr. Radcliff, I have a suggestion. Would you consider leaving him one of your famous notes, stating your friendship with Josef and your knowledge of his misdeeds? His fear would increase substantially knowing you were involved and serve to distract attention from the Underground, should anyone want to investigate the matter."

"That is a very Sicarius suggestion of you, Tommy. Annarelle must be wearing off on you. I will sign and seal a letter before I leave." Then Sana shifted her attention to Lady

Highsmith, and offered an escape from the group to start her new life, if she so desired. "Lady Highsmith, I don't expect you to risk your life any further…"

"I go where Jak goes." Lady Highsmith stated before any alternatives could be discussed. Sana let it be because she didn't know what to do with her anyway. She just hoped Lady Highsmith didn't distract Jak during battle.

Finally, the plans were laid out with the exception of the reconnaissance mission. The headmaster took over for Sana and commanded, "Annarelle, Slate, and Ibson will come with me to perform a reconnaissance of Minot. I don't want any surprises when the mission begins." Rosana also wanted Slate by her side, which was another reason she couldn't fault Lady Highsmith's declaration. Rosana softened the headmaster's command by asking, "Ibson, I'd feel better with your defensive magic protecting us, and I know its effectiveness is related to proximity. Are you willing to join us?"

"I'll slow you down, but I will come if you wish."

"Our plans are set. Do you all have your stratego medallions?" Nods of affirmation circled the table. Sana informed the rest of the group of their roles while the headmaster waited impatiently. There was a mission to start and the headmaster was anxious. "Jak, I will leave it to you to locate a suitable staging area for your troops outside of Minot. I will use the medallions to meet up with everyone after our reconnaissance mission is complete." Rose didn't want to start another mission without taking a moment to appreciate the friendships she had formed, despite the anxiousness of the Sicarius Headmaster, so she addressed the group. "We are special. Lattimer has much strength, but together we have more. We will fight him, and if one of us falls, let that death bring the others closer to freeing Malethya from his reign. I am proud to be counted in your company."

The group was unaccustomed to such sentimental statements from the Sicarius Headmaster, but Villifor broke the silence with a hearty, "I'll drink to that!" Stomachs turned and heads throbbed around the table as he hoisted his mug.

Slate understood the origin of the awkward statement and leaned in close, saying, "We will win, Rose. You will see them again." He gave her a hug while the others berated Villifor for reminding them of their current states.

Slate rose from the table and said, "Magnus killed my parents. Tonight I get the opportunity to pay him back." Rosana knew his personal grudge against Magnus was large, but she saw him push it back down and refocus with a deep breath. He was growing into the leader they needed him to be. "More importantly, though, we get closer to Lattimer. We won't fail. Ibson and Annarelle, it's time to go." They grabbed their travelling cloaks and packs for the journey ahead.

The Sicarius Headmaster followed Slate, Ibson, and Annarelle out of the basement and into the fresh, pungent air of the river docks. The group was largely silent; the headmaster approved. She had no desire for small talk. Instead, she ordered Rosana to watch their surroundings.

A light rain fell on the city. It wasn't heavy enough to keep boats at the dock, but the rain did warrant their cloaks. Fishermen were hard at work bringing in their morning catch. Rosana saw them sort the fish by throwing some into baskets whilst complaining amongst themselves, "Damn parasites spoil the meat… wasting fish is like throwing good coin away." She looked into one of the baskets as she walked by and saw a mottled appearance across its scales. The cause was unmistakable. The blight was spreading, and it wasn't just spreading to the trees. It was now affecting the fish in the river as well. Thankfully, the basket with the blighted fish was only a small portion of the fishermen's catch, but it was only a matter of time…

They headed north from the docks and Rosana took the opportunity to observe the city she knew so well. The streets she travelled were clean and the people smiled despite the rain. Even those that looked to have spent most of their lives avoiding a smile at least appeared to have softened their permanent grimaces into a semblance of happiness. Times were prosperous. It was amazing what a little coin could do for the morale of the city.

A small crowd gathered around a crier as he yelled to the masses, "Explosions rock the night, but Lattimer thwarts an attack on the infirmary! The Ispirtu Headmaster led a counterstrike onto infirmary grounds and the spineless rebels ran like the cowards they are! Lattimer proclaimed the attack to be orchestrated by the nefarious criminal Slate Severance! The former tournament champion continues his reign of terror against the people of Malethya that once cheered his name. King Darik promises to bring Slate to justice…" The man went on, but Rosana didn't have any desire to listen to Lattimer's propaganda.

Rosana looked over at Slate—he wore his cloak tight to cover his ghostly white skin. As much as it helped him in combat to prevent blood loss to any wounds, his paleness didn't do him any favors when he was walking around the city in the daytime. Rosana was thankful for the light rain that fell that morning. It made their traveling cloaks much less conspicuous on a day when plenty of eyes would be looking for Slate Severance. The rain made Rose think back to the rose garden blooming in the infirmary grounds. *Has it really only been a few short weeks since I broke Ibson out of the infirmary? So much has changed; now the rose bushes exist only in my memory and the infirmary grounds are a desolate barren memorial.*

They passed the ruins of a building that had been standing only a day before. *Is this the work of the Underground? Were soldiers and wizards here when their minds were freed?* It was impossible to tell how the destruction took place, but as they continued through the city, it was apparent that it wasn't an isolated incident. Ruined buildings and businesses speckled the city, changing her initial impression by the docks. The people in the heart of the city weren't smiling like the people on the docks. Their eyes darted around, and they hurried from building to building. The people of Malethya were a hard bunch, but the attacks of last night shook them noticeably. The damage may have been speckled throughout the city, but the after-effects of fear were in every darting glance, every hurried footstep, and every pair of eyes peaking from their windows.

Rose felt guilty, but the headmaster would

not let her dwell on it. A day of fear was a small price to pay in comparison to life lived under a blood mage, never knowing who around you was enslaved or when it would happen to you. She looked up to the top tower of Ispirtu, just visible in the distance. *Is Lattimer in there right now looking down on the city? If he is, he will be too far away to see the fear in people's eyes. The longer he sits in his tower, the more disconnected he will become from the people, and the less their lives will mean to him. Power corrupts and absolute power corrupts absolutely. He needs to be stopped.*

As they neared the edge of town, they spotted a caravan readying for departure to the north. A bribe to one of the merchants gave them a horse, cart, a space in the caravan, and a considerably lighter purse. It would have been easier, and a lot cheaper, to steal some horses, but Ibson was old and Slate hated horses with a passion rarely reserved for the creatures. Annarelle took the reins, and they rode north slowly, just one more group of travelers huddled in their carts trying to protect themselves from the rain.

After a couple hours of slow travel, Annarelle directed the horse away from the main road toward a small path into the woods. They were still significantly west of Minot, and following the caravan added significant time to their journey, but the relative obscurity afforded by traveling within the group made it worthwhile. After they split from the caravan, Slate directed Annarelle to drive toward a small farm on the edge of the forest.

Unaccustomed to visitors, the farmer saw them approach and greeted them kindly, if not a little bit skeptically. "Good day. What can I help you with? I don't have much extra food to sell as my crops are a little slow this year." *Has the blight traveled this far?*

"Would a horse and cart be of any use to you?" Slate asked with his cloak still kept tightly around his face.

"I don't have enough money to buy them from you. You might as well turn around if that's your business…"

"I didn't say anything about buying them. They are of no use to us anymore. They are yours…" He jumped off the cart and removed his hood. "…courtesy of Slate Severance." The farmer tightened his grip around his pitchfork at the sight of Slate's red eyes and pale skin. Slate tried to ease his mind by saying, "No need to do anything foolish, now. I know I look as scary as the stories about me, but I don't make a habit of attacking farmers without reason. Consider the horse and cart a gift. The only payment I require is that you spread the word that I'm not the monster people assume me to be."

The farmer remained skeptical but slowly reached out and grabbed the horse's reins. "Where will you go? There is nothing but woods and farms between here and Ravinai." Rosana and the rest of the group filled their travel packs with the supplies they would need for the remainder of the trip.

"I can't tell you, but I promise you won't see me again. If I succeed in my mission, your life will be unchanged and years from now you can tell your grandchildren about how you survived your encounter with the most dangerous man in Malethya." Slate patted the man on the shoulder. He flinched at Slate's touch and was obviously eager for them to leave. Slate obliged and started walking through the man's fields toward the woods. He called over his shoulder, "If I fail, I wouldn't worry about grandkids. You won't have the opportunity to have them. Enjoy the horse."

"You were doing so well with your public relations… right up until that last comment." Rosana chided Slate, even though his dark humor played well with his audience of Sicarius Guardsmen. Even Ibson chuckled a bit.

They entered the woods and headed east, relying upon Sana's training under Lucus to navigate the woods. She had learned to track her location based upon small signs of nature, such as looking for cool, damp-loving plants and fungi. Mushrooms and moss loved to grow on the north side of trees, where the tree trunks blocked direct sunlight for most of the day. After an hour of walking, they came across a blighted patch of trees. The disease must have been carried here some time ago, because the effect was widespread and devastating. Tree after tree drooped its wilted branches ever closer to the ground, looking as if they wished someone would just cut them down to end their misery. What the trees didn't know was that the coffin they craved would bring no solace, for the disease killing it spread along the ground as well. Grass and fallen leaves alike were various shades of brown, with some approaching black. The group took in the scene and Slate said, "This is why we are fighting. Blood magic always has consequences."

Regret threatened to overwhelm Sana but the defiance of the headmaster put an end to it. She refused to let Sana acknowledge fault. Sana had no way of knowing that her efforts to save Slate's life would cause the blight. Instead, the headmaster turned the conversation toward the task ahead, "The easiest way to stop blood magic is to kill Lattimer."

"You don't need to convince me of our course of action, but my motivation doesn't come from killing your brother." Annarelle looked at the headmaster with concern. "I want to stop this—or anything like it—from happening again." Her hard stare toward her headmaster gave no doubt that she disapproved the total lack of empathy with which the headmaster's comment had been delivered. "If you ever need to convince someone to join our cause, or to rediscover it, this would be a good spot to do it." Annarelle grabbed a healthy twig and flipped over a dead leaf, exposing a host of maggots feasting upon the dying trees.

Ibson cringed at the sight. "I hate maggots, but I think their feast will be short-lived. My mother always told me, you are what you eat." Rosana looked closer and saw that the maggots were mottled black, just as the fish had been. They would be dead in days.

Slate said, "Let's get back to saving the land of the living." Sana couldn't agree more. She led them away from the blighted patch of forest toward Minot, trying to push away thoughts of the disease. She had enough on her mind worrying about how to stop Lattimer, much less a blight she barely understood, even if she had caused it. The others must have been battling similar thoughts, because the trip was quiet and Sana soon realized they were close to Minot, so she brought the group to a halt. They had started their journey early enough in the morning that the sun was barely past its midpoint in the sky.

"We're close enough now that we'll have to

start watching for patrols. Our attack last night created confusion throughout Malethya, but I'm sure soldiers everywhere will be on high alert for a while. Magnus probably increased patrols to gain some form of control over the situation." Military commanders had used the tactic as long as battles had been waged. Following an attack, commanders needed to appear in control. Soldiers needed action and direction to feel safe and increased patrols at least added some benefit, however marginal.

"Do you think they will have patrols at the rock overlooking the town?" Ibson asked.

As the only person with some amount of Bellator training, Slate rubbed his head in thought. "He'll probably have a few patrols up there, but they will be sparse. The rock face serves as a natural barrier from attack, so he'll concentrate his patrols in the woods below."

"Does your head hurt?" Slate didn't usually rub his head when he thought through his plans. Rosana's training and her familiarity with Slate's tendencies picked up on the relatively common motion immediately. It may be common, but it wasn't common for Slate.

"I've had a headache all day. I shouldn't have drunk so much last night." Slate said with his winningest smile. "Let's go check out Minot." He left to scout ahead of the group before anyone questioned him.

The headmaster let the comment slide, knowing that Rosana could monitor his behavior as they approached the rock face. The headmaster wanted to use Slate as a warning to Lattimer's proximity. His debilitating condition could serve as a useful tool for her. Rosana cringed as the headmaster thought about Slate as a tool. Rose didn't intervene. Malethya needed the headmaster right now and the cold decisions that came with it. *Slate himself had said it.* She would monitor Slate and make sure his headache didn't worsen. If it did, she would enact one of Sana's contingency plans.

Annarelle's hand went up, signaling a stop. "Slate found a patrol up ahead." Annarelle used some hand signals to communicate with Slate and then told the group, "Stay quiet and watch your step. The coast is clear, but we don't want anyone finding our tracks."

The Sicarius Headmaster took the rear position in the group to monitor their tracks. Annarelle moved silently but was unaccustomed to the woods. Sana prepared a spell that she had used on numerous occasions to cover their feet with moss and mask the sound. In this instance, she watched the paths of her friends and cast the spell anywhere she saw tracks, covering them with moss. Annarelle was right to warn them to watch their step, but the Sicarius Headmaster hadn't stayed alive this long by hoping no one followed her path.

A few slow, arduous minutes later, the group met up with Slate near a tree surrounded by dense underbrush, providing good cover for the group. Ahead, the woods opened up to the rocks and then the blue sky of Malethya beyond. They had reached the cliff near Minot. "I only saw one patrol and it was an Ispirtu wizard. Hopefully it's one that spent her time locked up in the Ispirtu tower and feels out of place in the woods."

"Why didn't you just take her out?" Ibson asked. For as wise as the old wizard could be, he didn't know a thing about the ways of

Sicarius.

"I didn't want to take her out in case she's due to return and report soon." Slate answered succinctly, which could be an effect of the seriousness of their circumstances. But Rosana also noticed he held his hands near his sides. *Is he just relaxed or is he trying to avoid contact with his head?* Rosana was reminded of the times she—in the form of the Sicarius Headmaster—had watched Slate and Rainier play Stratego in the heart of Ravinai's city square. Each day brought a new challenge and an alteration of their physical appearance and mannerisms to sneak upon each other unannounced. Slate glanced toward Rosana. *He knows I am watching him. Game on.*

Annarelle expanded on Slate's short reply. "We need to work around the inconvenience of this patrol to maintain the surprise of our attack tonight. If we kill the patrol, he would be missed and found. If we incapacitate him, he'll wake up, and we'll find the town on high alert tonight."

"So we work around him, as you say. How do we do that?" Ibson asked. For the Sicarius Headmaster, it was like asking a master swordsman to explain how to unsheathe his sword. It simply wasn't worth her time. Annarelle handled it.

"If we were alone, we'd have to time the patrol and scout only when he was well-clear of our position. Since we have multiple people trained in the ways of Sicarius, however, we can watch both directions along the patrol route and signal if he draws near."

"I'll take the first watch in this direction." Slate signaled to his left and took off. *Predictable first move. When someone has your tail, the first goal is to put distance between yourself and your pursuer. He doesn't want the scrutiny currently directed toward him, and he's taken the position farthest from Rosana's watchful eyes.*

"Ibson, come with me to watch Minot," the Sicarius Headmaster said. "We will crawl along the rock face and peek over the edge, so that we minimize our profiles for anyone looking from below. Annarelle, you have the other direction in case the patrol doubles back."

The headmaster walked to the shadows of the tree line and dropped to her belly to crawl toward the edge of the rock face. It wasn't really any different than peeking over the edge of a rooftop in Ravinai. She had done that too many times to count on innumerable Malethyan nights. She didn't bother to wait for Ibson as he creakily lowered himself to the ground. She wanted to see Minot.

Her hopes of chaos and destruction were dashed the second she glimpsed the town. The ground was scorched and the trees were cut back from the town, but the wounds were old, caused during her previous visit to Minot. The buildings remained unharmed. Soldiers trained in the grounds of the Bellator complex with Hedok verbally abusing them between bouts. The Ispirtu complex teemed with activity, probably from wizards discussing their most recent finds in the library or preparing to head back to the cottage to make their next discovery. Ibson caught up to her and looked over the side of the rock. Rosana said to him, "Our mission in the infirmary didn't have any effect in Minot. We destroyed the blood in the Phylactery and yet Lattimer is strong as ever."

"That tells you something about Minot,

doesn't it, young headmaster?" Ibson's questions had a way of making Sana feel both elementary, like a first year student in Ispirtu, and at the same time challenged.

"It means Minot is more important to Lattimer than we ever guessed. He only staffed this place with soldiers and wizards that voluntarily subjugated their minds to him. When the Phylactery fell, Minot was left untouched."

"There is a lot of promise in you, headmaster. One day you might realize your full potential." Ibson smiled in the grandfatherly way that made Rose wish her father had. Brannon's gentle moments were few and far between. *Why do I warm to his praise?*

The headmaster changed the subject. "Have you prepared defensive magic for all of us?"

"Of course, my dear. I cast the spells before we reached the farmer's house. I didn't like the way he held his pitchfork."

Rose laughed before the headmaster could stifle it. Thankfully, she managed to do it quietly. *He didn't like the way the farmer held his pitchfork?* Between Slate, Annarelle, and the Sicarius Headmaster, the farmer would have been dead before he had the pointy end sticking in the right direction. They didn't need Ibson's help with the farmer any more than Rose needed her mom to clean a dirty smudge from her cheeks. Caitlyn always wiped her face regardless of her protests, and it seemed that Ibson would always make sure they were protected from the smallest of harms.

Sana's curiosity about defensive magic begged the question, "What pattern do you use to cast the defensive magic anyway? How is it effective against so many different types of magic?"

"It's questions like that that will keep you

alive long enough to realize that potential I was talking about." Then the smile on his face slipped and his eyes clouded momentarily. "Unfortunately, I am oath-bound to that topic as well. My secrets regarding defensive magic must remain my own until my oath has been fulfilled." Then the smile returned to his face. "Thankfully, the oath doesn't prevent me from using defensive magic."

"So you must fulfill this oath without speaking its nature to anyone? Why would you devote yourself to a cause with little chance of success? The person who forced you to make this oath has a sick sense of humor."

Ibson smiled and said, "My sense of humor isn't that terrible, is it? I forced the oath upon myself." Once again the smile faded and his eyes clouded as he gazed over Minot. Sana didn't interrupt his thoughts. She had a million questions, but none of them pertained to the mission at hand and the headmaster was getting anxious.

Magnus was somewhere down there with a vial of Slate's blood in his pocket. Lattimer might be around as well, but Slate wasn't cooperating with her efforts to determine his whereabouts. Helping Ibson wasn't the headmaster's priority, especially if he couldn't tell her the meaning of his oath or how to break it. He would have to pay the price of his oath on his own terms.

After a few minutes of contemplation, she decided on her next course of action. "Ibson, can you trade places with Slate? Tell him I need his council on how to apply his particular brand of chaos to the town of Minot."

The request brought Ibson's mind back to the present, and he patted her on her arm. "Of course, of course. Stay safe."

The Sicarius Headmaster never needed a reminder of her own mortality, but Ibson's farewell conjured the list of dead headmasters to her mind again. She knew her name would join the list eventually, but when? She had so much more to accomplish, so much more to teach Annarelle, although her protégé was progressing nicely. Her thoughts were interrupted when Slate joined her. With the speed of his approach, he must have flashed all the way from his lookout position.

"You called?" His winning smile was once again plastered all over his face. *Does his head feel better or is it just his current disguise in the real-life game of Stratego?*

The Sicarius Headmaster answered in alternating speech so that Slate would know this wasn't the time to banter. "Minot's defenses are still completely intact. How would you disrupt them?"

Slate looked over the town for a second and then answered, "Tommy will work with Annarelle to cloud the area with smoke by sending smoke orbs onto the town from this location, and I think Jak and Villifor's plan to harry the response of Magnus' troops will be sound. As for me…" Slate scanned the town and closed his eyes in thought. *Is he visualizing the future battle or trying to clear his head?* "I can't front an assault for the Bellator troops. There will be too many opponents for me to attack them head-on. Their numbers would simply overwhelm me. No, I'd be most effective working with you on a strategic strike. I could help you cut to the heart of the camp, find Magnus, complete the mission, and get out." He looked at her with apparent determination. *Magnus had killed his parents. He wants to complete this mission more than anything.*

"You will be less effective in Minot than you were in the infirmary. Magnus, Cirata, and Hedok are training troops to act with control as Furies. They are formidable." *Was Slate's commitment wavering?* Rosana studied his body language and facial features, but he wasn't giving anything away. His hands clenched his staff as if anticipating battle and his jaw was set with stubborn determination. *Maybe I've trained my student too well.*

"They still aren't as fast as me, they aren't as strong as me, and they still bleed. If they manage to get a glancing blow, I'll trade them a superficial, bloodless wound for a lethal one in return." Fearlessness intertwined the words of his impassioned speech. "They. Won't. Stop. Me." He emphasized his final words with pointing to the town and hitting his chest with his hand. *The man is a force of nature.* Rosana loved him for it, even if she didn't show it at the moment.

Sana acquiesced at the command of the headmaster, "Okay, Slate. I have several plans that call for a strategic strike, and I have seen all that I need from this rock. Let's gather the others and decide on the best option. I'll get Annarelle, you get Ibson, and we'll meet back a way. Do you remember where we were when you first spotted the patrol?"

"Yes, I'll meet you there." He slid back from the rock face on his belly, and she followed closely behind. When she was well away from the cliff edge and any watchful eyes from Minot, she turned to her right to track down Annarelle. After a minute of walking she saw a snapped twig and picked up Annarelle's trail. She made the call of a sparrow, knowing

Annarelle was near. A short distance ahead, she heard Annarelle's response in the form of a meadowlark's call. Annarelle joined her a few seconds later.

"Are we all clear?" the headmaster asked.

"The patrol is due back soon, but there aren't any signs yet."

"Let's not give him any. How is your knot tying?"

Annarelle's eyes narrowed. "Good enough to hold Ibson. What happened?"

The headmaster corrected her presumption. "They'll need to be stronger than that. The knots are for Slate." Shock covered Annarelle's face, and a member of Sicarius was difficult to shock. "Slate is hiding Lattimer's presence in Minot. We can't allow him to join the battle. His presence will only be a liability."

"How do you know?" Annarelle asked. The answer was simple; Slate had lost the game of Stratego. He had controlled his facial features, his body language, and his emotions, but his body still betrayed him.

"Slate's palms get sweaty when he is nervous. In his first guild tournament fight against Rainier, Slate told me his mouth dried out and his hands perspired so much that he was actually thankful for the leather wraps on his staff. People can tell a lie with a smile on their face, but the body is difficult to control." Rosana was happy to see Annarelle soaking in the lesson. "I questioned Slate, but I wasn't listening to his response. When he pointed to Minot and hit his chest to emphasize his point, he let go of his staff. The leather wraps were damp." There was only one logical conclusion. "Slate is fighting a battle in his head as surely as he fought Rainier in the guild tournament. Lattimer is in Minot."

They neared their meeting point in the woods. Annarelle asked, "What do you want me to do?"

"Just follow my lead, and when the time comes, tie some good knots."

From the bushes ahead, she heard the call of the sparrow and gave the call of a meadowlark in return, repeating the greeting. Slate and Ibson came out of hiding and Rosana took control of the conversation before they had a chance to alter her plans. "Slate, do you think this location will serve as an adequate staging ground for tonight's battle?"

Slate looked around, assessing the wooded area in which they stood. "We are outside the range of their patrols, but just barely. When Villifor first came to Minot, he staged his army in a clearing to the west of here, but Magnus was on that Bellator mission. I wouldn't want to be anywhere near that clearing with Magnus expecting an attack. It will be difficult for Jak and the others to get an army to this location, but provided they can, it will serve well." He then looked at Rosana and smiled without any of the tension she had just witnessed on the rock. The easy smile and thoughtful answer only confirmed his guilt. The battle in his head diminished as he distanced himself from Minot. Slate then said, "Of course, that assumes Jak can find us. How do you plan to signal him?"

"I don't plan to signal him. I plan to see him coming and to intercept him before he encounters any danger from Magnus. Annarelle, can you retrieve my medallions?"

"Yes, headmaster." She dug through her travel sack until she found the box containing the Stratego medallions. She unfolded the box onto the forest floor, exposing the map with pins marking the most recent locations of all her friends.

"I've never seen you use this before. I've always wondered how you used the medallions to track people." Slate hunched over the board to get a closer look at the map.

"Her particular use and identification for this spell is nothing short of remarkable." Ibson huddled over the map with Slate, his academic nature overpowering him.

"Annarelle, will you explain it to Slate? This is a weak area in your training and teaching others is an effective learning tool." Sana commanded her apprentice, and Annarelle nodded in affirmation. Sana slowly circled the group in observation of Annarelle's explanation.

"Each medallion has a pair, kind of like a twin. The technical name for it is entangled particles, but the headmaster would have to explain those details. When the headmaster casts a probing spell into the medallion in our possession, there is a ping or reflection from the stone's absent pair. The headmaster has become attuned to the signals and can map out a rough direction and distance on this map. Do you see here?" Annarelle pointed toward the pin marking Tommy. Slate and Ibson leaned in closer to look where Annarelle indicated. "The last time we used the medallions Tommy was in Ravinai. If I use it now…"

Thwack. The Sicarius Headmaster chopped down on the base of Slate's neck. The demon of Malethya, the man who inspired fear throughout the kingdom and attacked entire squadrons of soldiers single-stone-handedly, dropped unceremoniously onto the map.

CHAPTER NINETEEN

WHEN KNIGHT FALLS

Annarelle cinched the ropes around Slate and propped him against the trunk of a tree while the headmaster checked the knots. Rose thought they were too tight, but the headmaster jerked them tighter.

"What have you done?" Ibson demanded appropriately.

"Lattimer is in Minot, and Slate was hiding it from us. Lattimer's presence makes Slate a liability to the mission in his current state."

"So you just incapacitated him? He trusted you!"

"He is not the first man I have incapacitated. It was necessary." The Sicarius Headmaster refused to acknowledge regret in her actions despite Rosana and Rose sharing Ibson's sentiment. "As for the blow to the neck, you have yourself to blame. I prefer to incapacitate people with a weak spark spell, but your defensive magic made that option impossible."

"But Slate is our best weapon against Lattimer and his men! You've just handicapped all of us."

The headmaster had heard enough. "Calm down. He will wake up." *People always overreact to forced incapacitation. Slate probably needs a nap anyway.* "Besides, we haven't discussed our plan yet, and I will need you to relay it to him when he wakes up in a few minutes."

"Then speak." A skeptical Ibson waited to

hear the headmaster's intentions. Rosana took over the negotiations with a little help from Sana, since Ibson always responded well to logic.

"Lattimer is in Minot and Slate's mind is clouded with revenge. Magnus killed his parents, and he saw an opportunity to avenge their deaths. He is too important to send running headlong into battle against Lattimer before we've cleared his mind of the blood magic that still festers within. I feared that if I told Slate he couldn't be involved in the attack tonight, he would go rogue and attack anyway."

Ibson softened his position, but only partially. "Then tell me how you plan to overcome the loss of such an important part of our plan. How will we still succeed?"

"We need to separate Magnus from Lattimer. If we can make Magnus come to us while we occupy Lattimer, then Slate comes back into play. We can kill Magnus, destroy his totem with Slate's blood in it, and leave before Lattimer realizes our true target." Ibson appeared thoughtful, so the headmaster ordered Rosana to rush on before objections arose. "But I'm not done scouting yet. I only said that to Slate so that we could locate an appropriate staging area before I incapacitated him. I didn't want to put him, or you, in danger. I need to take Annarelle with me into the woods surrounding Minot. It will take most of the afternoon, but when we return, we will have decided upon the best possible plan. Will you watch Slate until we return?"

"Slate deserved to be treated better than this. I would not have thought you capable of such betrayal." Ibson was silent for a minute before adding, "But if I know one thing about you, it's that you wouldn't do anything to hurt Slate… at least not permanently. I will watch him until you return." Despite his willingness to help, his tone shared his disappointment in the headmaster's actions.

"Thank you, Ibson." Rose hugged the old wizard. "I'll write a letter to explain my actions." Rosana put pen to paper, recollecting the first day they met, when she had incapacitated him in his guild tournament tent and left a letter for him to find on his pillow. This time, she wrote:

Dearest Slate,

Your first mistake was trying to keep a secret from a Sicarius Guardsman. Your second mistake was dating a Sicarius Guardsman. Your last mistake, the mistake that finds you unconscious against a tree, was to assume that you had managed to trick a Sicarius Guardsman.
Please know that the decision I make now is not a mistake. You are important. You are important to me. I need you, but not as much as the people of Malethya need you. Don't let them down. Don't let me down.

I love you,

Rosana sealed the note and dropped it onto his stomach. She then lifted Slate's chin and gave his warm, motionless lips a kiss. Annarelle approached her friend and mentor, gently squeezing her shoulder. "I'm all packed up. Are you ready to go?"

"Of course, we have a mission to scout." Rosana let the headmaster answer so that her emotions wouldn't get the best of her. Sana diverted attention from Rosana's brief display of affection by casting the spell that affixed moss to her and Annarelle's feet, so that they would be harder to track. They left Ibson to care for Slate and began to travel through the woods, encircling Minot to approach from the opposite direction. Annarelle walked in companionable silence as they picked their way through the forest, carefully dodging tree limbs and stepping over ambitious roots that fought for space along the rocky forest floor. It wasn't until they had walked all around the southern edge of Minot and Rosana turned east, away from the city, that Annarelle finally realized something was amiss.

"We aren't going to scout Minot, are we?" Annarelle stated the obvious, since Rosana had just turned away from the town. "You lied to Ibson, but you didn't fool me. We aren't going back there to wait for the others. You are going against the plans of the team, the plans you made in the first place. Tell me why."

"You are right. We aren't going to Minot. Our mission has changed. Our new target is the hunter's cottage. Magnus is in charge of the operations within the library, the storage room, and the vault. It is the one place I know he will be. As for the original plan I shared with the team"—Sana paused to think through her response and then said—"that plan no longer offers the best chance to accomplish the goals of our mission. We need to kill Magnus and destroy the totem filled with Slate's blood. In truth, the plan I told the team was never the plan most likely to succeed, but it was the plan I hoped to enact. With Lattimer here, that plan is no longer possible."

"We could separate Magnus from Lattimer, just like you told Ibson." Hope crept into Annarelle's voice. She should have known better.

Now Rose spoke, "I know my brother better than anyone, and he is too careful to let something like that happen. He will keep Magnus close, and I suspect he will keep Phoenix close as well."

"That doesn't leave us with too many options," Annarelle protested.

"There are always options, it's just that sometimes the decisions associated with them are difficult to make. We are Sicarius Guardsmen. We do the job that needs to be done." Rose searched for an analogy. "How good are you at chess?"

"Good enough to hold my own. But I've seen you play," Annarelle admitted. "I could not beat you."

"When people play chess, they try to keep all their pieces on the board. In general, this is a sound strategy, but every good player knows that sometimes they have to sacrifice a rook or a knight to set up a larger play. We need to free Slate's mind to make a play on Lattimer... and we might have to sacrifice a knight to succeed." Rose said, while the headmaster ran through the list of Sicarius Guardsmen that had previously held her title. How many of them got the opportunity to choose when they added their names to the list? She could ask for nothing more.

"No..." Annarelle said, almost in a whisper.

The strength of her voice grew as she pleaded with Rose. "You aren't simply a knight on a chessboard. Slate would never sacrifice your life, and even if you want to use the chess analogy, the knight is the wrong piece. You would be the fractal-forsaken queen. Queens aren't sacrificed so lightly. Please reconsider…"

Rose hugged her friend. Decisions such as these were difficult, but this was the precise reason she had ceded more control to the headmaster; hard decisions needed to be made.

"You know I have considered every possibility, and this one is the best. We have weakened Lattimer with our attack on the infirmary and must strike now before he rebuilds his army. Even now, his army in Minot is formidable and a conventional assault will fail with Lattimer here to bolster their ranks. I'll have to sneak in and kill the target the Sicarius way. This is a mission for the Shadow in the Night, the Master of Chaos. I will walk into the cottage and blend into my surroundings. I am the master of my environment. No door shall bar my way. I could sit beside my own mother and she wouldn't know I was there." Rose's mind flitted quickly to Caitlyn. *If this is my final mission, I hope Annarelle will find a way to tell Caitlyn that I visited her regularly, in my own fashion.*

Sana, having calculated her odds of survival, grabbed Annarelle by the shoulders and looked her in the eye. "After this mission, there is a good chance you will be the Sicarius Headmaster. You have grown immensely in the months I have taught you, and I know you are up to the task." Tears streamed down Annarelle's cheeks as she fought to combat the news, and

Rose gave her another hug before the Sicarius Headmaster pushed her away to hear Sana's plan. Annarelle was a great friend, but she was a Sicarius Guardsman first, and she had a job to do. "You will not be entering the hunter's cottage with me. Instead, I need you to stay outside and watch who exits. Your first task is to kill any wizards traveling alone to Minot. I expect my plan will cause messengers to be sent and you must intercept them. I will not have sufficient time to complete my mission otherwise. Then, watch for Bellator soldiers carrying Magnus' dead body. If they do, you will know I succeeded in my task. If I don't exit the cottage, then presume this was my final mission. It will fall to you to bring the news to Slate and the rest of our friends."

Annarelle stared at her friend and mentor for a while before she set her jaw. "We always face long odds in our missions. What can we do to increase them a bit? Even if this mission is next to impossible, we don't have to make it easy for them. First, we have the tools of our trade." She dropped her travel sack to the ground and started laying out the contents. Disguises of several sorts lay on the forest floor, along with a coil of rope, a lock pick set, a few exploding orbs, a Sicarius mask, and a small arsenal of throwing weapons.

"Let's start with weapons." The Sicarius Headmaster drifted over the exploding orbs and various throwing weapons before her fingers ran over the hilt of her throwing knives, taking comfort from the familiar feeling of the catalpa etchings against her fingertips. "Phoenix and Magnus will have informed Lattimer about your aptitude with exploding orbs, and I must assume he will have devised a method to counteract your magical abilities. He could copy the spell that surrounds the walls of Ispirtu, and with blood magic, he wouldn't need to understand the pattern to replicate it here. I'll leave the exploding orbs, although I'm aiming to inflict as much damage as possible. That leaves my throwing knives. I'll take all of them." Sana decided against grabbing kunai and the other throwing weapons since most were best-suited for diversionary tactics that masked escape, but she didn't feel the need to tell that to Annarelle.

The headmaster loaded the folds of her Sicarius wraps with as many knives as they would hold, hoping she would get the chance to use them all. Then Sana cast a spell that coiled the rope across her shoulder, just as she controlled the vines in the forest. Annarelle looked at her questioningly, but Sana simply shrugged and said, "It's rope. You never know when you need some rope." Finally, she wrapped the lock pick set against her thigh using the same rationale as the rope. *Some tools I can't go on a mission without.*

"That settles your supplies. What about your disguise? Which of these costumes will hide the Master of Chaos?" Annarelle asked as she motioned toward the clothing worn by the prisoners in service at Minot.

"Last time I was in Minot, I used Josef and his prisoners to locate the hunter's cottage. That won't work this time, because I would be stuck working in storage all day, too far away from Magnus to ensure mission success. There is also the consideration that my brother will likely be watching the prisoners closely. He is not one to repeat mistakes." Sana pointed to the Ispirtu robes folded neatly on the ground.

"This time, I will be a scholar investigating the library." She pulled the robes over her Sicarius wrappings.

Annarelle picked up the Sicarius mask and handed it to the headmaster, but the headmaster refused. "Lattimer gave Phoenix a mask, so he has a mask on hand to replicate. If he can replicate it, then he can probably cast a spell with blood magic that detects it. If he has, I might as well set a security orb over my head when I walk into the hunter's cottage. I used this mask to infiltrate Ispirtu and join my father's side against Lattimer's treachery. He will know that this mask is a threat to his power. He will have some method to counteract its effects. Like I said, Lattimer doesn't repeat mistakes. For this mission, I will rely on Rosana's skills."

"Then at least let me alter your appearance a bit." Annarelle fixed her hair in a slightly eccentric style befitting the whims of a wizard and applied some makeup that de-emphasized Sana's cheekbones and strong chin, her most defining features. Afterward she sat back to evaluate her work, deeming it to be sufficient. "That looks better. You look just crazy enough to be one of Lattimer's followers. How else can I help?"

"There are only two things left for me to do. First, I'd like to review the information we stole from Minot the last time." They didn't have much information to work with, but she wanted to know the information she did have. One never knew when it would come in handy. Annarelle produced the painting rendered by the artistic stylings of Cirata Larasa and the storage list. She looked for deeper meaning in Cirata's painting, but it didn't seem

applicable to the hunter's cottage. Its setting
was the infirmary and none of the detailed gore
depicted in the painting created a connection
in her mind with her observations from the
cottage. The list, on the other hand, was
definitely applicable but also impractical.
What good was an ancient artifact if it was
buried in an endless sea of sand? Nonetheless,
she committed the entire list to memory. When
she was done, she said, "The last preparatory
task I have is right here." Sana pulled the
stratego medallion she had taken with her and
held it up. "This medallion is the other half
of the piece shot in Phoenix's leg during the
infirmary mission. I suspect my brother will
have ordered Phoenix to Minot from Ravinai.
Let's hope the tracker is still in place."

Sana pinged the medallion with a probing
spell and the signal from its counterpart was
immediate. Phoenix was close by, and based upon
the direction of the signal, he was within the
town of Minot. "The abomination is here."

"That's all the more reason not to carry out
this mission. It's too dangerous. Slate would
never wish for you to carry it out. You aren't
being yourself…"

The Sicarius Headmaster couldn't argue any
longer with Annarelle for fear that Rose would
side with Rosana's objections. She stopped the
argument with a reminder of the purpose of
their guild. "That's precisely why it must be
completed. This is Malethya and we are Sicarius
Guardsmen. We act when others fail to act. We
do what must be done, even if those we protect
never know our deeds. We are shadows. Shadows
never die, headmaster." She took the Sicarius
mask and shoved it into Annarelle's hands.

Annarelle looked down at the mask and slowly

nodded. By the time she looked up, the former Sicarius Headmaster had vanished into the woods.

CHAPTER TWENTY

A Lion in a Hornet's Nest

The Sicarius Headmaster waited patiently out of sight of the tiny hunter's cottage when a group of wizards finally exited the path from Minot, led by a red-haired wizard without a shortage of confidence. Disguise or no, Sana wanted to know if there was a specific trick to entry that the wizards used. Rose didn't put it past Lattimer to add a little security upon his arrival. It wouldn't do any good to get caught before she even entered the building. Without the Sicarius mask, that was a very real possibility.

The wizards walked up to the Bellator Guardsman at the door and she overheard the red-haired wizard say, "Step aside, fireball fodder." Well at least Rosana knew which tone of voice to use. The condescension Ispirtu wizards held for anyone that didn't hold the spark was alive and well in Minot.

"Say the password or you can see if your wit is sharper than my sword." He grabbed his hilt and unsheathed the sword an inch or two to emphasize the seriousness of the matter.

"Heed the raven's call. Now get out of my way." The wizards pushed past the guardsman into the hunter's cottage. The brief exchange provided Sana with the necessary password for entry and a sense of relief that no magical defenses were employed. Her training in magic was incomplete, and she couldn't possibly bypass a spell that Lattimer cast to protect the cottage. Fractal's blessings were upon her, so she tried her luck while the blessings remained.

Rosana made her way over to the path in the woods and approached the guardsman using the same path as the previous wizards. She left the cowl of her Ispirtu robes down, so that her face was fully exposed, fixed with an expression of supreme confidence that only a wizard can bare.

The guardsman saw her coming and scowled, "State your business." His previous encounter left him in a foul mood. *Such attitude toward a wizard can only be met with derision.*

"My business is not for your insignificant ears. Heed the raven's call, and tell me where I can find the wizard in charge of the library."

"Harrumph…" The Bellator soldier turned to open the door, presumably to lead Rosana to the wizard in charge. That wouldn't do.

"I said to tell me where to go. I don't need a chauffeur carrying a pointy stick."

The guardsman turned around with a cutting glare. "Just look for the only bastard more arrogant than you. He's got bright red hair that matches his temper. His name is Glennon."

"Hmm, maybe you aren't chauffeur material, but you have the makings of a butler. At least you know the names of the other help." Rosana patted him on the chest and was rewarded with an indecipherable grumble as she entered the hunter's cottage.

Rosana fought the momentary bout of disorientation she encountered when stepping into the library by quickly scanning the room while her senses reoriented themselves. Setting foot in a tiny cottage that transforms into a ballroom-sized library has a way of messing with your mind. Rosana spotted Glennon speaking with a small group of wizards at one of the tables in the middle of the library. She walked toward him purposefully while taking note that Magnus, Phoenix, and Lattimer were absent from the room. *Have I made a mistake by coming here?* Sana reminded her that any plan would have been a risk, and this one had the best chance of success. Rosana almost reminded her about the magnitude of the risk; she didn't want to throw her life away for nothing.

As she approached, Glennon looked up and folded his arms in front of him. "I haven't seen you before."

Rosana could play this part of the mission in one of two ways, and she had already decided her course after witnessing the encounter with the Bellator Guardsman. "No, Glennon, you haven't seen me before and when I leave this room you will promptly forget that I was ever here. I will require the aid of two wizards familiar with the library to retrieve texts for me. They will need to have very selective memories as well." Glennon degraded those below him, and such behavior was often an artifact of the organizational structure surrounding him. If he degraded those beneath him, there was an excellent chance that he was used to receiving similar treatment from his superiors. Rosana was banking on it.

"I am in charge of research in the library. Nothing happens here without my thorough understanding of the situation, especially since we have been placed on high alert." The same scowl remained on Glennon's face but that only encouraged Rosana. If she had guessed incorrectly, he would have responded with a fireball instead of conversation. Glennon was tough, but he would crack given the right situation. Rosana would make sure he understood that this was the right situation.

"I am here to research a special topic for the Great Redeemer. I will report my findings back to him and no one else. I've been assured that this conversation will satisfy your curiosity. Have I been misinformed? I would hate to return empty-handed…"

"You expect the aid of two of my researchers with nothing but empty words? I have been entrusted with research within this library for a reason." Rosana cut him off before he started to regain his authority.

"You conduct research in books and provide that information to those who can actually accomplish something with it. You are a tool, and a simple tool at that." *If it hurts me to hear Slate referred to as a tool, it had to cut even deeper to hear yourself referred to in that manner.* "You funnel the information to the Great Redeemer. As long as you continue to do this simple job, you will remain a useful tool in his eyes, but nothing more." The stern look on Glennon's face turned to something between being aghast and murderous. Finally Rosana was getting somewhere. "You mentioned that we are on high alert. Do you know why we are on high alert? No, because tools know better than to ask those questions. I didn't have to ask because I am one of the wizards who receive your funneled information. With this information, I am trusted to act on the Redeemer's behalf. I was told the reasons we are on high alert and I am here to find information of the most practical sort. Help me now or I will return to the Great Redeemer and inform him that he needs to find a new tool." *There. I have laid my bet on the table. Will Glennon call my bluff?* The Sicarius Headmaster's fingers were inches from a throwing knife and Rose fought to stay calm and control her breathing, so that she wouldn't be betrayed by sweat forming on her brow or the pounding in her chest.

With murder still in his eyes, Glennon said, "Take the table in the back. I'll send two junior researchers over to assist you." Rose contained a sigh of relief that threatened to escape and Rosana strode past Glennon without a further word. Her ruse had worked, and the power of self-preservation prevented Glennon from raising the alarm immediately, but she had no doubt the wizard would be working to verify her story by sending a wizard to Minot. Annarelle would intercept the messenger, but that only bought Rosana so much time before Glennon became anxious from the lack of response and decided to act. The mission clock began to tick.

She sat at the empty table Glennon had directed her to use. It offered a clear view of the prisoners working under the hot sun within the storage room, which probably explained why the other Ispirtu wizards left it empty. The sight of half-starved men and women working under the hot sun without breaks would inspire pity even within the heart of a wizard. It was best to avoid such distractions from their important research.

Shortly after sitting down, two researchers joined her table. Rosana recognized the man and woman immediately as part of the group that had entered the hunter's cottage with Glennon. They were obviously trusted friends of Glennon and would report the nature of her request to him immediately. Rosana spoke to them before they opened their mouths. *Control the conversation.* "I require texts on spark-based magic involving catalpa trees. Specifically, I know their power has been harnessed in the past and it may have been harnessed by our enemies. I need to know how. I expect you to return expediently." The two researchers left her alone while they searched through the book stacks with seasoned efficiency.

Sana had chosen catalpa trees as her cover story for a very simple purpose. She reasoned that the true story of Lattimer's battle with Brannon would be told within Lattimer's ranks of confidants, even if it wasn't shared with the general public. If Glennon heard rumors of such a tale, a detail in the story such as catalpa trees would be just specific enough to provide relevancy and vague enough to demand secrecy. It had the secondary benefit of potentially helping to stop the blight, on the off-chance that she stayed alive long enough to make use of the information.

The wizards returned in short order with several books on catalpa trees, making it easier for Rosana to avoid the death stares Glennon trained on her from across the library. She opened the first book and scanned the table of contents for something interesting, settling on a section entitled "Catalpa Trees and the Dilution of Magic," written by Koch, one of Cantor's students. Flipping to that section she read:

Catalpa trees innately treat magic as the human body treats a foreign object. They first try to counteract any spell that enters their roots or veins by dilution of the spark throughout the tree, minimizing the effect of the spell. If that fails, the tree then isolates and walls off the diluted spell at a localized level, thereby protecting the unaffected portions of the tree. Since catalpa trees have extensive root systems, any disease affecting one tree is dangerous to the entire grove. The magic-resistant response of the catalpa trees simultaneously protects the individual catalpa trees from lesser magic as well as the health of the grove through the sacrificial loss of individual trees affected by stronger magic.

Sana thought back to the spell she'd cast to save Slate from the blood magic being used against him by Lattimer. She had opened Slate's veins and forced his infected blood into the catalpa grove. The blood magic was too strong for a single tree to dilute on its own, and it spilled out of the tree. The infected blood was absorbed by the extensive root system of the trees in the grove. Now she understood the mistake she had made. Her spell had prevented the grove from isolating the infected trees and when the infected blood overran the defenses of the individual tree, the extensive root system put the next trees in danger. It moved on to the next tree and then the next tree and then the grass and every other plant it contacted. There could be no mistake about it. Sana had caused the blight.

All thoughts of the blight evaporated when Magnus emerged from the vault's stairwell with Cirata at his side. He was dressed in full Bellator armor, but held his helmet in his hand as he barked orders to the wizards and soldiers following him. "How much time do you need to solve the riddle of this wall? You've been studying it for months, and as far as I can tell you've made no progress whatsoever." None of his followers dared answer his question, so instead he redirected his anger. "Where's Glennon?"

"Here, General Pudriuz." Glennon spoke without any of the derision that he displayed toward the guardsman at the cottage entrance, leaving no question as to who was in charge.

"What progress have your wizards accomplished in penetrating the wall that protects the vault?"

"They are probing the wall around the clock and tracking the patterns they sense, but the pattern in the wall shifts constantly. By the time my wizards learn the pattern well enough to use it in a spell, it has already changed. We are hoping that the patterns begin to repeat so that we can predict them and penetrate the wall." Glennon hoped the truth would shield him from Magnus' anger. It didn't.

Magnus lifted Glennon into the air with one arm, demonstrating the leadership abilities of a hammer and confirming Rosana's prior approach to addressing Glennon with a firm tongue. "Your plan is to sit and wait and hope?"

Glennon backpedaled ineffectively, as his feet dangled above the ground, "I have made significant contributions within the library."

Magnus raised him higher. "Let me reiterate your directive, in case it isn't clear enough for you. The library is a collection of books, and while you find value in their writings, they aren't important enough to be protected from the outside world. The vault has real-live people walking around in it. For all we know, they are the very people who wrote the books you are so proud of reading. Find. A. Way. In."

With each word he squeezed Glennon's neck tighter, making his eyes protrude in an unflattering way. He released the wizard, and Glennon collapsed in a crumpled heap on the library floor, gasping for breath.

Magnus promptly turned his attention to Cirata. "Let's go check out what other failures await us in the storage room. If I'm still getting status reports when Phoenix shows up, I may not be able to contain my temper."

Rosana froze at her table. Phoenix was on his way. Was she being fractal-blessed with the opportunity to kill two of his generals? They were the only two people that Rosana had witnessed commanding Furies. *If I can kill them both and destroy the totems they have in their possession, Slate might finally be free from Lattimer's control.*

The Sicarius Headmaster disagreed vehemently. *Our mission is clear—kill Magnus.*

"Phoenix is a pitiful man who elevates himself by blaming you for the failures of those beneath you." Cirata stroked Magnus' arm while letting her icy stare linger on those she considered to be most egregious in their failures. "Would you like to take your anger out on some of the prisoners? I know that always cheers you up, darling."

Magnus contemplated the suggestion as he walked toward the storage room and Rosana. Rosana shifted the book she was reading to the right of the table so that she could turn her head slightly away from Magnus and Cirata. They were two of the only people who had seen her without her Sicarius mask in Brannon's office, and while Annarelle was highly trained in the art of disguise, there was no need to take unnecessary risks. The small physical act of masking her identity was the only course of action she could decide upon, while an argument raged internally between herselves.

We must wait! Rosana insisted. *Phoenix is coming. We could destroy both totems at once!*

The headmaster refuted her claims. *You jeopardize our mission with your greed. We came to kill Magnus, and we should do it while we have the chance.*

Sana didn't have a strong opinion on the matter. *Normally, I would agree with the headmaster, that we would be adding additional risk to the mission for questionable benefit. But in this case, I'm not so sure. Since we have already decided that the mission will be carried out with little chance of survival, it stands to reason that we should inflict as much damage as possible.*

Then it is a good thing that I'm in charge of this mission, the headmaster stated with finality. *Your objections are noted and ignored.*

Magnus neared and Sana calculated her odds of mission success. Magnus' path would bring him within ten feet of her table, well within range of her throwing knives. With his helmet off, it would be a sure kill. Upon his death, she would have to reach the totem and destroy it before the library turned into one massive fireball. It would work. It was amazing how simple missions could be when you didn't have to worry about surviving. The Sicarius Headmaster's hand slid under the Ispirtu robes and gripped the handle of a throwing knife.

Don't do it, Rosana objected. *We can kill Phoenix too! He's on his way here!* But they were on a mission and the headmaster always did what she thought needed to be done.

This is my call, the headmaster said coolly.

Magnus drew even with her table. The Sicarius Headmaster slid the knife out from beneath her robes in anticipation, keeping it hidden from view.

Sana readied her spell to ensure the knife flew straight. Rosana screamed in silent frustration.

Magnus and his group passed by the table, exposing the back of his neck. Her throwing knife would penetrate the base of the skull and sever the connection to the brain. At this distance and with the aid of Sana's spell, the target looked to be the size of a barn door. It would be nearly impossible to miss and instantly fatal. The time was now. Sana indicated her spell was ready. The Sicarius Headmaster moved to throw the knife.

Her arm didn't move.

Wait, Rose spoke. She never interrupted a mission.

What is this? the headmaster asked. *Why are you interfering with the mission? Free me now while there is still time!* Magnus approached the storage room.

We will wait, Rose answered absolutely. *You are all a part of me, but this decision is bigger than a mission. It must be mine to make. Lucus once said a sacrifice is freely given. I will sacrifice my life as he did, but I will make it count for as much as possible when I do. If I have a chance to kill Phoenix as well as Magnus, I will wait for it.*

The tension in the headmaster's arm didn't relax. *You have witnessed the effectiveness of my techniques. Your inactivity let Lattimer grow in power and you failed to obtain information about the phylactery or the vault.*

It wasn't until I took action that we spilt the blood of the phylactery and discovered a way to save Slate. We need to act. We need to act now.

Magnus passed into the storage room, rendering the argument moot since the headmaster's knife became temporarily ineffective. *We will discuss this more later,* the headmaster promised as she slipped the knife back under her Ispirtu robes. Rosana rejoiced silently, careful not to upset the headmaster or make Rose regret her intervention in the matter.

Inside the storage room, Magnus redirected his vitriol toward the Bellator Guardsman overseeing the prisoners. "Have the dogs found anything today?"

"It is the same as every other day, General Pudriuz. All we find is sand. We dig deep. We switch locations. We uncover broad amounts of sand over a large area. We take half-day excursions into the desert heat in hopes of finding artifacts. But it is always the same. Sand. Sand. Sand." Magnus' fist clenched, but he stopped short of hurting the poor soldier.

"Tomorrow, bury something before the dogs arrive and then tell them to search in that area. I want to make sure the prisoners will bring back an artifact if they find it. We need these dogs to fetch as well as dig." Cirata cooed at Magnus' wit. *Malethya will be a better place without the verbal banter of those two in it.* Magnus continued delivering commands to the soldier on duty and Rosana lost herself in her book to avoid attention. Cirata and the others were accustomed to wizards in the library being totally engrossed in their work. She needed to play the part to maintain her disguise.

The researchers assigned to help her returned

with a few more books, graciously diverting her attention from Cirata's fawning. "I found this text that fits your description rather well." The wizard half bowed to her as he left. Apparently, seeing Glennon berated twice in one day bred obedience among his friends. Rosana looked at the title, *The Application of Spark-Based Magic to Artifacts*, written by Julian, the second of Cantor's most favored students. A quick look through the index found an entire section referencing catalpa trees.

Once discovered, the ability of the catalpa trees to diffuse magic made them a prime target as a medium for creating magical artifacts. In particular, wizards with an aptitude in the defensive arts found catalpa wood to be of great benefit. They crafted minor talismans to ward off spells or reduce their effects, effectively acting as armor in a magical battlefield. A promising area of research within spark-based magic involves amplifying the effects of the catalpa tree. Rather than just diffusing magic, what if enough spark could be forced into the catalpa wood to make it immune to magic? The answer is unclear, but the implications are profound.

Sana thought back to her own experiences with using spark-based magic with catalpa wood. Forcing the catalpa wood to diffuse magic beyond its normal limits didn't make the trees immune to magic, it just created the blight. Suddenly the Blighted Knife, long lost in the storage room, made more sense. Some spark-based wizard had forced too much spark into the knife. It was a failed experiment in spark-based magic. *But why would someone choose to make a talisman from a knife? The object is contradictory to the purpose of the spell.*

Usually people created artifacts from objects that at least resembled their original purpose. Maybe the creator of the Blighted Knife had a sick sense of humor. She was about to read on, when she was interrupted by a loud announcement.

"General Pudriuz, a party approaches from Minot." The Bellator Guardsman standing guard outside the Hunter's Cottage announced before promptly returning to his post.

Magnus exited the storage room and walked right past Rosana toward the door to the hunter's cottage.

There goes another wasted opportunity, but maybe your defiance of me will bear fruit.

Magnus yelled to the wizards in the library. "You are Ispirtu's brightest. Act as if you possess knowledge lost since the days of the Cantor. No one will see weakness or failure when they come through that door. Am I understood?" The tone of his question left little doubt in the expected response.

"Understood, sir!" a chorus of wizards answered with forced enthusiasm. Wizards didn't like calling anyone sir, much less a man without the spark.

The Sicarius Headmaster slipped her hand beneath the table for quick access to her throwing knives while Sana assessed the situation. From the table she sat at to the entrance she was confident the Sicarius Headmaster could make a series of lethal, spell-enhanced throws that took out both Magnus and Phoenix in rapid succession. The trick would be ensuring that the totems they carried were destroyed so that Slate's blood spilled into the ground. A talented wizard could cast a spell in two seconds, so she would be relying on confusion in the aftermath of Magnus' death to buy her some time to cross the distance and destroy the totems. It was a risk, but a reasonable one. Her attack would come as a surprise. The researchers in the library would not expect an attack from within, even if they were on high alert.

The Sicarius Headmaster shifted her weight in her chair so that she could spring toward the door. She unsheathed a throwing knife. All eyes in the room looked toward the front entrance to greet Phoenix. The door swung open.

Lattimer entered the library.

Rosana watched in horror as King Darik, Phoenix, and a whole host of wizards and Bellator soldiers followed the ruler of Malethya. He dressed in the robes of Rose's father, but despite the family resemblance, there was no mistaking Lattimer for Brannon.

Lattimer carried the family scepter, but in his hands, the crystal swirled red. While carrying that scepter, Lattimer was no longer a wizard. Lattimer was a blood mage, and with his presence Rosana's heart sank. Despite the close proximity, her throwing knives were useless. She had thrown one at him while breaking Ibson out of the infirmary, and the knife had changed course at the last minute. Whatever spell protected him would also protect those close to him, so Magnus and Phoenix might as well be behind a brick wall. Even if Lattimer's spell didn't protect Magnus and Phoenix, she couldn't close the gap and destroy the totems before Lattimer killed her. The power of the scepter let him cast spells very quickly. The Sicarius Headmaster was right. Rosana should have killed Magnus when she had the chance.

When will you learn to trust me? the

headmaster said angrily. *This failure belongs to all of you.*

Lattimer addressed everyone in the library. "As most of you have heard, our enemies, led by Slate Severance, have struck. The attack was on the infirmary in Ravinai, but I have reason to believe the notorious criminal and his partners will target Minot next. Have any of you seen or heard anything suspicious?"

Rosana sneaked a glance toward Glennon and saw him staring back at her. Rosana knew the look. It was a look of indecision mixed with torment. Glennon wanted to mention her arrival, but he feared the ramifications of speaking up incorrectly. If Rosana was who she claimed to be, he would lose his position within the library, if not his life. Rosana cocked her head and pierced Glennon with a look of pure conceit, willing him to find the subservience he displayed in the presence of Magnus. Her look made him hesitate from speaking, and in that moment, Lattimer continued on.

"Good. I trust all of you will remain vigilant in this matter. Now…" Glennon had missed his chance; Rosana prevented exposure momentarily. Maybe a small fractal's blessing was upon her. Lattimer then continued, "…my sister is a master of infiltration and deception. Just to be certain, I will administer a quick test of obedience." Lattimer raised the scepter into the air and said. "Furies, assemble in rank and file order in front of Magnus."

She was a dead woman.

Everyone's eyes turned red, and they started forming lines in front of Magnus. Sana could act obedient, join a line, and hope no one noticed that her eyes weren't blood red. But that type of blind hope would leave her surrounded by a room full of Furies once she was inevitably identified. Her only other option was to go deeper into the hunter's cottage—either to the vault with its impenetrable wall or the endless storage room with its suffocating heat.

This time, the Sicarius Headmaster slipped from the table and headed for the storage room door before her other selves could debate the choice. Just as she crossed the threshold to feel the sun's heat upon her head, Rose heard her brother's voice. "It isn't polite to arrive unannounced, Rose. Mother would be deeply ashamed of your manners." Rosana was crushed. She would add her name to the long list of deceased headmasters without even accomplishing her final and most important mission. She urged the Sicarius Headmaster forward into the endless desert, aiming roughly for a nondescript rock formation about a mile away, although in the desert, distance was difficult to judge.

She pumped her legs as fast as she could, but she only made it a few hundred yards when she got short on breath. She started hyperventilating, and the increased effort only made things worse. She dropped to her knees and looked behind her to see Lattimer standing in the doorway to the storage room. Phoenix, King Darik, and Magnus stood behind him to enjoy the show.

Lattimer said, "It's a funny thing about breathing. People take the air around them for granted, but a spell that lowers the air pressure around you can cripple as quickly as one of your throwing knives across a hamstring." Lattimer must have altered the spell because Rosana's breathing started to return to normal. "Now that you know I can kill you at any time, why don't you tell me why you are here? And don't even insult me by throwing a knife. We both know how hopeless that is."

Rose stood up to face her brother, her father's killer. "I am here to stop a blood mage. I am here to stop the single biggest threat to Malethya since the days of Cantor. I am here to stop you."

Lattimer laughed at her defiant words, but it wasn't the fun-filled laugh of Rose's brother in his youth. It was too forced. *Stress? Anxiety?* The emotions Rosana would have associated with such a laugh didn't fit the profile of an all-powerful wizard. *What has happened to him?* Lattimer said to her, "You came here to stop me? It doesn't look like you thought that one through all the way, sister. As for my being a threat to Malethya, what have I done since taking power? I've fed the hungry, cleaned up the streets, and brought prosperity to the kingdom, just as I promised. Am I the threat, or are you? I believe you blew up half of Ravinai last night."

"I freed the minds of those that you enslaved!"

"Do you know who those people were? I have only involuntarily subjugated the minds of the soldiers and wizards that opposed me when I took power. I haven't involuntarily subjugated a mind since the battle for Ispirtu. Any other new leader would kill the remnants of the opposition immediately, but I knew I needed them. I knew Malethya needed..."

"You killed father!" Rose screamed the interruption. She was tired of the philosophical debate and the twisted rationales of a blood mage. If she listened any further, she might even start believing the fractal-forsaken bastard. "And you tried to enslave Slate!" Rosana added for good measure.

Anger finally cracked through Lattimer's voice. "Brannon held us back. He knew magic was dying in Malethya, and he left us vulnerable to attack. When the Disenites attack…"

Now Rosana laughed. "We have been held hostage by the threat of the Disenites since I was a child. They were defeated. They aren't coming back. They…"

"They are already here!" Lattimer shouted angrily. "A Disenite ship sits in the bay of Portswain as we speak. It could attack at any time." He saw the shock on Rosana's face. "You didn't know? The Sicarius Headmaster, with your entire information network spread across Malethya, didn't know about an army invading your own country." He laughed the same forced laughed as before, but now the anxiety made sense. "I built an army of Furies in the hopes that it would be strong enough to defend our land from invasion. In one night, you took out a third of my army. You might have doomed us all."

The Sicarius Headmaster hadn't checked the information network recently. She had been too busy preparing for the attack on the infirmary and then going to Minot. She was still processing her lapse as Lattimer turned to King Darik.

"King Darik, what is the penalty in Malethya for my sister's deeds?"

The king stepped forward and proclaimed the penalty, even though it would only be enacted at Lattimer's discretion. "The Sicarius Headmaster has disobeyed a direct order from her king and since led numerous attacks against the king's army. For such traitorous activities, Rosana Regallo is sentenced to death."

Lattimer looked at Rose. "Lucky for you, I am a more benevolent leader than Darik. Malethya needs the strong to lead right now. You are strong, but are you stronger than Phoenix?" Lattimer paused and excitement spread across the deformed face of Phoenix. "I need the Sicarius Guild to be rebuilt. Phoenix has not been as successful in that area as I would have liked, and it's because of you. There are enough stories and rumors of the Sicarius Headmaster still floating around Malethya that recruitment has been sparse. In order for him to succeed, he needs to stop the rumors. That means killing you. Phoenix, do you accept this mission?"

Phoenix bowed deeply and said, "My ordeals began when she sent me on a suicide mission. I would like nothing more than to end her life as she would have ended mine, if not for your redeeming intervention."

"Then rise as a Fury and kill the Sicarius Headmaster." Lattimer lifted his scepter toward Phoenix and simultaneously pushed his opposite hand outward toward Rosana. A huge pressure wave hit her and sent her hurdling through the air. She landed somewhere near the rock outcropping. While she tried to regain her senses, Lattimer amplified his voice to reach her. "For Phoenix's loyalty, I have equipped him with the same spell that I used to deflect your throwing knives and a few other spells to mitigate your tricks. To keep it fair, I've sent you toward the rock formation you so eagerly ran toward. Phoenix will chase you down tirelessly, but if you do kill him you will have a choice. You can return to me, subjugate your mind, and help me save Malethya by building a new Sicarius Guild. Because of your actions, I will need solid intelligence on the Disenites when they invade our land. Think of it as penance for your traitorous deeds." There was a pause before he said, "Of course, if you refuse to help me a second time, then you can stay in the desert and die. The choice is yours, if you live long enough to decide."

Rosana looked up, expecting to see Phoenix rushing headlong toward her, but he wasn't. Instead he ran toward the prisoners and raised his hand, screaming, "Attack the Sicarius Headmaster, you dogs!"

Now the spectator, Lattimer praised his servant. "Furies with minds! This is what will save us from the Disenites!"

The prisoners, who lacked the control of Phoenix or the soldiers under Magnus' care, sprinted forward with feral screams, yielding their digging implements as weapons. They were still a long way off, but they would close the distance quickly. Phoenix took up a position in the rear of the group, choosing to let the dogs sniff out their prey before closing for the kill.

Rose thought back to her decision in the library and the predicament she was now in. She should have listened to the headmaster. *Headmaster, this mission is yours. You have control. I will not intervene,* Rose promised. *Do what you need to do to get out of here.*

The Sicarius Headmaster threw off the Ispirtu robes to gain full access to her arsenal of knives and threw one straight toward the heart of Phoenix. Sana held the pattern of a falcon diving through buffeting winds and ensured the headmaster's aim was true. The knife flew impossibly straight, past the sprinting prisoners until it dove downwards at the last possible second to bury in the sand a safe distance from Phoenix. *Damn. Lattimer was telling the truth.*

The failed experiment at least narrowed the headmaster's options. She could climb the rock formation and hold her ground against the oncoming Furies, but they had the advantage of sheer numbers if she let them close in on her. Conversely, she could run to keep the advantage of distance, but they would run until they died. Collapsing in the sand, too weak to fight, was no way to die either. Then she realized something important. Her knife had flown past the prisoners. It would take a great deal of Sana's spark, but…

Knives flew from the headmaster's hand with devastating speed and Sana ensured they hit their marks. Knife after knife buried in the hearts of the oncoming prisoners. Without armor, they were just target practice. Then Rose spotted Josef, half-starved wearing a loosely-hanging decayed shirt that mirrored his soul. She thought the rips and tears across the fabric matched the lines of worry, doubt, and despondency that the man faced every night when he tried to escape, only to return at sunrise, pick up his shovel, and start digging again. She had promised she would try to free him from his enslavement and in return he helped her sneak into the hunter's cottage and later led the prisoners in an effort to mask their escape from Minot. Even when she made the promise, she knew there was little chance that she would actually be capable of freeing him from

Lattimer's control. Josef had voluntarily given control of his mind to Lattimer, so the bond didn't break when she destroyed the Phylactery. Judging by the gaunt look of his face, even taking into account the disturbing red eyes, Josef's last few weeks of enslavement had taken a large toll on the man. He had been through too much and didn't deserve to die today.

The Sicarius Headmaster put a knife in his chest without the slightest regret and Josef fell into the sand. Rose prayed a fractal's blessing that he would enjoy his freedom from Lattimer's control in the afterlife.

Lattimer compounded Rose's pain by saying, "Look at the savior of Malethya as she kills the very people she claims to protect. You condemn me for killing in the name of a higher cause. Now you do the same to save your own skin. I guess we really are family."

The remaining prisoners charged onward, stepping over the dead bodies that had fallen in front of them, and they closed the distance at alarming speed. Even more alarming, though, she was running out of knives. She had loaded up her suit with them, but she never intended to kill an entire barracks full of prisoners. Rosana started counting the remaining prisoners while the Sicarius Headmaster threw knives and Sana cast spells, but the bodies fell too rapidly to get an accurate account. Just as she was about to give up, the bodies stopped falling and six prisoners continued toward her. The Sicarius Headmaster had thrown her last knife.

With less than a minute before Phoenix and the remaining prisoners would reach her, Rosana, the master of her environment, looked around for the best place to spring a trap. She directed the headmaster toward a rock that jutted out from the other rocks in the formation, giving her some form of cover. As soon as she identified the location, the Sicarius Headmaster sprinted there while she was still out of range of Phoenix's darts. It wouldn't do to get paralyzed now, even if it was a lucky shot on a moving target. As she disappeared into the rock formation, Lattimer's amplified voice commented. "The Sicarius Headmaster disappears from view, but she has nowhere to hide. Who will emerge the victor in this Sicarius battle?"

The short sprint to the rock formation offered a much-needed surprise. Besides jutting away from the rock face to provide cover, the back side of the rock was easily scalable, even if her name wasn't Slate Severance. She climbed the rock and kept flat to her belly when she reached the gently sloped top of the rock formation, remaining hidden from view. Sana prepared her spell from her dwindling supply of spark, and waited.

The feral cries of the approaching Furies made their approach easy to mark, and she was ready as the group burst around the rock. Sana unleashed a powerful blue arc of electricity that jumped between the prisoners and left their scorched bodies cooking in the sand where they fell. Without any armor to transfer the spark, the spell would take considerable energy, so Rosana's location for the trap was ideal. Any further from the prisoners and she didn't know if she'd have the strength to reach them. A half second later, Rosana saw Phoenix round the corner and shoot a dart at her, but the Sicarius Headmaster had already started rolling down the back side of the rock. Just as

Rosana's view changed from Phoenix to the bright sun overhead, a dart flew inches past her nose.

The Sicarius Headmaster landed on her feet after rolling down the sloped rock and dove behind the nearest outcropping of rock, anticipating Phoenix to chase his weakened prey.

Instead, she heard Phoenix's voice call out. "Bravo! You managed to kill all the untrained dogs in camp. Now let's see how you fair against me. I am stronger than you, smarter than you, and unless I'm mistaken, I'm the only one with a weapon. Even if you manage to land a lucky blow against me, I will feel no pain. I will keep coming for you, and there are no shadows to hide you in the desert. It's time for the Shadow of the Night to die in the day's hot sun." The words angered the Sicarius Headmaster, but most of what he said was true. She was in a difficult spot, and he had the advantage. She kept her mouth shut.

While he spoke, Rosana tracked his voice. It sounded as if he was circling around the rock formation to her left. Sana took the information and directed the Sicarius Headmaster to head in that direction, rationalizing that Phoenix was Sicarius trained. Talking was a trainee mistake, and guardsmen that did it usually wound up dead before becoming guardsmen. Talking while walking and giving away your location was too stupid to be a coincidence. Sana guessed that Phoenix doubled-back in the direction started as soon as he finished speaking in the hopes of tricking Rosana. He wanted to come across her quickly and confront her head on, where he had the advantage.

The Sicarius Headmaster moved quickly and silently around the rock face and Sana took inventory of her options. All her knives were gone, but she had a rope and a lock pick. She was low on spark, but Lattimer's spells protected Phoenix anyway. With limited options, the Sicarius Headmaster decided on the rope as her choice of weaponry.

Rosana and Rose, meanwhile, reviewed what they knew about the storage room in silence, hoping to provide worthwhile input to the headmaster.

What did Ibson say about this place? Rosana asked.

He said it was created by a four-dimensional fractal that was folded to create the world we see here. I don't know what that means, Rose reminded Rosana.

And it was created to house magical artifacts, but this has to be the worst storage system ever created. I'd give anything for that Blighted Knife right now.

Rose sighed, *Ibson said that the prisoners could dig forever and have a zero percent probability of finding a single artifact because the desert is endless. It's hopeless.*

Their conversation stopped when the Sicarius Headmaster peeked around the corner and found Phoenix with his back to her. Sana had guessed correctly. The Sicarius Headmaster lunged forward and kicked the back of his leg, dropping him to his knees. Phoenix struck blindly behind his back while holding a knife, but the Sicarius Headmaster was ready for it. She wrapped the rope around his extended wrist and twisted it behind his back. She chopped down on his neck to incapacitate him, but Phoenix twisted just in time. As he twisted

away from her blow, he was forced to twist away
from the rope, pinning his arm against his back
and rendering the knife useless. The headmaster
took the opportunity to continue wrapping the
rope around him. The more he fought the more
entangled he became. After some struggling, the
Sicarius Headmaster stood behind Phoenix
holding the rope that pinned both his arms
against his body. She wrapped her free arm
around his neck and started to squeeze,
constricting the blood flow to Phoenix's brain.
He would pass out in seconds.

Phoenix threw his shoulder against the ropes
and dislocated his arm from his body. The pain
should have been excruciating, but Phoenix
accomplished the maneuver without a single
scream of pain. Before the Sicarius Headmaster
could react to the surprising tactic, Phoenix
pulled his dangling arm from the ropes, grabbed
a poisoned dart from his pocket and shoved it
into her leg.

The Sicarius Headmaster immediately lost all
strength and feeling in her leg, and she fell
to her side. The awkward, unanticipated motion
allowed Phoenix to twist away from her
chokehold. He collapsed to the ground a short
distance from her, gasping for breath.

The Sicarius Headmaster forced herself to her
feet, knowing she was in trouble. She needed to
carry all of her weight on one leg and if she
didn't kill Phoenix before he recovered, she
wouldn't be able to defend herself. She
desperately worked her way the short distance
toward Phoenix, dragging her leg behind her.
She watched in horror as Phoenix gulped life-
saving air and slowly regained his strength.
Just as she got close to him, he looked up at
her with unbridled hatred in his red eyes and

lunged at her.

The Sicarius Headmaster rolled backward and used Phoenix's momentum to throw him overhead. While the maneuver sent Phoenix to the ground again, the Sicarius Headmaster ended up in the sand as well and Phoenix, with two good legs, recovered much more quickly. He jumped to his feet and had the headmaster pinned on her back before she could even roll over and sit up. With his knees holding her arms, the Sicarius Headmaster was defenseless. She stared helplessly up at the bird-pecked, rat-eaten face of Phoenix and knew she wouldn't be getting a quick death.

The abomination jammed a second dart into the Sicarius Headmaster's good leg. With his prey crippled further, he took the time to pull his shoulder back into its socket with a sickening pop. Then Phoenix focused all the pent-up venom he had held inside since his ill-fated Sicarius mission, "I trusted you, and you sent me to my death. You don't deserve to be the Sicarius Headmaster." He then released a primal yell of victory and shouted, "I am the Sicarius Headmaster now!"

From the distance, Lattimer's voice returned. "Well done, my servant. You have proven yourself worthy."

Then Phoenix turned his contorted face toward her again. "But before I kill you, I want you to know exactly what I went through." He let the light gleam off the blade of his knife. "You may have noticed that the poison in your legs isn't spreading. It has a very localized effect. I didn't want to numb your entire body and prevent you the experience you so graciously gave to me. When I was attacked, the birds came first." He lowered the knife point toward her shoulder.

The Sicarius Headmaster knew it was her job to endure the pain of the superficial wounds being inflicted, and any other forms of torture Phoenix derived. She had been on the delivering end of torture on numerous occasions, but she only used the third tenet to get vital information when other means weren't suitable. She was livid at Phoenix's unprofessionalism. He was torturing her for pure pleasure. She refused to speak or scream out in pain. She would give him no satisfaction.

The Sicarius Headmaster's sacrifice allowed her other selves to think. Sana knew this was the end, but there was very little she could do about it. Phoenix was protected from her spells and he was kneeling on her upper arms, leaving her forearms just enough movement to scratch at his back, which was pointless since he couldn't feel the scratching anyway. Her odds of survival were zero.

The Sicarius Headmaster assessed Sana's assessment of their situation and came to a conclusion. With her death imminent, it was better to kill Phoenix in the process. She told Sana, *I have seen Ispirtu Furies turn themselves into exploding orbs. Can you do that? Maybe the explosion will be strong enough to overwhelm the magic protecting Phoenix.*

I'm low on spark, Sana said, *but wizards are capable of powerful magic if they aren't trying to stay alive while casting the spell. I could do it.*

Ready the spell, the Sicarius Headmaster commanded as Phoenix drove the knife tip into her body over and over again in shallow cuts that mimicked the pecking beaks of birds.

Phoenix continued his dialogue between knife

wounds. "I'm sorry I can't give you the full experience that I endured. The worst part about being attacked by birds is that you never know when or where the next attack is coming from. I am limited by the single knife tip to a single wound inflicted at a time, depriving you of the true pain I felt as birds pecked at my flesh."

Rosana kept conversing with Rose. She knew if she were left to her own thoughts, Rosana would think of Slate and her failure to help him. *Where did I go wrong? I was only trying to protect Slate and I ended up putting myself in the same position. This is all my fault.*

It's not your fault. I made the decision not to kill Magnus. Blame me if you must, Rose demanded.

Rosana was taken aback by the determination in Rose's voice. Normally she was quiet or even timid, but she obviously hadn't given up yet, despite the current circumstance. *No one blames you, Rose. We are all here to protect you, in one way or another.*

Rose had been thinking to herself ever since her previous conversation with Rosana. *This was a storage room. If someone was smart enough to fold a four-dimensional fractal in a way that created an endless desert, they surely would have put some thought into how they would retrieve the artifacts they buried.* The simple assumption made something click for Rosana. *I have an idea. Let's kill this bastard.*

What is it? Rosana asked, clutching for any idea in her desperation.

Ibson said there was almost a zero percent probability of locating an artifact by digging because of the vastness of this desert. Inversely, it begs to reason that there is an equal probability of finding an artifact in any given location. *What if they made the desert in such a way that they didn't have to dig for anything? What if you could reach into any part of the desert at any time and retrieve any artifact you wished? You would have a perfect storage system—accessible to you and inaccessible to everyone else.*

That sounds valuable… in theory. How would it work in practice, though? Rosana stopped scratching Phoenix's back long enough to reach into the ground. She let the sand fall through her fingers to demonstrate her point.

Phoenix had a point of his own he was trying to make. "The birds didn't just attack me in the shoulder, though. They were rather… indiscriminate… in their attack." He penetrated her skin with the knife point repeatedly, just deep enough to draw blood as he moved the knife around her body. The Sicarius Headmaster felt like a pincushion, but she refused to give him the pleasure of seeing her squirm. She held strong and endured.

Sana reported to the headmaster, *The spell is ready.*

Wait! Rose commanded.

You put me in charge and promised not to intervene, the headmaster said. *This is our only chance of killing Phoenix.*

No, there is still hope, even if you can't see it. Rose questioned Sana, *Do you have the spark left for a probing spell?*

Sana answered, *I can manage.*

Reach your hand into the sand and cast the probing spell as wide as possible.

You will fail. Sana will not have enough spark to kill Phoenix, and all of my efforts will be for nought. Don't do this, the Sicarius Headmaster urged.

Sana did as Rose instructed and was startled by what she found. *The sand… it's all connected. My spell reaches everywhere the sand touches.*

Yes, and now you need to concentrate on the Blighted Knife. Picture it in every detail. It has the same balance and etchings on the hilt as your own throwing knives. You know it well.

Sana did know it well and she concentrated on the item, holding it steady in her mind.

Phoenix said, "After the birds, I tried to escape into the forest and a stag hit me in the chest." He took the hilt of his knife and rammed it into her chest with all his strength. The Sicarius Headmaster felt a rib crack. "A stag running at full speed can do much more damage than I can, but you get the idea."

Rose said, *Now you need to bring your probing spell back in. Fold the spell on top of itself as you go. Fold the spell until it fits the exact size and shape of the Blighted Knife.* Rose prayed that she was right.

Phoenix continued his torture. "After the stag knocked me off my feet, the rats came. The rats were the worst." He ran his hand along his half-eaten face. "Rats can be quite ravenous when they eat."

Now close your hand.

Sana felt the familiar hilt of her throwing knife within her palm. She looked up at the abomination above her, pulled the Blighted Knife from the sand and swiped at Phoenix. With her arms pinned, she only managed to nick his side. Rose was distraught. *I went to all this trouble to get the knife and now I can't land a lethal blow.*

Phoenix saw the change in her eyes and looked down to see her holding the Blighted Knife.

"Well, that's some blade. Where did you pull that from?" He knocked it from her hand and looked at the superficial wound to his side. "Is this the best you could manage? It causes me no pain and the cut is so minor I won't even need an infirmary wizard to heal me after this. I do appreciate that you haven't given up yet, though. It makes my victory that much more enjoyable." Phoenix brought the blade of his knife toward her with the intent of carving her face in his own likeness.

So Phoenix will live… the headmaster said to Rose without anger. She was past the point of anger.

Rose saw the wound turn black as blight.

It spread quickly across his stomach and lower back and if it caused any pain, Phoenix didn't notice it. He brought the knife closer to her face and Rose willed the blight to spread faster. It spread outward in all directions.

The blade touched her cheek.

The blight touched Phoenix's heart.

CHAPTER TWENTY ONE

FROM THE ASHES

The Sicarius Headmaster rolled the corpse formerly known as Phoenix off her and touched her cheek. That bastard's knife had sliced a deep gash as he collapsed on top of her, a parting gift she gladly accepted. It only caused a fraction of the pain Phoenix had planned to subject her to and didn't result in her death. That was a win no matter how you looked at it. She untied a ribbon of cloth from her Sicarius outfit and applied pressure to her cheek to stem the bleeding.

Rosana looked down to find that her arms, shoulders, and neck bore the brunt of the bird attack, but Phoenix had graciously saved her face from the tip of the knife with the intention of leaving a blank canvas for his rat-inspired carvings. Even with that small grace, the superficial wounds he inflicted bled annoyingly. They wouldn't have caused her much concern, but her supply of spark was dangerously low. Sana didn't want to heal herself and use up the last of her spark, especially considering that bleeding wasn't even her primary problem.

Her legs still didn't work. She knew the effect of Phoenix's poison would wear off eventually, but how long would it take? How was she supposed to fight her way through Lattimer and an army of Furies if she couldn't even stand up?

"Phoenix, you have claimed your victory!

Return to me. I tire of this hot sun." Lattimer commanded with some agitation.

Rosana chose not to answer, hoping that silence would buy a few more minutes to recuperate. Phoenix had left her damn-near dead. She needed to rise up and escape, but first she had to complete her mission.

Rosana grasped the knife that had been used to torture her and propped herself up on one elbow to examine Phoenix. His face had gone completely black as the blight spread throughout his body. She didn't risk touching him in case the infection would spread to her. Instead, she used Phoenix's knife to cut the seams of his pocket. The totem bearing Slate's blood dropped to the sand.

The Sicarius Headmaster buried the knife into the vial and let the arid desert soak up the precious liquid. With each droplet that filtered through the sand, the headmaster could almost feel Lattimer's grip on Slate's mind lessening. She sighed in relief.

With the main objective of the mission successfully completed, the headmaster took the time to acknowledge Rose's accomplishments. *I still breathe because of you. You held onto hope when all I could see was defeat.* The headmaster paused. This sort of thing wasn't easy for her. *I always considered it my job to protect you from the darkness in the world. I never thought that your determination and hope would save me. I need you to lead. I need you for the darkest times when all hope is gone.*

Rose blushed at the compliment. She would have gone into a speech about how she needed all of her selves to be complete, but speeches were difficult for Rose. She trusted that her other selves would understand and instead quoted the headmaster, *A mission isn't done until we get back to safety. Save the compliments for then. Let's get out of here.*

The Sicarius Headmaster located the best weapon at their disposal and the cause of Phoenix's death—the Blighted Knife. She dragged her limp extremities over to the knife and wrapped the black blade in several layers of fabric, hoping the fabric would provide some protection against the blade. Rose contemplated returning it to storage, but Sana wanted to preserve her remaining spark, and she didn't know what obstacles awaited her. At the moment, this blade was her best chance of survival. She tucked the wrapped blade into the folds of her outfit.

"Phoenix, come to me!" Lattimer's voice echoed through the desert, and it left little doubt in Sana's mind about the nature of the order. Lattimer had ordered his Fury, Phoenix, to return to him and an immediate response would be expected.

Rosana roared, "The abomination you call Phoenix is dead once again. He could not kill the Shadow of the Night. Do you wish to send any more men to their deaths in this desert?"

Lattimer said, "Ah, what a delight! My sister still lives. We Regallos always were tough to kill. I applaud your fortitude and now leave you with a choice. Join me and reform the Sicarius Guild to protect Malethya from the Disenites, or die in the desert sun. Which do you choose?"

Rose never faltered in her response. "I would never join you, brother. No one who creates a creature like Phoenix can be allowed to rule. I will oppose you until the day I die."

"Then your choice is made." He then issued an

order to some soldiers. "Find her and surround her. I want you to watch her take her last breath as she bleeds beneath the hot sun." He then directed his voice toward her one last time. "Goodbye, sister."

Not yet, Rose thought.

It would take several minutes for the soldiers to reach the rock formation and she wasn't going to give up yet. She was immobile, or at least greatly slowed. Her chances of climbing the rock formation as she had done previously were slim. The soldiers would get to her first.

Rose said to her other selves, *We have access to any artifact from the days of the blood mages. We can do this.*

Rosana checked with Sana, *Do you have enough spark left?*

Sana said, *I'll need to, won't I? I knew what the Blighted Knife looked like, so it didn't take a lot of spark to retrieve. All I know of the other artifacts is a simple description from the list we stole in Minot. It will probably take a considerable amount of spark to cast the spell, and that's assuming that whatever artifact I retrieve will get us out of this predicament.* She didn't sound overly confident that it would work.

Rosana, who had memorized the list, responded right away, *The Closed Door—you can pass through the threshold and travel to your heart's desire.*

What good is a retrieving an artifact if we can't use it afterward? Sana mused.

It is the only chance we have, Rose said. *I doubt whoever made the Closed Door intended for it to remain shut. Just like this desert serves as a perfect storage room once you understand how it works, I'm sure the door opens quite easily, if we can figure out its secret. Sana, please retrieve the Closed Door.* Rose asked kindly, but with newfound command.

Sana thrust her hand in the sand and probed, extending the spell's reach to the edges of the desert with ease. The four-dimensional fractal, however it was created, was definitely meant for just such a spell. Then she concentrated on the picture of the door she knew best, the large doors to her father's Ispirtu office carved from the wood of a great catalpa tree. Rose's interest in catalpa trees began as a young child climbing the steps of the Ispirtu tower to visit her father and her early childhood fascination grew to include the etchings of the great trees on the hilt of her throwing knives. These experiences bled into Sana's image of the Closed Door.

Sana pulled the spell back toward her. She felt resistance, as though her commands weren't quite clear. Sana knew it was because her memory of the doors to Brannon's office didn't accurately describe the complete details of the Closed Door, but she couldn't help that. She poured in more spark, depleting her reserves past any point in her life. She needed to overcome the resistance to her spell. *If I die now, what is the difference? At least I won't give the soldiers the pleasure of watching me bleed to death.*

She imagined the desert folding inward upon itself, which was the closest description she could contrive for the foldings of a four-dimensional fractal. As it grew closer to her, she faced another problem. When she'd retrieved the Blighted Knife, she had closed her hand around the hilt and it appeared. She couldn't exactly grasp a door in the palm of her hand, at least not if she hoped to go through it afterward. Instead, she imagined the desert folding into the dry air above it. The top of the sand gripped the artifact within its vast hold, but Sana closed her eyes and poured more of her spark into it.

The barrier broke and Sana released her spell, collapsing to the ground. The only thing that kept her from passing out was the pain of the open wound in her cheek pressing against the sand below.

She opened her eyes.

Before her stood the most beautiful door she had ever seen. Huge wooden doors with immaculate etchings hung from a massive wooden frame that extended to either side of the door, almost forming a wall on either side. The etchings formed a maze of magical symbols. A wizard could spend a lifetime trying to decode their meanings. Along the bottom of the door, a small crack tantalizingly previewed a world beyond. The location wasn't discernable, but green grass contrasted starkly with the sand around her. The prize beyond the door was guarded by an intricate locking mechanism that surrounded a simple metal knob. She needed a closer look.

The Sicarius Headmaster lifted her head from the sand and dragged the dead weight of her legs behind her with the diminished strength of her once-strong arms. Seconds ticked by way too quickly as she inched her way to the door. In the distance, she could hear the sounds of armor clanking as the soldiers approached. Her other selves urged her forward.

At the door, she pulled herself up to a sitting position and got out her lock-pick set,

only to find it useless. The locking mechanism
lacked a keyhole or any other obvious picking
site. This was a magical artifact, so it stood
to reason that the answer to unlocking it would
be in the form of a spell.

Rose pushed the defeatist thought from her
mind. Sana didn't have the strength for another
spell and if generations of wizards hadn't
successfully opened it through magical means,
then she didn't want to calculate her chances.
The sounds of the armor grew louder.

Rosana scanned the etchings on the door, to
no avail, but then her eyes settled on the
hinges of the door. The top hinge had a slight
recess, a recess that looked suspiciously
familiar.

At the sight of the recessed hinge, the
Sicarius Headmaster laughed with joy. The
alternating, dreadful laughing sound filled the
hearts of all that heard it just as the first
Bellator Fury rounded the corner of the rock
formation and into view.

The Sicarius Headmaster knew this door.

She knew the trick to opening it.

The headmaster reached for the top of the
hinges and pulled upward, activating a
mechanism that slid the door into the
doorframe. *The hinges are the lock and the lock
is a decoy, just like all the symbols and
etchings on the door face. How many wizards had
devoted their lives to deciphering a secret
code that wasn't there?* The Closed Door had a
distinctly Sicarius feel to it. Wizards
expected a spell to seal the doorway, so the
maker of the Closed Door presented the wizards
who attempted to unlock the artifact with an
unsolvable magical riddle. The obvious riddle
hid the simple mechanical trick in plain sight.

In fact, it was the same mechanism that had protected the Sicarius Guild from unwanted visitors for time immemorial.

The design she had used to hide the Sicarius Guild in the basement of the arena must have been a highly guarded secret from the days of Cantor. She imagined the design came into the possession of one of the original headmasters and passed to each subsequent headmaster upon their death until it came into Rosana's possession. When it came time to design a place to house the Sicarius Guild, Rosana instructed the architect to utilize the design without knowing its origins.

More soldiers charged toward her and the first and most athletic of the Ispirtu Furies came into view. The sight of ill-intentioned Furies barreling at her from a short distance away didn't inspire confidence that they would stop at Lattimer's orders to simply observe her death. The red-eyes and howls of rage conflicted too deeply with their orders and her racing heart, so she started counting.

...1 She hopelessly urged the doorway to open more quickly. As it slid open enough to view a world beyond the threshold of the doorway, Rosana's eyes fixated on a tied-up Slate, surrounded by Ibson, Jak, and all their friends. Whatever they were discussing wasn't audible through the doorway, but it didn't take too much imagination to see Slate arguing with the others to be freed. No one noticed her.

...2 From a sitting position, she screamed to Lattimer, "You cannot kill a Shadow. I will come for you brother!" The door opened just enough for her to fall face-first through the threshold and into the grass beyond.

Her friends looked up to see her dragging her

legs across the doorway, which had already started to close. Lattimer's command, "Kill her!" was lost to the sound of fireballs already prepared by the raging Ispirtu Furies.

The door closed completely, sealing the sounds of the explosions on the far side of the door and leaving blissful silence.

CHAPTER 22

FINDING ANSWERS

Rosana closed her eyes and soaked in the life she had almost lost. Around her, blades of grass tickled her cheeks, the leaves rustled in the trees, and the birds sang joyfully, all welcoming her back from certain death.

"Rosana!" Slate yelled after looking up to the sound of her body hitting the ground.

"Cut me free!" he demanded of Jak.

Then the sounds of rushing footsteps approached and any further existentialist thoughts regarding the sanctity of her life were interrupted. Slate flashed toward her before any of the rushing footsteps could reach her and cradled her head. "She's hurt! Ibson, we need you!"

Ibson soon accompanied Slate and began probing her wounds in preparation for his healing spells, but Rosana ignored his actions. Instead, she looked up to Slate. Concern and worry were plastered over his face. He couldn't hide these emotions. The Sicarius Headmaster would have been displeased at the lack of control he exhibited, but Rosana ignored her too. Never before had she seen just how much Slate cared for her. He stared at her with so much compassion that he made the eyes of a Fury look kind. She would do anything for him.

"She's lost a lot of blood. Would anyone…" Ibson gave his prognosis.

"I'll do it." Slate said just before anyone else could answer.

"I don't want to mix the blood of a Perceptor with her right now. She has enough injuries without creating new problems. Jak, get over here. You've probably got a pint or two to spare in that body of yours." Ibson said, referring to Jak's massive frame.

"I'd gladly help, Ibson… even if she took all the fun for herself. From the looks of her, she decided against waiting for us before starting the battle. A pity… I was rather looking forward to ridding Malethya of a few Furies." He removed his broadsword from his back and sat down beside Ibson. Jak stuck out his arm and waited for a poke from Ibson's knife tip. A minute later, Ibson transfused blood into her body and her exhaustion faded a bit.

When Ibson finished, he propped her up. "It will take a few minutes for the poison to wear off and the function in your legs to return. As for the wounds, none of them were too serious, but the one on your cheek will leave a scar. You will be tired for some time."

A scar? I can deal with a scar. As for sleep, well, I will sleep when I am dead.

"Now, my dear, why don't you tell us how you appeared out of thin air…" Ibson prompted.

"Then you can tell us if you accomplished anything besides almost killing yourself," Villifor added with the tactfulness of a hammer.

"…and tell us where Annarelle is…" Tommy spat out, unable to hold in his concern any longer.

Rosana recognized the look on his face, since it looked very similar to the love Slate displayed for her a moment prior. "Annarelle will be here shortly and will think that I have died. I almost did. When she gets here, we need to be ready to leave. We could have Lattimer's

army on our heels all the way back to Ravinai."
Tommy let out a deep breath he probably didn't
realize he was holding. Villifor issued orders
to the Underground to pack up and prepare to
leave. "As for whether I succeeded on my
mission…"

Slate jumped in, "My head feels better than
it did overlooking Minot. It changed just a
minute or two before Rosana appeared."

"So you killed Magnus?" Jak asked.

"No. I killed Phoenix." Stunned looks
surrounded her, so she explained further. "I
infiltrated the hunter's cottage to kill
Magnus, but the odds of survival were low."

"You mean none. It was a suicide mission."
Slate looked at her severely and she didn't
argue. He was right.

"And I owe you an apology for knocking you
unconscious. I was willing to give my life if
it meant saving Malethya, but thankfully, I'm
still alive and able to apologize." She didn't
wait for Slate to accept the apology. She knew
he was so excited to see her he would have
agreed to anything. Rosana continued, "I
overheard Magnus mention that Phoenix was on
his way, and I got greedy in the hope I could
free Slate's mind for good. Phoenix showed up,
but he showed up with Lattimer. With Lattimer
present, not only was I unable to kill Phoenix,
but I had missed my window of time to kill
Magnus as well. It didn't take long for
Lattimer to discover my presence, and I fled
into the storage room."

"You were trapped in an endless desert and
you fought your way through a blood mage to
escape?" Tommy shook his head in amazement. "I
wouldn't want to get in a fight with you,
headmaster."

Rosana offered him a smile, even though it came out as more of an exhausted smirk. "Not exactly, Tommy. Lattimer sent Phoenix into the desert, pitting us against each other for the right to lead the new Sicarius Guild under his command. Phoenix sent the prisoners, who were busy digging for artifacts, after me. I killed them all, but ran out of knives and a great deal of spark in the process."

Tommy was still incredulous. "So you killed a fully-trained and fully-armed Sicarius Guardsman—a guardsman who couldn't feel any pain—without weapons or spells?" Looking around the group, the others had similarly impressed looks on their faces, with the exception of Slate and Ibson. Ibson looked sad, and Rose knew he was thinking of Josef and the other prisoners. He had met them in Minot and they had helped them escape the first time around. Now they were all dead, killed by the person they had helped save. Slate, on the other hand, had a more discerning look on his face. He knew the Sicarius Headmaster had done the killing and wouldn't feel any remorse, but Slate looked for signs of emotion from Rosana, Rose, and Sana. The man could handle complexity in his life.

"I got the drop on Phoenix, but he stuck my leg with a dart and quickly overwhelmed me. I was lucky in that he didn't just want to kill me. He wanted to make me suffer."

"That explains the state you arrived in…" Lady Highsmith offered.

"Yes, and while he tortured me I retrieved the Blighted Knife from the sands of the storage room. I nicked his skin with it and the blight spread to his heart, killing him as he started to carve up my face."

Now Ibson's level of interest in the conversation became infinitely more noticeable. "You retrieved an artifact from the storage room?"

"More importantly, I killed Phoenix and smashed the totem containing Slate's blood." Rosana didn't want to get bogged down in academic conversation with the old man, but she still felt the need to appease him a bit. "As for the artifact, I didn't summon one, I summoned two… and it was your description that let me do it. First, it was the Blighted Knife, and then I retrieved the Closed Door, opened it, and ended up here."

"Remarkable! How did—" Ibson began, but Villifor cut him off.

"I suppose you left both artifacts in possession of your brother? You know, the fractal-forsaken blood mage that is already too powerful?" Villifor's relationship with her had always been strained. They simply spent too much time as headmasters of opposing Guilds… plus, she didn't like the man.

"Some overzealous Furies consumed the Closed Door with a barrage of fireballs right after I fell through. Its charred remains won't do Lattimer much good." Villifor nodded his acceptance, which was still a long way from approval. In that instant, her former feud with the Bellator Guild caused her to tell a lie. Information was power after all, and the Blighted Knife wrapped in the folds of her robe was a powerful secret she might need later. Sicarius training dies hard. "As for the Blighted Knife, I returned it to storage after killing Phoenix. It was too dangerous to bring with me. It kills all it touches, isn't that right, Ibson?"

She looked down to her own hand. The tiniest of black flecks mottled the palm of her hand where she had touched the Blighted Knife. Sana sighed. *I knew this was a suicide mission, and my escape from the desert doesn't change that. At least when the blight takes my life, I will die knowing that my sacrifice accomplished something worthwhile. I'll be able to add my name to the list of headmasters with pride.*

She looked up to see concern in the eyes of the elderly wizard. "I was going to keep this a private matter, but since you brought it up, you are correct. You have been infected with the blight in your hand. I discovered it while healing your other wounds. I'm assuming this is the same hand in which you held the knife?"

"It was."

"You shouldn't have done this!" Slate condemned her. Rosana understood his outburst came from a place of love, but she would have none of it.

"I did what I needed to do." She was going to explain her actions further, but Ibson stepped in to placate them both.

"I wasn't able to heal the blight, but I didn't just leave it to spread." The news stopped both Slate and Rosana from arguing further. "When I probed Slate's mind, I understood that his mind battled the damaged blood from Lattimer's spell by preventing blighted blood from entering his brain. I applied the same principal to the tissue in your hand. It will fight to keep the blight in your hand, but I'm afraid my efforts weren't strong enough to stop the blight. It will progress slowly, and as the blight infects more of your body, it will become stronger. I'm sorry Rosana, but you will still die."

"How long does she have?" Slate asked.

"I'm afraid I can't venture a guess." Ibson said with a saddened face.

A short silence fell over the group until a messenger from the ranks of the Underground ran up to them. "Someone has approached our camp claiming to be the Sicarius Headmaster." He said this while looking at Rosana.

"It's all right, soldier. Bring her here." Jak commanded and everyone waited with anticipation but none as excited as Tommy.

Annarelle walked toward the group and announced, "Rosana is dead. I am the Sicarius Headmaster now."

The circle of the group opened to reveal Rosana sitting in their center. Tears of joy formed instantly on Annarelle's eyes and Rosana said, "Not dead yet… just dying."

Then Tommy enveloped Annarelle in a large bear hug. When he was done, Annarelle ran over with tears and questions bursting in equal amounts. Rosana fought through the pain shooting through her legs as they reawakened and forced herself to her feet, with a great deal of help from Slate.

She hugged Annarelle, but only briefly, saying, "If you made it back to camp, Lattimer's troops won't be far behind. His scouts will take some time to locate us, but we should get moving."

"Where are we going?" Slate asked. He was the leader of the group, but every good leader knew when to listen. Sana obviously had a plan.

"We are going to Ravinai to restock our supplies, which Tommy so graciously obtained from Mr. Radcliff. Then some of us will continue on. Tommy, you will stay back to run the Underground. Bolster their ranks and get them ready. A battle is coming." Tommy nodded with fierce determination before glancing at Annarelle. He was obviously hoping she would stick around, and Sana had the same thought.

"Annarelle, you will stay behind and serve as the acting Sicarius Headmaster. I don't know when I will die, but I know you are ready for the job. Stay in Ravinai. Tend the information networks. Recruit new members, continue to inform the wizard council until we have need of them, and most importantly, figure out how to kill Magnus. I expect a plan in place by the time we return."

She then turned to Villifor and Jak. "The two of you will be traveling with us and gathering new recruits. Malethya is a big place, and we can find help for our cause in more places than Ravinai." Lady Highsmith stared at her with expectation. "Lady Highsmith, I know you will be accompanying Jak. Just try not to distract him from his duties." Jak blushed and the worry disappeared from Lady Highsmith's face. Finally, she gave Ibson the option. "Ibson, you can leave us if you want. I obtained your help through rather forceful means, and you have been nothing but helpful."

"I will stay with you and help as much as an old wizard can. Will you tell me where we are going, though?"

"Lattimer divulged some information to me that I hope we can confirm through my information network in Ravinai. If it's true, it changes everything." Rose thought of the Disenite ships sitting outside of Portswain, bringing with them certain war for Malethya. Along with war, the Disenite ships also brought opportunity and, if Sana guessed correctly, a surprise. The Disenites would throw Malethya into chaos. No one thrived on chaos like the Sicarius Headmater.

"We go to Portswain. The Disenites have arrived."

REFLECTIONS

Rosana walked to Slate and the window that looked out over the harbor. She wrapped her arms around him, repeating the words, "There is still hope."

"What hope can a Disenite army bring?" Slate asked dejectedly. "We are already facing a blood mage, and now we have twice as many enemies to contend with. Do we just sit back and hope they all kill each other, leaving Malethya to us?"

Rosana appreciated sarcasm as much as the next girl, but borderline depression was an ugly trait in a hero or a lover. It was time to cheer him up. "Get the box from my travel bag and lay it out on the table." She cleared the table while issuing the command. Sometimes Slate just needed to do something to save himself from his own thoughts.

He got the box and brought it to the table, laying it in the center. Rosana opened it up to reveal a map with pins in it.

"Who are you tracking?" Slate asked.

Rosana pointed to all the pins on the map. "Do you notice any of our friends that I haven't been able to track?"

Slate looked at the map and then questioningly at Rosana. "Where is Rainier?"

"I haven't been able to track him for some time. The signal was so weak, I thought his medallion was broken somehow. What if it wasn't broken? What if he was just really far away?"

"Ping it." Slate commanded with hope in his eyes that didn't quite reach his face. Rosana understood. She had first speculated about Rainier when Lattimer mentioned the Disenite ship, but she knew she needed to be closer to ensure he was here. She needed to be in Portswain. Now she was and she almost couldn't dare to hope. Sana concentrated on her spell.

After a moment, Sana looked up.

"Well?" Slate asked.

Sana stood up, carried the medallion to the window and pointed. "Rainier is on that Disenite ship—the one flying the commander's flag."

Slate ran Rainier's last words through his mind. "He said he had to return to his tribe and he promised to bring back help." He shook his head and then broke into a huge grin. "That swindling tribesman has more secrets than even you, headmaster."

"Let's not get carried away, Slate." The headmaster smirked at him.

The joy of realizing their friend was within eyesight turned seriousness after a moment. Slate asked, "But why is he just sitting out there? Why doesn't he attack?"

Just then, Rosana felt a jolt in her hand and knew instantly what it meant. The bond between the Stratego medallion she held and the medallion in Rainier's possession had just been broken. "I don't know, but Rainier needs our help."

ACKNOWLEDGMENTS

Since I'm publishing *Shadow Cursed* simultaneously with *Severance Lost,* I could copy the acknowledgments from there, but instead I'm going to do something different. Instead, I'm going to thank all of my teachers, from school and in life.

First, I'd like to thank my first grade teacher Brian Hoffman, who rewarded a first grader with a blizzard from Dairy Queen after reading his first 100 books. I've never had ice cream taste as gratifying as that day at recess. Since then, I've had wonderful teachers that taught me I could do anything I wanted to do. Thank you Mrs. Gates, Mrs. Hackenmueller, Mrs. Pullen, Mrs. Patrick, Mr. Stoick, Mr. Goudy, Mr. Wik, Mr. Stewart, and everyone else from Monticello!

When I went to college, my honors engineering professor challenged me in every sense of the word, and by doing so, gave me the confidence that I could solve any problem, given enough time. I just needed to figure out which problems I wanted to solve. Thank you, P.K. Imbrie.

It wasn't until graduate school, when my doctoral advisor gave me the freedom to explore my own areas of research that I finally realized how challenging that independence could be. There are too many things in life to learn and not enough time to do it. Thank you, Paul Iaizzo.

Of course, all of the academic lessons in my life don't help a lot without some wisdom to go along with it. Whether it was my parents' guiding hand or my Wacky Wortz relatives during my formative years, I've been blessed with wonderful support in my life. Now I've added some great in-laws in Ron and Lora Vanderploeg, and I have some girls of my own, who teach me every day in new and amazing ways.

I hope all of you take the time to thank the teachers in your own life.

I also hope you've enjoyed my books so far. I've tried to write the type of book I like to read and if I succeeded, please tell me (email), your friends, or the millions on the internet by graciously writing a review. I am currently writing *Remnant Awakens,* my next book in the Fractal Forsaken Series. Please enjoy the sample chapter and check back at jllorenquill.com to track my progress or sign up for the mailing list for periodic updates. I can't wait to share the rest of the story with you!

OTHER BOOKS BY J. LLOREN QUILL

Severance Lost – Fractal Forsaken Book 1

Coming Soon
Remnant Awakens – Fractal Forsaken Book 3

Please enjoy a sample of the prologue and first
chapter from Remnant Awakens

PROLOGUE

Home. Most people took their home for granted. They grew up in a home and tired of it, so they moved away and tried to leave a mark on the world. When the world refused to be marked, they pined for the comforts of home after realizing what they had given up too late. Rainier had seen the story played out countless times during his travels through Malethya.

For those that put more thought into the word home, it was more powerful and meaningful. Home was transient; it existed wherever love took it. Home was the smell of a loved one's pillow or mother's fresh-baked pie. Home was a memory, painstakingly built on a small plot of land and forged through the tribulations of youth. People would do anything to preserve these memories. They would shelter their children from the hardships of life just to protect the dream of home. What was Rainier trying to protect?

Rainier looked across a battlefield riddled with bodies. Paladins lie next to Bellator soldiers and Ispirtu fireballs burned the great war-machines of Disentia. The ground would have been stained with blood if the Ispirtu wizards hadn't ripped open the earth in their onslaught and drained the battlefield of evidence. Beside him, his friends, a small contingent of the Resistance and the remaining Disenite troops under Rainier's command stood in opposition to Lattimer Regallo and his army of Furies. Lattimer had amplified his voice and posed a question to Rainier. The fate of Malethya hung in the balance. Who would he protect? Where was his home?

Growing up in the nomadic Tallow clan, Rainier was taught a different sort of home. Home was duty — the duty of the remnant. Home was honor. The remnant bore the honor of staying behind in Malethya after the Disenite army was defeated in the Twice-Broken wars. Home was vigilance. The remnant would watch Malethya for signs of blood magic. Home was sacrifice. The remnant would stay hidden in enemy lands and only return home if the threat of blood magic returned.

Rainier used to know what home meant. He never questioned the teachings of his tribe. When Lattimer revealed himself as a blood mage, Lattimer did what he was trained to do. He returned home to Disentia. He warned his people that blood magic had returned to Malethya and everything he once knew came unraveled.

CHAPTER ONE

HANG THE MESSENGER

"Rainier Tallow, you are charged with high treason." The pronouncement came from the high priest of the Disenite court. He stood as he spoke, which gave the priest an air of even greater authority within the courtroom, in case someone misconstrued the obvious – Rainier had no power here, and neither did the rest of his tribe that waited behind him, knowing that their fate was tied to his. "You have only been kept alive this long because you spoke the sacred words of the Oracles. Explain how you came to our shores and explain where you heard the sacred words. You will be killed if your answers do not satisfy my curiosity."

Apparently the Disentia Court had never heard the phrase *Burden of Proof*. "We set sail…"

A sharp, discreet elbow cracked him in the ribs, courtesy of his court-appointed priest. Rainier bit his tongue and then recalled the titles these fractal-forsaken bastards demanded to be called. *Had he just referred to a High Priest as a fractal-forsaken bastard? Ah well, the man obviously had an affinity for titles, so what was one more? Besides, the title fit a man that seized his ship, shackled him, and put him to trial. Rainier had expected a parade upon his homecoming, or at least a hot meal. Instead he got Mr. Robes-of-Righteousness before him.* "Your excellency," Rainier began again, "we set sail from Malethya two months ago to fulfill our duty to Disentia."

The high priest interrupted him. "What was

your duty? The court is unaware of anyone left behind in Malethya." The biting tone made it clear that the court was never left unaware of Disentia's plans.

This was starting poorly. What had Rainier done to deserve such anger? Rainier looked up at the priests in their elevated seats and tried to understand their perspective. Each priest on the court represented one of Disentia's tribes. Rainier came from the Marked clan, but when he located the heavily tattooed priest bearing the sacred ink, he didn't see a friendly face despite their supposed brotherhood. At best, his clan's priest could be described as skeptical, but he still awaited Rainier's words with an open ear. The priests representing the remaining clans – Scorched, Frozen, and Charged – were less welcoming still. But none of them approached the open hostility of the High Priest. Rainier decided to keep his explanation simple and to the facts while he tried to understand where the anger originated. "We are the Remnant. When Disentia's forces attacked Malethya, they attacked a people with a pagan's understanding of magic – they used the spark to cast spells and the pattern served only as a link in the process. The oracle that led the Disenite forces predicted that since the pagan wizards of Malethya didn't hold the pattern while using the least amount of spark necessary to cast a spell, they were destined to fall from fractal's grace completely. It would only be a matter of time before they forgot their own history and fell back into blood magic, the casting of spells using only the spark. This prophecy demanded that our priests and paladins cleanse the land of Malethya.

As the war continued on, the oracle's prophecy increased in strength as the pagan wizards used magic in battle against our holy forces and relied upon increasing levels of spark with every battle. Before the final battle of the war, the oracle made another prophecy – the war must end to save the land of Malethya from its own people. The pagans' use of magic would scar the land so greatly, that it could never be cleansed, recovered, or converted. The oracle commanded the Disenite forces to sail home and chose to stay behind with a group of brave paladins to cover the retreat of their friends, knowing their demise was already foreseen.

It was only after the Disenite ships sailed and the final battle began, that the oracle saw another vision – a vision of blood magic in Malethya's future. The prophecy would not be realized soon, he knew that war with the Disenites would leave the land of Malethya in great upheaval, so he ordered a small group of the remaining paladins to leave the final battle. They disappeared into the countryside, charged with the duty of watching Malethya for the return of blood magic to the land. I was born to their number and I now lead them. I am Rainier Tallow, leader of the Remnant."

"The tale you tell is quite astounding, Rainier. I question the validity of the tale, but it is interesting enough that I'll allow you to continue. But first, who was the oracle you speak of?"

"Trabon Tallow, my father." Muffled laughter filled the courtroom, but the serious priests managed to maintain their stoicism.

"So you claim to be the descendant of Disentia's most famous oracle and former leader of Julian the Immortal's troops." Mention of Julian the Immortal caused all of the priests to bow their head in reverence towards the man seated above the high priest. Julian had not spoken as Rainier's court-appointed priest had told him to expect. In Disentia, the pattern was power and words were a powerful pattern. Julian appointed the high priest to be the Immortal's Voice and to speak for him in public. The priest said the arrangement was intended to keep anyone from learning the pattern of Julian's speech and use it to control him. It was good to see paranoia wasn't limited to the leaders of Malethya. "That is quite the claim, but we'll get to that in a minute. You have yet to tell me how you reached Disentia's shores."

Rainier spoke clearly and assuredly in an attempt to push past the skepticism of the court, "The Remnant hid under the guise of a clan of nomadic tribesmen and watched Malethya for signs of blood magic. After waiting patiently, my father's prophesy became realized. At first, small towns were wiped out without any evidence, but as the blood mage grew in power, he grew more brazen. An army of Furies was observed during an attack on a small town, confirming the presence of the blood mage in Malethya."

"Excuse me, but I thought you said the Remnant was watching Malethya dutifully. Are you telling me that it took the presence of an army before you took notice?"

Rainier countered tactfully, given that the man held his fate in his hands, "With all due respect, your excellency, I ask you to consider the welcome I have received since my arrival." *Who steals a man's ship? Bastard!* "I thought it was important to gather more evidence before returning."

"Then please present the evidence you gathered while this threat to Disentia grew in power."

Rainier had to bite his tongue to keep a biting remark down. *What was he supposed to do - carve out the eye of a Fury and pocket it for his journey across the sea?* "I'm afraid I don't have any physical evidence, but I stayed in Malethya long enough to identify the blood mage. Lattimer Regallo has taken control of Malethya and is ruling the country from the shadows. He controls the mind of King Darik, he has an army of trained Furies at his disposal, and the people of Malethya don't even know he has taken power. You may judge that I stayed too long in Malethya, but I left as soon I could direct the Disenite forces to their target and not a moment longer."

"You stayed until you knew where to direct the Disenite forces? Do you presume to lead the Immortal's troops? I believe I am the Immortal's Voice and only I can appoint someone to that position." Laughter filled the courtroom and Rainier received another elbow from his court-appointed priest. "Now, how did you get to our shores?"

"The Remnant was known as a nomadic tribe within Malethya, but we were prosperous in our businesses, and we secured a ship at Portswain under the name of a holding company. It was kept in dry dock until I needed it. After identifying Lattimer Regallo as the blood mage, I returned to the Remnant and told them to prepare for our journey home. The ship was in harbor by the time we reached Portswain and we sailed straight here, at least until our ship was identified in Disentia's waters." Then his ship was stolen, he was imprisoned and half-starved before standing trial for treason, but he left out those details.

The high priest then said, "You were fortunate to be found by the captain you did. When you spoke the sacred words of the oracles, he did not recognize them, but he found an old flag from the Immortal's army and an oracle's ring while appropriating rations from your seized ship." *Appropriating rations? How about pillaging his ship?* Rainier kept his mouth shut and the high priest continued. "He brought the items to his superior's attention, and they are one of the few reasons you have been granted this trial. I would now have you speak the sacred words again, in front of the court's well-trained ears."

Rainier took a deep breath and recalled the words his father had taught him. Every time he spoke the words, he felt a deep truth within them, "The world is a pattern of ever-changing life. The pattern cannot be seen. The pattern cannot be described. It is only through familiarity with the world that a sense of the pattern can be understood. It is only through familiarity with life that the pattern can be predicted." Like they always did, the sacred words confused the fuck out of Rainier.

How can something be true and confusing? As contradictory as it seemed, Rainier didn't have to look too far into his past for an example. Rainier's best friend was his Teacher of the pattern and a walking testimony to the power of Blood Magic. Slate had an innate power to sense the pattern around him but his lack of training made him completely ignorant of it. His soul was true and he fought blood magic with the dedication of the Remnant, but he fought with power bestowed by Lattimer. He fought with the tools of the enemy. *What were Slate and his friends doing now? Had Sana healed Slate completely or was he still only partially saved from Lattimer's grip on his mind? Rainier longed to see his friends again, but he knew the best way to help them fight Lattimer was to return quickly with an army at his back. That sounded a lot easier to do before he got himself on trial for treason…best to get out of the noose before making too many future plans.*

The High Priest called upon the priest representing each faction of Julian's domain. They all wore expensive robes styled in the manner of their own faction. The stylistic differences contrasted sharply with the expressions on the faces of the priests. They all wore the same look of bemusement intermingled with condescension and indifference. *These were the people that held his life in his hands? How could they care so little about the proceedings? How could they care so little about him?* The high priest asked formally, "Scorched faction, how do you judge the testimony?"

The Scorched priest, dressed in an elaborate mix of yellows, oranges, and reds, stated loudly, "The words spoken burn with the heat of wizard's fire and smolder with the truth of an oracle. He speaks true."

Next to Rainier, his court-appointed priest exhaled slightly in relief and the High Priest moved onto the next priest. "Frozen faction, do you agree with that assessment?"

The Frozen priest stood and Rainier failed to appreciate the translucent robes that shimmered in all the wrong places. "The words spoken sting like a foot stepping on the morning frost and bite with the truth of an oracle. He speaks true."

The High Priest must have agreed with Rainier's aversion to the sight before him. "Thank you. Please take a seat." He then moved onto the next priest. "Charged faction, what did you hear?"

The priest stood in his robes that darted out in seemingly random directions like a lightning bolt. It reminded Rainier of the Sicarius Headmaster when she erupted in spark that knocked back Lattimer and allowed her to escape the clutches of the Blood Mage. The priest said, "The words spoken arc from one truth to another. He has the capacitance of knowledge reserved for an oracle."

"That only leaves one faction. Marked priest, what do you say?" the High Priest asked.

The Marked priest's plain robe emphasized the ink covering the priest's skin. Rainier knew the meaning of the tattoos instantly, since the Tallow tribe descended from the Marked faction. The Marked cover the portions of the body that describe their mission in life. The priest's inked skin declared his devotion to the pattern itself, the highest declaration a member of the Marked could make. The priest looked down upon Rainier and said, "The words spoken sting like the needle and hold with the permanence of ink."

The court-appointed priest next to Rainier almost choked at the proclamation and an audible sigh of relief could be heard from his tribe standing behind him. All four factions had validated the truth of Rainier's words. *Now they had to believe his story. When was the parade? Break out the confetti and pour the drinks.*

The Marked priest continued before any celebrations began. "However, the man speaking does not bear the ink of the Marked. He does not know the pattern and therefore cannot speak as an oracle."

Dammit. His father had always pushed him to name a Teacher, complete his training, and declare his devotion to the pattern. Rainier had actually named Slate Severance to be his Teacher, but he had severed that relationship before completing the devotion ceremony. Even though Slate's abilities as a Perceptor made him more than qualified for the role, Slate hadn't known his responsibilities as a Teacher, and Rainier wasn't anxious to fill him in on the process. The guy was already a tournament champion and all-around badass – he couldn't give Slate any more titles to fuel his ego. Besides, it hadn't seemed that important when they had been chasing down a blood mage; now it did.

"I have named a Teacher, but your statement is true. I have not completed my training."

Silence hung in the courtroom as Rainier tallied the implications. *Would the truth of the sacred words carry enough weight with the high priest to overlook his lack of formal training?*

Finally, the high priest stood up. "Rainier Tallow – The court has reached its verdict." He looked around the courtroom at his fellow priests and then raised his voice, no longer speaking as the high priest but as the Voice of Julian the Immortal. "You speak the undeniable truth of the sacred words and warn of a grave threat to Disentia. The sacrifices you and the rest of the Remnant have made in the service of

Disentia are commendable, but I fear your lack
of training and the time you spent away from
Disentia has led you astray. There is no threat
to Disentia. Before this trial, I spoke with
the oracles. They do not foresee a rise in
blood magic on our shores or any of our
neighbors. You have invoked the sacred words
and soiled the pattern with lies. You are
sentenced to death by hanging."

*What? They were going to kill him because he
didn't have ink on his skin, and his warning
caught them off-guard? Pattern-soiling or not,
Rainier didn't plan to go down that way.*
Rainier relied on his Sicarius training to play
the part of the confused and condemned prisoner
contemplating the end of his life. He hung his
head in his hands and shook it from side-to-
side, which gave him a chance to formulate a
plan. A paladin approached him from his right,
probably tasked with leading him back to his
cell. He would see a dejected, unarmed man too
shook up to defend himself. When he got close,
Rainier could incapacitate the man and steal
the short swords from his back before the
paladin realized he intended to fight back.
After that, things would get ugly. The priests
would surely cut him down since he was used to
facing the fireballs of Ispirtu wizards and
didn't know what spells to anticipate from the
priests, but if he was lucky he could bury his
sword into Mr. Robes of Righteousness before he
fell. The paladin neared and Rainier readied
himself to spring into action and strike a blow
into the soft spot of the paladin's neck when a
raspy, age-ravaged voice stopped the paladin in
his tracks.

Julian the Immortal spoke from on high, "As
my Voice has said, the boy will be sentenced to

death…unless he completes the oracle trials."

Boy? Rainier had put his pubescence years behind him, but he didn't want to argue with the old man when he was saving his life. Besides, everyone probably seemed like a boy to someone older than dust. Regardless, the simple act of speaking seemed to stir a spark of life within Julian and he continued. "He will be fed, prepped for the trials, and given comfortable rest while under guard. Tomorrow morning the trials will begin and determine his fate. If he passes the trials, he will obtain the title of oracle, his warning will be believed, and we will act."

The courtroom was stunned, but not by the words spoken by Julian but rather the fact that he spoke at all. The high priest recovered first. "While I speak for the Immortal, I cannot always interpret his wisdom correctly. I hang my head in shame and will receive any punishment for my failure you see fit." The high priest did indeed hang his head, but Rainier failed to see any shame on his face. It looked more like annoyance at the interruption and a healthy dose of fear – Julian was old but apparently still very powerful.

Julian spoke, "Learn from your shame and continue as my Voice. Redeem yourself by carrying out my orders and ensuring the boy is properly trained. Then, meet me in my chambers and we will prepare for war."

42160329R00237

Made in the USA
San Bernardino, CA
30 November 2016